WARM AND DEAD

DR. ZACK WINSTON SERIES
a Medical Conspiracy Thriller

MIKE KRENTZ

Relax. Read. Repeat.

WARM AND DEAD
(Dr. Zack Winston Series, a Medical Conspiracy Thriller, Book 2)
By Mike Krentz
Published by TouchPoint Press
Brookland, AR 72417
www.touchpointpress.com

Copyright © 2022 Mike Krentz
All rights reserved.

Softcover ISBN: 978-1-956851-34-2

This is a work of fiction. Names, places, characters, and events are fictitious. Any similarities to actual events and persons, living or dead, are purely coincidental. Any trademarks, service marks, product names, or named features are assumed to be the property of their respective owners and are used only for reference. If any of these terms are used, no endorsement is implied. Except for review purposes, the reproduction of this book, in whole or part, electronically or mechanically, constitutes a copyright violation. Address permissions and review inquiries to media@touchpointpress.com.

Editor: Jenn Haskin
Cover Design: Colbie Myles
Cover Image: Shutterstock

First Edition

Printed in the United States of America.

To the men and women emergency physicians throughout this land who show up in the ED every day and make super-human efforts to postpone death, restore life, eliminate misery. Sometimes they fail. They move on, to quiet a frightened child, relieve pain, straighten a broken limb, repair a laceration, or reassure the worried well.

The past two years have been especially daunting for you BAFERDs. I am both humbled and proud to count myself among your numbers.

CHAPTER ONE

Brutal pressure in her lower abdomen awakened the sixteen-year-old from a fitful sleep.

Much worse than the labor pains two days ago.

Deep breaths, no help. She needed to pee. Could her bladder burst?

She tried to get up, but sudden cramping around her pelvis forced her back onto the mattress.

More deep breaths. She rolled to one side. Swollen breasts heaved like water-filled balloons. Sticky liquid leaked from the left nipple.

Did she sleep through a feeding?

Put off the bathroom. Nurse the baby. Forget the pain.

Why isn't she crying?

Terror swept through the teenager's body. She squinted against the darkness in the dreary bedroom. The horrible truth exploded in her mind one second before her eyes focused on the empty bassinet.

Panic overcame pain. She fumbled for the switch on the bedside lamp and spent three tries to flip it on. Frantic eyes searched the room.

No baby.

A thunderbolt shot through her abdomen. She cried out. Pressed her knees to her chest. Fear fell over her like a weighted blanket.

The pain let up. Moisture between her legs. Underpants and sanitary pad soaked.

Find my baby.

She eased out of bed and started to the door. A wave of nausea and dizziness knocked her to the floor. Another jolt shot through her lower abdomen. Rivers streamed down both legs.

Heavy breaths. She fought off another wave, crawled to the door, reached for the knob, and tried to twist it.

Locked?

The chilly room turned frosty. She shivered. Why would they lock her in the bedroom? Who took her baby girl?

Another cramp in her lower abdomen doubled her over. She waited until it passed then stood, leaned against the wall, and pounded on the door.

"Help! Someone! Where is my baby?"

No response.

Faint, she slumped to a sitting position against the wall and pounded the door again. Her mind fogged.

"Help!" She broke into tears. Her voice faded. "Please, help. Nurse Emily . . ."

CHAPTER TWO

You can plan for life, but you can't outsmart it.

His dad's prescient words caromed in Dr. Zack Winston's mind as he arrived at Bethesda Metro Hospital at 7 AM on a freezing late-December morning for his twelve-hour ER shift. Zack had not outsmarted life, but he had preserved it. He survived the attack on his life, saved Bridget's, and exposed a medical cabal.

Killed his best friend and mentor, too. For cause justified.

A year later, Zack relished his routine emergency medicine practice and less reckless off-duty lifestyle. Approaching fifty, Zack Winston had finally grown up. No longer driven to seek or create drama in his life.

The sub-freezing weather and predicted snowstorm should deter the seasonal crunch of ill and worried-well people seeking pre-holiday tune-ups in the ED. Zack checked his phone, again. The weather would stay away until after his evening trip to Reagan Airport to pick up his daughters visiting from the west coast.

Zack's optimism seemed validated when the off-going emergency physician, Dr. Paula Cho, turned over a department almost empty of patients.

He should have known better.

Following turnover, the day-shift team gathered in the central workstation of the main treatment area. A dozen curtained patient cubicles, only one occupied, surrounded the workstation. In one of the cubicles, an internal medicine resident evaluated an octogenarian woman with a long list of non-acute medical conditions. Her son had left her at the ED triage desk with a packed roll-aboard.

"Positive suitcase sign," Zack called it. The family planned to enjoy Christmas without the burden of grandma's unpredictable mental status.

A blare from the emergency medical services radio commanded attention. The warbling voice and background siren indicated an incoming crisis.

So much for optimism.

"Montgomery County EMS, five minutes out your facility with a middle-aged male, cold-water drowning near Seneca Landing on the Potomac River. Water temperature at rescue fifty degrees. VF on our arrival, shocked three times with conversion to pulseless rhythm. Patient is hypothermic to touch. Warming blankets applied. We have him intubated on 100% oxygen, CPR in progress. Cardiac monitor sinus brady at thirty."

Zack spoke into the transmitter. "Copy all. Continue." A cold-water drowning converted from ventricular fibrillation to a slow but regular heart rhythm might survive timely treatment. Slim, but a palpable chance.

The warbling voice came back. "County Police on scene. Patient ID indicates he is a physician."

Icy fingers spread across Zack's chest. "Standing by in resus room."

Zack watched the familiar rush of adrenaline-charged nurses and techs scurrying to the resuscitation room to set up for their incoming patient. They moved faster than usual, a bit more frenzied.

Zack paused to catch his breath. High odds they knew this physician.

The approaching siren, at first faint, then more intense at the ER ambulance bay, clarified Zack's thinking. As he headed to the resus room, he spoke to the ER Secretary, Wayne Snodgrass. "Call the ECMO team."

When Zack entered the resus room, five heads turned in unison toward him. The looks on their faces showed they knew what he was about to say.

He told them anyway.

"Folks, if this victim is a local physician, we may know him. We can't let that affect our judgment or performance. Remember the first rule in a cold-water immersion. The victim is never dead until he's warm and dead."

The doors from the ambulance bay burst open. Two paramedics in blue coveralls pushed the gurney into the resus room.

Zack recognized the victim: Nate Young, a respected pediatrician on the hospital staff. He stepped back to allow the team to move Nate under the bright lights next to the equipment in the room. The paramedic who first treated the patient gave his report in a loud voice.

"Two joggers saw the victim face down just offshore by the C and O Trail. They called 911 and pulled him out of the water. They noted shallow breathing, started CPR. We arrived within ten minutes and found the patient pulseless, apneic, with V-Fib on the monitor. De-fib converted him to sinus brady on the third shock.

"Victim's truck was parked at the scene, engine compartment warm, suggesting he arrived a short time before immersion."

Zack scanned Nate's overall appearance. Purple cyanosis discolored the pediatrician's lips and ears. Looking under the warming blankets, Zack noted that Nate wore casual khaki trousers and a long-sleeved shirt. Both were soaked, as were his socks and winter shoes. Two nurses tunneled beneath the blankets to cut off the wet clothing.

Zack turned to the paramedic. "Was he wearing a coat or jacket when found?"

"None found at the scene."

Why would Nate Young go to the river in subfreezing early-morning air without a jacket?

An ED nurse relieved the paramedic performing chest compressions while a respiratory tech hooked the endotracheal tube protruding from Nate's mouth to a mechanical ventilator. Another tech changed out the EKG leads from the EMS portable monitor to the ED's multifunction readout screen.

A nurse called out. "BP sixty over palp, weak carotid pulse, no spontaneous respirations." The heart monitor showed a normal EKG pattern, but a slow rate of forty beats per minute.

"Temperature, please," Zack said. Nate's odds of recovery depended on his body's core temperature. The protective mechanism of hypothermia would decrease his metabolic demands so his brain could survive an extended period of oxygen deprivation.

A nurse inserted a rectal temperature probe and hooked it to a cable plugged into the multifunction display on the monitor screen. After what seemed too long a time, the number 89 flashed on the screen in digital red. Zack sensed the elation in the room. Definite chance to save Dr. Nate Young!

Zack raised his voice. "Warm him up."

The nurses piled heated blankets on top of Nate, replacing the ones from EMS.

A good beginning, but not enough.

Zack barked out orders. "Change out the pre-hospital IV fluid for heated saline. Start warm gastric lavage."

They were deep into a desperate attempt to save a colleague's life and Zack hadn't yet touched him. At the foot of the bed, he felt the soles of Nate's feet. Icy. No surprise. Nate's body was shunting all available blood to vital organs, allowing minimal circulation to the skin. They could pile blankets on him all day, but they had to warm up his core before he suffered vital organ shut down.

"Have we heard from the ECMO team yet?"

As if on cue, Wayne Snodgrass appeared at the door of the resus room. "Dr. Winston, Dr. Hartman on the line for you."

Zack picked up the phone on the resus room wall. The familiar baritone voice of Jerry Hartman, the ICU director who had come to Zack's support in a malignant malpractice case the prior year, filled his ear.

"What's up, Zack?"

"We have Nate Young in the ED, brought in by Montgomery County

EMS after cold water immersion, time unknown. On arrival, he's full code with no spontaneous respirations, no neurological activity, sinus brady on the monitor. Core temperature eighty-nine. How quickly can we get him set up for ECMO?"

The best hope of returning Nate Young to useful life would be to put him on extracorporeal membrane oxygenation (ECMO), a procedure to warm his blood by circulating it out of his body through a heated 100%-oxygen membrane apparatus similar to a heart-lung machine, then back into his body. In addition to the rewarming, the procedure would provide oxygen-rich blood to Nate's brain.

Jerry hesitated. "You realize the odds of success are slim, even with the hypothermia?"

"Gotta do it, Jerry. It's his only chance."

"On my way."

Zack hung up and spoke to Wayne Snodgrass. "Contact Dr. Prakash. Tell her she's needed in the ED, STAT, at my request." He wouldn't have to tell Sevati Prakash, Chief of Cardiology, why he needed her. She would respond on Zack's word alone.

"Core temperature ninety and rising," a nurse said.

"Better pulse," another one said. "Weak and thready at forty-six."

"Respirations?"

"None spontaneous," the nurse at the head of the bed said.

Zack spoke into Nate Young's ear. "We're going to get you warm and alive, friend."

The next ten minutes passed in a blur of continuous motion. Soon after Zack hung up the phone, Jerry Hartman and Sevati Prakash entered the resus room in tandem.

Zack gave them the history and current status of their pediatrician colleague while completing his exam on Nate Young.

"No signs of trauma," he said. "Odd, he wasn't wearing a jacket."

Wayne Snodgrass stuck his head into the doorway. "ECMO team ready in ICU."

"Let's roll," Jerry said.

The entourage departed the resus room in a flurry, pushing Nate's gurney and all accouterments in one synchronized moving mass, like an octopus in a feeding frenzy.

Zack stood alone in the resus room. Except for the remnants of open sterile packages, leftover tubing, and other detritus from a dramatic resuscitation, he might have wondered if the event had even happened. He heaved a sigh, hoping that despite overwhelming odds they had given a colleague a chance to live.

CHAPTER THREE

Emily Morgan pulled the blanket up to her neck against the chill in the drafty bedroom of the old colonial mansion in rural Maryland. She turned on her side and wiggled her bare posterior away from her bedmate. Dr. Adam Good, also naked, stopped snoring, snaked a hefty arm under the covers, and rested his hand on her breast.

Emily shuddered at his touch.

Within seconds he snored anew.

A faint but frantic voice from across the hall drew Emily out of sleepiness.

"Nurse Emily . . ."

The girl's cries, not the cold air, must have disturbed Emily's sleep a few minutes earlier. Now fully awake, she wiggled away from her bedmate, got up, grabbed her scrub pants and nurse's smock from the bedside chair, and dressed in a hurry.

"Whassup?" Adam's sleepy voice behind her.

"The girl," Emily said. "I'll go check."

"S'okay, Em."

Across the hall, Emily fished the keys from her smock pocket and unlocked the door to the girl's room. It opened only a foot before jamming against a body on the floor. Through the gap, Emily saw the girl's legs, spattered with blood. She leaned her shoulder into the door, shoved it open another six inches against the waifish weight, and slid through the gap.

She knelt beside the girl, noted her shallow respirations, and felt a weak pulse. A cursory look at the blood-soaked panties and the trickle of blood between the girl's legs gave Emily all the information she needed.

She shouted into the hallway. "Dr. Good. We need you. STAT."

The girl opened her eyes. Her voice croaked. "Where's my baby?"

Emily moved her away from the door, pulled the thin pillow from the bed, folded it in two, and placed it under the girl's feet to elevate her legs. She lifted the nightgown and pulled off the blood-soaked underwear and pad.

The girl thrust her knees to her chest. Her torso lurched forward. She shrieked, then expelled from her vagina a boggy mass like a spoiled tomato. A spurt of blood followed. The girl fell back onto the floor, half-conscious.

Emily shouted. "Adam!"

His footsteps lumbered across the hallway and into the room. He looked bizarre wearing only boxer shorts. His round, ruddy face scowled at Emily.

"What the hell?"

"Massive postpartum hemorrhage," Emily said.

The girl's skin had turned waxy gray. Emily thrust her hands into latex gloves pulled from the bedside table. She knelt in the blood on the floor between the girl's knees, spread the legs, and inserted a gloved hand as deep as she could into the birth canal. She leaned forward and pressed her other hand hard on the lower abdomen until she captured the soft, distended uterus between her two hands.

"Starting uterine massage." Emily jammed her hands together as hard as she could. A clot of dark red blood spurted onto her smock. She looked at Dr. Good. He stood by, arms folded over his chest, face stern.

His callous detachment disturbed her. "Call 911?"

The stoic physician placed a hand on Emily's shoulder. "Stop."

Emily hyperventilated, not from her frantic effort at uterine massage—their only chance to stop the bleeding—but from her disgust with Dr.

Adam Good. She shrugged his hand off her shoulder. "We can't stop. Please call 911."

His voice turned cold. "Do you really want to do that? How will you answer the inevitable questions?"

Emily's heart plunged. "We must do something. We can't lose this girl."

"We have the infant. We don't need the girl." He folded his arms and nodded at the moribund teenager spread-eagled on the floor in a pond of blood. "Let her go. Now."

From outside the room and down the hall, a baby cried. Emily removed her hands from the girl's body, fell back onto her haunches, and shrieked. "No!"

Dr. Good squatted beside her and put a stiff arm around her shoulders. "Hush. We mustn't frighten the other one."

CHAPTER FOUR

"THE HUNGER GAMES? On a Kindle? For a fifteen-year-old? You think she hasn't seen the movies?"

Monica Harris, emergency department head nurse, regarded Zack with kind, parental eyes. He'd used the lull after the resuscitation of Nate Young to discuss with the ED staff his choice for a combination birthday and Christmas present for his fifteen-year-old daughter, Annie. She would arrive that evening on the flight from San Diego with her older sister, Jennifer.

Wayne Snodgrass turned away from the computer keyboard. "Dunno about a Kindle, Doctor Winston. My teenagers read books on their phones—along with everything else important in their lives."

Zack frowned. "You guys have no idea how much thought I put into that decision. I read the books myself before I decided to buy them for her."

Monica gave Zack a kind smile. "We're trying to help. Maybe not something a divorced father gives his teenage daughter—especially if he hasn't seen her for a while."

How did she know Zack hadn't seen his girls recently? A nursing course on how to read physicians like a book?

Wayne picked up the theme. "Does she like to read? Most teenagers don't these days. They're into videos. TikTok, and such."

Zack didn't know the answer. He scrambled to hide his ignorance. "Well, she's a bit artsy. Likes music, uh, all sorts of music. I understand she's into fashion, but not sure what that means."

Blank faces looked back at him. Zack threw up his arms. "Oh, hell, I'll be honest. I don't have a clue because I haven't seen my daughters in five years."

Wayne cleared his throat. Monica looked at Zack with the same expression she would have for a patient suffering from terminal cancer.

Zack spoke to the floor. "That's why I wanted your advice. Because you have teenagers."

Wayne gave him a friendly look. "I can tell you something with near certainty. Whatever you give her, she will love it because it came from you."

Zack's smile vanished when the older man continued. "Then she will hate it, because it came from you."

"Well, that takes the pressure off," Zack said. "Seriously?"

"I have three teenagers from two different marriages," Wayne said. "None of whom live with me now. Been there, done that, Doc."

"How long will your daughters be here?" Monica asked.

"Annie, the fifteen-year-old, will stay until after the new year. Jennifer is twenty-two—in her first year of med school. She wants to be home for New Year's Eve. I think that involves a boyfriend."

"If your younger daughter is into music and fashion," Monica said, "you might win her heart with a pair of concert tickets. There's a K-Pop band coming to the Capital One Arena over the holidays week."

Zack blinked. "K-Pop?"

Wayne laughed. "You're hopeless, Doc." He pulled out his phone. "Look here." He motioned Zack to look over his shoulder as he played a YouTube video. A group of fancy-attired young Asian women cavorted on a stage while they sang a fast-paced song. Zack couldn't make out all the lyrics, although he recognized they were in English.

Monica's smile did not hide her pity. "K-Pop is popular music from

South Korea. It's a worldwide phenomenon. You can bet your daughter knows all the groups and most of the songs."

Zack folded his arms. "I've already bought the Kindle."

"That's great," Monica said. "You can donate it as a door prize for the hospital Christmas party." She and Wayne laughed.

Zack looked down. "I could go with her."

"Ew, no," a young nurse who had been listening said. "How gross to have your old dad with you at a concert, especially K-Pop."

Zack lifted his head. "She's getting the Kindle."

CHAPTER FIVE

Early morning light seeped through the makeshift nursery window as Emily wrapped a second blanket around the papoose-like bundle of two-day-old infant. She fought back a tear as she carried it down the foot-worn oak stairs into the spacious front room of the former colonial-style mansion she knew as The Good House.

Dr. Good had dressed in a hurry and left the house right after the death of the baby's mother. "Got a call," he had said. "Go back to bed, Em. Flossie and Roach will take care of the mess."

Emily had spent the rest of the early morning sitting with the infant in the former bedroom converted to a nursery. She had thought of contacting Dr. Kid, but what could he do? The baby seemed fine, happily unaware she'd just become an orphan. Emily had stayed in the nursery when she heard Flossie and Roach arrive and go into the deceased mother's room.

She listened to music through the ear buds on her old iPod to suppress the voices from the girl's room, especially the third person who had arrived after the first two. Spider. The middle-aged sultry man with piercing eyes terrified her.

Roach, the young man who looked more like a preppy college student than a loathsome disposer of dead bodies, stuck his head into the room. "Bring the kid downstairs."

Emily carried the precious bundle through the near-empty living room onto the expansive front porch with its four dramatic columns and wide steps down to a circular drive. Immediate chill infused her body, not so much from the frigid air as the scene in front of her.

Spider and Roach loaded the blanket-wrapped corpse into the back of a white Cadillac SUV. Spider growled when he saw Emily on the porch. "Get back inside."

She hurried into the house with the baby just as Flossie, the part-time nurse who sometimes helped at The Good House, came down the stairs. "All cleaned up and ready for your next delivery." She brushed past Emily and hurried out the front door.

Through the front window, Emily watched the two men complete their work and slam shut the rear door to the SUV. They exchanged a few words, then Roach and Flossie got into a black super-cab Ford F-150 truck and left.

Emily shuddered. She hated being alone with Spider in this isolated rural place.

He took a wicker basket from the back seat of the SUV and strode up the steps to the front door. Emily cringed. She figured him in his mid-forties, maybe ten years older than she. He looked younger with his perfect tan, groomed sandy-brown hair, and tall, confident posture. Spider could, no doubt, assume any charming persona he wished, but in this place, Emily considered him the meanest of the mean.

He leered at her when he entered the house and tossed the basket at her feet. "Put the kid in the basket." Emily realized she had not put on underwear beneath the scrub pants and smock when she'd left the bedroom to answer the mother's cries.

She turned away from Spider and placed the newborn into the makeshift carrier and arranged the blankets. From the pocket of her smock, she extracted a small bottle of formula from the nursery and placed it in the basket with the infant.

She did not look at Spider when she spoke. "She'll need to be fed soon."

"Yeah, right." He turned toward the stairs to the second floor and beckoned to her. "Come on."

Emily hesitated, confused. "The baby . . . ?"

"Leave it."

A tremor of fear shot through Emily's body. "What are you doing?"

Spider grabbed her wrist.

Shaking, Emily placed the basket with the baby on the floor.

Spider pulled her up the stairs, not constrained by her feeble attempts to resist. On the second-floor landing, she tried to calm herself.

Even if he . . . He won't kill me here. Unless . . . Get rid of two bodies at once?

Emily dug her heels into the threadbare carpet. Spider yanked her off balance and dragged her the short distance to her bedroom. He pushed open the door and shoved her inside. The momentum caused her to jackknife over the bed. She buried her head in the duvet, bracing for the inevitable assault.

Spider barked, "Stay here until I get back."

Emily turned to face him. Relief and confusion mixed with fear contorted her face. "But, the other mother . . ."

"Done. You're off duty now."

He left the room and shut the door. The lock clicked, then his footsteps receded down the stairs. She heard the baby's cries from the first floor, followed by Spider's stern voice. "Shut up, brat."

Emily rushed to the sealed bedroom window that overlooked the front of the house. She watched Spider carry the basket with the baby to the waiting SUV and thrust it onto the back seat. He started to close the door then hesitated, reached into the compartment, looped a seat belt around the basket handles then latched it. He went around the back of the car, checked the security of the rear hatch, then got into the front seat. He started the SUV and drove away via the long access drive that led to the rural road where few vehicles came by and even fewer noticed the turn-off to The Good House.

The House was a secret place, known only to its owner, staff, and clientele—some privileged, some not.

As soon as the SUV was out of sight, Emily ran to the bedroom door and tried the handle. Locked. She shook the door, then pounded on it. "Hello? Is anyone else here? We need to get out of here. Danger. Please. Help."

Silence.

She tried again, pounding harder. "Anyone?"

Someone must be here. They wouldn't leave the other woman alone so near to term.

Unless 'done' meant. . . .

She pounded the door. "Hello?"

More silence.

Sinking dread filled Emily's heart and soul.

They took her. I am alone.

She dropped to the floor next to her bed.

I must get out of this wretched place.

Of course, she could never leave. Dr. Adam Good had seen to that.

CHAPTER SIX

Zack hustled for several hours to provide optimal care while striving to reduce the number of unseen patients. He wanted to check on Nate Young. Plus, he needed to head to the airport when his shift ended. He didn't want to burden his relief with leftover day-shift patients when he couldn't stay to help clear them.

Just after noon, he thought he might get a break for a quick ICU visit to check on Nate Young.

Dr. Sebastian Barth entered the workstation in a dramatic flurry. A large man, the head of Bethesda Metro's obstetrics and gynecology department appeared uncharacteristically upset.

"Where is Dr. Cho?" His voice was stern, strident.

"She's off duty," Zack said. "Can I help you?"

Florid-faced and weary, Barth held up a two-liter plastic bag used in the operating room for collecting fluids during a surgical procedure. Dark red blood filled the bag.

"Can you guess what this is, Zack?"

Faced with an ED filling up with patients, and anxious about Nate Young, Zack was in no mood for games. He answered in one word. "Blood."

Barth scowled. "Not just any blood." He held the bag close to Zack's face. "This is what happens when an emergency physician misses an ectopic pregnancy. I wanted to show Dr. Cho the consequences of blowing off a teenage girl with lower abdominal pain and not considering a life-threatening OB emergency."

Zack had his own painful experience with the consequences of missing a ruptured ectopic pregnancy. His past error of omission had derailed a promising career as a US Navy physician. Unlike Paula Cho, at that time Zack had been unfit to practice medicine. Paula, on the other hand, was the most competent and conscientious emergency physician Zack knew.

"I have to believe there's more to the story," he said. "I will get in touch with Dr. Cho and relay your message. I'll get back to you or have her contact you."

Mollified, Barth spoke in a calmer voice. "You do that. But I expect to hear from either Dr. Cho or you by the end of the day."

"Will do," Zack said. "Especially if there were mitigating circumstances."

Barth plunked the bag of blood onto the counter in front of Zack, turned on his heel, and left the ER.

Piqued, Zack wanted to stop him, but life would be simpler if he just let the man go. He picked up the bag and handed it to a nurse. "Please dispose of this."

The nurse's hostile shrug communicated *do-it-yourself* displeasure. With a huff and a dramatic flair, she carried the bag to the utility area.

Embarrassed, Zack turned to Wayne Snodgrass. "Please make a copy of the ED record on the patient that Dr. Barth took to surgery."

Paula Cho would not miss a ruptured ectopic. There had to be an explanation. Figuring that she was already asleep after her night shift, Zack sent her a text message to call him when able to talk about a case from last night.

By mid-afternoon, Zack caught a short break from the steady flow of patients. A child receiving inhalation treatments for a severe asthma attack precluded him from leaving the department to check on Nate Young. Instead, he headed back to the "bunker" (the ER physicians' combined office/lockers/sleep room) with the copy of the ED record from the missed ectopic. He took his store-bought chicken Caesar salad from the fridge, tossed the high-carb croutons into the trash can, and poured low-cal dressing over the lettuce, chicken, cherry tomatoes, and Parmesan cheese.

As he devoured the salad, Zack skimmed for the pertinent details in Paula's meticulous note on the ER record. She had seen the patient, Abigail Watson, at 2:10 AM and discharged her shortly after 4 AM.

> *Abigail Watson, 14 YO white female with several day history intermittent lower abdominal pain, fluctuating both sides, with three bouts of diarrhea, mild nausea, no vomiting.*
>
> *Child brought in by caregiver as parents out of country. Caregiver produces proper documentation of medical POA.*
>
> *Sexual history: Menarche age 11, regular menses, normal flow, no pain. Denies sexual activity, specifically intercourse. Remainder of history unremarkable.*
>
> *Physical exam: Thin female in no acute distress, reticent but answers questions when encouraged by caretaker. General exam unremarkable. Abdomen: mild, nonspecific tenderness throughout the lower abdomen without guarding or rebound. Pelvic exam: external genitalia normal for age. Hymen virginal. Introitus admits one finger. Visual examination with smallest available speculum reveals no cervical or vaginal abnormalities. Bimanual examination complicated by small vaginal introitus and patient resistance. Mild right adnexal tenderness noted without mass.*

Zack looked in vain for documentation of either a pregnancy test or an ultrasound examination. The absence of both worried him. It suggested that Paula ruled out any possibility of pregnancy based on her history and physical examination—atypically cavalier for Paula Cho or any conscientious emergency physician.

But then Zack had the benefit of the retrospectoscope and Sebastian Barth's two-liter bag of blood.

His salad finished, he closed the record and headed back to the treatment area where another influx of patients awaited. The asthmatic patient had improved enough to go home. He discharged him, then started seeing new patients. For the time being, he had to ignore the niggling sense that he needed to learn more about Miss Abigail Watson.

—⋀—

By three in the afternoon, the ER had settled down and Zack thought it safe to run up to the ICU to check on Nate Young. He had one foot out the door when his phone buzzed. Paula Cho. He did an about-face and headed to the bunker.

"Paula, thanks for returning my call."

"What's this about, Zack?"

He told her about Sebastian Barth's rage in the ED, the incriminating bag of blood, and his own review of her care of Abigail Watson.

"Oh my God," Paula said. "How is she doing?"

Typical Paula, first thinking about the patient.

Zack had not asked. "I don't know. Sebastian didn't say. I presume she's out of the woods." He bit his lip. "As soon as we're done here, I'll check."

"I would appreciate that." A pause. "Hard to figure how that girl had an ectopic."

"I gathered that from your note." Zack's turn to pause. "And from the lack of a pregnancy test or ultrasound."

Paula's deep sigh rushed through the phone like a gush of wind. "Zack, if you had done that exam, you would think no possibility of that girl having intercourse."

Zack sighed. "Wouldn't be the first time I got fooled." He hesitated to continue but had no choice. "You know pregnancy is always possible in adolescence, no matter what you find on exam."

After a long pause, Paula answered in a subdued voice. "I'm mortified. Worst mistake I've ever made."

Zack replied in a gentle voice. "It does seem uncharacteristic. Was there anything else about the encounter; something that might have thrown you off track?"

"The whole thing was weird. She came in with a caretaker, not her parents. Her affect seemed . . . strange. Very reticent to speak, deferred to the caretaker before answering my questions. The caretaker was strange, but I couldn't put my finger on it."

"You're describing what we sometimes see in child abuse cases: quiet child, overbearing parent or caretaker. Child defers to the adult, from fear."

"I thought about that, and of course, I've seen it. This was . . . different. Not like any child abuse case I've encountered. This child, this teenager, seemed more oblivious than frightened. She didn't overtly hide anything. Seemed naive or ignorant about her body or her situation. I half wondered if she was mentally deficient." Paula paused, pondering. "I did a thorough physical exam. No signs of trauma, physical or sexual."

"That's interesting." Zack tried to visualize the scenario as Paula painted it. Would he have come to the same conclusion, or would he follow the standard guidelines for evaluation of lower abdominal pain in a young woman? A cardinal rule: always assume they are sexually active no matter what they say.

"I should have assumed she was sexually active and proceeded according to standards," Paula said.

Zack sensed that Paula was on the verge of breaking down. He tried to reassure her. "We can say that now because we know she had an ectopic.

To be honest, I can't say that I would've done differently at the time with the information you had."

Zack did not trust his own words.

"Thanks for that, Zack, but the fact remains. I screwed up."

He knew how it felt as an emergency physician to beat oneself up after missing a life-threatening diagnosis; in his case a life-ending error.

"At the very worst," he said, "you may have made an error in judgment. I would hardly call your care of this patient negligent."

"With all due respect, Zack, while I value your opinion, I'm more worried about Sebastian Barth."

"Call him, Paula. Tell him what you told me. I found him more reasonable than expected."

"Of course, I will. Then, whatever happens, will happen." A short pause. "I need his number."

Zack looked up Sebastian's number and gave it to her. Before hanging up, he tried again to encourage her. "Please don't beat yourself up, Paula. I speak from experience. None of us is infallible. I, for one, have no doubt you did your very best in this case. You always do."

"I appreciate that, Zack. Thanks for talking me through it." She hung up without further comment.

Zack spent a few seconds staring at the ER record. If Paula Cho thought this girl could not have been pregnant, she should have been right.

They were both missing something.

CHAPTER SEVEN

Bridget Larsen, JD, lifted the scarf over the keloid crossing her throat as the door to her spacious office opened. Associate Attorney Ange Moretti entered with their new client, Dr. Jeff Gibson. Bridget offered a hand to the doctor, then directed them to a small conference table.

She spoke in a hoarse voice just above a whisper. "Dr. Gibson, good morning, I'm Bridget Larsen, a partner in this law firm. I'm the lead defense attorney on your case."

The doctor glanced at Bridget's neck as he shook her hand. "Honored to meet you, Ms. Larsen."

Bridget raised an eyebrow. "Most physicians don't feel 'honored' to meet a lawyer."

The young doctor smiled. "You are well-known and respected in the emergency medicine community, ma'am. We're a tight-knit group. Most of us heard that you defended Zack Winston and almost got killed in the process."

Bridget blushed. "Zack saved my life."

Not that I remember it.

Bridget touched her neck where Zack had inserted a pen barrel to create an emergency airway and restore her breathing. She cleared her throat but spoke in a hoarse whisper. "We're here to talk about how to defend you in this suit." A year after the parking garage attack and its dramatic aftermath, she had not regained her full voice; a permanent result of the deformity in her trachea. "I'll let Ange explain the ground rules."

Ange leaned forward. "Even before her notoriety on the Winston case, Bridget was the most successful malpractice defense attorney in the National Capital Area." She glanced down before continuing. "The, uh, attack damaged her voice. She can't speak much above a whisper."

Bridget shrugged. "Not conducive to waxing profound in a court room."

"Which is where I come in," Ange said. "I'll be Bridget's voice in court, depositions, and wherever else she needs me." She glanced between Bridget and the physician. "Make no mistake, Doctor, her brain works as well as it ever did. You have the best legal advocate in the region, if not the country."

Bridget touched Ange's arm. "I can't let Ms. Moretti sell herself short," she whispered. "She's the brightest associate ever in this firm."

Dr. Gibson spread tremulous hands in an inclusive gesture. "The 'A-Team.' Good. I need all the help you can give me."

Bridget leaned back in her chair and nodded to Ange, putting her in charge of the remainder of the conversation.

Ange opened the file that she and Bridget had earlier reviewed in detail. She picked up a pen and tablet to make notes. "We have the records here, but we want to hear in your own words what happened."

The doctor looked down at the table.

"Take your time, Doc," Ange said. "Unlike the ER, we're not in a rush."

Dr. Gibson rubbed his eyes. Bridget noted a trace of tears.

"My worst nightmare." His voice trembled. "I'd give anything to relive that night."

He lapsed into silence.

Ange put down the pen. "Let's start with an easy question. You are an attending emergency physician at George Washington University Hospital, correct?"

"Yes."

"For how long?"

"Just short of eighteen months. I completed my residency there last year."

"How did you happen to be on duty at a rural hospital in Maryland on the night in question?"

"Moonlighting. Most of us do it. Supplemental income."

Bridget and Ange exchanged glances.

How much income does one young doctor need?

Ange continued, "That's a community hospital, the one in rural Maryland, right?"

"Yeah, and that's important background for this case."

"How so?"

"Minimal resources. Mostly primary care, some general surgery, routine OB." He looked at both Ange and Bridget. "No NICU."

"Neonatal intensive care unit?"

"Right."

Ange nodded. "Okay, so tell us about this case and why the absence of a NICU is relevant."

The doctor looked away. His eyes filmed over with tears.

Bridget touched his arm. "We're on your side here, and there's nothing you can tell us that we, or at least I, haven't heard before." She glanced at Ange, her eyes showing what she thought.

Big job ahead getting him ready for deposition, let alone court.

Dr. Gibson wiped his eye. "Sorry. I'm not usually emotional."

"First malpractice case?" Ange asked.

He scoffed. "Obviously."

"Not ours," Ange said. "We've got this, Doc. It's what we do." She leaned forward, her voice soft. "Just tell us what happened. Describe your thought process at the time."

The doctor blew out a breath. "Sixteen-year-old girl came into the ER, thirty-five weeks pregnant, obese, hypertensive, complaining of severe headache, dizziness, vomiting. All four extremities were swollen. Urine was positive for protein. Clear-cut diagnosis of preeclampsia."

"Also known as toxemia of pregnancy?"

"Right."

"How did she arrive? Ambulance?"

He shook his head. "Walk-in. The triage nurse took one look at her and brought her straight back to the OB room."

"What did you think when you saw her?"

"She was in danger of progressing to full-blown eclampsia. She needed to deliver that baby."

Bridget spoke in her chronic whisper. "Eclampsia would be an immediate threat to her and the baby, right?"

The doctor nodded. "Yes. We prevent that complication by delivering the baby."

Ange continued the interview. "You said the rural hospital has OB, right?"

Dr. Gibson nodded. "Yes."

"Yet you attempted a transfer to Bethesda Metro Hospital. Why?"

"Signs of fetal distress. The baby would be in trouble. Bethesda had the closest NICU . . ." The doctor's voice trailed off and he stared at the floor.

Ange gave him a moment to recompose himself. "Could you have delivered the baby?"

"Yes. That's part of emergency medicine training, emergency delivery. But I had neither the skill nor the equipment to manage a critical neonate."

"Hence the transfer," Ange said.

"Right. I first asked for the neonatal transport team, but they were on another mission to the south, so we called the local volunteer EMS squad." He shook his head. "I did everything I could to stabilize the girl and buy time, loaded her up with magnesium sulfate, and started a drip. EMS responded quickly. I thought she had a reasonable chance. At Bethesda

Metro, they would take her straight to C-section for delivery, then resuscitate the baby."

The young doctor hung his head. "She had a chance. I swear she had a chance."

"What happened?" Bridget's whispered voice tinged with empathy.

"En route to Bethesda, she had a seizure and went into severe cardiac failure. She died before they got to the hospital. They rushed her straight to OB where they tried to save the baby, but . . ."

Bridget and Ange allowed the silence in the room to absorb the doctor's grief.

Ange touched his arm. "Do you need a break?"

Dr. Gibson looked up; wiped his eyes. "I'm okay. Let's move on. Please."

Ange glanced at Bridget then continued, "Just a few more issues to clarify with you, Doctor, then we'll be done for today."

He bit his lip and nodded.

"The mother was unwed, correct?"

"Yes?"

"Did her parents come with her?"

"No." He shook his head. "That was the other problem. She refused to give us information about parents. Best we could tell she was a runaway."

"Did anyone come with her?"

"An older teenager, clean-cut, but . . . Strange affect. Said he was eighteen. I wasn't sure, but I couldn't take the time to challenge him, what with her critical condition. He swore he was not the father. The girl backed him up on that, but she refused to say who got her pregnant."

"No parents, no father, just this clean-cut youth who was maybe eighteen, or not?"

The doctor frowned. "Yeah. The guy said they lived in a commune in the country. I thought it might have been a cult or something like that. We called the County PD, but the guy split before they arrived. Walked out of the ED while we were attending to the girl.

"Turned out the so-called commune doesn't exist. It was all a lie." He paused and shrugged. "We never knew where she came from. It took law enforcement a day to figure out who her parents were. They live in Ohio and confirmed their daughter was a runaway. They hadn't seen her in over a year and had given up looking."

Bridget scoffed. "Yet they suddenly cared enough to file a multi-million-dollar lawsuit against you and the hospital on her behalf."

After escorting Dr. Gibson to the front lobby, Ange rejoined Bridget in her office. The two lawyers exchanged wary glances across the conference table.

Ange eyed Bridget. "Didn't you swear off ER docs?"

"A lifetime ago." She touched the scar on her neck. "Literally."

Before Zack.

How different would her professional and personal life be now if she had stuck to her guns and not let the other partners talk her into taking Zack's case two years ago?

Ange broke through. "Hello? Did you just go somewhere?"

Bridget winced and looked at Ange with a sheepish grin. "Yeah. Sorry." She cleared her throat. "So, counselor, what's your thought on this ER case?"

Ange shook her head. "This doc is in a world of hurt. Dead mother, dead baby. Any jury in the country will give the plaintiffs a huge reward to compensate for their loss. We'll have to settle. Can't risk a trial."

Bridget raised a hand. "Not so fast. I might agree—if the plaintiff were a bereaved husband and father. In that case, we would settle for whatever the doctor's insurance company agreed to pay."

She stroked her chin. "These parents may be impeachable. We need to look into their background. Why did their daughter run away? What did she run from? How much time and effort did they make to find her before they gave up? *Why* did they give up?" She scowled. "If my son ran away I would never stop looking."

"I don't know," Ange said. "I might feel otherwise if I had a child; but even if they are the worst parents in the world, estranged or not, they lost their daughter and their grandchild. How does that not constitute injury, at least in the legal sense?"

"Of course, injury. But there may be an opening, some mitigating circumstances. Maybe enough to reduce the amount of settlement if not to defend the case."

Bridget paused. "Plus, that cult/commune/whatever aspect. How does that relate to the illness and outcome? Did she suffer abuse there? Did she have prenatal care? Who was the guy who brought her in and then fled?"

Ange tilted her head. "I don't follow."

"Maybe this girl and/or the people with her share some blame for her preeclampsia. Goes to causation."

Ange leafed through the documents, then looked Bridget in the eye. "By going straight to injury and causation, are you concurring on negligence? Did this ER doc fail to meet the standard of care when he transferred the woman?"

"I don't know." Bridget rested her chin on her hands. "His rationale makes some sense. Remote location, limited resources. Fear of losing a neonate."

Ange folded her arms. "Seriously? If he had delivered the baby, he'd at least have a living mother. Transferring her, he lost both."

"He thought the transfer would save both mother and baby. He couldn't know she would crash en route."

"He should have considered it." Ange shook her head. "I don't see any defense on negligence or standard of care here." She scrunched her eyebrows. "Another thing. How do we find a medical expert who will agree to look at this case, let alone defend Dr. Gibson?"

Bridget looked past her. "Don't know till we try." She smiled.

"Of course, we try, but—" Ange leaned forward, looked straight at Bridget, eyes piercing. "Do you, uh, have someone particular in mind for our medical expert?"

Bridget looked away. "I might."

"Not . . . ?"

"He has experience with obscure circumstances."

Ange let out a long breath. "Really? Have you talked to him recently?"

Bridget studied the table. "Not for some time. Months." She looked up. "You?"

Ange shook her head. "That long ago or longer. I tried to keep up with him for a while, but constancy is not Zack Winston's strong suit."

She looked askance at Bridget. "He has a new girlfriend."

Bridget flushed. "I didn't know that." She glanced away for a second. "Not relevant to his potential role as an expert witness." When Ange didn't react, Bridget continued. "Zack has experience practicing emergency medicine in remote locations. You know, from his time in the navy in Japan."

"From which he carries a lot of baggage."

"We all have baggage, Ange."

Ange shook her head and smiled. "You've already decided, haven't you? You knew before we met Dr. Gibson."

Bridget smiled, sheepish. "Guilty, your honor. Only because I believe Zack can help us make a case for this doctor. It's the kind of hopeless situation that plays to Zack's strengths."

Ange waved her hand. "I'll concede on that point."

"You have veto power. If you think it's a bad move, or if it will make you uncomfortable because of your past relationship with him—"

Ange cut her off. "Not an issue. Ancient history." She thought for a few seconds. "You may be right. Worth a shot."

Bridget smiled. "Yeah, worst case we thank him for his service and regroup."

Ange looked away, thoughtful. After a moment, she turned to Bridget with penetrating eyes.

Bridget squinted at her. "Are you thinking something else?"

"Just wondering." Ange paused, uncomfortable. "Do you have another reason for contacting Zack?"

Bridget flushed and glanced upward before settling her gaze on Ange. "No."

Ange looked at her, silent.

"What are you getting at, Ange?"

Ange averted her eyes and shook her head. "Nothing."

Bridget touched her throat. "You'll call him?"

"Sure."

"Thanks." Bridget looked at her watch. "I missed my swim workout this morning. I'm going now to make it up. Call or text my cell after you talk to Zack."

"Will do." Ange left the room.

Bridget retrieved her gym bag from the closet and hurried from her office.

CHAPTER EIGHT

Just before four-thirty in the afternoon, Dr. Louise Ritchie, the new ED medical director, arrived to spell Zack for his scheduled Zoom call with Marshall Hilliard, US Attorney for the Eastern District of Virginia. Bridget Larsen's husband.

Since the dramatic events that almost killed Bridget and Zack, Marshall had led a task force investigating the medical cabal that traded in drugs and murder-for-hire. The former ED medical director, Dr. Dennis King, had been a key player, deft at making murder look like an accident or suicide. Zack had ended Dennis' life in self-defense when his former friend and mentor attacked him with a lethal chemical.

Zack respected his new boss, a woman approaching sixty; a quiet, consistent, yet firm leader. "Thanks for spelling me, Louise. I won't be long on this call." He waved his arm across the treatment area. "These patients are all stable, awaiting labs or consults. Sorry I didn't get to the three new ones."

A gracious smile crossed Louise's face. "I should thank you. I prefer seeing patients over pounding that danged keyboard or sitting in meetings with doctors who consider themselves experts on everything."

She's a pleasant change from Dennis King's arrogance.

Louise picked up a tablet and went off to see a patient. Zack noted the bounce in her step and lilt in her voice as she opened the cubicle curtain.

"Hello, there. I'm Dr. Ritchie. How can I help you today?"

Zack went to the bunker, pulled his laptop from the backpack he always wore to work, sat at the single desk in the room, and booted up. Once he'd opened the link to the Zoom meeting, he sat idle for fifteen minutes while the screen showed the rotating circle and message to wait for the leader to start the meeting.

He lost his patience and started a phone text to Marshall's secretary that he needed to get back to the ER. The screen came alive.

Instead of Marshall Hilliard's austere gray-templed southern gentleman visage, the friendly freckle-faced, red-headed image of the Deputy US Attorney, Fiona Delaney, a woman in her forties, filled the screen.

"Dr. Winston, thank you so much for waiting. Sorry to be late. We know you're on duty in the ER. Marshall had a last-minute conflict. He asked me to take the meeting."

Zack smiled. "No problem, ma'am. I have coverage in the ER, so I can devote whatever time you need." That wasn't entirely true. Louise would soon need to get back to her administrative duties, but Zack hedged his bet with the knowledge that the US Attorney's office was always in a rush to move on to the next meeting, phone call, Zoom event, or conference. Zack Winston would not be the rate-limiting step in that equation.

"Thank you, sir," Fiona said. "I'll cut to the gist."

She turned slightly away from her camera, to view what Zack assumed was a second computer screen. After a few clicks on her keyboard, she turned back to face the camera. "We've come across a person of interest to our investigation, relative to someone you once treated in the ER. Does the name Melody Snyder mean anything to you?"

Zack's body froze. His mind opened an image of the chartreuse, pink, and gray Nike running shoes worn by a former patient who arrived in severe respiratory distress. He would never forget the tragic death of Melody Snyder. Never.

"Doctor Winston? Are we still connected?"

Zack broke through his mental freeze. "Yes. She died in our ER, about a year-and-a-half ago."

Because I botched her airway.

Fiona allowed a short pause for Zack to regroup before she continued, "You saw her twice, right?"

Her tone seemed aggressive.

Is she interrogating me here?

He nodded. "Yes. I can retrieve her electronic health record now if you wish. Won't take a minute."

Fiona waved a hand. "We have a copy, thanks."

Zack wrinkled his brow. "What do you need from me?"

"We understand that on both occasions she arrived in anaphylaxis after bee stings while running on the B & O trail, correct?"

"Yes." Zack gulped. "The second time she was already in acute respiratory failure on arrival. We failed to establish an airway and she died."

Not we. I.

Zack had crossed his arms while talking. Did he sound as defensive as he felt?

Fiona smiled. "Relax, doctor. This isn't about your care in the ER."

Could have said so sooner, lawyer.

"Thanks. What then?" He uncrossed his arms, leaned back in the chair, and forced himself to calm down.

"Her husband, Douglas Snyder, brought her in the first time, correct? You met him after you resuscitated her?"

Zack recalled the handsome executive in the tailored suit, with a handshake and smile like a politician on the campaign trail. "Yes."

"Did anything seem unusual to you at the time?"

"Indeed. He had given her two EpiPen doses without effect."

Zack snapped his fingers. "Darn." He glanced away from the camera, sheepish. "I asked him to bring in the empty vials. I was concerned they may have expired or had some other issue that rendered them ineffective." He frowned. "He never brought them in, and I didn't think to follow up."

Trying to hide his chagrin, Zack said, "Lots of stuff happened in the ER that day . . . And afterward."

"Understood. We don't hold anything against you."

"I should have followed up."

Fiona looked away from the camera. Zack thought he saw a brief frown before her face took on a mask of professional decorum. She spoke in the direction she was looking. "Hello, sir. We were just getting started."

From off-camera, Marshall Hilliard's stentorian voice said, "I'll take it from here, Fi."

"Of course, sir." Fiona's face on the screen gave way to Marshall's.

"Hi, Zack," the US Attorney said. "Sorry for the delay."

"Hello, sir."

Hilliard looked away from the camera. "Thanks, Fi." He paused, as if waiting for his deputy to leave the room, then turned back to the camera. "Now, where were you?"

Zack summarized the conversation, emphasizing his regret for not following up about the Epi-Pens.

Marshall shook his head. "Would not have made a difference."

Puzzled, Zack stared at the screen.

Marshall consulted the other monitor. "The second time you saw Melody Snyder, she came in by EMS, right?"

"Yes, she was found down on the trail, alone. She was near death when we got her."

"Did you interact with Douglas Snyder after she died?"

"Yes. He was crushed at first but seemed to recover quickly."

Marshall tilted his head. "Really?"

Zack recalled Doug Snyder's reaction to his blurted confession about failing to secure Melody's airway. "At one point, he became angry, like a lion about to attack me."

Marshall said nothing.

Zack's squinted. "What's this about, sir?"

Marshall looked directly into the camera; spoke as if he were addressing a jury. "We believe that Douglas Snyder murdered his wife; that he was and may still be a principal in the cabal that framed and almost killed you; that would have killed Bridget were it not for your life-saving treatment."

Zack blinked at the screen. "Why would Douglas Snyder kill his wife?"

Marshall's expression went blank. "I'm afraid that's beyond your need to know, Doctor Winston."

What the hell?

A soft knock on the bunker door diverted Zack's attention from his computer screen.

Louise Ritchie stuck her head into the room.

"Sorry to interrupt. I have an ECOMS meeting in ten minutes and there's an overdose coming in five by ambo. Will you be done in time to take it?"

Zack looked at his watch. He'd been away from the ER for over a half-hour. His annoyance at Marshall's last statement demotivated him to spend any more time on the call.

He looked at Louise. "I'll wrap this up now."

She seemed disappointed. "Are you sure? I'd rather treat an OD than go to that meeting."

Zack had to smile. "I got it, ma'am. But we all need you in that meeting. Those other docs will badmouth us to hell and back if you're not there to defend us."

Louise shrugged. "The cross I bear." She closed the door behind her as she returned to the treatment area.

Zack turned back to the computer screen, his own expression blank. "I need to get back to the ER for an incoming patient."

Marshall nodded. "We can follow up later. Could you please research the possible deliberate use of bee venom extract to cause Melody Snyder's anaphylaxis? Anything else that might help us. Include anything you can remember about Douglas Snyder."

"Right." Zack positioned his mouse pointer over the *Leave* button on the Zoom screen. "Just one comment. With all the resources at your disposal, you have no clue as to Doug Snyder's whereabouts?"

Marshall forced a smile. "I'm sorry, Doc. You know I can't disclose everything. We have some ideas, but nothing concrete."

"Yeah. Got it."

"Expect to hear more from us, maybe soon."

The US Attorney's screen image disappeared, replaced by a notification:

The leader has ended the meeting.

Still annoyed, Zack shut down his laptop, returned it to his backpack, and hustled to the resuscitation room.

EMTs were transferring an unconscious female from their transport stretcher onto the bed. Zack noted her cyanotic blue skin and lack of responsiveness.

"Mixed overdose," a nurse said into Zack's ear. "Oxy and heroin."

Gowned, gloved, and wearing a clear plastic shield over her masked face, Louise Ritchie stood at the head of the bed, a curved-blade laryngoscope in her left hand, a plastic endotracheal tube in her right.

The patient was a young woman, maybe in her early twenties, wearing a tattered sweater and ragged jeans. A pair of worn leather snow boots encased feet with no socks. From both sight and smell, Zack deduced the woman had not bathed for some time.

He thought of his daughter, Jennifer, about the same age with a bright future ahead of her. Had this woman's future seemed bright once? Before some life trauma drove her to opioid abuse?

"Dibs on the intubation," Louise said in a voice tinged with glee. Without waiting for a response from him, she inserted the laryngoscope into the woman's mouth, lifted the jaw, sighted along the blade, and slid the tube through the vocal cords and into the larynx. A nurse inserted an air-filled syringe into a side port on the tube and pushed the plunger to inflate the small balloon that would keep the tube's tip in place in the woman's trachea.

Louise stepped back to allow another nurse to connect the endotracheal tube to a ventilator. Then she listened to both sides of the woman's chest.

"Bilateral breath sounds," Louise said with an air of triumph. "We've at least given her a chance to live by supporting her ventilation."

Zack stepped up to take over the resuscitation. "Nice job."

"Thanks," Louise said. She removed her personal protective gear. "Now I have to get to that danged ECOMS meeting."

"I got it here, ma'am."

She started out of the room, then turned at the door. "I long ago lost count of how many intubations I've done in the ER, but I've never done a cricothyrotomy on a non-breathing injured woman in a parking garage." She winked. "That honor is all yours, Doc."

Louise left the room before Zack could respond. He turned to the resuscitation in progress. "How many doses of Narcan so far?"

CHAPTER NINE

Thirty minutes after Louise Ritchie left the resus room, Zack transferred the overdose patient to the ICU. He phoned Jerry Hartman, who would receive the young woman in the unit.

"Unresponsive despite multiple doses of Narcan," Zack said. "Glasgow of five, pupils still constricted, on ventilator support. Nothing more to do here."

Jerry blew into the phone. "Nothing more to do up here either, except wait for the proper interval to get an EEG to support a diagnosis of brain death."

"You know you don't need an EEG for that," Zack said. "Clinical judgment suffices."

"Tell it to the personal injury lawyers, Zack. You know, the ones who advertise on billboards?"

"Understood."

"Another notch for the opioid gun," Jerry said.

"Not the last, I'm afraid. Sorry."

"No problem, Zack. You didn't shoot her up."

"Yeah, no telling what else was in the hit."

Jerry huffed. "Won't matter. Same outcome."

"Yep. Thanks anyway, Jerry."

Wayne Snodgrass entered the room. "Dr. Prakash on the other line for you, Doctor Winston."

Zack ended the call with Jerry and took the other one. "Sevati, what's up?"

"Can you come to ICU?"

"Doubt it. Just handled a mixed substance OD, and the department is slammed. What's up?"

"We have an odd physical finding on Nate Young. The intern found it."

"What?"

"Cannot say on the phone. I will wait until you can come up."

"May be a while."

"It is okay."

Wayne Snodgrass interrupted Zack. "Mrs. Young is in the quiet room."

Zack ended the call with Sevati, left the resus room, and ignored the main treatment area as he headed for the quiet room.

After the garish and stressful environment of the resuscitation room, Zack appreciated the low-light atmosphere of the quiet room. By design, if the patient's family was sequestered in this ephemeral space, their loved one's situation had turned dire. At least in this instance Zack could offer a glimmer of hope instead of his dreaded role, played many times in the past, as the Reaper's grim messenger.

He found Yvonne Young in the company not only of Monica Harris, but also a woman dressed in a charcoal business suit that might have come off the rack at Target.

Yvonne turned to Zack, with whom she'd socialized at hospital-sponsored events. Her wan expression conveyed both hope and despair.

Zack smiled and gave her a reassuring nod before he turned to the woman in the suit.

"I'm Dr. Winston. You are?"

The woman, who appeared to be late-thirties to early-forties, flashed a badge. "Detective Tina Ramirez, Montgomery County Police Department."

It seemed too soon for a detective to be on the case of a recent near-drowning. Zack scrunched an eyebrow. "Would you excuse us, please?"

As if on cue, Monica Harris ushered the detective to the door. "You can wait here in the hallway, Detective. Dr. Winston won't be long." The woman left without objection. Monica closed the door behind her and stood guard next to it.

Zack gave Yvonne a fraternal hug. "It's not all bad news." He directed her to the plush couch, then sat in the side chair.

Yvonne looked him in the eye. "How is he, Zack?"

"Alive. We've transferred him to ICU."

"Thank God!"

"Not out of the woods, but he has a chance." Zack swallowed hard. "It's a slim chance for full recovery, but we have him in the best possible place." He explained the resuscitation and ECMO. "He'll remain deeply sedated on cardiac bypass for at least twenty-four hours, probably longer depending on how he does." He swallowed again. "We won't know his ultimate outcome for weeks. Or months."

Tears filled Yvonne's eyes. "I didn't hear him leave the house."

"Is there anything you can tell me? Anything at all that might help us?"

A frightened look crossed Yvonne's face. She glanced at Monica, unsure. Monica took the hint and stepped out of the room.

Yvonne gestured toward the door. "That detective thinks Nate tried to commit suicide."

A shock wave coursed through Zack's body. "Suicide? That's ridiculous, least of all Nate." He rubbed his brow. "This only just happened. Why would they suspect anything like that?"

Yvonne buried her head in her hands. When she looked up, her eyes were moist.

"They were investigating him. Somebody accused him of, uh, taking advantage of, uh—" Yvonne broke down, shaking her head in violent motion side-to-side. Zack touched her hand. She grabbed on and squeezed hard. "They accused him of molesting his patients." She broke into tears. "Nate would never do that."

Stunned, Zack squeezed her hand. "How in the world—?"

Yvonne blotted her eyes with a tissue from her purse. "An investigative reporter contacted Nate yesterday. Said he had proof, witnesses, and victims. He was going to publish a story in Sunday's *Post*." She wiped tears from her eyes and cheeks. "Nate denied it, but of course he was upset. A story like that. The reporter had talked to the authorities, so when they heard what happened with him this morning, the detective came running."

Zack looked away and stared at the wall, his mind a jumble of thoughts and feelings. When the silence became unbearable, he put an arm around Yvonne's shoulder.

"Did you notice anything at all to make you think that Nate would try to harm himself? Did he seem depressed? Had he been drinking? Did he say anything?"

Yvonne took a deep breath and looked at Zack with pained eyes. "For about six months, he's been . . ." She shrugged. "Different. Distracted. When I try to talk to him about, whatever it is, he clams up. Swears there's nothing wrong." She scoffed. "I know my husband, Zack. Something is different about him."

Zack weighed his response. "Any chance he's been . . . You know?"

Yvonne about choked on her answer. "Seeing someone else?" She huffed. "I've wondered as much. He's been working more on nights and weekends. His medical group is minus one pediatrician, so I've figured he's covering more calls."

She gazed at the wall, processing her thoughts in silence.

Zack touched her hand. "I can't believe Nate would do that. Not the Nate I know. It has to be something else."

Yvonne turned to him, tears streaming down her face. "Like what? He stood to lose his whole career, not to mention his personal reputation and maybe his family. We have teenagers of our own. What were they going to think?" Her fists knotted in her lap. "Yes, Nate was depressed. But he didn't molest his patients and he sure as hell didn't try to kill himself."

"How can I help, Yvonne?"

Her nostrils flared. "Convince that detective Nate couldn't have done those things."

"I'll try."

Yvonne's expression softened. "What do I do, Zack?"

"Right now, we concentrate on keeping Nate alive. Whatever else happens, we deal with it. We will figure this out. We will do our absolute best to save Nate, in all respects."

Zack rose to leave. Yvonne stood and hugged him. "I can't lose Nate. I love him. I always will, no matter what."

"We'll get through this, Yvonne. You have a lot of support. Be strong."

Zack stepped out of the room and made way for Monica to re-enter.

"Stay with her as long as you can," he said. "I'm going to talk to that detective."

Zack found the detective waiting outside the treatment area. They approached each other. The detective spoke first.

"Excuse me, Doctor. Were you the treating physician?"

"Yes, I'm Dr. Winston, the treating emergency physician."

"What can you tell us about his condition?"

"He nearly drowned. He's not out of the woods, but we have reason to be hopeful."

"When can I interview him?"

Zack's annoyance over the accusations against Nate flashed.

Never, if I have any say in it.

He forced a calm voice. "I don't know. He's unconscious. No telling when or if he'll wake up."

"Can you tell me anything else about his condition?"

Zack shook his head; turned away.

The woman followed him. "Any signs of trauma? Evidence of self-harm?"

Zack stopped, turned, and put on his most congenial face. "I understand there are certain allegations pending about Dr. Young, and some concern that he attempted suicide."

The detective nodded. "Can you shed any light on that, doctor? Please understand, we've made no assumptions here, reached no conclusions. Just looking for truth."

Zack nodded. "I understand. We all have to do our jobs." He stroked his chin. "I can assure you this. No way did Nate Young ever molest a minor. It's inconsistent with his character. As for self-harm, I have no reason to believe he attempted suicide by drowning himself in near-freezing water. A man would have to be crazy desperate to do that."

"Was he?"

"Crazy desperate? No chance in hell, detective."

"Is that an opinion, or can you back it up with facts?"

Zack tilted his head. "Opinion, based on my knowledge of the man. As for facts, we'll get those as best we can once he wakes up."

IF he wakes up.

"Thank you, Doctor. I would like to keep in touch."

"Of course."

Zack started to leave then turned back to the detective. "Whatever you're chasing, you need to look elsewhere."

He spun on his heel and headed toward the treatment area.

CHAPTER TEN

When Zack returned from the quiet room to the treatment area, a full backlog of patients awaited him. No chance to go up to ICU. He spent the remainder of the shift striving to keep up with the steady flow of new patients, relying on his health-drink concoction to keep him nourished.

A lull near the end of his shift at 7 PM allowed him to retreat to the bunker to change clothes. For the first time since that morning, his thoughts returned to the imminent arrival of his daughters. He checked his phone to confirm their flight from San Diego would be on time, then changed out of work scrubs into casual attire consisting of slacks, a long-sleeved collared shirt, and a woolly sweater. As he pulled the sweater over his head, he wondered again why Nate Young had no outerwear with him at the river.

Unless....

Zack shook his head.

No way Nate Young attempted suicide by drowning.

When Zack returned to the treatment area, his relief had arrived. Zack gave quick turnover on the two patients still awaiting lab results then hustled up to the ICU. He had a little time before heading to the airport.

He found Nate Young in the same condition as after resuscitation early that morning. He was under moderate sedation, so at best his neurological examination would be unreliable. His physiological parameters looked good.

Good sign, but it's still early.

Zack looked around for Sevati Prakash or Jerry Hartman, but neither of them was present in the ICU. He told the evening charge nurse that Dr. Prakash had wanted him to look at something regarding Dr. Young.

The nurse shrugged her shoulders. "I didn't receive pass down on anything like that."

Maybe Sevati didn't want to share her observation with anyone but Jerry and Zack. He thought about calling Sevati or Jerry, but a glance at his watch told him he should get going to the airport. One could never trust the DC traffic, even on a weekday evening in late December.

Zack's phone buzzed as he opened the door to his Lexus in the physician's parking lot. He let it go while he jumped into the car, shut the door against the frigid air, started the engine, and turned on the heater. The phone stopped ringing. He glanced at the caller ID.

Angela Moretti.

Ange?

Zack had not heard from or spoken to his former girlfriend in, what, six months? Maybe more. He glanced at the dashboard clock. No time to return her call. He started to back out of the parking space, then hit the brake.

What if she's calling about Bridget?

He continued his egress from the parking lot as he activated the hands-free phone function. "Call Ange."

She answered on the third ring. "Zack. Thanks for returning my call."

"Is Bridget okay?" He quickly added, "Are you?"

Even through the phone he sensed her cynical smile. "We're both fine, Zack. Thanks for asking. This is a business call."

"Please don't tell me I'm being sued again."

"Nothing like that." She paused. "I'm calling for Bridget. Her voice, you know."

Of course, Zack knew, and Ange knew he knew. She had shone her phone's flashlight onto Bridget's neck in the darkened parking garage while Zack performed the cricothyrotomy that saved her life.

His foot came off the accelerator and he blinked at the memory. "Go on."

"She— We wonder if you could consult as an expert on a malpractice case."

Traffic on Old Georgetown Road slowed to a crawl on the approach to the Capital Beltway. Zack worried he might be late to the airport.

"Why me?"

"Bridget thinks you would be a good fit. We, uh, both do."

"What's the case?"

"Defendant is an emergency physician, Dr. Jeff Gibson."

"Don't know him. What's the story?"

Ange described how Dr. Gibson had been on duty at a rural Maryland ED when a pregnant teenager came in with preeclampsia. He had elected to transfer the patient to Bethesda Metro because the rural hospital had no NICU. The woman died en route, and the baby did not survive.

A vision of Sebastian Barth and his bag of blood crossed Zack's mind as he eased his Lexus into the fast lane heading south on the Capital Beltway.

"I don't get it," he said. "Why would you and Bridget consider defending this guy? He's dead meat. He lost a young woman and her baby. Even if we make a case against negligence . . ."

"Possible mitigating circumstances."

Ange described how the teenage patient seemed to be a runaway, brought in by a strange young man who fled the ED. Some mention of a cult that authorities could not substantiate. The parents surfaced days later. They initiated the lawsuit.

Ange's story reminded Zack of Paula Cho's description of the unusual circumstances of her ectopic pregnancy case. He shook his head. "Probably not related."

"What?"

"Sorry. I was thinking about another case." He accelerated the Lexus ahead of a slow-moving minivan driven by a soccer mom with a passel of kids in the back. He made it into the right lane as he approached the exit to George Washington Memorial Parkway.

"Not sure I can help you, Ange. Besides, my plate is pretty full. I'm on my way to the airport to pick up my daughters who are coming for the holidays."

"Really? That's great."

Some time ago, before his life turned to hell, Ange had called Zack out on his absent relationship with his daughters; the same night she ended their romantic relationship.

"Yeah, well, getting my life in order, you know."

"That won't be a problem for us, Zack. We won't need you till after the New Year."

Zack pursed his lips. "I'm not sure I can offer any value to your case."

Silence from the other end.

Zack had completed the cloverleaf turn onto George Washington Parkway before Ange spoke again. "Maybe you should talk to Bridget. She really wants you. We could all meet in person."

That shattered Zack's defensive wall, in a pleasant way. He feigned hesitancy in his response. "Couldn't hurt, I guess. I'll have to work around whatever my daughters want to do."

"Doesn't have to be soon."

How long had it been since Zack had seen Bridget? He couldn't remember. Months.

"How about I call your office in the next day or two. We'll work something out."

"Sure. I'll let her know."

Before Ange could end the call, Zack blurted, "How is she? How is Bridget?"

Another pause. "Truth? I worry about her."

"Why?"

"She's unhappy. Like she's going through the motions."

"Don't we all, sometimes?"

"Yeah, but this has been going on for some time. Did you know she's taken up triathlon?"

"No. I knew she was a runner. Marathons, as I recall." He pictured the marathon posters in Bridget's office.

"Now she's into the whole swim-bike-run bit. Spends several hours every day training or working out. Most mornings she hits the indoor pool at the aquatics center then comes to work smelling like chlorine."

Bridget always wears Chanel.

"Those workouts could be healthy," Zack said.

"They could also be addictive, avoiding some uncomfortable reality."

"She almost died, lost her voice, unable to speak in court. You know how she loved litigating."

"Maybe that's all it is. I worry there's something else going on."

Zack's phone buzzed. Call waiting.

Sarah.

"I gotta go. Almost to the airport. I'll think about all you said. See how Bridget seems when we meet."

"Okay. Thanks, Zack."

"No problem," Zack said. He ended the call.

Sarah had hung up before Zack got off the call with Ange. He hesitated, then buried the thought of ignoring it. She would keep calling until he answered.

"Call Sarah," he said.

She answered on the first ring. "Zack, are you on your way to the airport?"

"Halfway down GW Parkway. I should get there in time."

"Nervous?"

"Damn right. Wondering if this was such a great idea."

"A little late to worry about that."

"Not worried, just anxious, excited."

"You'll be fine once you see them." After a pause, she spoke in a sweet voice. "I look forward to meeting them."

Zack pursed his lips. "I know."

Longer pause. "So . . . when do you think that will happen?"

Zack let out a breath. "Sarah, we discussed this. I need to reunite first. I don't know how that will go after five years without contact. They may not be ready to meet another woman in my life."

He listened for a response but heard none. "I hope it will be sooner than later," he said.

The silence on the other end exceeded Zack's comfort zone.

Sarah spoke before he had a chance to say something stupid. "I just want to be supportive, Zack."

His head buzzed. "I know that. Like I know you can trust me to sense when the time is right."

"They're only here for ten days. Not a large window of opportunity."

Zack slowed for the exit to Reagan Airport. "Actually, Jennifer leaves in a week, on the twenty-ninth. She wants to be back in California for New Year's Eve. I believe it has to do with a boyfriend. Might be getting serious."

"I can find out more about that than you can, Zack. You know, woman to woman."

Zack huffed. "I'm at the exit to Reagan, so I need to hang up. I promise you will meet both my daughters before they go home."

Another prolonged pause. "Okay. Sorry if I made you angry. I just want to help."

"I know you do, and I'm not angry."

Much.

"Just stressed."

"I can help relieve that stress, you know."

Zack cringed. "Not while my daughters are here."

"Figured as much, Doctor Prudish." Huge sigh. "Whatever."

Zack flushed. "I have to go now, Sarah. I'll call you when I can. This will all work out."

He clicked off the call before she could respond.

CHAPTER ELEVEN

Emily spent the rest of the day locked in her bedroom. Throughout the long hours, she heard no one. No footsteps up or down the stairs. No activity on the front driveway. More ominous, no sounds from the room down the hall where the other young mother waited to go into labor. Emily had heard nothing from that girl's room, even after the commotion in the first mother's room.

The now-dead mother.

Dr. Good had cautioned Emily about waking "the other one." Why didn't she answer now when Emily called out?

Had there been another body in the SUV when Spider drove away this morning? One Emily didn't see?

"Done," Spider had said.

Where had Dr. Good gone? She hated that on the one hand she got so annoyed with his doting on her, yet she found herself uncomfortable in his absence.

Emily bowed her head and accepted that the other woman was no longer in The Good House. Maybe no longer alive. She looked out the window. Dusk, at 5 PM. December 22. Winter solstice. Shortest day of the year.

They often locked Emily alone in her room. She had long ago acknowledged the impossibility of escape from The Good House. Where would she go? To whom? At what cost?

Prison or death, depending on who caught her and where.

Emily had a chance once, but no longer. She should have faced the consequences of her indiscretion as a nurse-midwife trainee, taken her punishment, and paid the price.

Instead, she had allowed Dr. Good to spirit her away to this purgatory.

"Criminal negligence and an eighteen-year statute of limitations for a dead infant," he had told her. "I alone can save you."

She loved him so much then; she thought they would stay together forever. Before she discovered his true nature.

Alone in the darkening room, Emily knotted her fists, scrunched up her face, and held her breath for as long as she could stand. At the cusp of passing out, she let out all the air in one long, mournful wail. She allowed her heart and soul to feel and suffer her feelings about Adam Good, for what he had done to her, and what he did to desperate women who deserved hope and salvation, not abuse by an evil profiteer.

The sound of a vehicle approaching the house shook Emily from her introspection. Through the window, she saw the familiar black F-150 truck park in the driveway.

Roach oiled himself out of the driver's side. He looked like a throwback to John Travolta in *Grease*

Emily's day had just gotten worse. She spat his name at the window. "Roach."

He walked around to the passenger side and pulled a thin, pale, shaken young woman from the vehicle.

My God, she looks barely twelve years old.

The skinny girl's protruding abdomen suggested a late third-trimester pregnancy. Emily swallowed hard. Another addition to Adam Good's dark enterprise.

The front door opened and closed, followed by two pairs of footsteps on the stairs and hallway. One heavy, one light. They stopped in front of Emily's room. The lock turned, the door opened, and Roach wormed into the room. He pulled the young girl behind him by her wrist.

A blush of hope crossed her terrified face when she saw Emily.

"New arrival," Roach said. He guided the girl to sit on the bed. "This is your nurse."

The girl whimpered. Emily reached out to her. "I'm Emily."

The frightened waif shrank away. Emily sat on the bed next to her. "Don't be afraid. I'm here to care for you."

The girl leaned toward her, a slight movement.

Emily took her hand. "What's your name?"

The girl pulled back, shook her head, and looked down. "I'm . . . no one."

Emily eased closer. "Okay. How about I call you 'Missy'?"

A half-smile flitted across the girl's face. Her whole body quivered. "I like it."

"Well, Missy. It looks like you're going to have a baby. Any idea when it's due?"

Missy's body froze and her eyes widened. "A baby?"

A grim picture emerged in Emily's mind. "That's right." She made a motion over her own abdomen as if to draw a pregnant person. "In your tummy."

The girl looked blank. "A baby?"

Emily pursed her lips and nodded.

"In my tummy?"

"That's right. Looks like it's going to want to come out pretty soon."

The girl recoiled like a frightened kitten, the surprise on her face turned to terror. "Come out? From my tummy? A baby?" She placed a hand on her abdomen. "How?"

Emily shot an angry glance at Roach. "How indeed?"

"Dang if I know," he said in a detached voice.

Emily took both of Missy's hands. "You'll be fine. I'll help you when the time comes, and I'll get you ready for it. You don't have to be afraid."

Missy took deep breaths. Her face relaxed some. She leaned toward Emily; gazed at her with wondering eyes. "Thank you, Nurse Emily."

"You're welcome." She stood the girl up. "Now let's go see your pretty new room."

A glimmer of light appeared in the girl's eyes. "Room? I get a room?"

"You sure do."

"I've never had my own room." Her face morphed from smile to frown. She started to cry. "I'm scared."

"I'll be right here across the hall. I won't let anything happen to you." Emily dabbed the tears from the girl's face. "Now let's go see your very own room."

Roach leaned against the wall with arms folded, a far-off look on his face. Emily glowered at him as she walked past to lead Missy into the hallway.

"Bastard," she said under her breath.

He didn't change position or expression. "Bitch."

Emily devoted an hour to getting Missy calmed down, evaluated, and settled in the room where the previous tenant had died that morning. By the time she was done, the young girl had begun to trust her.

She assessed that the girl was either mentally challenged, emotionally traumatized, or both. In nursing school, before the calamity that changed her life, Emily had gained some basic knowledge in neurodevelopmental pediatrics. She estimated Missy's chronological age at fourteen, but that she functioned at a mental age of six or seven. The girl had no knowledge or insight into male/female relations, pregnancy, or the birth process. When asked about family, she clammed up, stared at the floor, and acted as if she did not hear the questions. Emily asked her if she'd ever had a boyfriend. She squeezed her eyes shut, pursed her lips, and shook her head side-to-side with vigor.

"Daddy said no other boyfriends."

A disturbing image of how "Missy" might have gotten pregnant arose in Emily's mind. That question must wait for another day.

She fed the girl a light supper, put her through a warm bath, and found bed clothes that were only a size too big. After two bedtime stories, the girl fell asleep.

Exhausted, Emily tip-toed out of the room and went downstairs.

Roach sprawled on the couch smoking a joint.

Emily stood next to him, hands on hips, a scowl on her face. "Dr. Good doesn't allow that in the house."

The young man stretched his arms and legs and yawned. "Yeah, well, he's not coming back."

"What?"

"Something came up. He's gone for a while."

Emily nodded toward the stairs. "Does he know about . . . ?"

"Yeah."

"What if she goes into labor, or worse, and he's not here?"

"You deal with it."

Emily pursed her lips. "That girl doesn't belong here. She's too high risk. No prenatal care, poor nutrition, no hygiene, and mentally . . ."

Roach took a long drag on the joint and blew smoke toward the ceiling. "She stays here. You deal with it."

"If she delivers a baby in distress . . . ?

Roach let out an exasperated breath. "Deal with it. Get Dr. Kid if you must."

"She could lose her baby; her life."

Roach shrugged. "Then we take care of it. Like the other ones."

Ones? Plural?

A hot flush flowed through Emily's body. This was too much. Squaring her stance in front of Roach, she blurted. "No. I won't do it. I can't do it. We can take her to an ER. Drop her off and leave. No one needs to see us."

Roach scoffed. "No."

She folded her arms; stood her ground. "Wouldn't be the first time."

Roach vaulted off the couch. Half her age but almost a head taller than Emily, he bent his head to put his face so close she almost gagged at the pungent scent of weed.

"What is it about 'no' you don't understand, nurse?"

She backed away, spread her stance, kept her arms crossed, and stared at the punk kid in front of her. "I won't do it. I'm done with all this."

Roach tilted his head. A forced smile grew on his lips. "You have no choice, and you know it."

Emily pictured herself vaulting past him, rushing out the front door, into the woods.

As if reading her thoughts, the youth grinned and reached into his front pocket to extract a cell phone. He poked the screen, then held it in front of Emily.

"You will do as Dr. Good demands, or I press this number. You won't make it fifty yards into the woods."

She recognized the speed dial that she had thought only Dr. Good knew. A "code purple," emergency summons.

Emily was trapped. "Fine."

Roach returned the phone to his pocket, then reached behind his back. His hand came out holding a pistol. "Dr. Good said I can use this if I need to."

At once terrified, Emily turned away and climbed the stairs. At the top, she looked back at Roach. He had resumed his sprawl on the couch, the pistol no longer in sight.

She went to check on Missy. The girl was still asleep, clutching her pillow like a teddy bear. Emily returned to her room, lay on the bed, buried her face in her pillow, and sobbed.

CHAPTER TWELVE

Zack stood halfway down the corridor from the Delta Airlines passenger arrival area, trying to look relaxed as he craned his neck to find his daughters amid the bustling throng of holiday travelers. How much had they grown and changed since last he saw them at ages ten and seventeen?

He scowled at the memory. He had taken an hour break from a medical conference he attended in San Diego. They had spent half that time looking for a place to eat before settling on food-truck fare. He had sensed that they couldn't wait to get away, back to their own lives. Was he projecting his own discomfort at the time?

What if I don't recognize them?

He pulled out his phone. Call or text? He didn't know the protocol. If he missed the girls off the plane, he would have to call his ex-wife Natalie and endure her condescending reprimand. He could do without that.

Zack checked the arrivals board one more time. The nonstop flight from the west coast had arrived twenty minutes ago. Five minutes passed. His anxiety peaked. He reached for his phone to call Natalie but stopped in mid-motion when an attractive young woman approached him.

"Dad?"

Zack stuffed the phone into his pocket. "Jennifer?" He swallowed hard. "I hardly recognized you. You've. Grown."

He took in her attire, casual but tasteful, probably expensive. What else should he expect from a first-year Stanford medical student whose mother happened to be a La Jolla psychiatrist who catered to the rich and famous?

Jennifer wrapped him in a hesitant but affectionate hug. "It's been too long. I've missed you."

Zack let go and studied his older daughter. "Wow. You look fabulous. Very, uh, professional."

He glanced past her. *Where was Annie?*

A teenage slouching version of Lisbeth Salander drifted toward them. *Annie?*

Zack failed in his effort not to gawk at his younger daughter's ear and lip rings, nose stud, and spiked jet-black hair with streaks of violet, blue, and fluorescent yellow. Purple eye shadow completed the look. She wore multi-holed jeans and a tight halter top that revealed red bra straps.

After a few seconds, he moved forward and hugged her. She halfway returned the hug, stiff and uncertain.

"Hi, Dad." Voice flat.

They stepped apart, both uncomfortable. "You've certainly changed, uh, grown since I last saw you."

"Duh. I was in grade school then."

"I know. It's been too long."

Annie looked at Jennifer as if asking to be rescued. Zack looked at Jennifer with an identical expression. He wondered if he could talk Jenn into staying the full ten days.

If she noticed the matched pleas for help, Jennifer didn't let on to Zack or Annie. Her mother's clone, including that detached inscrutability. Annie would have been "Daddy's girl," except she was so young at the time of the divorce.

What, if anything, did she remember about her dad?

Zack forced himself into tour-guide mode and started walking toward the concourse exit. "You girls have checked luggage?"

Jennifer angled her head and chuckled. "Yeah, we couldn't stash all our girly stuff into these two backpacks." She grinned and cast him the same sarcastic raised eyebrow he'd seen many times from Natalie.

Chagrined, Zack led them to baggage claim. Both retrieved suitcases large and heavy enough to support a permanent move to the northeast. He assisted them in rolling their baggage toward the curb where he intended for them to wait while he retrieved his Lexus.

A blast of frigid air struck as they walked through the sliding glass doors to the sidewalk. Neither girl wore a coat.

"It's been unseasonably cold here," Zack said. "I hope you brought warm clothes."

Annie opened her suitcase on the sidewalk, rustled through the crammed, disorganized contents, and extracted a tattered denim jacket with padded lining.

Jennifer hugged herself but left her suitcase closed. "Maybe we should go to the garage with you."

"Good idea."

Annie stuffed her belongings back into the suitcase and forced it closed. They went back into the terminal. The girls' luggage would not fit onto the escalator, so they found an elevator to the upper level and a closed walkway to the parking garage. Zack second-guessed himself for not making that choice in the first place.

None of them spoke until Zack drove the Lexus out of the parking garage.

Zack had turned the car northbound onto George Washington Parkway. Jennifer sat beside him in the front seat staring out the window into the crisp night air that offered a decent view of the Washington Monument across the Potomac River. Annie sat behind Jennifer in the back seat. From the instant she buckled her seatbelt, she had stared at her phone.

Zack frowned at his earlier naiveté.

Of course, a fifteen-year-old has a phone.

He reclaimed his voice. "How was the flight?"

"Long," Jennifer said.

Zack glanced into the rear-view mirror, still befuddled by his daughter's appearance, attire, and attitude.

"How was it for you, Annie?"

She answered without looking up from her phone. "Long."

"Did either of you sleep?"

"Not really," Jennifer said. "I don't sleep well on airplanes. I did some studying."

"Studying? On holiday break?"

"Medical school is harder than in your day, Dad."

Zack forced a laugh. "Hopefully, you've inherited your mother's knack for science. That was almost my undoing. You know, back in the dark ages when I studied medicine on hand-written parchment."

He smiled at how easily he could reprise the sarcastic banter he'd had with Natalie.

Even in the darkness, he sensed Jennifer's blush. "I'm sorry," she said. "That didn't come out like I meant it."

Zack smiled in her direction. "No problem. It's no secret I got into medical school by the skin of my teeth as an alternate, whereas your mother was AOA and Summa Cum Laude in college. She had her pick of med schools."

Jennifer sighed. "I consider myself lucky to be at Stanford."

Zack smiled. "You will do well there." As if he had any facts to support his opinion.

He glanced into the mirror. Annie continued to stare at her phone. "What did you do on the plane, Annie?"

"Watched a movie." She still didn't look up.

"What movie?" Zack made it a personal challenge to unlock her gaze from that screen.

"*Logan.*" Eyes glued to the screen.

"Ah, yes, the demise of Wolverine." Zack chuckled, more to himself than his daughter. "What did you think about Laura finally acknowledging him as her father?"

Bingo!

Annie's eyes shot off the screen and contacted his in the mirror. Her expression approximated that of a person seeing her reflection for the first time. Then it was like a veil slipped over her face and she looked back at the phone.

"Kinda cheesy."

"I thought it was cool."

Jennifer regarded him with suspicion. "I don't believe you'd watch a movie like that one, Dad."

"You'd be surprised what a single man with 300 cable channels and a 65-inch UHD TV will watch. I'm a big fan of all the Marvel movies. Jessica Jones is my favorite. Luke Cage a close second."

In the mirror, a dismissive shrug from Annie. "Weenies."

Zack turned the car onto the Capital Beltway. No one spoke until he took the exit onto Old Georgetown Road into Bethesda.

"I'll bet you girls are hungry. They don't serve decent food on airplanes anymore."

"We had snacks with us," Jennifer said. "But we could both stand some dinner."

"Whatever suits your appetites, we have it in Bethesda. Italian, Greek, Mediterranean, Mexican, or plain old American burgers."

"Only Beyond Burgers for me," Annie said. "I'm vegan."

Zack glanced at the mirror and wondered what other surprises she had in store for him over the next ten days.

"I think we can find something to everyone's liking at my favorite Mediterranean restaurant."

"Whatever," Annie said.

CHAPTER THIRTEEN

Just after 6 PM that evening, Bridget squeezed her Range Rover next to Marshall's Mercedes SL 450 in the two-car garage of their luxury townhouse in the Cameron Station neighborhood of Alexandria, VA. As usual, her husband had taken more than his fair share of space—a not-so-subtle declaration that the US Attorney for the Eastern District of Virginia deserved more space than a mere malpractice defense lawyer, no matter how successful and lucrative her practice.

Story of our marriage.

Why would Marshall be home before dinner for the first time in two weeks? Then she remembered they had promised to attend their son Dustin's tournament championship basketball game at Bishop Ireton High School.

"Damn," she said aloud. She had barely enough time to shower, change clothes, and leave. They would have to get dinner after the game. At least the residual chlorine smell from her swim would dissipate in the youth-sweat environment of the gym.

Inside the home, Bridget rushed upstairs and full-on collided with Marshall coming out of their bedroom. He reached out to catch her as she stumbled backward. He missed. Bridget's back struck the railing, and she slid to a sitting position on the floor.

She started to apologize, then noticed the roll-aboard suitcase in her husband's other hand. She pointed at it. "What's that?"

Marshall glanced away, then helped Bridget to her feet. "I have to go to Richmond."

Bridget stepped back. "Now? What the hell?" She hated how her deformed voice squeaked when she wanted to sound assertive.

Marshall assumed his sonorous authoritarian tone, as if he were addressing the Supreme Court. "The case we've been working. The judge moved the pre-trial motions to tomorrow morning. We received notice this afternoon."

"We?"

"The team working the case."

Bridget's eyes narrowed. "Can't your deputy handle it?"

Marshall shook his head. "Not with that misogynist judge. He'll tear Fiona to pieces. I need to be there for support." He paused and avoided eye contact. "Plus, I have other meetings in Richmond later in the day."

A flush rose in Bridget's face as her throat tightened. She could not speak above a whisper. "We promised Dustin. His game."

Marshall reached to touch her shoulder. She drew away.

"I called him and apologized," he said. "He understands."

Bridget scoffed. "Sure he does." She stepped around her husband toward the bedroom, then turned in the doorway to face him. "How are you getting to Richmond?"

"Driving. Too late for AMTRAK."

"When will you be home?"

"Tomorrow night, if all goes well."

"And if it doesn't?"

Marshall shrugged, sheepish.

Bridget crossed her arms. "Did you forget Grant's flight from Boston tomorrow?" Bridget had not planned to entertain her stepson without his father.

Marshall narrowed his eyes. "He might as well learn now that a lawyer, especially a Harvard lawyer, has to make sacrifices."

Bridget's mouth gaped. "He's a law-school freshman. You haven't seen him since his college graduation."

Marshall harrumphed. "Can't be helped, Bridge. I'll make it up to him."

Bridget's jaw tightened. "Fine. I'll go to Dustin's game, and I'll meet your other son's plane. We'll see you . . . whenever."

"Bridge . . ."

"Not now, Marsh. I need to get moving."

She stepped toward the bedroom, then turned back to him. "How's that task force doing? The one investigating the medical cabal?"

The task force Zack Winston is on.

Marshall pursed his lips; raised an eyebrow. "Not much I can talk about. The cabal went deep underground after Dr. Dennis King's death. There seem to be several arms, or cells. We have a new lead we're chasing down." He smirked. "Your Dr. Winston might help us with that."

MY Dr. Winston?

Marshall looked at his watch. "I have to go and so do you." He turned and descended the stairs, hefting the roll-aboard behind him.

Bridget called after him. "Be safe."

She almost meant it.

—⋀—

Later that night, Bridget pulled into the empty garage after attending the basketball game. Marshall's car was gone, as expected. With a glint in her eye, she parked her Range Rover in the middle of the space and shut down the engine.

Leave it here and take the Metro to work tomorrow. Let him find his own parking spot when he gets home.

IF he comes home.

She glanced at herself in the rear-view mirror. "How old are you, Bridget?"

She started the car, backed out, and returned the Range Rover to her side of the garage, leaving enough space for Marshall to park his beloved Benz.

She paused before getting out of the car, remembering how kind he'd been to her during her recovery from the attack and surgical repair of her trachea.

Bridget had never doubted Marshall's love. Just his loyalty. She should have had a clue about his character years ago, when he took up with her while still married to Grant's mother.

What does that affair say about my own character? Does it matter that we ended up together? Had our own child?

Bridget knew the answer. Their subsequent life did not justify what they had done. She had acknowledged and forgiven herself for her part, and committed to fidelity and motherhood, including being stepmother to Grant Hilliard.

Marshall, on the other hand, repeated the same behavior. Fiona Delaney was just his latest dalliance. Albeit predictable, it hurt Bridget. Yet she remained loyal.

A vision of Zack Winston drifted into consciousness. She erased it and got out of the car.

Inside the house, Bridget relished the silence and solitude. Flush from their victory, Dustin and his teammates had gone to a celebratory party hosted by their coach. The man was not only an expert in the art of high school basketball but also possessed keen insight into the teenage psyche. None of his players would get into trouble that night. They could party at his house under his watchful eye, and—as he had shared discretely with their parents—he would lock them in for an all-night sleepover. No cruising the streets in the dark hours for them.

Bridget finished off the salad she'd made the previous night, untouched by either Marshall or Dustin. What to do with the rest of the night by herself? Marshall would be in Richmond by now. What plans had he made for the night? He wouldn't call, a practice he'd stopped two political appointments and many years ago.

Out of sight . . . ?

Another vision of Zack Winston burst into Bridget's mind. She vanished it with a head shake and wave of her hand. No denying she had feelings for Zack. He had saved her life. Even before that terrible night, he had become not only her client but her friend. After a rough start and several backslides, they had developed a melding of minds and formed a productive partnership that triumphed over a wicked plot to destroy Zack's career and his life.

She had jeopardized her own career by using Marshall's confidential documents to defend Zack. Had near-death and permanent damage to her voice been her punishment?

Bridget remembered little of what had happened in that parking garage after she, Zack, and their colleagues had celebrated their legal victory at a DC restaurant. Of late, snippets had risen into consciousness. The psychiatrist she'd finally agreed to see had advised that she try to remember. Recalling the event would help her deal with the ongoing terror of being alone in dark places, and her constant compulsion to look behind when approaching her car—even in her own locked garage.

The night was still early for someone who thrived on less than six hours of sleep. Bridget poured herself two fingers of Lagavulin single-malt scotch and settled onto the living room couch. After a couple of sips, she closed her eyes and allowed the visions to surface.

They came in brief disconnected flashes: Unlocking her car door. The sudden heat of Dennis King's breath in her left ear as he grabbed her from behind. His grumbled voice. "Zack," and "slut." Then, nothing.

No. Something else first. A new memory rose into her consciousness: A sharp blade, a surgical scalpel, drawn across her throat.

Bridget's eyes popped open as she grabbed the front of her neck. Dr. King had slit her throat and left her dying on the concrete next to her car. Zack and Ange had found her not a second too soon.

Had Zack later killed Dennis in self-defense as the authorities decided, or was it retaliation for what his former mentor had done to Bridget?

She got off the couch. "No more memories tonight."

Bridget downed the rest of the scotch, bounded upstairs to change into cold weather running gear, and charged out the front door. A better solution than getting drunk and battling horrific memories: conquer the frigid darkness with physical prowess. As her feet pounded the asphalt and sidewalks, she reflected that taking up triathlon training had been a healthier choice than seeing the psychiatrist. Cheaper too, if you didn't count her aquatics membership, Peloton, and the new top-of-the-line Trek racing bike.

As her breathing deepened, Bridget felt a flush of energy course through her body. The angst she'd felt since arriving home from work gave way to clarity and resolve.

"I deserve better than you, Marshall Hilliard."

Her thoughts went to Dustin, already accepted into the pre-law curriculum at Georgetown. On track to follow the legacy of both parents and his older brother at Harvard Law. She knotted her fists and picked up the pace. The effort drove all distractions from her mind.

Back home, Bridget changed into sweats, combed out her long blond hair, and reclined on the bed. No need to shower since she was the only one home. She picked up her phone and scrolled through the contacts.

Her finger lingered over Zack Winston's number. She almost punched it, but then continued scrolling to Dominic Zimbaro. She chuckled at the memory of Zack referring to her firm's freelance investigator as "Dominic Soprano." Dom could be a twin to TV's infamous mobster, and he was not above bending rules to get vital information to support Bridget's clients. With a final determined grunt, she punched the number.

Dominic answered on the second ring. "Ms. Larsen?"

"Sorry to call so late, Dom." She paused, unsure of what to say.

"No problem, Ma'am. What can I do for you?"

Bridget pursed her lips.

Don't turn back.

"A job. It's not firm business. I, uh, want to hire you on a personal basis. Your usual fee."

After a moment of uncomfortable silence, Dominic replied. "Go on, please."

"Do you have any contacts in Richmond?"

CHAPTER FOURTEEN

A wave of exhaustion washed over Zack as he and his daughters finished their dinner at the Mediterranean restaurant. He had expended most of his emotional energy during his ER shift, exacerbated by Nate Young's near-drowning and the dust-up with Sebastian Barth over Paula Cho's missed ectopic case. Those challenges paled in comparison to the stress of seeing his two daughters after such a long interlude, compounded a hundredfold by his fumbling attempts to reconnect with them, especially Annie.

He'd made some progress with Jennifer, who was old enough to have a vague memory of their early family life. She'd matured enough to realize that he did not bear all the blame—contrary to the emotional poison that Natalie had fed the girls during and after the divorce. Jennifer and Zack had common ground, her journey toward becoming a doctor like both her parents. He wondered if her interest in neurosurgery represented an emotional break from his specialty of emergency medicine and Natalie's career in psychiatry. Or was it a synthesis?

"I thought I wanted to be a cardiothoracic surgeon when I entered med school," Zack said. "Then I got into the clinical years, and I liked every specialty." He scoffed. "Even psychiatry."

When Jennifer didn't react, he continued. "I was an adrenaline junkie. Emergency medicine became the perfect choice."

"I don't think I could take all the night hours and holidays away from home and family."

"On the other hand," Zack said, "as an ER doc when you're off duty you are totally off. You can spend time with family and not worry about being called in to crack open someone's skull to evacuate a blood clot on their brain after they got drunk and rammed their car into a bridge abutment."

Jennifer frowned. "That's harsh, Dad. Sounds like resentment."

Zack considered her words then forced a smile. "Yeah. Maybe. You see enough self-induced tragedy, you can get judgmental." He pursed his lips. "Plenty of alcohol-related traumas in the ER."

Jennifer shot him a piercing look. "Pot to kettle, Dad?"

Zack silently cursed Natalie as he raised his glass of sparkling water to his daughter. "I don't know what you've heard, but, yeah, I succumbed to that alcohol demon near the end of my navy career. Damn near ruined me, but I beat it." He looked her in the eye, speaking truth. "From time to time I indulge my passion for fine wine and single-malt Scotch. It's a hobby, not a habit."

Jennifer forced a smile and raised her glass of cola. "Okay, Dad."

"One word of advice about med school. Don't make your career choice until you get into the clinical years. Sample everything. You may be surprised what stirs your passion. If you can't be devoted to your medical practice through the course of a career, you need to do something else."

Jennifer nodded. "Got it."

Annie had spent most of the dinnertime staring at her phone while picking at her vegan salad. She deflected Zack's conversation attempts with either shrugs or monosyllabic answers. He wondered if she'd listened to his conversation with Jennifer.

"What about you, Annie? Any idea what you want to be when you grow up?"

She shot him a look that said she considered herself already grown up. "I like the arts." She glanced at Jennifer. "None of that science junk."

Zack considered that he'd sired a right-brained daughter and a left-brained daughter. Had he not known better, he might wonder if they both came from the same mother.

Annie's eyes returned to her phone.

Zack lost his patience. "Please put the phone away for a few minutes and talk to your dad."

When she looked up, her face reflected both surprise and anger. "Yeah, sure."

A strained five-minute conversation followed. Zack learned that Annie didn't care much for school, didn't want to talk about her friends, and didn't know what she wanted for her birthday or Christmas.

"Have you seen 'The Hunger Games'?"

"Boring. Like who would do that?"

"Sacrifice herself for her family, for her little sister?" Zack glanced at Jennifer. No help coming from her.

"It's a lame story."

"It's based on a Japanese classic, 'Battle Royale,' a book and a movie."

"Whatever."

Zack fought to quell his dismay. What garbage had Natalie fed these girls? She had initiated the break-up, accused Zack of being emotionally unavailable, and left him for another man. After the divorce, he resigned from his successful emergency medicine practice and joined the navy as a flight surgeon. That had meant a considerable loss of income, which Natalie claimed was a ploy to reduce the child support he paid. Zack countered that she made enough as a psychiatrist to support herself and their daughters in a lifestyle to which he could only aspire.

He had later apologized, attributing his tirade to the stress of being divorced by the woman he loved. Natalie never bought into that apology or proclamation of love. She told him that if he ever decided to be truthful with himself, he might someday enjoy a real committed relationship.

Zack had dismissed that as "psychobabble."

And now I'm seeing a shrink three days a week to help me deal with the tragedy of Noelle, the true love I met and lost in Japan.

He was about to probe Annie about her interest in the arts when his phone buzzed. He glanced at the caller ID.

Sevati Prakash.

News about Nate?

"I'm sorry, ladies. I need to take this call from the hospital." He rose from his chair. "Go ahead and order dessert. I'll be right back."

He walked toward the entrance and answered. "Sevati?"

"Sorry, Zack. I was about to hang up when I remembered you are with your daughters."

"It's okay. We're just finishing dinner at a restaurant. What's up?"

"I was told you came to ICU looking for Jerry or me. I assume it was about Nate. I am calling from home, so we can talk."

"What did you find?"

"The intern found them when he did his complete exam. Needle tracks in the web spaces between the toes."

"Huh?"

"On the left foot, between the first and second, and again between the second and third toes."

Stunned, Zack rubbed his forehead. "That makes no sense. IV drug abusers use that route sometimes. But Nate? No way." He closed his mind to the niggling thought that maybe Nate used drugs to deal with a secret fetish. Could the accusations be true?

"Did you find any other needle tracks, any signs of chronic abuse?"

"Only the ones between the toes," Sevati said. "I saw them myself. So did Jerry Hartman."

"You did a tox screen?"

"Of course. We will get preliminary results tomorrow."

Zack squeezed his eyes shut, thinking. "Did you give a narcotic antagonist, Narcan?"

"Yes. No change in his status."

"This makes no sense, Sevati."

"You understand why we did not want to discuss over the phone in the hospital?"

"Of course." Zack peeked into the dining room. Jennifer cast him a Natalie-like scolding expression as desserts arrived at the table.

"Okay, Sevati, thanks for the call. I have to get back to my daughters." He rubbed a hand through his hair. "Once I get them settled at home I'll go to the ICU and see for myself."

"It can wait until tomorrow."

"No, it can't."

Zack could hear her huff through the phone. "Priorities, Zack. Nate will still be there in the morning."

Et tu, Sevati?

"Okay. Please call if there's any change. No matter the time."

Sevati agreed.

Zack hung up and returned to the table. He shifted his brain into a different compartment.

"What music do you like, Annie?"

CHAPTER FIFTEEN

Sometime later, Zack introduced his daughters to his swank man-cave. The apartment's living room sported black leather furniture facing the 65" UHD smart-TV attached to a wall across from the mini-bar and walk-in chrome and black kitchen.

"The couch opens into a queen-sized bed," he said to Annie. "I thought you might like it."

She shrugged. "Whatever."

He showed them their bathroom off the living room, then escorted them to his home office in the spare bedroom. "Another fold-out couch," he said to Jennifer. "Hope that's okay."

"It's fine, dad." Jennifer stared at his height-adjustable desk with the gaming desktop computer and 49-inch curved monitor. She smirked. "Won't I be in the way of your work?"

Zack shook his head. "I have a desk and laptop in my bedroom. This room is all yours while you're here. I won't intrude."

Once he got the girls settled, he glanced at his watch: 10 PM.

He rubbed his forehead. "So, uh, there's a patient in the ICU, a physician I know. We admitted him from the ER this morning. Near-drowning. Still in a coma. I should go see him. Would that be okay? I won't be gone long. Give you girls some time to settle in, maybe call your mom to let her know you got here in one piece, I mean two pieces?"

Annie rolled her eyes and crossed her arms. "Whatever."

Jennifer moved closer to him; touched his arm. "That must be awful. Of course, go." She shot Annie a stern look. "We'll be fine."

In the ICU, Nate Young remained unconscious. His skin color had improved because the heart-lung machine delivered enriched oxygen to his bloodstream. The near-normal complexion made the unmistakable needle tracks between the toes of his left foot easy to recognize. Like Zack had seen in hard-core IV drug abusers whose arm veins were long since destroyed, or who endeavored to hide their habit from others. Except Nate's arms and groins, typical sites for IV drug injections, were unharmed.

Zack had known Nate for several years. The man could not have been a secret drug abuser and still maintained his practice and standing among his medical peers.

I've been fooled before. Fooled others myself. You never really know someone.

He checked for results from the toxicology screen, but they were still pending. He called Sevati to confirm that his examination matched hers. He promised to meet with her and Jerry Hartman the following morning. The girls would be jet-lagged, their bodies still on Pacific time, and probably wouldn't get up until noon. Zack could go to the hospital and still be back at the apartment to fix them a late breakfast.

When Zack opened his apartment door just before 11 PM, the girls had taken over the living room. They had found the snacks Zack had stocked for their visit, but they had shunned the potato chips and dip for the veggie tray that he had bought as a last-minute afterthought. Jennifer sat in Zack's recliner, watching a movie on the TV. Annie spread out on the sofa, ear buds plugged into her phone.

Neither one moved when Zack entered.

"Guess you two are on west coast time," he said.

Jennifer looked up and paused the movie. Annie kept her ear buds in place and stared at her phone. Zack fought off the urge to rip it from her hands.

"I need to get to bed," he said. "I have to go into the hospital in the morning, but I expect to be back before you two get up."

Jennifer smiled. "Yeah, I definitely plan to sleep in."

Annie made no indication she'd heard him.

"Anything you need before I retire?"

"We'll manage, Dad," Jennifer said. "Good night."

In his bedroom, Zack changed into sweatpants and a long-sleeved running shirt. He sat on the edge of his bed, fighting the sudden fatigue and anxiety that washed over him.

He needed Noclle.

He sat at the small desk, pulled open the drawer, and extracted the leather-bound journal he had purchased at his psychiatrist's suggestion, to write notes to his deceased second wife. Three months had passed since his only entry.

Zack's psychiatrist had urged him to communicate with Noelle through the journal.

"She was the only person in your life with whom you allowed vulnerability," the shrink said. "Even though she's dead, you should communicate your feelings to her. Otherwise, you'll bury them. They'll come back to hurt you later when you least expect it."

Zack found the exercise too artificial to be helpful. He would prefer a return to when he could conjure the "ghost" of Noelle from his mind into pseudo-reality. Had it been so crazy to converse with her, even to see her, as if she were alive and present? Of course not. Even his shrink concurred, after the fact.

Once he had suffered and recovered from the tragedies of the last year, "Noelle" told him he no longer needed her in that way. She urged him to become close friends with a living woman, Bridget. On an intellectual level, Zack recognized that Noelle was neither a ghost nor a paranormal companion. She arose from his subconscious, encouraging him to make healthy life choices free of the defenses and buried memories of his past.

It worked, sort of, even after the realities of normal life interrupted his companionship with Bridget.

Zack opened the journal and re-read his first letter dated in late September.

CHAPTER SIXTEEN

September 27

My dear Noelle,
   My shrink says I should write to you directly as the best way to unburden my soul. I tried doing it on her couch, but she called me out for being defensive and dishonest. You never let me get away with that . . . one of the reasons I loved you so fiercely.
   "Loved?"
   I still love you, more than ever, and I miss you every day. I wish I could see you again, even in my imagination like before you made me let that go.
   I yearn for our real conversations, when we were on liberty, sipping scotch on a hotel veranda, overlooking Hong Kong, or Cairns, or . . . well, you know.
   I'm supposed to get past that horrible night you died on Kitty Hawk.
   "You died."
   I still find that so hard to say. Sometimes I close my eyes and we have you in the OR and I believe I can save you. If only I'd tried harder. That's not true. You were dead already when the rescue swimmer picked you out of the sea and the helo brought you back to our deck.

All the people I've saved in my career, I couldn't save you.

"Enough," you say. "Cut the self-pity, Zack."

Okay!

I'm supposed to let the memory of our happy days heal the hole in my heart. I try to reorganize my mind so that the happy memories stay. I try to relish those, but reality lurks just beneath them like a killer shark in shallow water. When I'm tired, or weak, or down, I'm back in that OR, kissing your lifeless lips and telling you goodbye and it hurts so damned much I wish I could die just to be with you again.

I'm crying now. Maybe you see it. Maybe you see everything I do, hear everything I say, know everything I think. Would you still love me, knowing everything about me? You loved me once in spite of me. Would you still?

I had to quit for a few minutes, dry my eyes, you know.

Maybe the shrink's plan will work despite my resistance. The terrible nightmares come less often. Sometimes I see you as I did when my heart stopped before Dennis resuscitated me. I saw you reach for me and I thought we would be together again. I wanted that.

I wish I had died in that ER. To be with you again.

Hell, Noelle, this won't work. You're not here. Just me and this damned pen and paper. I will never see you again in this life. Loss is the only reality I have left. I even lost having Dennis to hate after I killed him. I tried to save him in the end. That didn't work either.

I could swear you just said, "Bridget." At least I saved Bridget's life. For what? She's gone too. Haven't seen nor talked to her in months. Ange neither.

Why do the women in my life always drift away?

If you were here you would kick my ass, remind me that I have more left in my life than missing you. I can see the fire in your eyes and hear the cutting edge in your voice when you say it.

"Get your shit together, Zack."

Another thing I love about you. Even in death, you refuse to tolerate my self-destructive melancholy.

Okay, I'm snapping out of it, just as you would want me to do. First thing, I'll invite my daughters to come to Bethesda for a visit. I haven't seen either of them in so many years. I thought about them after I almost died. I realized that I need to reestablish my relationship with them.

"Don't talk about it, Zack. Do it."

I hear you. You would refuse to have another word until I complied. I'll close now and get in touch with them. Maybe they can come during the Christmas holidays and we can also celebrate Annie's birthday on the 24th. I think she'll be sixteen.

Yes, I just did the math. Annie, my younger daughter whom I barely know, will be sweet sixteen. Scary that. Maybe Jennifer can be the buffer. She's twenty-two. I don't know her so well either.

"Quit procrastinating, Zack."

Okay. I'll do it right now.

I love you. Always.

Zack

Still here. I can't close without telling you something else, because I am bound and determined to be completely honest no matter how hard it is for me. Here goes . . . I have a new girlfriend. Her name is Sarah and I think she wants to be serious. I haven't told her about you and I can't do it because she's never going to be you and as soon as I tell her that she will know it and I don't want to hurt her so what am I going to do?

Now I'm done. Bye, love.

Zack turned to a fresh page in his journal. He reached back into the drawer to extract the 5" x 7" framed photo of Noelle in her US Navy service dress white uniform; the official photo he had carried along with her ashes from Japan to Michigan for burial amid family and friends.

The only picture he had of her.

He swallowed the surge of guilt welling up from his gut as he recalled shoving it into the drawer a few seconds before Sarah emerged from the bathroom the first time he slept with her. Because he didn't want to talk about Noelle with Sarah? Or because he didn't want Noelle to see what he was doing? He shook his head.

Because he was betraying Noelle's memory.

He held the photo in both hands and admired Noelle's radiant beauty. Her umber complexion and jet-black hair, all the more delightful against the crisp whiteness of her uniform. He kissed the image, then replaced it where it belonged atop the desk. He would leave it there, even when (if?) Sarah returned to his bed. He wanted Jennifer and Annie to see it. He wanted to tell them all about the true love of his life.

Natalie be damned.

Zack picked up the journal and wrote.

December 22.

Dearest Noelle,

They are here. Jennifer and Annie are in the next room watching TV. I have them for ten full days. Well, Annie for ten. Jenn "has" to go back for New Year's Eve. Boyfriend. Yikes. Last time I saw her she was in high school. Now she's a Stanford medical student. Yikes.

I don't know what to think about Annie. She turns 16 in two days. Full Goth and an attitude to match. Impenetrable shell. A small victory that I got her to look up from her phone by mentioning a Marvel movie. Wondering if I can get through to her in ten days. Scary. You could. The two of you would hit it off from the start. Maybe that's how I should approach it. What would Noelle do, or say?

A prominent pediatrician on our staff, Nate Young,

nearly drowned today. Cops suspect suicide because he was about to be exposed in the news as a child molester. I'm not buying that. Don't know if he'll survive or what cognitive function he'll retain if he does live. Difficult job to care for a colleague. Harder without knowing the why.

Five minutes have passed while I stared at the wall opposite my bed. I was thinking about Nate but then my mind drifted to a phone call I got today. Ange. Calling for Bridget and herself. They want me to be a defense expert on an emergency OB case. Not sure what to make of that.
Okay, yeah, it's not about the case, it's about. . . .
Seeing Bridget, you say? Yeah, you got it.

Pen in hand, Zack stared at the wall, then at Noelle's photo, then back at the wall. He couldn't think of what else to write.

His phone buzzed.

Sarah.

He'd forgotten to call her after he got home with the girls. He looked at the time. Almost midnight. He would usually be asleep. He let the call go to voicemail.

Zack closed the journal and replaced it and the pen in the bedside stand. He studied the photo of Noelle, as if he needed to memorize how she looked alive, not the dead woman he'd kissed goodbye on the ship.

After a quick trip to the bathroom and a check on the girls in the living room (neither had moved), he got into bed and shut off the light. He lay on his back and stared at the ceiling until his eyes drifted shut. In that twilight moment between awake and asleep, he heard Noelle's voice.

"Go to Bridget, Zack."

CHAPTER SEVENTEEN

Annie looked up from her phone and took out one ear bud when Jennifer stood and approached her dad's bedroom. Her sister tapped twice on the door before he opened it. He wore running shorts and shirt, but his rumpled hair and fogged eyes suggested he'd been asleep.

"Sorry, Dad," Jennifer said. "Where do you keep the bedding?"

His eyes flinched. He rubbed his forehead with the back of his hand. "Cripes, some host I am."

He stepped into the alcove next to the bathroom and opened a narrow closet. "Here." He started to reach into the closet, but Jennifer stopped him.

"We have it from here, Dad. Go back to bed."

He blinked his eyes and looked at his watch. "Okay. I'll see you when I get back from the hospital in the morning."

He smiled at Jennifer. "Good night, Jenn."

He shot a pointed look at Annie. "Good night, Annie."

Annie smirked. "Night."

Zack went back into his bedroom and closed the door.

Annie glared at Jennifer. "How can you be so nice to that yoyo?"

Jenn gave her a sisterly smile. "He's our dad."

"*Was* our dad."

"*Is* and always will be. We make the best of it."

Annie scowled.

"Get over the anger and hate, sis. Makes you look ugly."

Annie rolled her eyes. "You didn't want to come here anymore than I did. At least I'm not pretending I like it."

Jenn shook her head and blew out a breath. "Okay, little girl. Whatever you say."

"Don't call me 'little girl.'"

"Quit acting like one and maybe I will."

Annie crossed her arms, pulled her legs up to her chest, and stuck out her lip. "I hate him."

Jennifer sat next to her on the couch and put a hand on her knee. "How can you hate a man you don't know?"

"Because of what he did to mom, to us."

"You can't believe everything mom says."

"Oh, no? You know something different?"

Jennifer turned to face Annie. "I'm willing to give the man a chance. He chose to bring us here. Didn't have to do it. Maybe he really wants to make things right. At least get to know him before you decide to hate him."

"He's a nerd and a moron. Did you see how he looked at me at the airport? Like I was a freak. He brings us all the way here, drops us in this place, then leaves. He's doing it again tomorrow. What are we supposed to do cooped up in this cave?"

"He'll be back by the time we get up. The way you sleep, you may not wake up till dinnertime." Jenn smiled. "And you don't look like a freak. You're just, different. Give him some time. He'll warm up."

"I can't believe I'm wasting my winter break on this crap."

Jennifer flushed. "Cut the BS. Get your head straight. I did it. You can too."

Annie picked up her phone and replaced the ear bud.

Jennifer pulled out the ear bud. "Fine. Be a jerk. I'm going to bed." She tossed a sheet, blanket, and pillow at Annie. "Enjoy the couch."

Annie put the bud back into her ear and turned away. "Whatever."

After Jennifer went to bed, Annie used the bathroom, removed her eyeshadow and makeup, threw the covers onto the couch, and climbed under them. She didn't bother to open up the bed.

Her phone buzzed. Text from Conner. She opened it.

What up girl
This place is so lame
Mighta guessed
Miss you
You too wanna hold you
Want you to
Any news about you know what
Too soon coupla days maybe
You'll tell me
Duh
PIR
K Night ♥
Night ♥

Annie shut off her phone, got up to plug in the charger, and turn off the room light. When she got back into her makeshift bed, she buried her head in the pillow and whimpered.

CHAPTER EIGHTEEN

Missy had been frightened in the room by herself. Annoyed by the girl's crying, Roach had insisted that Emily share her room with the young girl, to which Emily readily agreed. She complained when Roach started to lock the door behind him.

"What if she goes into labor and I need to get to the supplies?"

Roach had cast a scornful look at the pregnant waif rocking back and forth on the edge of Emily's bed. "Then you call me and I might let you all out." He left the room; closed and locked the door.

Tucked close to Missy in the bed, Emily put an arm around her. Soon the girl fell asleep with her head on Emily's chest.

She awoke to Missy pushing on her shoulder. "Nurse Emily, I peed myself."

Emily opened her eyes to early dawn peeking through the window. She had forgotten to tell the girl about the bedpan under the bed.

Missy stood beside the bed, shoulders slumped, head down, hands against her cheeks. Rivulets of liquid ran down the inside of her legs.

Emily recognized the sweetish smell of amniotic fluid, not the typical ammonia smell of urine. She sat up and pulled the girl to her.

"Missy, your water broke."

"My? Water? Pee?"

The girl had no concept of the birth process. Emily needed to roust

Roach and get Missy into the combined delivery/bedroom across the hall. She got out of bed, put on her nursing smock, took Missy by the hand, and started toward the bedroom door.

All of a sudden, Missy screamed and bent over, grabbing her abdomen. "I have to go potty."

In one fluid motion, Emily rushed to the door, pounded on it, called out for Roach, and switched on the overhead light. Missy had slumped to the floor, her face pale. Bloody amniotic fluid ran from between her legs.

This is girl is going to deliver soon. I don't even know her gestational age.

Emily screamed for Roach.

He burst through the door. "What?"

Emily spoke in a scathing voice. "She's going to deliver. I need to get her to the room." She pulled Missy to her feet and supported her with an arm.

Roach had taken a step back in the doorway, eyes wide, mouth gaping.

Emily considered that the youth had never seen a woman give birth. "Help me get her to the room, damn it, then call Dr. Good."

Roach grabbed Missy from the other side and the two of them helped her across the hall as she doubled over again with pain.

They got Missy onto the delivery room bed.

"Dr. Good's not available," Roach said.

Emily glowered at Roach. "Then you're going to help me deliver this baby."

"I don't—"

"Shut up and do what I say."

Roach stepped back; raised his hands. "I can't—"

Missy screamed again.

Emily spoke into Roach's ear, reminded herself the youth was a decade and a half younger than she. She spoke with a deliberate, authoritative voice.

"You all don't want another dead body in this hole. If she dies, it's on you."

Roach relented. "What do you need?"

"There's an OB pack on a shelf in that closet. Get it and put it on this bedside table."

She turned to Missy, who lay on her back. Emily looked into her eyes and spoke softly. "Missy, you're going to have your baby now. It's going to hurt some, but we'll help you get through it. When it's all done, you'll be a mom with a brand-new baby."

Missy broke into tears. "I don't want to be a mom."

Roach placed the OB pack on the table. "Should have thought about that sooner."

Emily turned on him. "Shut up. You don't talk. You do what I say."

Roach raised his hands in submission.

She pushed an arm across his chest. "Out of my way. See that bassinet in the corner? Put some clean blankets in it. You'll find them in the closet. Then stand by to receive the baby." That made her think. "Call Dr. Kid. We'll need him here for the baby."

"Not available."

Good and Kid both not available?

"What the hell is going on?"

Roach stared at her, silent.

A cry from Missy seized her attention. Emily opened the OB pack, then took out and donned a sterile latex glove. She spread Missy's legs and did an internal exam. The cervix was fully effaced and dilated to nine centimeters.

This birth is going to happen in the next few minutes.

Emily shed the latex glove and applied a fetoscope to listen to the fetal heartbeat. Ninety beats per minute.

Baseline bradycardia. Fetal distress.

Missy had another contraction. The baby's heart rate dropped to sixty beats per minute and stayed there. Emily felt like someone was stabbing her brain with knitting needles. She looked at Roach. "We have a huge problem here. Please call 911. She needs a hospital. Now."

Roach paled; shook his head. "Can't."

Emily pleaded. "If she doesn't get this baby out now, they both could die."

Roach shrugged and shot Emily a helpless look.

Missy had another contraction. The fetal heart tones accelerated to 110. *We may be okay after all.*

Emily donned a pair of gloves and examined Missy. The cervix was fully dilated. She could feel the baby's head in the birth canal. Birth imminent. No choice.

She turned to Roach. "Okay. We'll do it here. Now." She wished they had a source to give Missy oxygen for transport in her blood to the fetus.

What to do after she delivered the baby?

She looked at the open OB delivery kit and had a bold idea. Glancing at Roach, she nodded toward the bassinet. Apprehensive, he took up his position to receive the baby.

Emily positioned herself between Missy's legs and established eye contact. "Missy, listen very carefully. The next time the pain hits, grit your teeth, gather all your strength, and push as hard as you can toward your bottom. You need to push the baby out of your bottom. Do you understand?"

The girl's eyes bulged and her lips quivered. Her arms and legs trembled. Tears ran down her face.

"It's okay," Emily said. "That's how babies come. You push it out through your bottom. Got that?"

Wide-eyed, Missy half-nodded.

"I'll coach you from down here, but you have to do the work. It's the only way we get this done."

Missy squeezed her eyes shut. "Here it comes."

Emily looked at Roach. "You coach too."

Missy shrieked.

Emily spoke in a loud voice. "Don't cry, Missy, push. Push, push, push, push, push!" She glowered at Roach, and the two admonished together. "Push, push, push."

Missy got the idea and pushed to the end of the contraction.

"That was very good, Missy." Emily did a quick exam. The baby's head had advanced further. "A few more times and you'll have it. When the next one comes, give it all you've got."

Missy started to hyperventilate as the next contraction began. Emily glanced at Roach and together they coached, "Push, Missy. Push, push, push, push!"

To Emily's relief, the baby crowned at the vaginal introitus. "One more time will do it, Missy."

"Push, push, push, push, push." Emily and Roach had gained a rhythm. With the final push, the baby's head popped out. Emily immediately turned it and used the bulb suction to clear its airway.

It didn't take a breath.

She decided not to wait for another contraction. She grabbed the baby's head between her hands and pulled straight down toward the floor. A shoulder emerged beneath Missy's pubic bone. Emily lifted the baby's head toward the ceiling to free the other shoulder, then slid the newborn out of its mother.

Missy flopped back onto the bed, exhausted.

"You have a baby girl, Missy."

Except it was blue and not breathing. Emily quickly clamped the umbilical cord in two places and then used the #10 scalpel from the OB kit to cut the cord between the clamps. Instead of returning the scalpel to the kit, she slipped it into the pocket of her smock. She carried the baby to the bassinet and rubbed it with vigor until it finally let out a weak cry. She handed it to Roach with instructions to wrap it in blankets and continue stimulating it. Then she returned to Missy, quickly delivered the placenta, and threw it into the trash.

The baby continued to make weak cries.

Emily sidled up to Missy, stroked her hair, and whispered into her ear. "Now we're going to get you and your baby out of this hell hole."

She turned back toward Roach, slipping her hand into her pocket, and seizing the scalpel. His attention was on the newborn as he continued to stimulate it.

The baby let out weak cries. Its color was somewhat improved, but still more blue than pink.

Emily looked Roach in the eye. "Now you're going to take us all to the hospital."

He stepped back. "No way."

"Yes way, and here's two reasons why." She stared him down. "First, if this baby dies your bosses lose a lot of money, right?"

He shrugged, defiant. "The clients won't pay for a sick baby anyway. We should just waste it."

"Make it three reasons, then. Two, if we take the baby to the hospital and it lives, it's still worth something to somebody. Think of it. You could be the winner here."

Roach scrunched his forehead. "I don't see that happening."

"Three," Emily said as she whipped out the blade and plunged it into the side of his neck, "you might get to live. Otherwise, I'll slice your carotid artery and you'll die right here along with this baby."

Roach reached for his neck but almost dropped the baby. He recovered in time to keep the newborn from falling to the floor.

Emily extracted the knife from his neck. She had aimed for the muscle behind the critical carotid artery and jugular vein. A slow trickle of venous blood ran from the wound toward Roach's collarbone.

Emily pointed the scalpel at his throat. "See? You didn't let the baby fall to the floor. You want to save it. You're not a killer, son." She pointed the knife at his neck to punctuate her point.

Keep him on the defensive. Don't let him realize he can disarm me.

Roach's gaze swept from Emily to the baby to the new mother and back to Emily. Resignation mixed with empathy crossed his face. "You win, lady. You didn't need to fucking stab me."

"Let's move." Emily pointed to the door. "You take the baby. I'll be right next to you with this knife ready to slit your throat if you try anything."

She directed him to grab a gauze pad from the OB kit. "Keep pressure on that neck wound."

Keep his hands busy so he can't take a swing.

Emily turned to Missy, who sat up in the bed, her mouth gaping open. "Get out of bed and take my hand down the stairs, Missy."

At the bottom of the stairs, Emily saw Roach's pistol on a side table next to the couch where he'd been asleep. She went for it but couldn't let go of Missy. In one swift motion, Roach dropped the gauze pad, held onto the baby, and seized the gun. He turned and pointed it at Emily.

"Make no mistake who's in charge here, Nurse. Now let's get to that hospital."

Within minutes they were in Roach's F-150 speeding toward the nearest rural hospital. Missy and her baby sat in the back seat. Roach drove with one hand. His other pointed the pistol at Emily's chest.

CHAPTER NINETEEN

Zack got up at 6 AM, took a quick shower, dressed, and tip-toed to the kitchen.

Annie stirred on the couch. When Zack turned around, she shifted position to her side, facing away from him. He whispered her name, but she didn't stir.

Asleep, or pretending?

Zack scribbled a note and left it on the kitchen counter.

> *Ladies,*
> *Gone to hospital. Back by 8. Help yourselves to whatever.*

He started to put the pen down, then continued writing.

> *Think about what you want to do today. We can tour museums, monuments, shops, anything you want.*
> *Love you,*
> *Dad*

Zack entered the ICU just before seven. He almost collided with Dr. Sebastian Barth hurrying out. Both men stopped, surprised to see each other. Zack tried to remember the last time he'd seen an obstetrician in the ICU.

Responding to Zack's raised eyebrow, Barth spoke first. "Cho's missed ectopic went into DIC overnight. She has no clotting factors left. She may bleed to death."

Zack sucked air through his teeth. "Damn. Does Paula know?"

Barth looked past him. "Yeah, she's been very"—He pursed his lips—"concerned. With reason."

Zack started to respond, then noted the quizzical look in Barth's eye. Emergency physicians were almost as rare in the ICU as obstetricians.

"I resuscitated Nate Young yesterday. Something doesn't add up about his case."

"I've heard the rumors." Barth looked in the direction of Nate's bed. "Shame. You never really know someone, do you?"

Zack stepped back; cocked his head. "You don't believe he . . . ?"

Barth shrugged. "Just saying you never really know someone. He could be as pure as a saint, but you know that saying about smoke and fire."

Zack's anger flared. "Well, I don't believe it. Neither does his wife."

Barth tossed his head. "You could be right. I don't know." He moved past Zack. "Got a delivery about to happen." He stopped and turned. "Hey, tell Paula Cho not to kill herself over this case. We all make mistakes."

"Thanks, Sebastian. She'll appreciate that from you."

Barth shot another look in the direction of Nate's bed. "Hope he survives, and I hope you're right about the rumors being false." He left the ICU.

Zack watched him for a few seconds then went to the workstation to review Nate's chart.

The pediatrician's physiological parameters had remained stable throughout the night. No surprise since he was still on ECMO, intubated, and on the ventilator. Jerry Hartman had been in to see him just before midnight. He had noted in the chart that Nate seemed a bit "lighter," meaning not so deep into coma.

A night nurse had recorded that Nate seemed to respond to simple commands like a hand squeeze or opening his eyes. Both phenomena could be reflexes of an impaired brain, but also a reason to hope.

Zack went to Nate's bedside and spoke into his ear. "Nate, it's Zack Winston. I hope you can hear me."

No response.

"We're going to get you through this." He slipped his fingers into Nate's open palm. He wondered if he could reproduce what the night nurse had reported.

"Nate, squeeze my hand."

Nothing.

He spoke a bit louder. "Nate, squeeze my hand."

No response.

Zack resorted to a procedure he'd learned in medical school. He rubbed his knuckles hard over Nate's sternum, hoping to produce enough pain to bring him out of his unconscious state.

Nothing.

Determined, Zack leaned over and looked into Nate's face. "Not giving up, friend. Open your damned eyes."

Nate's eyelids flipped open and he looked straight at Zack. He was sure Nate recognized him.

"That's better," Zack said. "Good to know someone's in there." He grasped Nate's hand, to which Nate returned a slight squeeze.

"Well, all right. We'll have you out of here in no time, Nate. Hang tight. Now get some rest."

Zack started to withdraw his hand, but Nate held it in a firm grasp. The monitor showed his respiratory and heart rates accelerating. Zack looked him in the eye. "Hang on awhile longer, bud. Keep going like this, and we'll get you off these machines soon."

Nate's eyes widened.

Responding to the rapid heart and respiratory rates on the monitor, the night nurse appeared at Zack's side. "You've gotten my patient all riled up, Dr. Winston."

Zack offered a chagrined smile. "Sorry."

"Dr. Barth couldn't get any response out of him."

Zack turned so fast on the nurse that she shrank away from him. "Barth saw him?"

The nurse looked confused. "You two were talking in the entry. I thought he told you then."

"He said he was here to check on the patient in DIC after a ruptured ectopic."

The nurse relaxed. "Yes, he saw her too."

"Is Dr. Barth taking care of her?"

The nurse shook her head. "No, sir. He transferred her to Dr. Hartman when she went into DIC."

"Jerry Hartman is her attending?"

"That's right."

Nate Young went into a full-blown seizure. His head, arms, and legs twitched in uncontrolled spasmodic jerks. The oxygen saturation reading on the monitor dipped below 95%.

"Ativan," Zack yelled.

Another nurse had already started giving the sedative. Within seconds, Nate stopped seizing and lapsed into unconsciousness.

The unit secretary called from the workstation. "Dr. Winston, we called Dr. Hartman. He wants to speak to you."

Zack took the phone and related the events that had just transpired. "No telling what, if any, additional brain damage that caused."

Jerry's voice was sleepy. "Another episode could kill him."

Zack agreed.

"We need to put him into medical coma," Jerry said.

"I see no other choice," Zack said.

He heard rustling of bed covers, followed by Jerry's tired voice. "Hey, Zack. What are you doing in the ICU this time of morning? What about your daughters?"

"Sleeping in. I just wanted to check on Nate."

"Well, thanks for stirring the pot. Now get out of there before you cause more trouble. Be with your daughters."

"Right."

"Give me the nurse so I can order the medical coma."

Zack did as requested, then went back to Nate Young. The pediatrician remained unconscious, his vital parameters returned to normal.

Before leaving the ICU, Zack looked in on the girl with the ectopic pregnancy. She was sedated. He reviewed the girl's chart. An extensive note from Jerry Hartman documented her crash into disseminated intravascular coagulopathy (DIC), a condition that could cause abnormal bleeding and shock; a huge risk for someone recovering from a ruptured ectopic with significant blood loss already. The girl had been in hypovolemic shock by the time the complication was discovered.

Of course, Jerry Hartman was doing all the right things for her. The girl's survival would depend on the extent of irreversible end-organ damage she'd suffered after she went into shock.

Zack scanned the physician's notes for this day and the day before. Sebastian Barth had not written a note since he transferred care to Jerry Hartman yesterday evening. No documentation that he had seen her this morning.

CHAPTER TWENTY

At the rural Maryland hospital, Roach stopped the truck in the ER driveway. With his gun hand, he shoved the shift knob into park. He poked the gun into Emily's ribs.

Missy whimpered in the back seat.

Roach spoke in a firm voice. "Get out of the car, get the waif and her kid, and walk into the ER. I'll be one step behind you. One word, one movement I don't like . . ." He glared. "You'll be toast. You, the girl, and the kid."

Emily did as she'd been told, one arm around Missy holding her limp baby, and scuffled as best she could toward the ER entrance. Roach walked beside her, his arm behind her as if to help. She felt the barrel of the gun against her back.

As soon as the automatic doors opened, Roach said, "Stop here."

Emily stopped and called out, "Help, help. We have a newborn in distress." A nurse and technician ran up to them. One took the baby and hurried to the treatment area. The other went to Missy, taking Emily's place in supporting the teenager. As she helped Missy toward the treatment area, the nurse turned to Emily and Roach. "You all need to register them at the front desk." She pointed to a small counter ten yards away. A young man there beckoned to them.

Emily started in that direction, but Roach grabbed her arm. "We're out of here."

She pulled away from him. "No. I need to be sure they're okay."

Roach briefly showed her the gun. "We are leaving. Now."

As Emily hesitated, the doors to the treatment room opened and a young man wearing a scrub suit and white coat came out and headed toward them.

"I'm Dr. Gibs—" He stopped mid-word and mid-stride as he and Roach stared at each other in obvious recognition.

"You," the doctor said. He turned and shouted at the front desk clerk. "Call Security. Now."

Emily looked at Roach. "What—?"

Before she could finish, he stepped behind her, wrapped his arm around her chest, and held the pistol to her head.

The doctor moved toward them.

"Another step and I shoot her," Roach said. The physician backed off. Roach dragged Emily backward through the front doors.

The doctor shouted. "Call 911."

Still pointing the gun at Emily's head, Roach backed up to the F-150, opened the driver's side door, and twisted his body to push her into the opening. "Get in, move to the other side, and stay still."

Emily climbed over the center console and sat in the passenger seat. Roach followed her into the truck, turned on the ignition, jammed the vehicle into drive, and lurched it forward just as a fat security guard approached from behind, gun drawn.

"Stop!"

Roach jumped on the brakes, pushed the gearshift into reverse, and backed the truck into the security guard, knocking him to the ground. Then he slammed the transmission into drive and accelerated, burning rubber as he drove away from the ER.

Emily looked through the back window. The security guard writhed on the ground. She turned on Roach.

"What did you just do?"

Roach shrugged. "What I had to do."

"The hell you did." She buried her head in her hands.

I cannot, must not fall into the hands of the authorities.

She trembled. "You have no idea—"

To Emily's surprise, Roach touched her shoulder in a tender gesture. "Yeah, I do." He glanced at her, half-smiled. "I know your whole story. We all do."

"What? How? Why?"

Roach smirked. "Cuz you're Doc Good's special nursling. Anything happens to you, we're all toast."

Emily glanced at the gun that Roach still held in the hand that gripped the steering wheel.

"Then why did you threaten me?"

Roach shrugged. "You gave me no choice. Couldn't risk losing you. We're supposed to never let you out of the house. If you got away . . ." He shook his head. "I'd be toast."

"Why, then?"

"I did it for that girl and her kid. Figured they need to live."

Emily stared at him. She believed what he said. "They are in good hands now." She thought about the scene in the ER lobby. "What was with you and that doctor?"

Roach shook his head. "You don't need to know."

The car approached an intersection. Roach turned the truck in the direction of The Good House. "Be quiet. I gotta make a call."

Instead of using the hands-free mode, he punched a number on his phone and held it to his ear. "Spider, Roach. We got a problem."

Emily listened as Roach told Spider about Missy's delivery, the baby's distress, and the trip to the hospital. He cringed as Spider replied. Emily couldn't hear what Spider was saying, but the irate tones from the receiver told her plenty.

"I know," Roach said. "Yes, sir. Understand. On our way." He clicked off the call, then made an abrupt U-turn to head back in the direction from whence they had come.

"What's going on?" Emily said.

"Change in plans."

"What?"

"Don't ask so many questions."

Roach continued back to the prior intersection. A Montgomery County Police vehicle running with lights and siren approached from the opposite direction and turned toward the hospital. Roach made a turn in the opposite direction and accelerated onto a narrow rural road that headed into the countryside, away from the small town and the hospital.

Emily gripped the handrest in fear. "Are you going to kill me?"

Roach laughed out loud. "What was it about 'Doc Good's special nursling' you didn't get?"

Somewhat mollified, Emily tried to still her beating heart and nervous brain. "What, then?"

"Can't go back to The Good House. Might be blown. Thanks to you."

"Where?"

Roach let out a long breath of air. "God, woman, would you please shut up? It's all good, pardon the pun. You'll see."

Emily stared out the windshield at the winding, narrow road ahead. Torrents of fear washed over her.

CHAPTER TWENTY-ONE

Zack returned home from the hospital to a silent apartment. He noted the time, half-past eight in the morning—five-thirty in California. If his daughters were typical, they would sleep until noon. Pacific time. He would give them another hour or two of sack time and then get them up, groggy or not.

From the kitchen, Zack's coffee pot beckoned. He wondered if either of the girls drank coffee or were they tea drinkers like their mother. Morning light through the window enabled him to make his way through the living room to fresh caffeine without turning on the lights.

Annie stirred on the couch when he walked past her.

"Whaa?" She opened one eye and looked at him askance as if he were an intruder.

Zack touched her shoulder. "Just dad. You can sleep longer if you want." He had a thought. "You can go sleep in my bed. It will be quieter and darker."

Her face scrunched. "Ew. No thanks." She turned away from him.

"Okay," he said. "Offer stands if you get too uncomfortable there." He eased the blanket up over her shoulders. She nestled her head into the pillow.

Tonight, he would open up the sofa bed instead of allowing her to sleep on the leather.

What dads do, I guess.

Zack carried his coffee mug into his bedroom. He left the door ajar so he would hear the girls whenever they got up. He booted up his laptop and logged into the hospital's VPN to access Nate Young's electronic record. Maybe the toxicology results would be back by now.

His phone buzzed. The caller ID showed *Unknown* and a number with a *703* area code. Arlington County, VA, just across the Potomac from DC. Assuming it was a spam or robocall, Zack ignored it and turned his attention back to the computer. He pulled up Nate's current record. No tox results.

They should have a preliminary by now. He intended to call Dr. Eric Wolfe. The head of pathology at the hospital was also Zack's friend and running buddy. Eric could access the status of Nate's labs even if not formally reported in his record.

Just as he picked up his phone, it buzzed again with the same unknown 703 number. Maybe it wasn't spam. He answered the call.

"Hello, Zack."

He recognized the raspy voice at once. "Bridget?"

She cleared her throat, but her voice didn't change. "It's been a century, I know. Sorry."

Zack cleared his own throat as he searched for the right response. "No sweat. I didn't answer the first time because the number—"

"Changed it. Too many crank calls after . . ."

"Makes sense." Silence. "What's up, Bridge?" He shook his head. "I mean, how are you doing?"

"Same. Voice is gone forever." She tried in vain to clear her throat. "I manage."

A brief image of his frantic restoration of her airway crossed his mind. "So sorry to hear that. I'd hoped . . ."

"I'm alive. I owe you for that, BAFERD."

Zack chuckled at her use of the familiar acronym, common in the emergency medicine community. She had used it to buoy his confidence in the darkest hours of the bogus malpractice trial that had almost cost him his life. It stood for "bad ass fucking ER doc." Zack took it as the ultimate compliment and endorsement.

The line went silent.

"Why did you call, Bridge?" He remembered his earlier conversation with Ange. "You twisting my arm to help out on your new malpractice case? Ange told me about the missed ectopic. To be honest, your doc is in deep doo-doo."

A pause. "Different but related. I hope you can help me figure out a call I got from that doctor early this morning."

"Huh?"

"Did Ange tell you the mitigating circumstance? About the girl being a runaway brought in by a youth who fled the ER as soon as he got the chance?"

"Yeah. Not sure how that helps the doc's case."

"Not the issue of the moment." She paused to clear her throat. "The physician, Dr. Gibson, just called to tell me he saw the same guy in the ER early this morning." Another pause. "He had a woman with him, maybe a nurse." She paused again. "They brought in a teenager who had just delivered an infant in distress." Her voice broke. "Damn. Hang on."

Zack waited while she tried to clear her throat.

"Sorry. As soon as Dr. Gibson recognized him, the guy grabbed the woman, put a pistol to her head, and ran out the door. The staff called Security and 911, but the pair got away in a pickup. Backed the truck into the security guard as they fled. Almost killed him." She coughed. "By the time Montgomery County PD got there, the youth and the woman were long gone."

"What happened to the newborn and its mother?"

"The baby died. The mom is either mentally or psychologically impaired. The police were still interviewing her when Dr. Gibson called me."

"Any idea where they came from? Doesn't sound like a typical home delivery. Who was the woman? A midwife?"

"Like I said, the youth and the woman split. Currently at large."

Zack thought for a moment. "What's that got to do with me?"

"I don't know that it does, but it got me thinking about your case last year; how it wasn't about the malpractice claim at all." She paused a few beats. "I decided to call and see what you think."

"Really? You said the police are already involved. You and I are not investigators. It doesn't matter what we think."

A tap on his door got Zack's attention.

"Come in." He said it loud enough so Bridget would hear.

Jennifer poked her head into the room. "Sorry, Dad. Didn't know you were on the phone. Where do you keep the coffee mugs?"

Zack smiled. Maybe not all her mother's daughter after all. "Cabinet over the coffee maker. Logical, right?"

Jennifer smiled back. "Thanks. We're both getting up now. Don't want to sleep away our vacation."

"Okay. I'll be done here soon." He turned his attention back to the phone. "Sorry, Bridge."

Her tone seemed less serious. "Ange told me your daughters are there for a visit. Good for you."

"Yeah, better late than never, right?"

"Do not beat yourself up, Dr. Winston. Families are hard, as we both know."

Zack wasn't sure what she meant. "Yeah."

Bridget cleared her throat for what seemed like the twentieth time in the conversation.

How does she live with that, a constant reminder of what happened to her?

"I had another reason for calling."

"Shoot."

She hesitated. "I'm at the airport to pick up my stepson, Grant, coming in from Boston. I don't know if you've made plans with your daughters, and I know teenagers can be a challenge. Especially under separated family circumstances."

"You got that right. No plans so far. Figured we'd play it by ear."

"Such a dad. Typical."

Zack feigned a chuckle. "So?"

"Marshall's out of town for . . . I don't know how long. Maybe a few days." She paused. "If I remember right, Grant is the same age as your older daughter. You know Dustin. He's younger. Going on eighteen."

"Yeah. Jenn's a freshman in med school and Annie turns sixteen on Christmas Eve. Similar ages."

Bridget cleared her throat, again. "If you and your daughters don't have evening plans, I thought you might like to come over for dinner with the boys and me. Introduce your girls to someone who might know what teens like to do around here." A pause. "You and I could talk more about the Gibson case, or, you know, just catch up."

Zack did not hesitate. "Of course. What time?"

CHAPTER TWENTY-TWO

Emily lost all sense of geography as Roach drove erratic twists and turns through the Maryland countryside. Yellow-brown fields ran along both sides of the roads, with occasional spots of melting snow. They passed sporadic farmhouses set back from the roads. No one would look twice at a black Ford F-150 around here. They were as common as roadkill.

At one point, Roach did an abrupt U-turn when he saw a Montgomery County Police cruiser sitting at an intersection a few hundred yards away.

Emily wondered why the cop didn't give chase.

Roach answered the unspoken question. "Guess he didn't see me. Our lucky day."

As Emily's geographical disorientation increased, so did her fear. A sense of impending doom gnawed at her stomach. Could she coerce or entice Roach to let her go? Being alone and lost without resources seemed a better option than whatever immediate outcome lay ahead of her—despite Roach's assurance that Dr. Good would always protect her.

Where is Dr. Good?

Roach stopped at the end of a rural road. He scanned both directions, twice, then turned onto the main thoroughfare and blended into the traffic, careful not to exceed the speed limit.

Emily recognized the Potomac River on her side of the car. They were heading south, toward the District of Columbia.

"We're going to DC?"

Roach stared straight ahead.

The surroundings became familiar to Emily as they drove through the populated area on the outskirts of the National Capital Region. She spotted a street sign, Clara Barton Parkway. A few miles later, it became Canal Road. That route would take them along the Potomac River into Georgetown.

A chill ran through Emily's body. Georgetown University Hospital lay just a mile or so ahead. Her breath quickened and sweat broke out on her forehead.

A vision of a dead, blue newborn flitted across her mind. How many years ago?

She could still feel Dr. Good's hand on her shoulder. "Run, Emily. Meet me at the loading dock. Stop for nothing."

What had Adam Good done in the interim, before he drove up to the loading dock in his Mercedes to spirit her away to his "safe house," a nondescript nearby rowhouse? He admonished her to stay there, answer to no one, and wait for his return. When questioned, he had refused to answer.

"Just do as I say. You will be all right. You are in my care."

Emily hid there for a week before Dr. Good came in the middle of the night and drove her to The Good House. Over the next five years, she'd never left that house without him, Spider, or Roach with her, not as her companions, but to assure that she spoke to no one and did exactly what they said. True, Adam Good doted on her, swore his undying devotion, and assured her that only his love could keep her safe from certain imprisonment, maybe death.

Would Adam Good help her now? Could he?

Where is he?

Roach drove the truck on a meandering path through the residential area. He scrutinized each street and the vehicles parked there as he passed.

Emily suspected but did not want to believe his intended destination.

As if on cue, Roach turned onto a familiar street and parked halfway down. Emily stared at the same townhouse she'd remembered in her dark, sleepless hours. Dr. Good's "safe house."

"Get out," Roach said. "Go straight to the front door. Don't look around or slow down."

Emily inched the car door open, searching up and down the street for an escape route.

"Move it," Roach said. "I'm right behind you with the gun."

Maybe Dr. Good waited for her inside the house.

Emily left the car and sprinted to the house. When she reached the threshold, someone opened the door. A hand pulled her into the front room. She turned around and put on her best smile for Dr. Good.

Spider's malicious face glared at her.

Roach hurried inside and closed the door. Emily looked between the two men, then scanned the room.

"Your protector is not here," Spider said.

He shot a wicked look at Roach. "It's just the three of us."

CHAPTER TWENTY-THREE

While Annie and Jennifer finished getting ready for the day, Zack cooked his signature omelet for breakfast: three eggs, bacon and sausage bits, mushrooms, spinach, and a mix of cheddar and gouda cheese.

Annie emerged from the bathroom, her face decorated with two shades of eyeshadow, nose ring, and black lipstick. She looked at the stove, scrunched her forehead, and turned up her nose.

"Are those for us?"

Zack had forgotten Annie was vegan. He made a quick recovery. "Well, two of them are, for Jennifer and me. I was going to ask what you'd like instead."

"Yeah, right." She opened the refrigerator. "Uh, any fresh fruit in here?"

Zack tried for a pleasant voice. "Why, yes, there is. I put fruit in my smoothies for taking to the hospital when I work." He shot her a "gotcha" smile. "Second shelf. Fresh strawberries and pineapple. Also, you'll find bananas on the counter. I can make you a smoothie if you want."

Annie shrugged, but Zack caught the hint of a smile at the corners of her mouth.

The timer on the toaster oven chimed. Zack pulled out four slices of toast and placed them on a small plate for Annie. "Multi-grain toast, no butter. Right?"

This time she smiled for real. "Yeah. Thanks."

Jennifer joined Zack at the small table. "Omelets always work for me." She shot her sister a condescending smile. "Someday you'll figure it out."

Annie scoffed. "No way." She fixed herself a bowl of fresh fruit and sat at the table.

"So," Zack said. "What would you girls like to do today? We can tour monuments, museums, you know, the touristy thing."

"Kinda cold for outdoors stuff," Annie said. "Winter and all."

Zack smiled. "Especially if you didn't bring a proper coat. We could go shopping for one. You've already dissed my other birthday gift."

Annie's eyes flickered. "Might be okay."

Jennifer smiled at Zack. "Sounds great, Dad. We love retail therapy."

Like mother, like daughters.

Zack cleared his throat. "For tonight, we've all been invited to dinner in Alexandria at the home of my lawyer friend, with her and her sons. The older one is a freshman at Harvard Law, the younger a senior in high school."

Annie's face darkened. "I don't want to meet your girlfriend."

Zack spread his hands, almost apologetic. "She's not my girlfriend, and she's married."

"Didn't stop you before," Annie said.

Zack swallowed the rage that flared inside him. Another Natalie lie. He was about to tell his daughter that it was her mom, not he, who had cheated. He stopped himself short.

Do not fall into that trap.

"Bridget and I are friends. We worked together on a case last year. She's asked for my help on another one. You might enjoy meeting her."

Annie glanced at the ceiling. "If you say so."

Jennifer shot Annie a "knock it off" look. "We'd love to meet them, dad."

Annie scowled and dug into her fruit bowl. "Whatever."

She ate a spoonful, then looked up to smile at Zack, eyes twinkling. "Thanks for the coat idea. I do need one."

Score one for the dad.

CHAPTER TWENTY-FOUR

Emily and Roach sat at opposite ends of the couch in the townhouse living room.

Spider sucked on a beer in the easy chair across from them. After a swig, he leaned forward and glared at Roach. "What happened?"

Roach gestured toward Emily.

Emily scoffed. "He should never have brought us that girl. She was too high-risk."

Spider raised an eyebrow. "He? You think junior here decides anything on his own?"

Her anger rising, Emily waved him off. "Whatever. The girl didn't belong at The Good House."

"Yet, she was there," Spider said. "Your job to deal with her." He moved forward, livid face less than a foot from Emily's. "What happened?"

Against her will, Emily leaned away from Spider's frontal attack. "The girl went into premature labor and delivered a baby in distress. No surprise, given her poor health and malnutrition."

She tried to stare Spider down, but he didn't flinch. "The baby needed emergency medical treatment. She was going to die if we didn't get her the right care."

Spider's eyes narrowed as he turned to Roach. "Why didn't you waste the kid?"

Roach pointed at Emily. "She threatened me with a knife."

"Knife? Where would she get a knife?"

"It was scalpel from the OB set."

Spider broke into a sarcastic laugh. "A scalpel? You couldn't disarm her?"

Roach looked at the floor, nervous. "Didn't try. I thought she was right. About the girl and the baby."

"You thought?" Spider rubbed his forehead. "We don't pay you to think, little man." He shrugged. "You are dead meat when Doc Good finds out what you did."

Emily looked up. "He doesn't know?" Doctor Good would support her, for sure.

Spider scowled at her. "I'm the one asking the questions here." He leaned back in his seat. "So, you took the girl and her kid to the ER. Oh, wait. Not just any ER . . ." He pointed at Roach. "The same place you went six months ago with that other girl."

Roach raised a hand. "At Dr. Good's direction."

"The doc didn't send you there this time, did he? You think he would send you to the same place? Man, you are beyond stupid. You have shit for brains and Jell-O for balls if you let this woman control you with a damned scalpel and, what? Empathy?" He pointed at Roach's face. "Not another word out of you unless I ask."

Roach sat back, crossed his arms and legs, and stared straight ahead.

Spider rubbed his eyes and turned to Emily. "You're only a shade less stupid than this kid. That baby only lasted a few minutes. But the girl . . . Now that's a problem."

Emily gasped. "The baby died? How do you know?"

"We know everything." He shot her a wicked smile. "Missy."

"Why did you ask us what happened, if you already knew?"

"A test. For honesty." He leered. "You passed."

Spider looked at each of them. "Here's the real question. Did that girl know where she was, at The House? Any chance she could have told the authorities where she'd been? Maybe the location? Did she hear your names?"

Emily and Roach both shrugged.

"I don't know." Emily looked Spider in the eye. "I doubt it. She's mentally deficient, psychologically impaired, but I can't promise . . ."

Spider raised a hand. "Got it. You don't know."

He turned to Roach. "You're positive that ER doctor recognized you?"

"Definite. As soon as he saw me, he had his staff call security and 911."

Spider blew out a long breath. "Now we have two new problems. That makes three altogether." He rose from his chair. "So, we deal with them."

"What do you need from me?" Roach asked.

Spider scoffed. "Consider yourself 'furloughed' till further notice. Get out of here. Lay low. Leave that truck in a garage, out of sight. Don't come near this place, The House, or any of our other sites."

Roach looked crushed. "Look. I want to help. Make amends for whatever I did."

Spider shook his head. "You're too hot right now. That doc will have described you to the cops. Can't risk anyone else ID'ing you. We'll call you when this blows over."

Roach stood and started to protest, but a glare from Spider silenced him.

"Get out of here," Spider said. "Go play your other life."

Roach left the house.

Emily heard his truck start up and drive away. She was alone with Spider. That terrified her more than fear of discovery. She wished she still had the scalpel, although she doubted it would deter Spider for more than a millisecond.

Spider approached the couch, took her arm, and yanked her up. "Now I deal with you. Come."

Emily tried to jerk her arm away, but he held on with a vise-like grip. He spat out the words. "You can come as told, or as forced. Up to you."

She calmed herself. Better not to resist until she got the right chance.

Spider led her up two flights of stairs to an isolated bedroom on the third floor. He stopped at the door and pushed her across the threshold. "It's got a bathroom." He let go of her arm. "You stay here until we decide what's next for you."

Emily turned to face him. "Where's Dr. Good?"

"He's indisposed for now. I'm in charge, as always." He gave her a slight shove further into the room, then closed and locked the door behind her.

Minutes later, she watched through the bedroom window as he drove away in his Cadillac SUV. She hadn't noticed the vehicle when Roach had pulled up to the safe house. Despite the terror in her heart, Emily said a silent prayer of thanks that Spider had left her alone in the room.

She had feared worse.

CHAPTER TWENTY-FIVE

Later that afternoon, Zack drove his daughters to Pentagon City Fashion Center for the promised shopping expedition.

Annie picked a black vegan-leather jacket with a zippered front, wide button-down lapels, long zippered pockets, and a narrow waist belt. Zack thought it impractical for DC winter cold, but Annie reminded him she lived in San Diego, not the frigid northeast. She added a white blouse and a front-fly faded denim skirt to complete her new ensemble.

Zack protested that the mid-thigh-length skirt was "way too short" for a girl her age.

Jennifer overruled him.

His older daughter accepted Zack's offer to buy her new clothes as well. She picked light blue denim jeans, a matching denim shirt, and a tailored dark blue blazer with long, narrow lapels. She used her own money to buy silver-toned large loop earrings, "to accessorize."

They spent another hour touring shops in the mall. Zack resisted the urge to add to his own extensive wardrobe, reminding himself the day was for his daughters, not him. He shot frequent glances at his watch as the time approached to head to Alexandria for dinner at Bridget's.

When he told the girls it was time to go, they both opted to change into their new apparel.

When they emerged from the dressing room, Zack broke into a wide smile. Each daughter was, in her own unique way, beautiful—in Zack's unbiased opinion. Annie's Goth-like makeup and hairstyle worked well with her new clothes, as if they were designed for her special flair. Jennifer's bearing in her new outfit exuded an aura of casual professionalism that would serve the future physician very well. Zack swelled with pride looking at them. He stuffed the sudden notion that he'd had little or nothing to do with their aura.

Genetics play a role too.

As they walked toward the exit to the parking garage, Zack's phone buzzed. Caller ID indicated Jerry Hartman.

"I need to take this."

Jennifer shot him a *Really, dad?* glare then shrugged. "Fine. We'll window shop."

Zack turned away. "What's up, Jerry?"

"We got Nate Young's tox results. Unidentified opioid."

"Not Fentanyl?"

"Nope. Probably a derivative. We'll have to wait for more extensive assay to know the exact substance. I'm suspecting carfentanyl."

"Dang," Zack said it loud enough that both his daughters turned from the shop window and stared at him. "That's an elephant drug. One-hundred times the potency of Fentanyl."

"Yeah, I know. It would explain the needle tracks between his toes."

"Or doesn't."

"What do you mean?"

"It doesn't add up, Jerry. Do you believe Nate Young is a drug user?"

"No. But I never thought of Dennis King as an assassin either."

Zack stared into the distance. Jerry was right. You never really know someone.

"How's he doing?"

"Stable in the medical coma. Can't really assess him beyond what we see on the monitor."

"I wish we could talk to him."

Jerry sighed. "He's nowhere close. We need to get him off ECMO before we think about waking him up and extubating him. I won't consider either until after Christmas. You know how light staffing is over the holiday." He paused. "We might get him off ECMO and the ventilator by New Years, but I wouldn't bet on it."

Zack frowned. "I'll stop by to see him tomorrow."

"Don't you have daughters visiting?"

"Yeah, but they sleep late. I'll come over first thing in the morning. I assume you'll be there."

"I'll let you know. Meanwhile, enjoy some family time." His voice edged toward sarcastic.

Another thought hit Zack. "Hey, before we hang up. You're taking care of a young woman, patient of Sebastian Barth's. A ruptured ectopic, went into DIC post-op. She came in through the ER when Paula Cho was on duty. I'm curious how she's doing."

Long pause before Jerry spoke. "She died."

"Hey, stranger."

A familiar voice from behind interrupted Zack's response to Jerry's shocking news. Zack turned, his eyes assaulted by the shock of red hair, freckles, and red-lipstick smile of Sarah O'Brien, Zack's current fling.

He scowled and pointed to his phone.

"Oh, sorry." Sarah put fingers to her lips. "Didn't mean to interrupt." She pointed to Jennifer and Annie, window shopping a few stores away. "Are those your daughters?" Without waiting for an answer, she moved off in their direction. "I'll go introduce myself. Take your time."

"Wait," Zack said.

"What?" Jerry Hartman said.

"Sorry, Jerry, I wasn't talking to you. I have to go now, but I want to know more about the girl who died."

"Not much to tell. She had DIC. Went into acute respiratory distress and progressive multiple organ failure. No chance to save her."

"I need to follow up, for Paula Cho's sake."

"Fine."

Zack saw that Sarah had struck up a conversation with his daughters. He walked toward them.

"Be with your daughters, Zack. This can all wait until after Christmas."

"Maybe not." He had reached the three women. "Gotta go. I'll see you tomorrow, Jerry."

"Or not." Jerry clicked off.

Sarah turned to him as soon as he pocketed his phone. "They're beautiful, Zack. I can't wait to get to know them better."

Zack glanced at his daughters. Both wore inscrutable looks. "That would be nice, but we have someplace to be now."

He made a show of looking at his watch, then spoke to the girls. "We're already running late, and the traffic . . ." He put hands on both girls' shoulders to usher them away.

He felt the heat from Sarah.

Jennifer turned to Sarah. "Very nice to meet you, Sarah. We'd love to catch up with you during our stay."

Sarah amped up the charm. "Wonderful. We'll arrange something." She fake-smiled at Zack. "This workaholic will want an excuse to go to the hospital. We three can have some women-time."

Zack threw up his hands. "Fine. We'll work something out. Right now, we need to get going. We have an appointment in Alexandria."

Sarah looked at him with a pinched expression. She spoke in a sarcastic voice. "Of course, you do."

The girls and Sarah traded phone numbers, she bade each of them goodbye, gave Zack a peck on the cheek, then turned and walked away.

Zack pointed his daughters toward the exit. "Let's move it."

"Interesting woman," Jennifer said. "Did you see her following us not long after we got here to the mall? Like she was stalking us."

Zack stopped in his tracks. "Really?"

"I saw her too," Annie said.

CHAPTER TWENTY-SIX

Grant Hilliard, Bridget's stepson, had walked out of airport security bleary-eyed and a bit disheveled, hefting an overfilled backpack. He'd confessed to Bridget that he'd gone straight from an end-of-semester bash to Logan Airport for his early flight to DC.

After a short, quiet ride from Reagan to Alexandria, they arrived at the Hilliards' townhouse just as Dustin rushed out the door. He planned a day with friends, exuberant at the beginning of their holiday vacation.

Bridget told her son and stepson to be ready to host her doctor friend and his daughters for dinner that evening.

"Sure, Mom." Dustin headed down the street to a neighbor's house.

"I need a nap," Grant said. He slung his backpack over his shoulder and lumbered up the stairs to the guest room.

Abandoned by all three of the men in her family, Bridget retrieved a briefcase from her home office and headed to work.

On the way home from the office that afternoon, Bridget stopped at the Alexandria Aquatics Center for her daily swim workout. Several lifetimes ago, she had been a high-school swimming champion. After the last meet of her senior year, she had pitched her gold medal into a dresser drawer and vowed never again to swim in competition. She had burned out on the early-morning workouts and constant pressure to excel; neither of which had helped her social life.

She had kept the self-promise throughout her adult life, turning to distance running to maintain physical fitness and feed her competitive spirit. Running was a less complicated sport that earned her a nice collection of marathon completion certificates to hang on the wall in her law firm office.

After she recovered from Dennis King's near-fatal attack, Bridget found that running, while still an abiding interest, no longer fueled all her inner needs. Maybe being so close to dying had triggered some compulsion to run away from death's doorstep. Cycling added to her running routine helped for a while, but Bridget felt the need for more. Within months, she decided to emulate some of her more driven male colleagues and take up triathlon. Not Ironman, but the more civilized Olympic distance.

Bridget's return to swimming after decades away from the sport had surprised her. She still had the "it" that made her competitive. More than running or cycling, swimming depended on technique over brawn or power. In her first open-water triathlon swim, she had come out of the water first in her age group.

—⋀—

Home from the aquatics center, Bridget relished the residual endorphin high from her moderate-interval swim workout as she prepped the ingredients for her pasta Bolognese. She felt like a giddy co-ed at the prospect of treating Zack Winston to her signature dish.

She'd not heard from Marshall since he left for Richmond. She didn't care.

Bridget added two more garlic cloves to the four called for by the recipe.

No such thing as too much garlic.

Just as she started mincing, Dustin burst through the front door. Bridget turned to greet him, brandishing the chef's knife like a weapon.

"You're late."

"Sorry, mom." He shot her that winning smile that always mollified her anger. "I'll make it up to you as soon as I change."

"Wake up your brother. He's been asleep all day. You two can set the table. I'll do the rest."

Dustin came back downstairs ten minutes later. "Grant's taking a shower."

"Please set the table."

He gathered plates and silverware but stopped before taking them to the dining room. "So, mom. I know we're having company, but, uh, some friends—"

"No."

He thrust out his lip. "You didn't even hear what I had to say."

"If it means skipping dinner, the answer is 'no.' I promised Dr. Winston that his daughters would get to meet boys closer to their own age."

"What about after dinner?"

Bridget scraped the minced garlic into a small bowl next to similar ones containing her pre-measured ingredients. "What's so important that you're willing to renege on your commitment to us this evening?"

Dustin adopted the pleading look that had worked for him since age two. "Some friends are going to the Georgetown basketball game. They have an extra ticket."

Bridget shook her head. "They'll have to find someone else."

"Geez, Mom. Might as well still be in school."

"You'll survive."

Bridget opened one of the two bottles of Chianti Classico on the counter and measured out a cup and a quarter. With her *mis en place* done, she lit the burner to preheat the cast iron skillet.

Her phone rang. Dominic Zimbaro.

"Hang on a second, Dom." She turned to Dustin. "I have to take this call. Please start browning the ground sirloin. You know the drill. If I'm not off the phone when it's browned, add the garlic, oregano, and red chili flakes, and stir it all together. If I'm not done by then, come to me for further directions."

Dustin shot her a sly smile. "And in return . . . ?"

"*Maybe* you can go with your friends to the Georgetown game. *After* dinner."

Dustin raised the wooden spoon like an Olympic athlete brandishing a javelin. "Thanks, mom."

"Remember to grind the oregano between your hands when you add it."

Bridget went into her home office and closed the door. "Hi, Dom. Sorry to make you wait."

"No problem, ma'am." Brief pause. "I, uh, heard from my contact in Richmond."

"And?"

"Your husband and his deputy had separate rooms in the hotel last night."

Bridget let out a sigh of relief. "Thank you for that."

Dominic took a deep breath. "Except, according to the maid my man, uh, interviewed, Mr. Hilliard either made his own bed this morning or never slept in it."

Marshall hadn't made a bed since he lived in his parents' home as a high school student. He found the practice a "waste of time if you're just going to get into it again."

Bridget's stomach went sour. "Anything else?"

"He never went to the hearing. A black SUV with tinted windows picked him up at the hotel. His deputy went to the hearing without him."

What the hell?

"The SUV dropped him back at the hotel this afternoon. He went to his room and hasn't come out."

"What about his deputy, after she went to the hearing?"

"My guy didn't see her, but he verified that she's still checked into the hotel."

Dustin appeared at the door. "Mom, the meat's browned and I put the other stuff in like you asked."

Bridget blew out a long breath. "Thanks, Dom. I have to go now." She thought for a second. "I, uh . . . Tell your man to stand down. I got what I needed."

"Will do, Ma'am, if you're sure."

"Yeah, I'm sure. Please send me a bill for your services."

"No charge, ma'am. This one is on us."

"That's very generous, but you don't have to do that."

His voice exuded empathy. "You've been good to us over the years. Happy to do it. Have a good evening, ma'am."

Bridget thanked him again, hung up, and returned to the kitchen.

Good evening indeed.

CHAPTER TWENTY-SEVEN

Zack parked his Lexus on the street in front of Bridget's townhouse. He closed the Waze app on his phone and made a show of turning the phone off and putting it in his pocket. He turned to the girls, this time Annie in the front seat, Jenn in the rear, both scrolling on their phones.

"No phones while we're guests in someone else's home. Turn them off and put them away."

Jennifer smirked, turned off her phone, and put it in her purse.

Annie stared at Zack like he was an alien creature. "Seriously, Dad? What century were you born?"

"Seriously indeed. You've been glued to that thing since you got off the plane. It won't kill you to separate from it for a few hours."

"Hours? You said we were having dinner. How does that take hours?"

Zack glanced at Jennifer for help, even though by now he knew she wouldn't triangulate for him. To his surprise, this time she came to his aid.

"Come on, sis. Be nice. We don't want dad's friend to think we're spoiled brats."

Annie stuck out her lip. "Maybe I do."

"Shut off the damned phone and put it away. Now." The intensity of Jennifer's retort surprised Zack, but it had the desired effect on her younger sister. Without another word, Annie complied.

Jennifer didn't let up. "Shitcan the 'tude, sis. Be nice, like you are with mom's friends."

Annie glared at her sister for a few seconds, then gave in. "Fine."

Zack opened the car door. "Well, okay. Now that we're all on the same page..."

Although nervous about seeing Bridget again, and unsure how his daughters would interact, Zack relaxed within ten minutes of Bridget greeting them at the front door and introducing Dustin and Grant. Zack and Bridget resumed their prior friendship and camaraderie without a hiccup. Jennifer and Grant hit it off at once and soon found common ground in their ambitious career plans. Annie and Dustin ignored each other as they ate in silence.

When Dustin pulled out his phone and started scrolling, Annie shot an "ah-ha" look at her dad and followed suit.

Bridget and Zack looked at each other and shrugged, neither one interested in stoking an argument with their respective teenagers.

Jennifer filled the void as she spooned another helping of Bridget's pasta Bolognese onto her plate. "As a future physician," she said to Grant, "I'm supposed to distrust future lawyers."

Grant smirked. "It worked out for your dad and Bridget. You know your dad saved her life, right?"

Jennifer did a double-take. "I did not know." She looked at Zack, curious. Annie looked up from her phone, also curious.

"Long story," Zack said.

Annie said to Bridget, "Is that how you got that thing on your neck, and why you can't talk well?"

Horrified, Zack was about to reprimand her rudeness, but Bridget stopped him with a slight raise of her hand. She smiled. "Your dad is quite the BAFERD."

Zack blushed.

"What's a BAF— whatever?"

"He's never told you?"

Annie shook her head.

Zack motioned for Bridget to stop.

"Your dad is a genuine bad-ass fucking ER doc." Bridget looked at Zack. "One of the best."

Despite her halting voice, Bridget told Zack's daughters the story of Dennis King's assault on her. "If your dad hadn't found me in time, or if it had been someone less skilled, I'd be dead."

Annie and Jennifer regarded Zack with newfound reverence.

"We had no idea," Jennifer said.

Zack shrugged. "ER doc is what I am. You do what you must."

The conversation continued throughout their dinner. Zack sat back and admired how Bridget brought Annie out her shell and got her to talk about her life and things important to her. He also noted that Jennifer and Grant had become more engaged in their own tete-a-tete. Conflicted feelings of satisfaction and longing washed over him. It felt almost like a real family. Except they were not a family.

He excused himself to the bathroom.

When he returned, Dustin had left to join his friends for the Georgetown game. Bridget and Annie were clearing the table and talking while Jennifer and Grant loaded the dishwasher. When the tasks were done, Bridget pulled Zack aside. "Grant is meeting some friends later in Old Town. He asked Jennifer to go with him, but she won't go without Annie. I hope that's okay with you."

Zack scowled. "Annie's too young for that."

Bridget chuckled. "You need to get to know your daughter, Zack. Don't be put off by the teenager attitude. She's quite mature for her age."

"All the more reason not to trust—"

Bridget raised a hand to stop him. "You can trust Grant. I do. Even if I didn't, he wouldn't risk his standing at Harvard by doing something stupid. She'll be safe. They will stay awhile then he'll bring them back here."

She paused, glanced away, then looked him in the eye. "Meanwhile, you and I can . . . talk."

An unexpected rush rose in Zack's chest. "I suppose . . ."

"Look," Bridget said. "It's early. He'll have them back by ten at the latest."

Zack smiled. "I trust your judgment, counselor."

CHAPTER TWENTY-EIGHT

Emily found herself locked into a ten-by-twelve-foot top-level bedroom with sloping ceilings, a dormer window, and a small bathroom with a glass-enclosed shower. The window was sealed shut. Not that it mattered, because she saw no way to descend from the outside to the ground level. The same was true of the bathroom window.

Like Rapunzel, Emily was trapped—without the long hair. Or any other means of escape.

During her first stay in this place, Dr. Adam Good didn't lock her in a room by herself. They became lovers. She expected to spend the rest of her life with him.

Emily scoffed. That dream had come true, but not the way young, impressionable Emily Morgan had fantasized it when she fled a bloody scene and waited on the loading dock at Georgetown University Hospital for her savior to snatch her away from the jaws of justice. Now older and much wiser, Emily had been Good's prisoner since her first night in this house.

Such a difference that frantic half-hour had made in her life. Emily closed her eyes and allowed the images to invade her mind.

Student nurse-midwife, just short of graduation, unsupervised.
Difficult delivery.
Blue baby.

Not breathing.
911.
Mouth to mouth.
Nothing.
Paramedics.
Airway obstructed.
Code 3 to the ER.
Dead baby.
Dr. Good. "Run, Emily."

"Failure to treat an obstructed airway in a newborn," he later told her. "Not certified as a midwife. Operating outside the scope of training. Prominent, wealthy political family. They won't want money. They will force you into prison for criminal negligence. You can never go back. Never leave this house. Someone will recognize you; turn you in. You won't survive. Only I can save you."

She had burst into tears, overcome with despair.

Dr. Good held her tight. "I will take care of you, my love. Always. You are safe with me."

Now staring out the window at the growing dusk, Emily felt not at all safe.

Where is he?

CHAPTER TWENTY-NINE

Bridget refilled Zack's wine glass, then her own. She hoped he didn't notice how her hand trembled.

"What's wrong, Bridge?"

Of course, he noticed.

She shook her head. "Long day."

He looked skeptical. "Your hand was shaking."

She tried a reassuring look. "Happens when I'm tired. The neurologist says it's a lingering effect of the hypoxic brain injury."

Zack raised his eyebrows, not buying it.

Can't bullshit a bullshitter.

He touched her arm, sending electricity through her body. She fought off a sudden urge to pull him close. She needed to break the spell.

"It often helps to go for a run. I don't suppose . . ."

"I always carry a gym bag in my car." He furrowed his brow. "You know it's freezing outside, right?"

She smiled. "All the better, right?" She tugged at the neck of her sweater. "Getting a little warm in here."

Zack responded with a wistful smile. "Right. Okay, a run it is. I'll go get my bag."

Each decked out in top-line cold-weather running gear, they circled Bridget's neighborhood, strides and paces matched. As the fog of their breaths commingled if front of them, Bridget recalled the last time she had run with Zack. Four months after she survived the attack, she had just resumed a regular running routine. Heading south on the Mt. Vernon Trail through Alexandria, she had looked up and spotted Zack running toward her. Why so far from his home? She knew the answer. They closed the distance and hugged each other like long-lost friends.

They had jogged to a nearby coffee shop, where they spent the next two hours engaged in animated conversation. She told him how solicitous Marshall had been during her recovery, devoting every spare moment to looking after her physical and emotional needs.

She had detected a note of envy or regret in Zack's reaction. Soon after that, they parted ways with promises to stay in touch—which, of course, they hadn't done.

Why does living get in the way of life?

Between the frigid air, their heavy breathing, and Bridget's impaired voice, they couldn't carry on a conversation beyond a few words.

"Doing all right?" Zack asked.

"Yes. You?"

He gave her an engaging smile. "Excellent."

They completed a three-mile loop in forty minutes before stopping in front of Bridget's home. As they drank from water bottles, Bridget motioned toward the door. "Still some time before the kids return. Let's get warm."

Zack smiled. "Great plan."

Inside, they each took a few minutes to cool down and dry the sweat from their faces and hair; Bridget in her upstairs bathroom, Zack in the guest bathroom on the first floor where he had changed earlier. He doffed his Gore-Tex outer jacket but kept on the long-sleeved Lycra shirt and thermal pants. He thought about changing back to his street clothes but decided against doing that without showering first.

Zack sat on the living-room couch and waited for Bridget. When she came downstairs, she had removed her outer clothing. She wore Spandex tights and a form-fitting Lycra top. Zack tried his best not to ogle her.

He failed. Her cycling-toned thighs and broad swimmer's shoulders complemented the natural curves of her body.

Bridget caught him staring but didn't seem to mind. "I've just the thing to warm us up." She offered a smile and wink as she went to the small bar, giving Zack a full view of her derrière. She retrieved a bottle of Laphroaig single-malt scotch and poured them each a Glencairn glass with one rock and two fingers of the whisky.

She handed him a glass, sat on the couch beside him, raised her glass, and affected a bad Scottish brogue. "A little taste of the burning hospital, eh, bro?"

He clinked her glass and looked her in the eye. "Here's looking at you, pal."

They both chuckled and drank. An uncomfortable silence descended on them.

Zack straightened his posture and set his glass on the coffee table. "So, about Dr. Gibson."

Bridget set hers down and turned to face him, hands in her lap. "Okay, I know we're not detectives or investigators, by occupation at least. Except, we both are by temperament. Aren't our mutual occupational duties to seek truth?"

Zack nodded. "Why this case?"

"Something's rotten, Zack. I can smell it." She raised her glass. "You can too."

"So what if we do? Not our job."

"Wasn't our job to discover the truth and blow the whistle on Dennis King either. No one else was going to make that connection."

"For which we both almost died."

Bridget frowned. "For God's sake, Zack, we can't let that control the rest of our lives. Otherwise, what good did it do to survive?"

He stared at her for a moment. "What are you suggesting? You know the cops are all over this. Surely they have a BOLO out for that youth that brought the girl to the ER." He crossed his arms. "It doesn't involve us."

Bridget sipped her drink.

Zack followed suit, thoughtful. He put down the glass. "We've had some, uh, atypical OB cases at our hospital. One involved a girl with a ruptured ectopic pregnancy. She died today from complications. One of our best physicians, Paula Cho, missed the diagnosis in the ER. The girl came in with a guardian and no parents. Paula thought she may have been mentally challenged. At the very least, naive about her body. Couldn't say how she got pregnant."

"Was the caretaker a young male?"

"No, a thirty-something woman."

They sat in silence for a few minutes, each sipping scotch and processing what they'd just realized.

Zack broke the silence. "Okay, Bridge. I'm hooked. We can talk to Dr. Gibson."

"And the young mother, if we can find her."

Zack shook his head. "What are you getting me into now, counselor?"

CHAPTER THIRTY

Sitting in the back seat of the Range Rover, Annie tuned out the animated conversation between Jennifer and Grant in the front. The two had obviously connected. What would Tall Paul in San Diego think about his girlfriend flirting with this preppy rich boy? On the other hand, Annie discerned no significant difference between Paul and Grant, who could be clones of the cool dude type that made her older sister act like an infatuated teenager.

How shallow.

Why did Annie need to be here with them? She wasn't into preppy parties. Her dad had all but forced her, even though she made it clear she didn't want to go. The man was so transparent. Anyone could see he wanted to be alone with Bridget.

How weird is that, Dr. SO-Cool?

Annie couldn't fault her father's attraction to Bridget. What a neat lady. Since Annie arrived in DC, Bridget was the first person who got her right away; didn't pass judgment on her appearance like the others. She was sincere and genuine, interested in Annie as a person. Such a shame about her voice. Yet her dad seemed mesmerized by her. What a doof. Bridget deserved better than Zack Winston. Her husband, maybe. Except she seemed to have hots for dad.

Her phone buzzed. A text from Conner.

Hey girl you fall into the Potomac
Annie scowled.
No why
Waiting for news
Got none give it a rest

She didn't want to think about it until she had to, which wasn't tonight. Maybe tomorrow she could get away to a drug store or something.

What doing
Going to a preppy party with my sister and some guy she's totally into Lame

The car stopped; backed up as Grant parallel parked it.

You meeting a guy too
:O=

The door on her side opened. Jennifer spoke into her ear. "Cut the text and get out. We're here." Annie felt almost relieved.

Gotta go bitch sister dragging me from car

She ended the text without waiting for his reply.

They sat at a long table in an upscale pizza restaurant in Old Town with about a dozen preppy types crammed along both sides. Grant and Jennifer sat squeezed together at the head. Annie sat at the end of the bench next to them. The boy on the other side ignored her, kept his back turned two-thirds while he chatted up his friends.

Your loss, jerk.

Annie searched the menu for anything vegan. She saw only two possible choices, a roasted vegetables antipasti and a dish she'd never heard of, Tonno e Fagioli. Except that one had anchovies and tuna. *Dang.*

She turned to the waiter standing with hands on hips beside her. "I'll have the roasted vegetables, please."

"You have to choose three," he said.

Arrogant preppy a-hole.

"Fine. Give me the artichokes, broccoli, and eggplant."

A voice from her opposite side interrupted. "You should try the escarole instead of eggplant."

Annie turned to see a young guy, not at all preppy, dressed in a tee-shirt and blue jeans. Long wavy hair and sideburns made him look like a visitor from a past era. Cool. He seemed closer to her own age than the others around the table.

"Seriously," the guy said. "You'll be glad you did."

"Okay," she said to the waiter. "What he said."

The waiter rolled his eyes and made a show of scratching out and revising her prior order.

The cool guy stepped close to the waiter; stared him down. "I'll have the same."

Chagrined, the waiter finished the order and left.

"Mind if I join you?" the guy said to Annie. He scowled at the person next to her on the bench. "I promise to be better company than this dude's back."

Without waiting for a reply, he gave the other guy a semi-polite shove and squeezed onto the bench between him and Annie. She sidled over, leaving one butt cheek hanging off the edge of the bench.

The guy greeted several others at the table as he sat down. He turned to Annie. "Haven't seen you here before." He reached out a hand. "Tyler Rhodes."

Annie shook his hand, which felt warm and friendly. "Annie Winston."

"What's your story, Annie Winston?"

She nodded toward Jennifer. "My sister and I are here from California to visit our dad."

Tyler smiled. "Ah, the old 'gotta go visit the dad instead of being with my friends over the holidays' routine. Such a drag, right?"

Annie smiled back. "Yeah. For sure."

"Been there," he said. "Finally just cut the old man off. He was never any good. Tried to make me into something I'm not." He shrugged. "Haven't seen him in five years."

"That's how long it's been since we've seen our dad."

Tyler raised his eyebrows. "Really? What brought about the change?"

She shook her head. "Long story, most of which I don't get."

"Parents," Tyler said. "I don't plan to ever be one."

Annie blushed. "Yeah, uh, me neither. I hope."

Tyler looked askance at her, just as the wait staff returned with the food. Annie felt suddenly famished. She dove into her vegetables like a rat on a hunk of meat. Besides, with her mouth full she wouldn't have to follow up on the parenting conversation.

"You vegan?" Tyler asked.

"Yeah, for two years now."

He nodded. "Me too. Three years."

For a few minutes, they ate in silence, each casting not-so furtive glances at the other. Annie felt a strange warm sensation inside her. Nothing like she'd felt with Conner, even though they'd been doing it for two years now.

Tyler finished his vegetables and turned to her. "What else do you do besides sacrifice yourself for your parents?"

Annie smiled. The evening was going better. First Bridget, now Tyler. Two people she liked. Two people she wanted to get to know. "Nothing much. Mostly into art and stuff."

He turned in his seat to face her. "Tell me. I want to know more about you, Annie Winston from California."

CHAPTER THIRTY-ONE

Zack and Bridget made plans to try to meet Dr. Gibson the following morning. When she got up to refresh their drinks, Zack raised a palm to his forehead.

"Cripes. I forgot. Tomorrow is Annie's birthday."

Bridget stopped in mid-pour. "And Christmas Eve. I forgot as well."

Zack felt a spinning sensation, as if he spiraled back to earth from outer space. He raised a hand. "Easy on the refill for me. I have to drive my girls home."

Bridget laughed as she poured him a full measure. "Says the man who once forced me to take an Uber home from his place after a few single malts."

Zack looked at his watch: 9 PM. Grant had promised to get the girls back by ten. Zack could probably metabolize another drink in that time. If not, Uber would work.

"Fine. We can decide when they get back."

Bridget handed him his drink and sat next to him, closer than before. He found her mixed aroma of dried sweat and Chanel more intoxicating than the scotch. He made no effort to move away from her. He wasn't sure which of them initiated the slight movement that brought their shoulders and thighs in contact.

They clinked glasses and stared into each other's eyes. Zack took a deep breath. "So?"

Bridget stiffened and lowered her head. "Marshall's cheating again."

"What? I thought that stopped after your attack."

"It did." She scoffed. "Now that I'm back on my feet, he seems to have that need again."

Zack touched her arm. "You deserve better."

She placed her hand over his. "I know." She leaned toward him. Their faces almost touched. On impulse, Zack bent to kiss her.

Bridget pulled back. "No. Not like this." She stared into his eyes, her own orbs deep pools of mixed longing and grief. "Please, just hold me?"

Zack reached out and pulled her into him. "I'm here for you, Bridge. Always."

She looked at him and tilted her head. Their lips moved together.

The sudden noise of the automatic garage door opening forced them apart like a bolt of lightning.

Bridget bounced away. "The kids are home early." She moved to the chair beside the couch.

The door from the garage opened. Zack and Bridget both turned at the same time.

Marshall Hilliard stood in the doorway, his shocked face crimson red.

—⋀—

Zack, Bridget, and Marshall had suffered through thirty agonizing minutes of forced small talk when Grant arrived home with Zack's daughters.

"Sorry we're late," Grant said. "Had a hard time peeling Annie away from Tyler Rhodes."

Annie's cheeks flushed and her chin dipped toward the floor.

Marshall came out of the bathroom. Bridget introduced him to Jennifer and Annie, whereupon the US Attorney put on his fake southern charm.

"Such beautiful young ladies you have, Dr. Winston." He winked at the girls. "Take after their mother, no doubt."

Tipsy from a few beers, Jennifer giggled.

Annie's mouth dropped.

"Indeed, they do," Zack said, his voice strained. "I need to get them home. Tomorrow is Annie's birthday. We want her well-rested for the gala we have planned."

Annie and Jennifer both swung their heads to Zack.

"Gala?" Annie scoffed. "Really, Dad."

Bridget intervened. "I hope you have a wonderful day." She looked at Zack. "I'm sure your father will make it special for you."

Zack forced a smile.

Bridget reached out a hand and touched Annie's shoulder. "It's been a genuine pleasure to meet you, Annie. I hope to see you again before you go back to California."

Annie beamed. "Me too."

"I'm sure we can arrange that," Zack said.

Bridget turned to Jennifer. "You too, future Dr. Winston."

Marshall harrumphed. He turned to his son. "Grant, did I hear you mention Tyler Rhodes?"

"Yeah," Grant said. "He showed up at the restaurant. Seems that he and Annie have much in common."

Marshall lifted his eyebrows, skeptical. "Does he have college plans, or did his 'year off' after high school tarnish him forever?"

"Apparently not. He's enrolled at Georgetown. Pre-med, though, not pre-law like his brothers."

Marshall shot Zack a cold smile. "Well, someone has to be the bottom-feeder."

Zack didn't retreat. "Reminds me of a riddle I once heard. What do you call a thousand lawyers at the bottom of the ocean?"

Bridget stepped up to him. "We've all heard it, thank you, Doctor."

Zack didn't heed the warning. "A good start."

His was the only laugh that followed.

Bridget shook her head. "Typical BAFERD. Ready, fire, aim."

Zack did a double-take at the unaccustomed sarcasm from her.

Did she do that for Marshall's sake?

He shuffled his feet. "We need to get going. Thanks again for the evening, Bridget, and Grant." He reached a hand to Marshall. "Good to see you again, Mr. US Attorney."

"Always a pleasure, Zack. See you at the task force next week."

Zack blinked. He'd forgotten. "I may have to miss it. The girls will still be here."

"By all means, Doc." Marshall smirked. "We'll try to muddle along without you."

"I'll walk you all out," Bridget said.

Zack glanced at her attire. "No need, counselor. It's cold out there."

"I would be remiss as a southern lady if I did not see a gentleman and his daughters to their vehicle."

As they walked behind the girls to the Lexus, Zack touched Bridget's hand. She pulled away. He spoke out the side of his mouth. "Are you okay?"

"I'll be in touch."

"Please do." He gave her hand a quick stroke as he reached for his keys.

CHAPTER THIRTY-TWO

When Bridget re-entered the house, Marshall sat in the easy chair next to the living room sofa, sipping his second shot of Makers Mark. No sign of Grant. Bridget figured he'd gone to bed.

Marshall set his glass on the table, sat back, folded his arms, and crossed his legs. "Well, that was interesting."

Bridget went to the bar and poured herself another Laphroaig. She turned to face him. "What?"

"Guess I made enough noise in the garage for the doc to get his dick back into his pants before I came through the door."

Bridget wanted to throw her glass at him but wouldn't stoop to the raging woman role. She let the jibe roll past her.

Typical litigator's ploy, taking the offensive.

"Welcome home," she said. "Didn't expect you until tomorrow at the earliest."

He glanced at the couch where Zack had been sitting. "Obviously."

Bridget's anger and frustration buffeted her attempt at mindful control. "I object to your tone."

"I object to finding my wife sitting sweaty and sexy with a guy. That one in particular."

Bridget blew out a breath. "Cut it, Marsh. You know nothing was going on here."

He scoffed. "Then why did I walk into a pheromone-rich environment?"

Ah ha. An opening.

"I wouldn't know about that. You're more attuned to pheromones than I am."

The counterattack caught Marshall by surprise. He drew back. "What's that supposed to mean?"

Bridget advanced to stand over him where he sat. "Where were you last night, Marshall?"

He took a sip of whiskey. "Richmond, as you know."

"Where in Richmond?"

Marshall's eyes narrowed. "What's your game, Bridge?"

She ignored his weak attempt at diversion. "Where?"

He furrowed his brow, feigning that he didn't understand the question.

Despite her chronic hoarseness, Bridget spoke in a deliberate tone, as if addressing a hostile witness in court. "Where in Richmond were you?"

"My hotel, of course. Traffic was a bear. We got in later than expected."

Bridget tilted her head. "You were in your hotel room?"

"As I said."

"No, that's not what you said. You said you were in your hotel."

He waved her off. "Same difference."

Marshall quaffed the rest of his whiskey; got up to pour another. When he was done, he did not resume his seat but stood in front of Bridget. They were about the same height.

She stared into his eyes. His glance flicked away then met hers. "Yes, my hotel room."

"All night?"

"Of course."

"Where was Fiona?"

He scowled and shrugged. "How would I know? Her room, I suppose."

Bridget finished her drink and returned the glass to the bar, but didn't pour a refill. She stood squarely in front of him, hands on her hips. "What did you do this morning?"

"Listen here, Bridge. I don't appreciate your cross-examination game."

She put a hand to her mouth. "So sorry. I thought I was asking reasonable questions from a wife to her husband." She stood her ground. "Did you make your own bed this morning? In your hotel room?" She cast him a friendly "gotcha" smile.

Marshall's face turned red. "What's going on, Bridge?"

"That's my question to you, Marshall Hilliard. Based on what I know, you're sleeping with Fiona. Again."

He erupted. "Never." He approached within two feet of her. "How dare you make such an accusation. You know nothing, Bridget."

She kept her poise. "I know you didn't sleep in your hotel room last night. Seems a logical conclusion that you slept in hers, or someone else's." She shrugged. "Doesn't matter whose."

Marshall stepped back. "I will not condone this reckless attack. How could you know whether a bed was made in a random hotel room in Richmond?"

She shook her head. "I cannot reveal my sources, but I assure you I have proof."

"Bullshit you do." He turned away toward the staircase. "I'm going to bed."

Bridget blocked his path. "Not in my bed. Not tonight. Maybe never again."

He moved closer to her, his face livid. "You wouldn't dare."

"Try me."

Marshall glared. "Never going to happen, Bridge. Least of all now."

Something in his tone alarmed her enough that she lost her mental advantage and stepped back. "Explain."

Marshall puffed out his chest and brought himself to full height. "The reason I came home tonight, instead of whatever you imagined I was doing, was to tell my dear, loyal wife that I had certain closed-door meetings in Richmond this afternoon."

Was he bullshitting her?

She folded her arms. "And?"

"Tomorrow, with the full support of my party's leadership and the governor, I will announce my candidacy for Attorney General of the Commonwealth of Virginia."

Bridget deflated like a balloon against a shard of shattered glass. She turned away, sat on the couch, pursed her lips, and glared at her husband. "So, of course . . ."

". . . not a hint of marital discord allowed, much less any separation crap."

Bridget could take on the formidable Marshall Hilliard in a divorce settlement with a good chance of winning or breaking even. She would have no leverage against the powerful party leadership that would close ranks behind him. They would dig up even the tiniest grain of dirt to use against her. They wouldn't have to search far.

I'm screwed.

Bridget mustered what resolve she could, drew in, and blew out a deep breath. "I get it."

"I thought you would see the light. You're a smart woman."

She glared at him with cold, steely eyes. "You're still not sleeping in my bed. Grant's in the guest room, so you can have the couch."

The two of them stared at each other, neither giving ground. The front door opened and diverted their attention.

Dustin halted in the doorway, home from the basketball game. His alarmed eyes bounced between his parents. "What's going on?"

Bridget's heart sank. She took a step toward her son. "Nothing, hon. We were just going to bed."

She turned to her husband, took his hand, and led him toward the stairway. "Come on, Marsh. Let's get some sleep."

CHAPTER THIRTY-THREE

Riding in the back seat of her dad's Lexus on the drive from Alexandria to Bethesda, Annie pulled out her phone to text Conner. He had texted her three times since she went into the pizza place with Jennifer and Grant.

> Whassup dude?
> Pissed
> WTF
> *You left me hanging*
> Give me a break I told you what I was doing
> *Too busy hanging with preppy kids to worry about me*
> Get a grip or I'm out

No response. Annie was about to sign off when Conner responded.

> *Sry miss you worried*
> Don't
> *But what if you know*

Annie didn't want to think about that. She'd had a good time this evening. Didn't need to let Conner, or reality, spoil it.

Quit sweating it dude we deal with it if we have to no since worrying.

WARM AND DEAD

How can you be so cool

Annie thought about Tyler. She figured he wouldn't be all anxious like Conner.

What do you want me to do thinking don't solve it

As if on cue, her phone buzzed with an incoming text from Tyler. They had exchanged numbers at the end of the evening. She switched text windows.

Hey girl what up
Not home yet
Liked meeting you tonight
Me too

She switched back to the chat from Conner.

You mad

Annie groaned so loud that Jennifer glanced at her from the front seat.

Give it a rest dude

She switched back to Tyler's next message.

Wanna see you again
Me too
Redundant
LOL yeah want to see you again too
Tomorrow
Dunno xmas eve and all plus my birthday
Sweet 16 happy birthday
I'm 18 but thanks
Sure you are and YW

Annie switched back to a string of texts from Conner.

Don't blame me for being worried
Hello
OK sry
WTF don't you answer you with somebody

Annie shook her head, annoyed.

Yeah my sister and my dad I haven't seen in 5 years
Sry
Gimme space OK we deal with whatever when I get home
Yeah OK miss you
Me too
Call me
Can't
:-(

This had gone beyond annoying.

Gotta go bye

She didn't wait for his response, closed that chat window, and resumed with Tyler.

Still there
Yeah waiting for you to get back from the other guy
??
Figure some dude in CA misses you
Are you like prescient or something
Nah just been around
Okay yeah dude in CA blew him off friggin' juvenile
Happens when you turn 18 ;) you start looking for real men

You know any
Meet me tomorrow I show you
Dunno if I can
Can if you want
I'll figure out something
Looking forward to it
I'll text you in the AM
Anytime I seldom sleep
Kbye
:-*

Annie clicked off and sighed.

Zack and his daughters entered the Bethesda apartment just after midnight. He hugged Annie. "Happy birthday, my girl."

She drew away from his hug and looked at him with a half-smile. "Thanks, Dad."

Jennifer noticed Zack's discomfort at the mixed message. "Annie doesn't do hugs. Don't take it personally, Dad."

Zack smiled at his younger daughter. "Okay. Sure. Happy birthday, Annie."

To Zack's surprise, Annie reached out and hugged him.

Jennifer chortled. "I meant she does hugs only if she initiates them."

Zack shrugged. "Whatever works. I'm cool with it."

The girls exchanged looks that said, "weirdo."

"Using the word 'cool' identifies you as not cool, Dad," Jennifer said.

Zack chuckled. "At least I'm not a boomer."

"Okay," both girls said in unison.

"What do you want to do tomorrow for your birthday, Annie?"

Annie scoffed. "You told Bridget you had something planned."

"Yeah, well, I lied."

"Duh. That was obvious."

"Seriously, what do you want to do?"

Annie squared her stance in front of Zack. "Here's the deal, Dad. Because I was born on Christmas Eve my birthday usually gets lost in the holiday cheer." She shrugged. "So, no big."

"We should do something to make it special for you this year."

Annie's face scrunched. Zack could almost see the wheels churning inside her mind.

"Do you need to go to the hospital tomorrow?"

Zack hesitated. "Don't have to." He ran a hand through his hair. "But I should see that doctor I told you about."

Both girls looked at him, curious.

"Can you tell us more about him?" Jennifer asked.

Zack told them the story of Nate Young.

"That ECMO think sounds interesting," Jennifer said.

Zack lit up. "You girls could come with me. We'll go out for breakfast afterward. There's a diner in Bethesda you would like."

Annie shook her head with vigor. "No way am I going to a hospital. Yuk."

Jennifer brightened. "I want to go." She scowled at Annie. "You can wait in the lobby if you want."

Annie crossed her arms. "No hospital. Not on my birthday. Not any day if I can help it."

"Okay," Zack said. "Maybe Jenn and I go to the hospital, then come back and pick you up for breakfast."

Annie kept her arms crossed. Zack discerned the wheels still turning in her head. Did she have an ulterior motive?

"I want to sleep in," Annie said. "It's my birthday and I want to sleep in. I hate going out for breakfast. They never have anything I can eat." She shot Zack and Jennifer a sweet smile. "You two go to the hospital and go to breakfast. Take your time. I'll sleep till noon." She gave Zack a sly smile. "Take us out to dinner for my birthday."

Zack and Jennifer exchanged glances. She gave him a slight nod. "Okay," he said.

He looked at Jennifer. "Can we go around seven in the morning?"

She frowned. "Can we make it eight?"

"If you think you want to be a surgeon, you need to get up early. It's how they do."

Jennifer huffed. "Fine. Seven o'clock it is."

Zack planned to ask Jerry Hartman to wait in ICU until he and Jenn got there. Jerry would enjoy showing off for a future doctor, especially one as pretty as Jennifer.

After Jennifer and her dad had gone to bed, Annie stretched out on the couch and texted Tyler.

> Still up
> *Duh told you I don't sleep much*
> You free in the morning
> *For you sure*
> Meet somewhere
> *I'll pick you up*
> Where
> *Where you staying*
> Not here somewhere in bethesda
> *Where*
> Hang on

Annie did a Google search for "pharmacy near me." She found one that looked within walking distance, with a Starbucks nearby.

> Starbucks on woodmont I'll text you the address

Time
She did some quick calculations in her head
Nine
See you there
Don't be late I won't have much time
Ooh sneaky Love it
Just be there
You got it
Nite :-*
Nite :-X

She clicked off and set her phone on the table next to the couch and opened the bed. Just as she had settled down to sleep, the phone buzzed. Figuring it was Tyler, she picked it up—only to be disappointed that it was a text from Conner.

Annie ignored it.

CHAPTER THIRTY-FOUR

December 24, Midnight

Dearest Noelle,

So much happened in just one day. Where to begin?

I saw Bridget. We . . . have something. I don't know what, but it's real. Scary. Something almost happened. Our kids were out together. Bridget and I . . . Well, we kissed. Then her husband walked in. What if he hadn't interrupted us? Would we have . . .? I don't know.

He's cheating on her again. Bastard. I would never—

Maybe it's good he came home when he did. He suspected something. Takes one to know one?

Damn it, Noelle, what the hell was I thinking? I can't be with Bridget. Not while Marshall is in her life. It's not right.

I want to be with her. You know that. You've known it for a long time. You gave me permission once. Except it wasn't you, it was my inner desire.

I need to stay away. I can't see her again. Not unless. . . .

Zack's phone buzzed. A text from Bridget. He glanced at the time, after 1 AM.

Dr. Gibson dead. Call me after 8 AM. Marsh gone to office by then.

She had just sent the message. She would be near her phone.

What? How? I'm up. Call me?

For five minutes, Zack stared at his phone.
Bridget did not call.

CHAPTER THIRTY-FIVE

Emily startled awake after midnight. Footsteps on the stairs. It took a few seconds before she remembered she was in the Georgetown house, not The Good House.

The footsteps got closer; someone coming to her room. She had dozed off around ten. A light sleeper, she had not heard a car arrive, had not heard the front door open or close. Who was in the house and how did they get in?

Dr. Good at last? She didn't want him to see her clad only in underwear. Not before he did a lot of explaining.

The footsteps stopped in front of her door.

Emily sat on the edge of the bed and pulled the quilt around her.

The lock turned.

She faced the doorway and smiled. She didn't want Dr. Good to see her sad. That would not go well for her.

Spider stepped into the room and shut the door behind him. His lascivious leer assaulted her vision. "I came in the back way."

Emily shrank away from him. She tightened the quilt around her.

Spider paused a moment, curious. Then he broke into a demonic laugh. "You think I came to . . . ? Oh, that is rich."

He grabbed her under an armpit, yanked her up, and faced her. Boozy breath defiled her nostrils. "You're not my type. Plus Dr. Good would kill me if I tampered with his precious nurse doll."

Despite his assurance, naked fear coursed through Emily's body. She willed herself to be strong, straightened her spine, and stood tall. "It's late. I'll thank you to get out of my room."

Spider scoffed. "Sure. Just wanted to be sure you didn't, you know, try anything stupid while we left you alone." He gripped her arm. "You've shown yourself not to be trustworthy of late."

She yanked her arm away and pointed at the door. "Get out."

He backed off. "Don't try anything stupid now. I'll be just downstairs, and I'm a light sleeper." He left the room and closed the door behind him. A key turned the lock.

She sat back on the bed, fists knotted, fighting tears. For a minute she hyperventilated, then slowed her breathing, relaxed her fists.

No more tears!

A new sense of focused calm welled up within her.

"I must get out of here. Tonight."

Emily waited almost an hour before she allowed herself to believe that Spider had fallen asleep downstairs. She tried her bedroom door. Locked. She must find a way to open it, without making much noise. On television shows, she'd seen people open a locked door with a credit card.

Dr. Good had never allowed her to have her own money, let alone a credit or debit card. She didn't even own a purse.

What to do? She knelt at the door so she could look directly at the lock and consider options. Hairpin? Didn't have one. Paper clip? Nope. She went into the bathroom and searched the medicine cabinet, drawers, and shelves. All empty. Someone had swept the room before she was locked into it, eliminating any option for escape.

Or self-harm?

Back in the bedroom, Emily sat on the bed. She spotted the clothes she'd put on the previous day before they took Missy to the ER. Scrub pants and a nurse's smock in a heap on the floor where she'd left them before climbing into the bed. She picked up the smock and checked the front pocket. She smiled as she closed her hand around the small fob that contained keys to OB closet's medication locker at The Good House. Two flat metallic keys about an inch long.

How could she use those on the bedroom lock?

She took the keyring to the door and studied the lock. After a couple of minutes, she sat back on her haunches, defeated. Nothing fit. She took a few deep breaths.

I am getting out of here whatever it takes. Even if I have to break down the door. I'll do what I must to deal with Spider.

Looking back at the doorknob, the obvious solution came to her. It would mean taking a huge risk, so she needed to be ready if Spider came up the stairs. She put the keyring on the floor by the door, then hurried to get dressed. Thinking she might need a weapon against Spider, she went back into the bathroom and searched. The shower curtain. It was hung on a rod that she easily lifted out of its sockets and collapsed. A handy club.

Back at the bedroom door, she laid the makeshift weapon next to her and removed one of the locker keys from the ring. She first needed to scrape a layer of old paint from the edge of the corroded bronze collar around the doorknob. Then she forced the point of the key between the collar and door and used the keyring as a pivot point. After several tries along the circumference of the collar, it popped away from the surface, revealing the lock mechanism beneath it.

Emily took the other locker key and used the point to loosen the two screws on either side of the lock mechanism. She tugged on the doorknob and pulled it back against the heads of the screws. A few more turns on each screw and the doorknob would come apart. Then she could undo the mechanism that held the door closed.

No way to keep it from making noise when it came apart. Emily rehearsed the steps she must take to get out and be ready to protect herself. She placed the shower bar between her feet and the door, crouched over it, held the doorknob in her left hand, and with her right finished loosening both screws. As planned, the doorknob came apart in her left hand. The lock mechanism remained in the door. Emily placed the doorknob on the floor, picked up the shower bar, stood, and pushed the lock mechanism through the door. It came out of the hole and landed on the hallway floor with a clattering *thunk*.

Emily eased the now lockless door open and crept into the hallway. She crouched at the top of the stairs, expecting Spider's full-on assault. Nothing happened.

For the first time in years, Emily Morgan felt free.

The sense of freedom lasted less than a minute as Emily took stock of her situation. She'd escaped the locked bedroom. Now what? Where would she go? With what?

She stood at the top of the stairs, still clutching the shower bar, and thought about what she must do next. Her thinking always worked better if she planned three steps at a time.

First, make sure Spider was not a threat.
Second, find her coat downstairs,
Third, flee this place.
Figure out the rest after that.

Emily sidled down the stairs, alert, shower bar raised and ready to strike. When she reached the second floor, a light shone through an open bedroom door.

Spider.

She crept towards the landing for the stairs to the ground floor. The sound of snoring from Spider's room stopped her short. She turned and hugged the wall to the open door and peeked inside. Spider sprawled across the bed in his underwear.

Emily crouched, not sure why, and crept into the room to where Spider's clothes lay on the floor. She set the shower bar on the carpeted floor and picked up his jeans. She glanced at Spider. Still asleep.

Searching for his car keys, Emily explored the left front pocket of his pants. Something sharp stabbed her finger. She gasped and froze in place, casting a glance to where Spider still slept, snores and all.

Her finger came out of the pocket with a drop of blood. She wiped it on her pants, then reached back in with great care and pulled out a medication vial, the kind with a cut-off glass top typical of single-dose medication to be drawn into a syringe for injection. The jagged edge of the vial had poked into her finger. The empty vial had no label.

Another glance at Spider confirmed he was still in deep sleep. She reached into the other front pocket of the jeans and found the keys. She put the broken medication vial and car keys in her smock pocket, took one final glance at the sleeping Spider, and slipped out the bedroom door.

She stopped in the hallway.

Should have looked for a wallet.

Where would she go without money? Emily looked back into the room. Spider stirred. He rolled over to face the doorway where she stood. She ducked behind the wall, holding the shower bar ready to swat him if he came through the doorway. He started snoring again.

Emily stole as quietly as she could down the stairs to the front room. Looking out the front windows, she couldn't see Spider's car parked anywhere within view.

What to do? Three things.

First, get out of the house.

Second, wander the street until she found Spider's car.

Third, drive into the countryside.

Fear gripped Emily's heart and she couldn't move. She would be out on her own for the first time since . . . She couldn't remember.

They would find her. She didn't know all the details, but she understood that their network extended wide and deep. What would they do to her? What if Dr. Good was gone for good?

Spider would be in charge.

The thought of becoming Spider's personal concubine without Dr. Good's protection drove Emily into action. The house's rear entrance faced onto a narrow alley that lead to another street. She would find Spider's car on that street.

Then she would just drive. As far away as she could. She would drive to Alaska if she had to. At least Canada.

She had to hurry.

One, get out of the house.

Two, find the car.

Three, drive away.

She had to flee the unreal, terrible world in which she'd been a prisoner ever since Dr. Good "saved" her.

Dr. Evil.

You can do this, Em!

She clutched Spider's keys and hurried through the kitchen to the back door. When she was three feet away from the door, someone on the other side unlocked it.

Roach.

Roach had come back. She was doomed.

Must hide. Must. Hide.

Emily ran back into the living room as the back door opened. She dove behind the couch. Slow footsteps ambled through the kitchen, into the living room, and headed straight to her hiding place.

Roach had seen her!

She cowered in terror as the footsteps walked around the couch. A familiar voice spoke in soft, kind tones.

"Emily, what are you doing behind the couch?" Dr. Good reached down and helped her to her feet. "What's with the shower bar? What keys are you holding?"

Emily pointed to the stairs. "Spider. He—"

Dr. Good pulled her close to him and hugged her. "You're okay. You're safe." He lifted her face close to his. "I've come to take you home. To The Good House."

CHAPTER THIRTY-SIX

Longing for sleep while also fighting it, Bridget clung to the edge of the king-sized marriage bed. With her back turned to him, she sensed Marshall sprawled on his back, sleeping without interruption; no cares, no worries to keep him awake.

The freedom of never admitting guilt, least of all to himself.

She finally fell into a deep sleep, only to awaken minutes later to the disruption of Marshall turning on his bedside lamp and getting out of bed. She kept her eyes closed, feigning sleep until he padded into his bathroom. One of his nightly trips to urinate, a burden that Bridget considered his due for refusing prostate surgery.

When she heard the shower start, Bridget got out of bed, donned a robe over her pajamas, stuck her phone in the pocket, and used her bathroom that adjoined Marshall's. Finished, she went down to the kitchen and pushed the button to start the coffee brewing—almost an hour before the 6:30 AM programmed time.

Bridget opened her phone. Zack Winston's text stared at her like an abandoned puppy. She started to return it when she heard Marshall's footsteps on the stairs.

Why was he up so early?

He arrived dressed in business attire carrying his suit jacket, which he tossed onto an armchair. He eyed the phone in her hand.

"Texting your boyfriend, Bridge? Can't wait till I'm out of the house?"

Bridget's finger jumped off the text window and slid to the phone button. She gave Marshall a withering scowl. "Calling Ange. She texted me after we went to bed. Our physician client died."

Marshall raised his eyebrows. "Really? Strange. What from?"

"Don't know. That's why I'm calling Ange, to see what we need to do or who we need to see to figure it out."

"You have a date with me this afternoon."

Bridget clicked off the phone before it could ring Ange's number. She huffed. "I'll be there, ready to gaze up with awe at my spouse, the future Attorney General."

She pocketed the phone and placed her hands on her hips. "Why are you announcing on Christmas Eve? Seems an odd choice."

"The party publicist thinks we'll get good airtime over the holidays. People can take only so much glad tidings and good cheer."

"As a voter, I'd find it offensive."

He grinned. "One of several reasons why you're not my publicist." He turned serious. "Speaking of whom, she recommends you wear blue. Put on your royal blue suit with a pale blue blouse. Complements your blond hair. Leave the blouse open at the neck. She wants viewers to see your scar. Makes my 'get tough on crime' platform personal."

Bridget felt she might puke. "She?"

"For God's sake, Bridge, get over it. We have a campaign to run."

"We?"

He moved close to her; placed a hand on her shoulder. "You and I are a team, like always."

Bridget moved away, squared to face him. "Let me be really clear here, Marshall Hilliard. I will do what I must to help you get elected because you and your party will make my life hell if I don't. But you and I are no longer a team. Not in real life. I'm done."

Marshall stared at her, eyes smoldering. "Be careful what you wish for, Bridget."

"Back at you."

He moved closer and stood in front of her, arms folded, eyes narrowed. "Since we are being 'really clear,' let me make a point. No scandals during my campaign. No paparazzi photos of my wife hanging out with some ER doc, or any man. No late-night excursions or out-of-town trips with Dr. Winsome or anyone. You got that?"

Bridget mimicked his stance and gaze. "I suggest you give that counsel to the candidate. Based on recent and past experience, you are more vulnerable to embarrassing disclosures than I'll ever be." She glared at him. "And his name is Dr. Winston."

Marshall pointed a finger at her face. "Watch yourself. Fair warning."

"Ditto."

He glanced at the kitchen clock. "I have to go. Breakfast meeting with the campaign team." He picked up his suit coat and headed toward the garage, turning at the door. "My office, one-thirty. Don't be late. Blue suit, open collar."

Without waiting for a response, he went through to the garage and slammed the door behind him.

"Fuck you very much," Bridget said to the closed door.

She went back to the kitchen, picked up her phone, and called Zack.

CHAPTER THIRTY-SEVEN

Zack awakened to his phone ringing.

Bridget.

He answered. "What the hell happened with Gibson?"

"Huh?" Sarah's voice.

Zack squeezed his eyes. *Son of a—*

"Were you expecting someone else, Zack? Lawyer friend perhaps?"

He sat on the edge of the bed; ran a hand through his hair. "No. I was expecting a call from Jerry Hartman."

"Who's Gibson?"

"You wouldn't know." He looked at the clock. 6 AM. "Why did you call, Sarah?"

"Sorry. Figured you'd be awake. Just wanted to touch base before your day fills up."

"Already has."

She blew into the phone. "Look, Zack. You have no cause to be curt with me."

Zack sighed. "Yeah. You're right. Sorry." He made his voice pleasant. "What's up?"

"I enjoyed running into you and your daughters yesterday. They seem like fine young women."

"Is that what you did? 'Ran' into us?"

"Well, I don't care for that insinuation. You have ten seconds to get nice or I'm hanging up."

Zack was seriously tempted to stay silent, but he spoke after five seconds. "Sorry again. I'm just waking up. We got home late then stayed up for a while."

"Okay. I'll let it go. This time."

After a pause, her voice sounded firm. "I want to see them again, Zack. It's important."

Zack wanted to ask, "important to whom?" but he decided against it.

"Today is Annie's birthday."

"I knew that. You have plans?"

He rubbed his eyes with his free hand; stared off into space.

Might as well give in now. She's not going to quit until I do.

"Would you like to join us for dinner this evening?"

Sarah gushed. "That would be wonderful. Thanks for asking me."

"Our pleasure." Zack hoped his voice did not sound as sarcastic as he felt.

"Where and when?"

"Not sure on details yet. Jennifer and I are going to the hospital to meet Jerry Hartman." He paused. "Do you know about Dr. Nate Young?"

"I heard about it. Terrible thing. You just never know someone, do you?"

Zack squeezed his eyes together again. "He's on ECMO. I wanted to see him, and I thought Jenn might be interested. She's a medical student."

"I know."

How did she get so much information from a brief encounter with my daughters?

"Annie's still doing that teenager 'sleep till noon' thing. We may do something after that. When they get up, we'll finalize our plans. I'll let you know. Dinner somewhere in Bethesda, I expect."

"Good luck getting something on the spur of the moment. Christmas Eve and all. How do you know anything will be open?"

"Good thought. Thanks."

"Tell you what, Zack, since you're being so nice and letting me join, how about I make the arrangements. Just give me a time. You know I love to plan things."

"Plan" as in "control."

"That would be great. Thanks. Let's shoot for six o'clock."

"Budget?"

Zack smiled. Untethered, Sarah would go for the top drawer. That might impress his daughters, or it might not. He thought of Annie's counter-culture aura. On the other hand, their mother made more money than Zack could ever dream.

"Just don't buy any buildings."

He thought of Annie's Goth style and dietary preference. "Vegan has to be an option. And no dress code."

"Great. I know just the place."

I'm sure you do.

His attitude softened. "Hey, Sarah. Thanks. I mean it. Just let me know where."

"Happy to help." Another pause. "Thanks for letting me in, Zack."

He drew a breath. "You're welcome."

Zack clicked off and went to the bathroom. He talked to his image in the mirror. "If I find her so irritating, why do stay with her?"

"Fantastic sex, for one."

"Beyond that?"

"She has a good heart, despite her overbearing attitude."

"True. Deep down a good person."

"Just not a permanent partner."

"No, that would be Bri—" He couldn't finish saying her name.

"Off-limits."

"Yeah."

"So, in the meantime, Sarah."

"Yeah. One could do worse. Much worse."

Zack shook his head as if to clear it. One thing to talk to oneself in the mirror, but an actual dialogue? What would his shrink say about that? What would Noelle think?

He tiptoed out to the kitchen for a cup of coffee. Annie didn't move.

Oh, to sleep like that again.

Back in his bedroom with a mug of Starbuck's French Roast, Zack texted Jerry Hartman to verify they would meet at Nate Young's bedside soon after 8 AM. Jerry confirmed via return text, reiterated that Zack didn't need to come in, and emphasized that he should spend the day with his daughters.

Zack texted back.

Med-student daughter Jennifer coming with me. See you at 8.

He showered, dried off, wrapped the towel around his midsection, and passed into his bedroom to get dressed.

His phone blinked. Missed call. Bridget.

Without getting dressed, Zack sat on the bed to call her. When she answered, his awareness of being naked under the towel created an unexpected yet pleasant warmth. Her whispery voice sounded sensuous to his ear.

"I was in the shower when you called. Didn't expect we'd talk this soon."

"Marshall left for work earlier than usual. Lots going on in his world."

"Anything you can share with me?"

"Later. Right now, I'm perplexed by Dr. Gibson's death."

"What happened?"

"He died while on night duty in that rural hospital."

"How?"

"Don't know. He went to take a nap while the ER was empty. Sometime later, a nurse went to get him for a new patient, but he was dead in the bed.

"His wife found Ange's business card in his wallet, so she called her. Thought her husband's lawyers should know he died. She suspects something."

Zack blinked. "As do you."

"The case has felt strange since we first interviewed Dr. Gibson."

"As you know, counselor, feeling something doesn't hold up in court."

She huffed. "I trust my instincts, *Doc*. So should you."

Zack was unsure if she meant he should trust her instincts or his. Probably the former.

"Okay, but we need facts. Do you know what they did with the body?"

"Mrs. Gibson told Ange they took him to your hospital since there was no other doctor available to do the death pronouncement."

Zack flipped to the emergency physicians' duty schedule on his phone. "Paula Cho was on duty in the ER." He looked at the clock. "She may have already gone home. I'll call her now in case she's still there."

He hung up with Bridget and caught Paula just as she was starting her car in the ED parking lot.

"Did you get a Dr. Gibson from that rural ER in Maryland last night?"

"DOA, Zack."

"Any idea of cause?"

"Cardiopulmonary arrest. Etiology unknown."

A thought crossed Zack's mind. "Did you get a tox screen?"

Her voice sounded piqued. "Of course. Drew the full battery of blood and urine tests, just in case."

"You're a competent physician, Paula."

"Tell that to the girl who died from DIC."

"I heard about that."

"Jerry Hartman said she went into multi-organ failure."

Zack heard a short sob on the other end of the line.

"Not your fault, Paula."

"Yes. It is."

"No. It isn't. We should talk."

"Not now."

"Are you okay? You're not . . . ?"

"Of course not."

"When do you work again?"

"After Christmas, the 26th. Day shift."

"Go home. Get some rest. Be with your family. Forget about the ER and that girl. Maybe we can talk on the 26th."

"Nice of you to offer, Zack, but not necessary. I'll be okay. Just need time to process. All a part of being an ED doc, right?"

"Don't we know it." He paused. "One other question. What became of Dr. Gibson's body?"

"Morgue. Dr. Wolfe is going to do an autopsy today, in his role as associate medical examiner."

"Thanks. Now go home. Stand tall, BAFERD."

"Thanks, Zack." She hung up.

Zack punched the speed dial for his friend and running partner, Dr. Eric Wolfe, Chief of Pathology at Bethesda Metro. He learned that Eric planned to autopsy Dr. Gibson later that morning. Zack asked if he could attend. Eric consented.

Jennifer will get to see ECMO and an autopsy, all in one morning. What more could a first-year med student want?

He called Bridget.

CHAPTER THIRTY-EIGHT

Zack and Jennifer had coffee and bagels in the kitchen. On the nearby couch, Annie never stirred. Zack tilted his head toward her and gave Jenn a concerned look.

"She does that," Jennifer said in a low voice. "Sleep of the dead. Trust me, you do not want to wake her. She'll be fine."

Thirty minutes later, they walked into the Bethesda Metro ICU where Jerry Hartman waited for them.

Jerry offered a hand to Jennifer. "Pleasure to meet you, Dr. Winston."

Jenn blushed. "Oh, I'm not a doctor yet, just a first-year med student."

"At Stanford," Zack said. He beamed with pride.

Jerry smiled. "Well, the medical world needs a new Dr. Winston." He gestured toward Zack with a sardonic smile. "This one isn't all that good. I'm guessing he hasn't explained ECMO to you."

Jennifer chuckled. "Actually, yes."

Jerry scoffed. "Well, let's be sure he covered it all." He led her and Zack into the small conference room where he offered coffee in Styrofoam cups. A tray of Danish sweet rolls sat in the middle of the table.

"Help yourselves to Danish, Doctors Winston. Just be prepared for the wrath of the nurses if you do. They always claim first right of refusal." He laughed.

Zack grabbed one of the sweet rolls. Jennifer and Jerry abstained. "I can handle nurses' wrath," Zack said. "It's an ED doc trademark."

"Whatever," Jerry said.

He went to a dry-erase board and drew a basic sketch of a human heart with tubes running to a machine. "ECMO, or extracorporeal membrane oxygenation, is like a heart-lung machine. We take poorly oxygenated blood from the body, run it through an oxygen-rich environment in the machine, then return it to the heart. Our current patient, Dr. Nate Young, came in after a cold-water near-drowning. Almost dead.

"Your superstar dad got ROSC, or return of spontaneous circulation, and wisely called us to put Nate on ECMO to warm his blood and keep it super-oxygenated to hopefully spare his brain from permanent damage due to low oxygen."

Jennifer nodded. Zack was pleased by her obvious fascination.

"If he remains stable through Christmas, we'll get him off the ECMO in hopes that his heart and lungs will oxygenate blood well enough on their own. Once we cross that bridge, we can try to wean him off the ventilator. If he breathes on his own and perfuses his brain, he may be out of the woods."

Jennifer raised a hand. "You don't know yet if he's had any permanent brain damage, right?"

"Right. All we can say for sure is he got the best care from the point of discovery to now. I like his chances."

Jennifer looked at Zack. "Superstar, huh? Is that the same as BAFERD?"

Jerry looked between them, puzzled.

Zack held a finger to his lips. "Shh. Trade secret. Non-ED docs won't understand it."

She laughed. "Got it."

At Nate Young's bedside, Zack showed Jennifer a wall chart depicting the parameters used to calculate a Glasgow Coma Scale (GCS) based on a patient's best eye opening, verbal response, and motor response. "Eight or less signifies some stage of coma. Best score is fifteen, which is where we all are right now."

"Well, most of us," Jerry said. "I seldom see an ER doc with a Glasgow better than thirteen."

Zack ignored the jibe. "When I saw Nate yesterday, he was about a nine or ten. His current GCS is three, because he's been super-sedated in a medically induced deep coma."

Jennifer looked puzzled. "If his score was above coma yesterday, why the super-sedation?"

"Your dad caused him to have a seizure," Jerry said. "We had to put him down lest he seize again. That could be fatal."

Zack huffed. "He had a seizure, but I didn't cause it."

Jerry clapped his shoulder. "We know that. Dang but you're getting a thin skin, Doc."

Jennifer was studying the GCS chart on the wall. "I understand the three behaviors of eye-opening response, best verbal response, and best motor response, and I get those are scored according to the stimuli that produce them, like voice commands. But what does response to pain mean? What pain?"

"We induce the pain," Zack said. "As a diagnostic maneuver."

"You inflict deliberate pain on your patients?"

"It's simple maneuvers," Zack said, "like rubbing over the sternum, pushing on the glabella just above the nose, maybe twisting a nipple."

"Ouch," Jennifer said.

Jerry Hartman chuckled. "At least he didn't describe what ER docs call the 'testicular compression test.'"

Jennifer scowled. "That seems cruel."

"Yeah." Zack offered an apologetic shrug. "But it works."

Jennifer seemed unconvinced.

Anxious to change the subject, Zack showed Jennifer the needle tracks between Nate's toes. "We often see these in chronic IV drug users." He turned to Jerry. "Tox screen results?"

"Nothing yet," Jerry spoke to Jennifer. "We're also concerned about metabolic abnormalities that may have contributed to his seizure yesterday." He turned back to Zack. "Labs are all normal or at least in the expected range, blood gases included."

Zack stroked his chin. "Something new gone wrong in the brain? Could we have missed a head injury in our rush to get him on ECMO?"

"Or a cardiac event," Jerry said. "We'll get an EKG and cardiac enzymes."

Zack frowned. "Yeah. Good. Maybe an ECHO?"

Jerry nodded.

"Then CT his head?"

"I'd go for an MRI," Jerry said.

"Trust your judgment on that."

Zack's phone buzzed. Text from Bridget. He spoke to Jennifer. "Bridget's in the lobby. We'll meet her there then go down to pathology for the autopsy on Dr. Gibson."

He turned back to Jerry Hartman. "Let me know if you find anything new."

Zack pointed Jennifer toward the ICU exit, then stopped to look back at Jerry. "Carfentanyl?"

Jerry shook his head. "Only if he got it after you saw him yesterday."

The two physicians exchanged grim looks.

"I'll get that advanced drug screen expedited," Jerry said.

As they left the ICU, Jennifer asked, "Is it unusual to have two doctors go hard down in such close time to each other?"

Zack stopped in his tracks. He hadn't thought of that. What possible relationship could the fates of Nate Young and Jeff Gibson have, if any?

He shrugged. "Could happen. No obvious connection between our two, but bears investigating."

CHAPTER THIRTY-NINE

Annie waited for several minutes to be sure her dad and Jennifer wouldn't return to the apartment for something, then she rolled out of bed, made up the couch, took a quick shower, did her makeup, and dressed. She was out of the apartment by five minutes after eight.

The five-block walk to the pharmacy took only ten minutes at her brisk pace. Once inside, she hesitated.

Why do this now?

She could just go have good times with Tyler. Deal with her situation, and Conner, after she returned home. What difference would a week make?

On the other hand, worry-free she could have a better time with Tyler, and Conner would still be there in California.

Finding out now works to my advantage.

She strolled to the family planning section of the drug store, picked out the cheapest pregnancy test, and added a pack of condoms.

Just in case. . . .

Annie left the pharmacy with her new purchases stuffed into her purse. She walked the short block to the Starbucks where she had asked Tyler to meet her, ignored the line at the counter, and went straight to the restrooms in the back of the store.

Ten minutes later, as if in a trance, she stuffed the used test materials into the trash and walked out of the restroom. She had advanced to the front of the line at the counter before her mind crashed back to earth.

"What can I get you?" The barista shot her an impatient look.

Annie shook herself. "Uh, grandé latte with soy milk, please." She paid from the cash her mother had given her for the trip and stuck a dollar bill in the tip jar. Then she stood in place, gazing toward the front of the store.

"Next," the barista said.

Annie took the hint and got out of the way.

While she waited for her order, Annie reviewed her thinking since the positive pregnancy test in the restroom. No way did she want to spend the rest of her life with Conner Galloway. Yeah, he was hot, and he turned her on, and he thought he loved her, but she didn't love him. Never would. Didn't want to be tied down anyway.

Annie knew she had options, especially back home in California. She wouldn't hesitate to use them.

Should she tell her mom?

Not.

Her dad?

Never.

"Grandé latte with soy milk for Annie," someone said.

She shook herself, retrieved her drink, and found an empty table in the rear of the store. She sat facing the front door so she would see Tyler when he arrived.

If he arrived. Of course, he would. He was hot for her.

Story of my life.

Her phone buzzed. Mom.

"Why aren't you with your dad and Jennifer?"

"Hi, Mom. Nice to hear your voice too."

A pause. "I called to wish you happy birthday."

"Thanks, Mom."

"I called Jenn first. She said you stayed at dad's place instead of going with them. What's up with that?"

"Just needed to sleep. Jet lag."

"Really. How's it going?"

"Good."

"Is dad being good to you?"

"He's okay. Clueless, but trying."

"Sounds about right. What are you doing for your birthday?"

"Dad's taking us to dinner."

"And the rest of the day?"

"Hanging out."

"You should get out and see some of the monuments and landmarks there."

"Mom, it's freezing here."

"Yeah, well don't spend the whole time cooped up in your dad's apartment. And don't stay by yourself anymore. Get to know your dad."

"He took us shopping yesterday. Got some new clothes."

"Figures. The man thinks he has to spend money to show his love."

"Works for me."

Tyler came through the door, saw her, waved, and came over. He started to speak, but she pointed to the phone and mouthed, "My mom."

He backed away to the ordering line.

"Annie," her mom said, "what's going on? Are you not at your dad's apartment?"

Even three-thousand miles away the woman had pinpoint radar.

Oh, well.

"I had to go out to the drug store for, you know, women's stuff." Technically not a lie. "It's so cold I stopped at a Starbucks on the way home."

She winked at Tyler in the line.

"You shouldn't go out on your own there. You don't know the place."

"Mom, it's like a few blocks from Dad's place. Gimme a break. I'm sixteen now, you know."

"Well, your dad should be more responsible and not leave you there alone."

"He had to go to the hospital. Jenn wanted to go with him. I hate hospitals."

"Listen, Annie. An emergency physician only 'has' to go to the hospital when he's on duty, which your dad isn't."

Her attitude annoyed Annie. "A doctor friend of his is in the hospital, intensive care. That's why he went."

"Yeah, it's always some reason. Just don't stay by yourself again. Go with him. Don't let him act out like that."

Annie had no idea what her mom meant. She saw Tyler approaching the table, drink in hand.

"Okay, mom. I'm going to head back to the apartment now. Dad and Jenn should be home any minute."

"Okay. Have fun. Happy birthday. I love you."

Tyler sat down next to her.

"Love you too, Mom."

She clicked off the call, turned to Tyler, and kissed him on the lips.

CHAPTER FORTY

Neither Emily nor Dr. Good spoke on the drive from Georgetown to The Good House. She couldn't tell if he was angry or distracted. When they walked in the front door, he motioned through the foyer toward the stairs.

"Go freshen up. I'll make coffee. Come down when you're ready. We need to talk."

She looked at him askance and held her ground. "I don't need 'freshening,' thank you."

Good shrugged. "Well, I do. You can make the coffee."

He turned away and ascended the stairs.

Emily eyed the front door. How far could she run before he caught her? Her shoulders slumped. She wouldn't get far through the woods on foot. Especially as cold as it was outside. She would need a vehicle to escape.

Fifteen minutes later, they sat across from each other at the kitchen table. After a long sip of coffee, Adam Good looked at her with eyes that seemed both concerned and irritated.

"Do you have any idea what your little excursion to that ER almost cost us?"

Emily stared into her coffee for several seconds before she looked him in the eye. "I know what it caused that poor girl and her baby." She pursed her lips. "Her dead baby." A beat. "I know that I would do it again."

Good reacted as if she'd slapped him. "What did you say?"

Her breathing quickened. "You heard me."

His face evolved through incredulity, anger, and hurt before settling on empathy. He spoke in a kind voice. "Emily, love, we're not here to salvage damaged babies."

A deep well of anger, suppressed for years, flamed inside her. "Or young mothers who hemorrhage?"

Dr. Good looked down at the table. "Not if we have no further use for them."

Emily held out her hands, palms up. "You don't see the blood on these hands, but I do."

He tried to smile, but only half-succeeded, his face frozen in a pitiable grimace. "Please, no dramatics. Look, I know it's been a challenge these last few days—"

Emily pounded the table, causing it to shake and spill both their coffees. "Challenge? What do you know about challenges? Look at your hands. No blood. You leave all that to me, and those two jerks. And Flossie. You disappear, expect us to do horrid things, then come back when it's all over. I . . ."

A gush of tears and remorse overcame her. She buried her head in her hands.

Adam Good reached across the table to touch her shoulder. "Dear Emily, I . . ."

She jerked away. "Don't touch me."

He withdrew his hand, rose from his chair, and stood over her. When he spoke, his voice sounded calm and kind, like a wise, loving father.

"What's really going on here, Em?"

She looked up, her face wet with tears, nose dripping, eyes covered with a teary film. In Dr. Good, she saw the man she had trusted once, the man whose obsession had become her personal prison, like Christine Daaé and the Phantom.

An intriguing thought hit her. What if she could. . . .

Emily stared off into space, wearing a vacant look. "I needed you last night."

"I had some issues to manage. I'm sorry. I wanted to get there sooner."

She stared at the floor. "You didn't get there soon enough."

Don't overplay it.

Dr. Good drew a deep breath and exhaled slowly. "What?"

Emily forced tears. "Spider . . ."

Good grimaced. "Did he . . . ?"

She nodded her head. A tear ran down her cheek.

Dr. Good's voice tinged with anger. "When I'm done with him, he'll never lay another hand on you."

Emily looked at him. Plaintive. "When you came to the Georgetown house, I was running away."

His voice softened. "I know. You had Spider's keys, which I returned to him." Adam put his hand on her shoulder. "You never have to run away from me, Emily. Never. I'm your savior, remember?"

She stood, faced him, and fell into his arms, sobbing. "Oh, yes. Yes, you are." Inside she smiled.

Sweet revenge!

CHAPTER FORTY-ONE

When Zack and Jennifer met up with Bridget in the hospital lobby, he took immediate note that she was dressed in a dark-gray business suit over an open-collared yellow blouse, similar to what she would wear in court. A red scarf covered the scar on her neck. Since her recovery from the attack, she'd worn more casual clothes to her office or on social occasions but always covered her neck.

Jennifer and Bridget hugged each other like best friends. Zack offered Bridget a handshake. She ignored that and pulled him into a stiff embrace.

She turned to Jennifer. "Has your dad always been a little, uh, rigid?"

Jennifer laughed but did not reply. Zack figured she didn't know the answer.

When they got off the elevator on the basement floor, Zack led the way to the morgue. He stopped at the door and turned to the women. "Are you okay with seeing this?"

Jennifer groaned. "Seriously, dad? I did cadaver lab in gross anatomy last semester."

Bridget scoffed. "Have you forgotten I spent two years in medical school before realizing the law is a nobler profession? My favorite first-year subject was anatomy, second-year, pathology."

She smiled at Jenn. "I did cadaver lab, plus got to see some autopsies."

"Right," Zack said.

He led his companions to Dr. Eric Wolfe's office.

After introductions, Eric said to Zack, "How many days till pitchers and catchers report?"

"Uh," Zack tried to calculate the number of days between Christmas Eve and mid-February. "About fifty?"

Eric shook his head. "You're losing the edge, Zack. Fifty-three, to be exact." He turned to Jennifer. "Not only are your dad and I running buddies, but we share a passion for baseball; including hopeless causes like the Washington Nationals."

Jennifer smiled. "Padres fan. My mom has season tickets."

Of course, she does, Zack thought.

Eric turned to Bridget. "Good to see you again, Judge."

Bridget smiled. "Likewise, Dr. Death."

"Cha-ching," Eric said. "Okay, without further ado . . ."

He led them into the autopsy room, where they all donned hospital gowns, hair covers, and surgical masks. Eric added a face shield to his own protective attire. "You all won't need to wear a shield unless you plan to get really close."

"I'll take one," Jennifer said.

Zack failed to hide his pride in his daughter.

"Zack? Judge?"

Both Zack and Bridget declined.

"Okay," Eric said. He approached the autopsy table where the exposed body of Dr. Jeff Gibson lay on the stainless steel. A young man in similar protective attire stood near the head.

Eric stepped up to the left side of the body, then motioned Jennifer to the other side. "Okay, Dr. Jenn, you can be my assistant." He motioned to the young man. "Mr. Sawyer, our diener here, will help you."

Zack and Bridget stood at the foot of the table. He noted Jennifer's smile at Eric's special treatment, even from behind her mask.

No doubt about his daughter's enthusiasm for medicine. Zack somewhat recalled his own youthful zeal the first time he'd ridden in a paramedic ambulance as a pre-medical college student at the University of San Francisco. Eons ago.

Eric spoke to the diener. "Microphone on?"

The young man nodded.

"Let's begin." He raised his voice some. "Body is that of a well-developed, well-nourished Caucasian male, recorded age thirty-six."

He spoke in a normal voice. "Dr. Jenn, if you and Mr. Sawyer could please roll the body toward you."

Zack thought Jennifer hesitated for a second before touching the corpse, but she quickly recovered. Eric examined the back of the body.

When the late Dr. Gibson was returned to the supine position, Eric continued. "No external trauma or lesions noted."

He did a more detailed examination of the mouth and other body orifices. "No signs of trauma to mouth, genitalia, or rectum."

Eric retrieved a scalpel from the instrument tray next to him, then gave it to Jennifer, handle first. "Would you like to do the honors, Doctor?"

Jennifer's eyes widened. She looked at Eric. "Really?"

"I promise, you can't hurt him. I'll show you where to cut."

Ninety minutes later, Eric, Zack, and Bridget left the autopsy room while the diener led Jennifer through the technique of closing the Y-shaped incision on the front of Dr. Gibson's body.

"No obvious manner of death," Eric said. "The guy was healthy and fit."

"Paula drew a tox screen in the ER," Zack said.

Eric looked at his watch. "Which results we won't get until after Christmas. It's nearly noon, and I'll bet the lab is already on holiday staffing."

"Any clues at all?" Bridget said.

Eric ran a hand through his rumpled hair. "Toxic substance of some sort. Young healthy guys don't suddenly crump for no reason."

"Any way to expedite that tox screen?" Zack said. "You are, after all, the Chief of Pathology and an associate medical examiner."

Eric blew out a long breath. "I'll see what I can do."

"Box seats to the Nats home opener say you can get us preliminary results today."

Eric smiled. "You're on."

CHAPTER FORTY-TWO

Annie and Tyler sat side-by-side in the Starbucks booth, shoulders and legs touching. The cafe was a bit chilly, worse whenever customers arrived or departed through the front door. Annie snuggled closer to Tyler, enjoying the warmth of his body against hers, his man-scent filling her nostrils. When he faced her, his eyes seemed to gaze into her soul. She'd never felt like this, certainly not with Conner.

"How much time we got?" His touch on her thigh sent an electric surge straight to her pelvis. She flinched at the thought of another life growing inside there.

Tyler removed his hand. "Sorry."

She replaced his hand. "Don't be."

His brow wrinkled a bit. "You flinched."

She shook her head. "Not about your touch."

"Something." He looked deep into her eyes. "What?"

"I, uh, can't say."

"Can't or won't?"

She pulled her hand away. "Hey. Don't pry where you don't belong."

He shook his head. "Okay, Annie Mysterious. Where do I belong?"

"We've just met."

"No, we just met last night. Today is another day. We're friends now, right?"

She squeezed his hand. "At least."

He put his arm around her; pulled her closer. "Maybe more?"

A surge of longing gushed within Annie. She smiled. "Maybe." She tilted her head; parted her lips.

They kissed.

"So, how much time we got?"

Annie took a deep breath. "My dad and sister think I'm at his apartment. I need to be there when they return."

"So, Annie Enigma, how much time do we have before I take you home?"

"How big is your car?"

"Big enough."

She stood up, grabbed his hand, and pulled him out of the booth. "Let's go."

A blast of frigid air greeted them when they left the cafe. It hit Annie like a warning flash.

What am I doing?

They walked a block to a new Prius.

"Nice," Annie said.

"My dad's car," Tyler said.

Just as he opened the door for her, Annie's phone buzzed. A text from Jennifer.

"Shit."

"What?"

"My sister." She opened the text.

Rise and shine, muffin. Leaving hospital now. Dad and Bridget taking us to lunch. On our way to pick you up. Be in front of the apartment building in ten minutes

Annie huffed. "Crap. Please take me to the apartment. Fast." She returned the text.

Thanks for advance notice :(be there when I can

She jumped into the car. Tyler had already started it. "Move it."

"Relax. It's only five blocks."

Annie turned to him, eyes ablaze. "I said move it."

Four minutes later, she opened the door to get out of the car, then leaned over to kiss Tyler's cheek. "Thanks."

"I want to see you again. Unfinished business."

She got out of the car. "Me too. I'll text you. Now get out of here."

Annie slammed the door without waiting for his answer. She rushed into the apartment lobby; went to the restroom to straighten her clothing and comb her hair. She wiped her mouth.

Coffee breath.

From her purse, she took two breath mints and sucked them with vigor. She willed herself to relax, then went back into the lobby and watched through the front door until her dad's car drove into the circular driveway. Jennifer sat in the front passenger seat.

Bridget must have driven her own car.

After her dad stopped the car, Annie counted to ten then threw the building door open and made a show of rushing to the car and opening the back door.

"Can't believe I made it," she said in a panting voice.

"Just get in," Jennifer said.

As Annie got into the back seat, she spotted Tyler's Prius parked across the street.

Alone in the back of her dad's car, Annie texted Tyler.

Saw U lurking
Looking out for you
I'm not a child
Don't I know it [lewd emoji]
Don't be gross
Says not a child

Ha ha
When can I see you again
When do you want
Now
Seriously
Tomorrow
Christmas gotta be with my dad and sis
Next day
K
When
Text me
K
Be thinking about you
Me too :-*

    Annie clicked off her phone and stared out the car window. A warm flush ran through her, followed by a chill up her spine as she thought about the pregnancy test.
    Her phone buzzed. Conner. She sighed, wanting to ignore it.
    He'll just bug me till I answer.

Hey
Hey
Any news

    Annie sighed, shaking her head. Conner wouldn't survive this.

You can stop worrying
You mean
Stop worrying
You got the test
Yeah
And
No worries
Hell yeah

:-)
Good news
Told ya not to worry

Annie's dad drove the car into a parking garage and she lost the cell phone signal. She clicked off and stuck the phone in her pocket.

As soon as the three of them walked out of the garage, Annie's phone buzzed.

She turned it off.

CHAPTER FORTY-THREE

Zack's Google search for vegan-friendly restaurants in Bethesda landed the foursome for lunch at Raku-An Asian Dining & Sushi in the downtown area. Bridget had arrived before them and procured a table.

As they awaited their orders, Jennifer gushed with excitement about attending her first autopsy.

"Ew, not at the table," Annie said.

"Get over it," Jennifer said. She continued talking.

At an appropriate interval, Bridget changed the subject by turning to Annie. "Did you sleep late like your dad thought you would?"

Annie blushed. "Not really. I just laid on the couch and watched TV."

"What did you watch?" Zack said.

"Nothing you would know about." Annie turned back to Bridget. "Did you watch the autopsy too?"

Zack huffed. "You might be surprised what TV shows I know. I'm a Marvel fan, remember?"

Bridget sucked on an edamame, indicating to Annie that she couldn't talk while eating.

Jennifer looked at her sister with narrowed eyes. "C'mon, Annie. Tell dad what you watched."

Annie looked down and sighed. "Nothing."

Puzzled looks darted among the other three.

Jennifer folded her arms. "Out with it."

Annie squirmed; glared at her sister. "I went for a walk." She looked at Bridget, as if seeking help. Bridget just smiled at her.

"You went for a walk by yourself?" Zack said. "In a strange town?"

"Really, Dad? I'm not a baby."

Zack started to reply, but Jennifer interjected. "She goes all over San Diego by herself."

Bridget turned her smile on Zack. "Really, 'Dad.' How dangerous can it be walking around your posh Bethesda neighborhood in broad daylight on a freezing weekday in winter?"

Annie beamed at Bridget as if she'd found her guardian angel.

Zack made a lame attempt to recover. "Well, if you weren't going to sleep in, you could have come with us."

"To a hospital *and* an autopsy?" Annie screwed up her face. "Double yuk."

Bridget caught Zack's eye across the table. "I believe Annie can take care of herself."

Zack scowled. "Outnumbered three-to-one. So be it." He turned to Annie. "It's okay if you want to do stuff by yourself, but you must let me know where and when—before, not after." He gave her a stern look. "I'm still the dad. Got it?"

Annie rolled her eyes and spoke in her most sarcastic voice. "Got it. Dad."

Next to her, Bridget glanced at her watch, then looked toward the kitchen. "They're taking their time with our food."

"We ordered a lot of sushi," Zack said. "Are you on a tight schedule?"

"I have to meet Marshall at his office by one-thirty." She chewed her lip. "Can't be late."

"Sounds important," Zack said.

"It is. For him."

Zack started to respond, but Bridget waved him off. She turned to the girls. "What plans do you have for the rest of the day; and for your birthday, Annie?"

Both girls looked at Zack.

"Uh, some touring this afternoon, then back home to rest up, then a birthday dinner at the Woodmont Grill." He turned to Annie. "I've checked and it's vegan-friendly."

Jennifer glanced at Zack, then spoke to Bridget. "Would you, your husband, and sons like to join us?"

The blood drained from Zack's head. Had Jenn forgotten that Sarah would join them for dinner? Maybe she hadn't forgotten. Maybe didn't realize what conflict that could cause. Maybe she didn't care.

Bridget put him at ease. "That would be lovely, but not tonight. We have a family tradition. Catered Christmas Eve dinner with standing rib roast and all the fixings. Then we open presents; the boys go off to do their own things. Dustin meets friends for midnight Mass. I think Grant has a date. After they leave, Marshall and I get soused, and . . ." Her voice trailed off. "No one gets up until noon on Christmas day, at the earliest."

Jennifer looked down at the table.

A reaction to Grant having a date?

"Sounds like fun," Zack said.

Bridget touched his arm. "It is. You should try it yourself sometime."

"Can't. I lack the spousal component."

Bridget's laugh seemed forced. "You can fix that, Zack."

He looked her in the eye. "Not the way I'd like."

The arrival of their food broke the spell between them.

Zack picked up a tuna roll. "Usually, being sans spouse or kids—other than this year—I volunteer to work the ER on Christmas Eve."

"How noble," Bridget said.

"You wouldn't believe what we see on those nights. Christmas does not bring tidings of great joy to everyone. The ED attracts a horde of unhappy people, misery, conflict, trauma." He frowned; looked into the middle distance. "The most tragic are the unexpected sudden deaths. At least one every Christmas Eve." He shook his head. "Talk about misery."

As if muted, the others sat in silence and ate.

Talk about a buzzkill. Will I ever learn?

Bridget reached into her purse, produced two twenty-dollar bills, and set them on the table by Zack. She pushed back her chair. "Sorry, but I need to get going. I cannot be late for Marshall's big announcement."

Zack's mouth dropped. "Announcement?"

Bridget forced a smile. "Watch the news later if you get the chance." She stood and headed toward the door, putting on her coat as she went.

Zack picked up the money; pushed back his chair. "I'll be right back," he said to the girls.

He caught up with Bridget at the front door and pushed the two bills into her hand.

"First, you're not paying. Second, what announcement? Third, what's got you so rattled?" He barred her path through the door.

"Zack, I have to go. Now."

"Fine. I'll walk you to your car." He waved at the girls, mouthed, "I'll be back," and followed Bridget out the door. The frigid air reminded him he'd left his coat at the table.

"What's going on, Bridge?"

Bridget shook her head. "Go back to your daughters, Zack. Have fun. This doesn't concern you."

Zack huffed. "Anything that causes you discomfort concerns me."

They had reached her car. Bridget paid the parking meter with her phone app, then turned to Zack. "Marshall is cheating, for sure."

"What are you going to do about it?" He reached for her hand.

Bridget pulled away; opened her car door. "Nothing. I'm trapped, Zack."

"How the hell—?"

She got into the car, closed the door, put on her seatbelt, and rolled down the window. She turned to Zack with tear-filled eyes.

"Watch the news, Zack."

"But—"

Bridget started the car. "Goodbye, Zack." Her voice carried a cold tone of finality. She raised the window, eased out of the parking space, and drove away.

Zack felt like a sad circus clown as he shivered in the cold air and watched the car until it turned off the street.

His daughters appeared on each side of him. Jennifer handed him his coat. "What's wrong, dad?"

He turned to her. "What about—?"

"I paid the bill. We were both worried about you. And Bridget."

CHAPTER FORTY-FOUR

Emily spent twenty minutes in the shower, for no reason other than the privacy it provided for introspection. The plumbing in the old colonial manse had to be nearly a century old. The dense fatigue of the previous stressful night combined with the warm water made her sleepy. She put in the plug and allowed the tub to fill, then shut off the water and reclined in the tub. She laid her head back and stared at the ceiling, noting the cracks that had developed there over the years.

Dr. Good's obsession with her had controlled every aspect of her life for five years. It weighed on her chest like a block of ice. If she allowed this captivity to continue, her future would mimic the ceiling over her head, crack after crack, until the whole thing collapsed. How could she have been so foolish? How did she not see sooner what that man was doing, had done, to her?

His stereotyped reaction to her lie that Spider had raped her had lifted the final scale from her eyes.

In the early days, Emily thought she did good work. Good's mysterious network took in wayward pregnant girls with no homes, no family, no friends. Emily cared for them until they delivered, then Dr. Good and/or Spider and Roach would take the babies to foster homes.

So they said.

As soon as the young women recovered from giving birth, the men would take them to half-way houses or similar facilities where they could begin their re-entry into new lives, unburdened with the responsibility of destitute single parenthood.

So they said.

I believed everything they told me.

Dr. Good offered the choice of early-stage abortion on rare occasions, but only to women he chose.

By what criteria? Undesirables? To whom?

He made sure Emily never risked getting pregnant. Whenever they had sex, he demanded she take precautions beyond the oral contraceptives he gave her.

"No pill is foolproof," he said.

She suspected he had another life that he never mentioned, about which Emily was afraid to ask. Probably he was married, maybe had children. Maintained a legitimate medical practice?

Activity in The Good House had dwindled in the last year. They often had only one pregnant woman in residence. Sometimes, like now, there were none. Dr. Good had been away from The House more often and for longer periods of time. Spider or Roach would be there, with Dr. Good coming only to deliver a baby or perform a rare abortion. Afterward, he would stay, serve her elaborate meals, bathe her, take her to bed, and make tender love to her. The next day, he would leave again. Each time he promised to cherish and protect her.

Always.

If there were no women in residence, Spider or Roach would lock Emily in her room and leave her alone with sandwiches or leftovers. At least she had a commode and sink. Days later, Roach would return with a new "client." Then the cycle would begin again.

She thought about the west wing of the house. Sometimes Emily saw Dr. Good and the woman named Flossie entering or leaving through the door to the connecting hallway. That door was always locked to Emily. Adam had forbidden her from trying to enter. What did they do in there?

Weird sex? Except he and Flossie never betrayed any attraction to each other. Experiments of some sort?

Emily had to find a way into that wing. Somehow. No more giving in to Good's rules. She must find out what he did there.

He had been with her the night that girl hemorrhaged to death. Then he disappeared. Until today. Would he stay tonight? Christmas Eve? Emily hoped not.

Emily would prefer to be locked in her room. Alone.

The bathwater had gone cold. Naked and soaked through in the drafty bathroom, Emily felt a sudden chill.

Dr. Good would not enter her bed tonight. Never again. Her decision, not his. She drained the tub, stood, and dried herself.

Back in the warmer bedroom, she dressed in her nursing smock but kept her shoes off. She eased out of the room and tiptoed across the hall to the OB room. With no current occupant, the door was unlocked. Emily went to the supply area, took the key that she still had in her pocket, and opened the drug locker. She used a second key to unlock a small drawer along the bottom. Inside, she found several small plastic bags containing white powder. She took one and slipped it into her pocket.

After re-locking everything, Emily slipped back into the hallway. She intended to return to her room but stopped when she heard voices from downstairs. Dr. Good, and Spider.

Emily crept halfway down the stairs. Dr. Good and Spider didn't hear her because they were in animated conversation.

Spider's voice. "We need to tighten the noose. Soon."

Dr. Good's voice was pleasant. "Yes. Nice job yesterday."

"Wasn't hard."

"Two to go."

Spider's voice, sneering. "Maybe only one after tonight."

"I won't ask how."

Spider's voice sounded low, as if he suspected someone listening. "You don't need to know. Just watch the news tonight."

"Okay. Timeline on the main event?"

"The Bobbsey Twins have it for action."

Dr. Good's voice was deferential. "When?"

"Twenty-four hours. Forty-eight, tops."

"The moving parts need careful management. Timing has to be perfect."

A long pause, followed by Spider's voice, turned ominous. "We'll do it. Won't wait for perfect."

A shorter pause before Dr. Good spoke again. "Ready to spring the trap once that's done?"

"Like I said, watch the news."

Spider's voice turned low. "Our client needs another specimen."

"Don't have another one. And in this weather . . ."

"Expand your search. Otherwise, set up the *in vitro* . . ."

Dr. Good's voice dropped. Emily strained to hear what he was saying. She inched forward. A board beneath her foot squeaked.

"What the hell?" Spider's voice.

Chairs skidding back. Dr. Good's voice. "I got this."

Emily fled up the stairs trying not to make noise. Dr. Good's footsteps hit the bottom step just as she turned down the hall, scurried to her room, dove under the bed covers, and turned onto her side away from the door.

"Why is your door open, Emily?"

"Whaa?" Emily stretched her arms as if awakening from deep slumber; smiled at Adam Good. "Whassup?"

"You keep the door closed when you're in your room."

Emily squinted at the doorway. "Oh. Sorry. I was so sleepy after my bath, and all that happened to me last night, I decided to take a quick nap. I forgot to shut it."

Dr. Good moved forward and sat on the bed next to her. "Do not lie to me."

She reached for his hand. "It's the truth." Her face and voice soft, she said, "I'm exhausted. After what I went through . . ."

He patted her hand. "Fine." He glanced at the door. "Spider's here. Stay in your room until I tell you to come out."

Emily gasped. "Spider? Here?" She reached for him. "Please, don't let him . . ."

Dr. Good smiled. "Nothing to fear."

He stroked her hair. "Now get some rest. I'll make us a nice dinner after he leaves. Then you and I can, you know."

He plans to stay the night.

Emily squeezed his hand. "Thank you." She thought she might vomit.

He kissed her lightly on the forehead, then left her room. He closed and locked the door behind him.

Emily pursed her lips and squeezed her hands into fists.

Tonight. Tonight, I free myself.

CHAPTER FORTY-FIVE

With traffic worse than expected and the street blocked off for police escorts, Bridget arrived at the US Attorney's building five minutes late. Sweating despite the cold air, disheveled, and uncomfortable, she scurried past the banks of lights and TV cameras in the lobby, only to be accosted by a gaggle of reporters.

Christmas Eve. Slow news day.

"Ms. Larsen, what's your husband's big announcement?"

"Is Marshall Hilliard running for AG?"

"Why is the governor here?"

The governor? Damn.

Bridget charged through the reporters, bypassed the closed elevator, and aimed for the stairs like a sheep fleeing a pack of wolves. Hardly the image the next Attorney General of The Commonwealth would want, or condone, from his wife.

She got hold of herself, stopped, and turned at the foot of the stairs. She pointed to the red scarf covering her neck. "Sorry," she said in a hoarse whisper. "Can't talk."

Many of the media reps present knew about or had reported on the attack against her a year ago. They backed off. Bridget turned and hurried up the stairs toward Marshall's second-floor office.

"Best wishes, Ms. Larsen," someone said.

It sounded almost sincere.

Bridget ran fingers through her hair to loosen and tidy it before she entered Marshall's space. The doors opened onto a wood-paneled foyer. Marshall's receptionist stood and escorted Bridget down a hallway to her husband's office. When they passed Fiona's office, Bridget glanced inside. Empty. With any luck, the Deputy US Attorney was in court or had taken the day off and Bridget would not have to deal with her.

In his office, Marshall stood with a group of men and women, all similarly attired in dark business suits. No Fiona.

No wonder he wanted me to wear royal blue.

Marshall's fleeting frown and narrowed eyes betrayed his displeasure that Bridget had not complied with his fashion mandate. In a blink, he put on a smile and moved toward her. "There she is," he said in his practiced Southern-gentleman drawl. "Looking radiant as always."

They hugged briefly, stiffly, then Marshall directed her toward the governor. "You know Governor Jacobs, of course."

Bridget lit her best smile and extended a hand. "Of course. Good to see you again, sir."

The governor ignored the proffered handshake and gathered Bridget into a warm hug. "How are, you darlin'?"

Put off by the whiff of whiskey on the man's breath, Bridget broke away from the hug. "I am well," she whispered. "And you?"

"Couldn't be better, knowing we're running the best candidate ever for AG." He leaned toward her and spoke in a conspiratorial tone. "Someday soon, you will be First Lady of The Commonwealth of Virginia. The wheels are in motion."

Bridget put on her best Southern lady smile, albeit she hailed from California. "Why thank you, sir. That would be grand, but for now, I'm happy to be a simple defense attorney."

The door from Marshall's private kitchen opened. Fiona made a grand entrance in a Jackie Kennedy-like pink suit. Bridget scowled. Did Fiona not see how the attire clashed with her sangria-colored hair?

Fiona carried a tray of beverages in her free hand. She handed Marshall a glass of iced tea, then distributed drinks to the other dignitaries in the room.

When done, she came up to Marshall and Bridget.

"Hello, Mrs. Hilliard. Sorry I didn't fix a drink for you. Didn't know if you were coming."

"Fiona, nice to see you again." Bridget offered a handshake.

Fiona eschewed the hand and tried to hug Bridget. "How is our favorite defense attorney?"

Bridget swallowed the bile rising in her throat and stepped back. "Splendid, thank you."

She wheeled away, leaving Marshall and Fiona standing awkwardly together, and approached the current attorney general. The man was a longtime acquaintance from early years when he and Bridget faced each other across courtrooms as prosecutor and defense attorney. Unlike the sleazy plaintiff's attorneys she often dealt with in her current practice, this man had earned and kept her respect and professional admiration.

The two attorneys greeted each other with warmth.

Before they could talk, Fiona commanded everyone's attention. "They're ready for us downstairs."

The governor and attorney general preceded Marshall and Bridget out of the office and down the hallway to the same staircase that Bridget had climbed as she fled the waiting reporters and TV cameras.

Marshall squeezed Bridget's hand, not affectionate.

"Lose the scarf," he said.

At the top of the stairs, Bridget stepped aside to allow Marshall to descend first. She followed, assuming the role of doting bride. Her hand moved to her neck to secure the red scarf over the old wound. At the bottom of the stairs, she smiled, waved to the audience, and strode to her place next to but just behind her husband.

First Lady, my ass.

CHAPTER FORTY-SIX

Zack fumed as he watched the evening news. In the video clip, Bridget gazed at her husband with feigned admiration while the man pontificated about his commitment to justice for all Virginians. He promised a robust law-and-order agenda. Bridget's painted-on smile and vapid eyes told Zack all he needed to know about her earlier reference to being "trapped."

Jennifer emerged from the spare bedroom. "Shouldn't we go, Dad? You told Sarah we'd be there at six. That was ten minutes ago."

Zack waved a hand. "For Sarah, all times are approximate." He kept his eyes on the TV screen.

Annie, whose disregard for punctuality rivaled Sarah's, came into the room, dressed in her signature makeup with extra ear-piercings.

"Is that Bridget on TV? Cool."

She plunked onto the couch next to Zack. "Is her husband famous or something?"

"Or something," Zack said.

He'd seen all of Marshall Hilliard he could bear, so he clicked the remote to turn off the TV.

"Let's go. Even in Sarah-time, we're almost late."

Sarah had arrived at the restaurant on time. She waited in a booth by the front window.

"I took the liberty of ordering sushi rolls for appetizers."

She looked at Annie. "A veggie roll for you, Miss Vegan Sweet Sixteen. You'll especially like the Ponzu sauce."

Annie beamed. "Thanks."

Zack started into the seat opposite Sarah, but she patted the seat next to her.

"Go ahead, Dad," Jennifer said with a sly smile. She guided Annie into the seat by the window across from Sarah, then followed her into the booth.

Zack half-shrugged and moved into the seat next to Sarah.

"I ordered white wine to start," Sarah said. "A Pouilly-Fuissé, from actual France." She winked at Annie. "Your dad can afford to splurge on his girls."

Zack furrowed his brow. "Uh, you know Annie's underage, right?"

Sarah waved her hand in a dismissive gesture. "Nonsense. I'll bet she has an ID." She smiled at Annie. "California girl and all."

Zack had no idea how to respond, so he peeked at the wine menu. No surprise, Sarah had ordered the most expensive white wine, a mere $140. He figured the total bill would approach $1,000 by the time Sarah was done, but . . . for his daughters it seemed a good investment.

"For the record," Annie said. "I don't have a fake ID and I don't drink alcohol."

"All the more for the rest of us," Sarah said with a chuckle.

Zack glanced at the ceiling.

Think of this like a weekend night ER shift. Sooner or later, it ends. Might as well get some fun out of it.

The server arrived with the ice bucket of chilled white wine. Zack pointed to the menu, "For the red wine, we'll have the Chateauneuf du Pape."

He winked at Sarah. *I'll see your $140 and raise you $10.*

Sarah winked back. "Save room for champagne with dessert."

The lady did have her charms.

The girls seemed oblivious to the repartee between Zack and Sarah.

He figured they were used to expensive dining excursions with their mother and whichever current escort in San Diego. Zack and Natalie had been married ten years. Her second marriage didn't last two, a source of some vindication for Zack.

Sarah poured a generous quaff into three of the wine glasses, then raised hers. "A toast to the birthday girl, who had the cruel misfortune of being born on Christmas Eve—thanks to Dr. Doofus here."

Annie giggled.

Zack ignored the jab. He raised his glass as Jennifer raised hers and Annie picked up her water glass. "To my beautiful daughter. Happy Sweet Sixteen. It's really special to share this night with you. I love you."

Annie smiled, genuine. "Thanks, Dad. I love you too."

Sarah gulped a large portion from her glass.

Still uncomfortable, Zack followed suit.

Jennifer sipped from hers.

"How well I remember my Sweet Sixteenth," Sarah said. "I lost my virginity that night. Twice. With two different boys."

Halfway into his second quaff, Zack almost choked. The sting of alcohol attacked the back of his nose, but he managed not to spew wine all over the table. For almost a minute, he couldn't speak.

Annie and Jennifer stared at their plates.

Zack glared at Sarah.

"What?" she said in a mocking tone. She put a hand on his leg. "You have so much to learn about women, Zack. I wonder if you'll ever catch up."

Zack shot Sarah a condescending smile. "I expect to have fun trying."

Nice recovery!

Sarah batted her eyelids at him. "Don't we know that."

Desperate to shift the focus, Zack picked up the dinner menu. "Let's see what they offer to feed our growing selves." As he buried his head in the menu, he heard Sarah whispering to Annie, but he couldn't hear the words.

To his further embarrassment, Zack's phone rang in his side pocket. He'd forgotten to turn it off.

"Sorry." He pulled out the phone to turn it off. Caller ID indicated Eric Wolfe. News about Dr. Gibson?

"I, uh, should take this. It's the hospital."

"So much for cellphone rules," Annie said with unconstrained sarcasm.

All three women laughed.

Zack turned in his chair to face away from them as he answered the call. "Eric. What's up?"

"Working late on Christmas Eve is what's up. I got your preliminary tox report on Dr. Gibson."

"And . . ."

"Unidentified opioid."

"What?"

"Yeah."

"Needle tracks?"

"Between the toes."

The noise in the crowded restaurant gave way to a shrill alarm inside Zack's head. He could not ignore the similarity to Nate Young's case. "You know about Nate Young, right?"

"Yeah. We're on the same wavelength here. I'll bet a pair of Nats World Series tickets it's the same substance in both of them."

"Safe bet, friend. When if ever will the Nats be in The Series?"

Nevertheless, the results seemed too coincidental to Zack. "Can we meet?"

"Not tonight. I'm already in trouble at home for being late for the family Christmas celebration. Not tomorrow either. Come see me early on the twenty-sixth."

"Got it." Zack had a thought. "I may ask Bridget Larsen to join us. Dr. Gibson was her client, and she—"

"No problem. See you then."

"Thanks, Eric."

Zack clicked off. He was about to call Bridget when a firm tap on his shoulder got his attention.

"Time's up, Doc," Sarah said. "No more work on your daughter's birthday."

Zack put his phone on vibrate and returned it to his pocket. He swung around to face his daughters. "Have you decided what you want for dinner?"

Two hours later, they had finished dinner, two bottles of wine, and desserts. A half-empty bottle of champagne sat in a bucket of semi-melted ice. The restaurant lights came up. They were the only diners still there. The wait staff had begun clearing the other tables. The server hovered nearby, their bill in his hand.

"I think this place is closed," Sarah said.

"We're keeping the staff from Christmas Eve with their families," Jennifer said.

Zack motioned for the server, who presented the bill. True to Zack's prediction, once he added a 20% tip, the total came to $910. He plopped his credit card on top of the little tray, which the server processed and returned in record time.

He smiled at Annie. "Best thousand dollars I've ever spent."

"I want to come back out here for my birthday," Jennifer said.

Zack wondered if his speech was as slurred as hers. Never mind, because neither of them could hold up against Sarah when it came to drinking. Zack had found her more congenial, pleasant, and—to be honest—alluring as the evening went on.

The foursome weaved their way out of the restaurant, then huddled close in the chilly outside air.

"I'm not getting into a car with you or Jennifer driving," Annie said to Zack. "I ordered an Uber." She looked at Sarah. "Do you want me to call one for you?"

Sarah gazed into Zack's eyes. "Do I?"

Zack looked at his watch. "It's only ten. Would you like to join us for a nightcap at my place?"

Sarah smiled, triumphant. She took his hand. "I would love to, Zack."

CHAPTER FORTY-SEVEN

Bridget and Marshall stood with arms around each other's waists in the doorway of their home to see Grant and Dustin off on their Christmas Eve activities. Grant backed Bridget's Range Rover out of the garage and turned onto the street. Bridget and Marshall waved.

As soon as the vehicle was out of sight, Bridget released and stepped away from her husband.

Marshall's phone buzzed. "I have to take this."

"Sure, you do." Bridget went back into the house, closing the door hard behind her.

Who calls on Christmas Eve? One guess.

She went to the mini-bar and poured herself a generous portion of Laphroaig with a single rock. She glanced at the bottle of Makers Mark bourbon next to the scotch bottle. "He can make his own damn drink," she said aloud.

Bridget started to clear dishes and leftovers from the dining room table. A couple of sips of the single malt on top of the Tignanello Sangiovese wine from dinner calmed her, a bit.

Just put up with the stupid election. Then. . . .

She heard Marshall come back into the house and pour his drink. He joined her in the kitchen, an inscrutable look on his face.

Bridget looked at him askance. "Who was on the phone?"

He swallowed a draft of his bourbon. Paused. "So, uh, Fiona's coming over to give us something."

Bridget exploded. "What? You invited her here? On Christmas friggin' Eve? You miserable son-of-a-bitch."

Marshall spoke in a deliberate, steady tone. "She invited herself."

Bridget's eyebrows peaked. "Has the word 'no' fled your vocabulary, Mr. Iwannabe-Attorney-General?"

"She promised not to stay long. Just wants to give us, actually you, something. For Christmas."

"Bullshit."

Marshall raised his hands as if guarding against an attack. "Please, Bridge. Can we just get past it?"

"Past what, Marsh? You want me to make nice to your girlfriend on Christmas Eve just because she has something for poor widdle me, the estranged wife? No way in hell."

The doorbell rang.

Bridget glared at Marshall. "What, did she call from the driveway?"

"Please, Bridge."

"No. You can talk to her on the porch, but she doesn't come in the house." She turned to the sink. "I'm doing the dishes."

As Bridget started to load the dishwasher, she heard Marshall open the front door and step out, a friendly greeting in his voice.

A heaviness descended over her.

Why make a bad situation worse?

She stopped what she was doing, walked through the living room, and opened the front door. Marshall and Fiona stood a yard apart, both in obvious discomfort and shivering.

"Fiona," Bridget said in her most pleasant hoarse voice. "Marshall said you might be over. Please, come in from the cold."

After an uncomfortable exchange of pleasantries, Fiona presented Bridget with a bottle of Aberlour 16 Year single-malt scotch.

"Merry Christmas, Bridget." She shrugged. "I know nothing about scotch, but Marsh, uh, Marshall told me you like single malts and my research indicated this was the best."

Bridget did not recognize the brand, but she noticed the three-digit price tag that Fiona had left on the bottle. She forced a smile. "Thank you, Fiona, but . . ." She shook her head. "Why?"

Fiona forced a smile. "We know how much Marshall's candidacy will put a strain on you, especially since . . ." She cleared her throat. "So, we, uh, just wanted to let you know how much we appreciate you."

"We?"

Fiona glanced at Marshall. "The whole office."

Nice recovery, Fi.

Bridget gestured toward the sofa and chairs in the living room. "Please join us for a drink."

Fiona blushed. "I'd love to, but . . . I have other people to see yet." She shuffled her feet. "If I could just use your bathroom, then I'll be off."

"Sure," Bridget said. "Use mine. Top of the stairs. Be sure to use the first one. Otherwise, you'll land in Marshall's, and Lord knows what vile germs are living in there."

As if you haven't already been exposed to them.

While Fiona was gone, Bridget folded her arms and glared at Marshall. "What the hell, Marsh?"

He shrugged, sheepish.

When Fiona came back downstairs, Bridget and Marshall saw her to the door.

"Merry Christmas, and thanks," Bridget said to her.

"I'll walk Fiona to her car," Marshall said.

Bridget fake-smiled. "Of course, dear."

She closed the door behind them.

Take your friggin' time, jerk.

CHAPTER FORTY-EIGHT

Sarah, Jennifer, and Annie sat together on Zack's couch while he stood at the mini-bar opening the prized bottle of Remy Martin XO he'd saved for almost a decade. Glancing across the room, a pang arose in his chest.

If only Bridget was there instead of Sarah.

Would never happen, and Sarah has her own charms. Love the one you're with.

Zack's phone vibrated in his pocket. He pulled it out and held it below the counter to look at the caller ID.

Bridget?

He answered.

"Zack. Sorry to bother you." Her chronic whispered voice trembled.

"No prob—"

"Something's wrong with Marshall."

"What?"

"He can't speak. Just gibberish."

"Since when?"

"Ten minutes."

"Anything else? Can he move his arms and legs?"

A pause, then her raspy voice. "Not moving his right arm."

Adrenalin exploded in Zack's brain and coursed through his body, rendering him stone-cold sober. "Are your sons there?"

"No." Her voice was barely audible.

"Did you call 911?"

She croaked, almost inaudible. "They put me on hold."

"Hang up. I'll call for you."

"Thanks."

"I'll call you back."

She clicked off.

Zack dialed 911. From across the room, Sarah, Jennifer, and Annie all stared at him, wide-eyed.

After a two-minute hold, he identified himself to the 911 operator as Dr. Winston, emergency physician, and gave her Bridget's address. "Sounds like a stroke in progress. Can you give me an ETA?"

"Might be a while. All units are busy tonight. Christmas Eve."

Zack knew very well. Undermanned and overutilized, the regional EMS system would be stressed throughout the holidays.

He hung up and called Bridget. "They may be awhile. Can you drive him to the hospital?"

"He can't walk. I can't lift him."

Zack looked at Annie. "Call me an Uber. To Alexandria. Now."

He spoke to Bridget. "I'm coming to you. Stay on the line with me."

"You don't have to—"

"I'm coming."

He looked at Annie. "Did you get that Uber?"

"Five minutes."

"I'll wait downstairs."

He kept his phone to his ear, grabbed his coat, and headed toward the front door. Sarah stood in front of him.

"Do you need us to—"

Zack stopped his forward momentum, held the phone against his leg to cover the microphone, and looked at the three women. "I'm sorry. Bridget needs me. Medical emergency."

Sarah's concern appeared genuine. "Need help?"

"No."

She looked disappointed. "So, uh . . ."

"Stay here. I'll be back."

He kissed her on the cheek, then did the same with Jennifer and Annie. "Happy Birthday, Annie."

"Not one I'll ever forget. Go, Dad. Bridget needs you."

Zack charged out the door, sprinted down the hallway, ignored the elevator, and ran down the stairs two at a time.

"On my way, Bridge."

CHAPTER FORTY-NINE

Bridget put her phone on speaker mode and set it on the coffee table in front of the couch where Marshall half-sat, half-laid.

She forced her voice louder, albeit raspy and painful. "I'm on speaker, Zack. What can I do for Marsh while we wait?"

"How is he?"

"He can't move his right arm or leg now. His face looks funny, the right side droops."

"Sounds like an evolving stroke. Do you have any aspirin in the house?"

"Maybe. I can look."

His voice became distant, like he was holding the phone away to speak to someone else. "Cameron Station, Alexandria."

He came back on the phone. "What's your exact address?"

She told him and he relayed it to the Uber driver.

Then back to her. "Try to give him one adult aspirin."

Bridget ran up the stairs to Marshall's bathroom. In the back of the medicine cabinet, behind some prescription medications, she found an old bottle of Bayer Aspirin. She grabbed it and ran back downstairs.

Marshall now lay slumped on the couch, eyes closed. He appeared unconscious.

"Marsh?" She shook him.

He opened his eyes; didn't seem to recognize her. Unintelligible syllables rolled around the drool that ran out the right corner of his mouth.

"Zack, he's getting worse."

"Try to get the aspirin down him. Can he swallow?"

Bridget hurried to the kitchen and filled a glass with water. She returned to Marshall, sat next to him, and lifted his shoulders and head. She asked, "Can you drink this?" her voice barely audible. She put the glass to his lips. He didn't sip.

She picked up the phone to talk into the speaker. "He's not taking water, Zack."

"Don't force it. We don't want him to aspirate. Crush the pill and put it on his tongue, as far back as you can."

Bridget ran back to the kitchen, grabbed two spoons, and crushed the aspirin pill between them into a fine powder. With the powder in one of the spoons, she thrust it into the back of Marshall's throat. He gagged and spewed spittle and aspirin dust all over himself and her.

"I heard that," Zack said. "Hopefully, he retained some."

"What else can I do?" Her strained voice would quit at any instant.

"Keep his airway open. Make sure he's moving air."

"Okay. Seems good."

"I'm at least twenty minutes out." A brief pause. "Do you know CPR?"

"Yes."

"Where are the boys?"

"Dustin's at Mass with friends. His phone is off. Grant went on a movie date. I'll try him next."

"Okay. Hang in there, Bridge. Either EMS or I will be there soon."

Marshall started to gag. His face turned blue.

"He's gagging. Can't breathe."

"Clear his airway. Lift his jaw forward. Stick your finger in his mouth and sweep for a foreign object."

Bridget positioned herself over Marshall. She pulled his chin forward, which seemed to improve his breathing. She reached a finger into his mouth and swept from back to front. Nothing.

"Breathing a little better. Unconscious."

"Keep his airway open. I got an update from 911. EMS is en route. They should get there before I do."

At first, Bridget thought she only imagined the approaching siren, but it became louder.

"I hear a siren."

"Wonderful. Keep me posted."

The siren grew closer, then stopped. Flashing red lights through the window threw an eerie glow across the room.

"They're here, Zack."

CHAPTER FIFTY

As promised, Adam Good fixed dinner for Emily. Broiled New York strip, garlic mashed potatoes, and steamed fresh vegetables.

"Merry Christmas, Emily." He raised a glass of Mollydooker Australian Shiraz.

She smiled and raised her glass. "Merry Christmas, Adam." Without taking a sip, she set the glass down and stared at the table.

Good frowned. "Are you okay?"

Emily raised her head, nodded, and smiled at him. "I was just thinking how grateful I am to you, for taking care of me. Not just tonight, but, you know, ever since..."

"Always." He sipped his wine.

Emily took a small sip of hers. "I know."

"I love you, Emily."

She squeezed his hand. "And I, you."

He finished the glass of wine. "I need to go soon."

She batted her eyelids. "I hoped you would stay."

He stroked her arm. "I suppose..."

A half-digested bite of steak rose in Emily's throat. She fought it back. "I would like it very much, even if just, you know, for a while." She gazed into his eyes. "Please."

He pondered for a few seconds, then rose, took her hand, and gestured toward the stairs.

Emily rose, stood close to him, and loosened his belt buckle.

"How about you go, uh, get ready. I'll pour you another glass of wine. You're going to need it for what I have planned upstairs." She patted his cheek. "My 'Christmas special.' Satisfaction guaranteed."

Adam smiled, pulled her close, covered her lips with his, and thrust his tongue into her mouth.

Emily fought off the urge to bite it in two. She gave him a gentle push back and winked. "Go get ready, Adam."

He turned and hurried up the stairs.

In the kitchen, Emily poured a full glass of wine and dumped in the packet of white powder from her pocket. She swirled the liquid in the glass to be sure the powder fully dissolved, then sniffed the mixture. No telltale odor. She hoped the taste would be unaffected as well.

Outside, night had fallen, and the predicted freezing drizzle had started to fall. Emily took a deep breath and went upstairs cradling the glass of wine like a live grenade.

CHAPTER FIFTY-ONE

Zack opened the car door before the Uber ride he'd redirected stopped in front of the Inova Alexandria Hospital Emergency Room. He jumped out and hurried into the ER and headed toward the resuscitation room.

"Zack!" Bridget's hoarse voice from the nearby waiting room.

He went to her, took her in his arms, and pulled her close. He let go and gazed into tear-streaked eyes.

"What's happening, Bridge?"

"They took him for a CT scan."

"How is he?"

Bridget shook her head. "It's bad, Zack."

She looked away; stared at the floor, breaths coming in shallow rapid spurts.

Zack helped her to a chair, took the one next to her, and put a hand on her shoulder. "What did the doctors say?"

Tears flooded her eyes. "Massive stroke. Critical. He may . . ."

"Got it." He swallowed hard. "How are you doing?"

"How do you think? I'm a mess."

"Mom!"

Bridget and Zack looked up to see Dustin rushing toward them, with Grant a few steps behind.

"Thank God you're here," Bridget said.

"Came as fast as I could after I got your text in the theater," Grant said. "Had to search for Dustin in the church during Mass because his phone was off."

Bridget hugged him.

A look of terror crossed Grant's face. "How's dad? What's going on?"

"He's had a stroke."

"Bad?"

"Yes."

Dustin stood apart, fists knotted, eyes moist. Bridget went to him and embraced him. Neither one could speak.

Feeling intrusive, Zack touched Bridget's elbow. "I'll go talk to the ER doc on duty."

She reached up to squeeze his hand. "Thanks."

He left the three together and hurried toward the ER. A triage nurse stopped him. "You can't just go in there. You have to register first, then I need to evaluate you."

Zack snorted. "I'm not a patient. I'm Dr. Winston, an emergency physician. I need to talk to the physician on duty."

The nurse drew herself up to full height. "Wait here. I'll see if he's available."

"Right," Zack said. As soon as she disappeared through the double doors to the main ER, he followed.

"You can't come in here," the nurse said.

Zack held up a hand. "It's okay, really. I'm an emergency physician with clinical privileges at this hospital. I mostly work at Bethesda Metro, but I have covered shifts here in the past."

The nurse gave him a skeptical look. "I'll go with you."

Zack went to the physicians' work area. The doctor there looked familiar, but Zack didn't know him. Their multi-hospital physician group had grown so large that not all the doctors knew each other.

The physician on duty turned when Zack approached him.

"Dr. Winston?" He took a few seconds to adjust, waved the nurse away, and stood. "I'm Lou Weathers. I attended your talk at the last regional ACEP meeting." He cast Zack a doubtful smile. "I'm guessing you're not here to relieve me so I can go home and surprise my family for Christmas."

Zack shook his head. "Sorry. I'm here about Marshall Hilliard. His wife is a, uh, friend and colleague."

Dr. Weathers ran a hand through his hair and sighed. "Yeah, okay."

He pulled Zack away from the crowded work area into the resus room. "Acute CVA. I'm thinking intracerebral bleed based on presentation. Wife said they were in a heated argument when he experienced a sudden left-sided headache. Then he became aphasic, spoke gibberish. Progressed to right-sided monoparesis, upper arm, then a full right hemiparesis including a right facial droop."

"I was on the phone with her at the time," Zack said. "Figured an evolving stroke. Told her to give him aspirin, but he coughed out most of that."

"Good thing," Weathers said. "If I'm right about a hemorrhage . . ."

Zack recalled one of his favorite axioms about never treating a patient he couldn't see. Aspirin would be contraindicated in a hemorrhagic stroke because of its anti-clotting action. "Right." He scowled. "He lost consciousness just before the medics arrived."

Weathers nodded. "Yep. They established an airway, oxygen, IV, the usual grab bag, then hustled him here. He arrived comatose and hypertensive. Blood pressure was 250 over 130, pulse 100, respirations 20, and shallow. Dense right hemiplegia, completely paralyzed on that side, and with no reaction to painful stimuli."

"Pupils?"

"Mid-position, sluggish."

"So, no signs of increased intracranial pressure."

Dr. Weathers frowned. "Not yet."

Zack thought about the earlier TV image of a confident Marshall Hilliard announcing his candidacy for attorney general, flanked on one side by the governor of Virginia, and on the other by his loyal wife. He pursed his lips.

A nurse approached them. "Hilliard is back from CT."

Zack went with Dr. Weathers to the bedside.

Marshall Hilliard seemed a mere avatar of the man who had glared at Zack from the doorway to his garage. Just last night?

Zack spoke to Weathers. "Mind if I do a quick exam?"

"Be my guest. I'll see if we have the CT results yet."

It took only a few seconds for Zack to validate the other doctor's examination findings.

Except for the pupils.

He called out in a loud voice. "Lou!"

Marshall's left pupil had dilated while the right one remained mid-position. Weathers shone a light into both eyes. The left one did not react.

Zack had moved to the foot of the bed. He ran his fingernail along the sole of Marshall's foot. The big toe extended toward the patient's head.

"Babinski sign. He's herniating," Zack said.

The pressure inside Marshall's head was squeezing the soft brain matter through the opening at the base of the skull where the brain meets spinal cord. Unchecked, this herniation would squash the brain stem that regulates vital functions.

Marshall Hilliard would die in minutes.

"Call neurosurgery," Lou Weathers told his staff. "Set up a mannitol drip. Hyperventilate him."

"CT is up," a nurse said.

Lou and Zack looked at the images that appeared on a video monitor.

"Intraparenchymal hemorrhage, left parietal lobe," Weathers said.

"Mass effect, fifteen-millimeter mid-line shift, transtentorial herniation," Zack said.

The two doctors traded fatalistic looks. Marshall Hilliard's odds of survival to useful life, nonexistent.

"Neurosurgery on the line, Doctor Weathers."

Lou hurried to the phone.

Zack headed toward the waiting room. "I'll go talk to the family."

CHAPTER FIFTY-TWO

Intense emotions churned inside Bridget as she paced the waiting room. Dustin sat with his head in his hands. Grant stood in a corner, hunched over his phone.

Talking to his mother?

Would these young men lose their father today? Would Bridget lose her husband?

She squeezed her eyes tight. Mere hours ago, she had wished herself rid of Marshall Hilliard.

Did I cause this?

She didn't need to blow up at him when he came back into the house after seeing Fiona to her vehicle.

If I had kept my mouth shut it would have passed.

Could their marriage survive the vile things they'd said to each other then? Could any marriage rise above that quagmire?

She looked in the direction of the resuscitation room. Moot questions now.

Bridget had already decided that the marriage was doomed, that she had to get out of it for the sake of her own wellness and integrity, politics be damned. She was about to tell him so when Marshall clutched his head in sudden pain and the world went into a spin.

What now?

"Bridge."

Zack's voice behind her, gentle yet foreboding.

She read his face and shrank away. "Please, no."

"I'm sorry, Bridge."

Grant and Dustin approached. Bridget turned from Zack and put her arms around them. She looked at Zack. "Is he . . . ?"

Zack shook his head. "He's alive." He bit his lip. "But it's not good. Not good at all."

He led them into a small room, nicely decorated, like a funeral parlor. As Zack talked, Bridget watched his face, his mouth, his lips as he pronounced clinical words, their meanings painfully clear in context.

"Massive brain hemorrhage. Brain Swelling. Intracranial pressure. Vital functions. Craniotomy."

She raised a hand. "Stop, Zack. Please. I get it."

Zack pursed his lips. He sat there, looking at Bridget and her sons with abject empathy. Grieving along with them.

She remembered. "Where are your daughters, Zack?"

"Home. They're fine."

"Annie's birthday."

"We celebrated."

"Go to them." She gestured to the ER. "What happens here will happen with or without you."

He shook his head. "I need—"

She stopped him. "You need to be with your daughters, Zack."

He heaved a deep sigh. "And you with your husband."

Dustin darted a curious look at Zack.

"We'll be okay." Bridget stared into the distance. "Take it as it comes."

A tall man appeared in the doorway, neatly dressed in brown slacks, an open-collared button-down shirt, and a tweed jacket. Graying temples gave him an aura of wisdom and distinction. He looked at Bridget.

"Mrs. Hilliard?"

She nodded.

"I'm Dr. Pittman, head of neurosurgery." He looked at Zack with a curious expression.

Bridget gestured toward Zack. "This is Dr. Winston, a family friend . . . and advisor."

The men exchanged handshakes. Bridget thought it an odd formality under the circumstances. "This is our son, Dustin, and Marshall's son, Grant."

Dr. Pittman nodded, then sat across from her. "I've examined your husband and looked at the CT scan. He's had a massive brain hemorrhage that's caused severe swelling and pressure inside his head. Sometimes we can perform a craniotomy; go in and evacuate a clot to relieve the pressure in the brain."

He paused; pursed his lips. "This one runs too deep. If I operate, I risk making him worse. I could put him into a permanent vegetative state or cause his death."

Bridget furrowed her brow. "You can't do anything?"

"Not surgically. We'll admit him to ICU, take measures to reduce the pressure in his head, maintain his vital functions as close to normal as we can, keep him oxygenated . . ."

Bridget stopped him with an upraised hand. "Got it. When can I see him?"

"They'll transfer him soon. I suggest you go up to the ICU and wait there. It won't be long."

Bridget nodded.

The man stood to leave. He turned around at the door and spoke in a stiff voice, "I'm sorry, Mrs. Hilliard. Not a very merry Christmas for you all." He scurried out the door like a cockroach.

Zack cringed. "Neurosurgeons aren't known for their social skills."

Bridget waved him off. "Go home. Be with your living daughters."

He nodded. "Is there anything else I can do for any of you?"

"I'll walk with you to the door." Bridget turned to Dustin and Grant. "Be right back and we'll go up to ICU."

At the ED door, Zack called for an Uber.

Bridget hugged him. "Thanks for being here."

Zack winced. "Always." He patted her back. "Keep me posted."

"Of course." She sighed. "You and I both know how this will end."

He raised a quizzical eyebrow.

"Marshall will either die and I'll be a widow, or he won't, and I'll be . . . I don't know." She gestured toward the waiting room. "Either way, our lives change."

"I know."

Bridget clenched her jaw. "Dustin and Grant will lose their father."

"I know."

To Bridget's relief, a car appeared in the driveway. She didn't want to continue the conversation.

Zack hugged her, pecked her cheek, and headed to the car.

Bridget watched until it drove away, then she went back into the ED.

CHAPTER FIFTY-THREE

Her dad had called on his way to the hospital in Alexandria. Annie watched as Jennifer finished her drink, then took the glass to the kitchen.

"He won't be home for hours," Jennifer said. She looked at Sarah. "You don't have to stay. We can get you an Uber."

Sarah shrugged. "I'm fine with staying till he gets back. I'm curious to find out what happened."

"Okay," Jennifer said. "I hope you don't mind if I go to bed."

"No problem." Sarah turned to Annie. "You can go into your dad's room if you need to go to bed too."

Annie shook her head. "I'm wide awake."

"We can chat if you're up to it," Sarah said.

"Good night," Jennifer said. "Merry Christmas."

"Merry Christmas," Annie and Sarah said in unison.

Jennifer went into the guest room and closed the door.

Annie and Sarah made small talk for several minutes before Sarah's tone turned serious. "I guess you won't soon forget this Christmas."

Annie smiled. "You got that right. Big change from the boring ones with mom. She is so, so, structured. Her whole life is organized; routine. Not like dad. He's more, uh . . ."

"Spontaneous?"

"I was going to say 'flighty.'"

Sarah laughed. "Like most ER docs. They all suffer from ADHD."

Annie liked Sarah. "That's my dad, for sure."

Sarah cast Annie a penetrating gaze. "How about you? Are you more like your mom or your dad?"

Annie spread her hands over herself, indicating her attire and makeup. "Duh. What do you think?"

"Daddy's girl, for sure."

They both laughed.

"How are you liking your vacation so far?"

The question caught Annie off-guard. "Good. For the most part."

"The other part?"

Something in Sarah's eyes told Annie she could trust this woman, but she wasn't ready to confide in her. "It's complicated."

Sarah tented her fingers. "Long time since I was your age, but I remember. It can be very confusing." She gave Annie a conspiratorial wink. "Especially when it comes to boys."

"Yeah," Annie said. She gazed off into the distance, wanting but unwilling to share her dismay.

Sarah moved closer to her on the couch, speaking in a low voice, "How far along are you?"

Annie almost convulsed. "Huh?"

"How far along are you?" Sarah looked at Annie's abdomen.

"How did . . . ? How do . . . ? "

"How do I know? I'm a nurse with OB experience and a sensitive woman. I often work with ladies your age. We develop a sense." She shrugged. "Call it an educated guess."

Annie rocked in her seat. Tears formed at the corners of her eyes. "You guessed right." She turned toward Sarah. "I just found out for sure today.

Sarah enfolded Annie in a warm hug, like a sympathetic, motherly aunt. In a departure from character, Annie did not back away.

"You can talk to me about it. I won't tell a soul. Least of all your dad."

Their talk filled the hours until Annie's dad walked through the door.

CHAPTER FIFTY-FOUR

Bridget awakened to a gentle hand on her shoulder.

Marshall.

She groaned. "You're home late."

A firmer nudge on her shoulder, followed by a female voice. "Mrs. Hilliard?"

Bridget blinked. Her eyes slowly adjusted to the stark environment of the ICU waiting room. She half-lay on an uncomfortable sofa. A thirty-something woman dressed in blue scrubs and a wrinkled white lab coat stood over her.

Bridget shifted to a sitting position and addressed the woman. "Yes?"

"I'm Dr. Anderson, the intensivist taking care of your husband."

Something in the woman's voice alarmed Bridget into full wakefulness.

"Is he okay?" She glanced at Dustin curled up asleep in a soft chair. Grant stretched out full-length on his chair, staring at his phone. "Should we—?"

The physician shook her head. "Your husband's condition is unchanged. I need to talk to you about his labs."

"His labs?" Bridget straightened her posture, as if on a witness stand. Something in the doctor's tone put her on the defensive.

"Specifically, his coags. His coagulation studies." She gestured toward the chair next to Bridget. "May I?"

"Of course."

The doctor sat. "I understand he takes Xarelto, a blood thinner. For atrial fibrillation, right?"

Bridget scowled.

Where is this going?

"Yes."

"Can you tell me more about that? How long has he been on it?"

"Almost three years to the day. He had an episode at a Christmas party. Got lightheaded, almost passed out." She rubbed her forehead. "Chest pain too."

"Had he been drinking?"

Bridget smirked. "Oh, yeah."

"Go on."

"We called 911. EMS took him to the ER, where they diagnosed atrial fibrillation. The ER doc called it 'holiday heart.'"

Dr. Anderson nodded. "Did he require cardioversion, electric shock?"

Bridget shook her head. "No. It converted on its own."

"Then what happened?"

"They admitted him for cardiac monitoring. He spent Christmas day in Coronary Care. The next day they did a heart catheterization. Cardiologist said no evidence of heart attack, so they sent him home."

"On Xarelto."

"Right."

Dr. Anderson moved closer to Bridget. "Any recurrence of the A-Fib since then?"

Bridget shook her head. "Not that I know."

The doctor scowled. "You would know if your husband had another episode, right?"

Bridget stiffened.

Why do I feel like I'm being cross-examined?

"If he were home, yes. He travels a lot. I don't always know what's happening then." She stared past the doctor.

"He would tell you, right?"

"Not always." Bridget huffed. "It's how we roll, Doc."

The doctor drew back and consulted the tablet with Marshall's ICU chart on her lap. Her voice softened. "Does Mr. Hilliard take his medicine as prescribed?"

The stress, the uncertainty, the late hour, the lingering effects of alcohol, and this doctor's attitude got to Bridget. "I assume so. I don't monitor his compliance. He's a grown man. I'm not his keeper."

Least of all lately.

Dr. Anderson raised a conciliatory hand. "Sorry. I don't mean to offend."

"How about you just tell me what you want?"

The doctor let out a long breath. "Sure. His coags are way out of whack. Before the critical event happened, he was predisposed to abnormal bleeding because his body's coagulation function was severely impaired. He couldn't form a normal clot. That contributed to his brain bleed."

Bridget frowned. "But, why . . . ?"

"That's what I'm trying to figure out."

Now Bridget let out a long breath.

Dustin stirred, sat up, and looked at Bridget and the doctor. Grant straightened, rubbed his eyes, and blinked. Both looked between Bridget and the doctor, their faces strained.

"What's going on?" Dustin said. "Is dad . . . ?"

"He's the same. This is Dr. Anderson. She's asking for some clinical information." Bridget turned back to the physician. "Okay, Doc, what's going on here?"

The doctor tapped the stylus on the tablet. "I'm getting there. Sorry, but we have to be methodical. I'll be as succinct as I can."

Bridget glared at her.

This woman should have gone into law. She'd make a great prosecutor.

"Does Mr. Hilliard have any history of high blood pressure?"

"Not that I know."

"Has he been depressed lately?"

What the heck?

"On the contrary, he's pumped up about running for office. Jubilant."

Dr. Anderson put down the tablet and looked Bridget in the eye. "For reasons yet to be determined, he had a spike in his blood pressure. That spike caused a blood vessel inside his brain to tear. Ordinarily, his coagulation system would clot that off, with minimal damage. But because he was overly anti-coagulated, the bleeding continued, uncontrolled, resulting in massive, irreversible hemorrhage inside his brain."

The blood drained from Bridget's head. She slumped back in her seat.

Dustin rushed to the seat beside her and offered a bottle of water. "Mom, are you okay?" He turned to the doctor, terrified.

"She's fine," Dr. Anderson said. "Just worried about your father."

Bridget took a few swigs of the water, felt better, and sat up. Sheepish, she looked at the doctor. "Marsh and I had a fight just before this happened. Big argument. Angry words. Could that have spiked his blood pressure?"

The doctor looked at Bridget with empathy. "Perhaps." She touched Bridget's shoulder. "But no way can you blame yourself, okay?"

Bridget shrugged.

Dustin put his arm around her.

"The root cause," Dr. Anderson said, "is the abnormal coag function. We have to consider anti-coagulant overdose."

Bridget shook her head. "No way in hell did Marshall Hilliard overdose himself on Xarelto."

The doctor nodded. "That leaves us with another possibility."

Bridget stiffened; her fists clenched. "I don't like what you're implying."

"I'm not accusing anyone, ma'am. It could have been accidental."

The doctor looked between Bridget and the boys. "Could we get his current bottle of Xarelto and any other meds he's taking? We need to compare the prescribed dose, the date of the prescription, and the number of pills remaining in the bottle. To figure out if he took more than the prescribed dose."

"And if he didn't?"

"Then we look elsewhere."

Bridget stood and looked at Grant and Dustin. "You guys go to the house and get Marshall's meds from his medicine cabinet. Bring everything you find there. Call me if you have any questions."

She turned to the doctor. "They won't be long. You'd best be thinking about your Plan B."

The doctor stood and spoke in a flat tone. "Of course. Thank you."

Bridget went with Grant and Dustin to the ER entrance where Grant had parked her Range Rover. She faced them both at the door. "No speeding. We don't need you guys in the hospital too."

She turned and walked back into the hospital.

CHAPTER FIFTY-FIVE

Zack heard earnest voices inside his apartment when he unlocked the door. As soon as he pushed it open, the conversation stopped.

Annie and Sarah sat together on the couch, looking like two teenagers caught doing something they shouldn't.

He didn't care to imagine why they would act guilty. "Did I interrupt something?"

Sarah patted Annie's leg. "Girl talk. You wouldn't understand."

Zack forced a smile; raised his eyebrows. "Probably not." He moved into the room. "Well, Merry Christmas." He looked at Annie. "Not what I had planned for you and Jenn."

Annie stood and gave Zack a hug. "Merry Christmas."

He was too surprised by the show of affection to respond.

Annie moved back, perhaps also surprised. "What's happening with Bridget's husband?"

Zack shook his head. "Not good."

"Stroke?" Sarah asked.

"Worse. Intracerebral hemorrhage. Massive." He turned to Annie. "Severe bleed inside his brain."

Tears welled in Annie's eyes. "I feel so bad for Bridget."

Zack sighed. "Me too."

Sarah asked, "How's she holding up?"

Unexpected emotion caught Zack's breath. "She's . . . okay, under the circumstances."

The door to the guest room opened. Jennifer came out dressed in a nightgown, eyes bleary. "I heard you come home. Bad news about Bridget?"

Zack summarized what he'd told Annie and Sarah.

Jennifer hugged him. "I feel so bad for her." A pause. "How are you doing, Dad?"

The question caught Zack by surprise. He choked out his response. "Doing all I can to help. But . . ."

Sarah placed a hand on Zack's shoulder. "You can't save everyone, Doc. Lord knows you try."

Uncomfortable silence filled the room until Zack broke it. "Thanks for staying, Sarah. You didn't need to do that. Especially on Christmas Eve."

"No place else I needed to be. Happy to do it."

She shot a pointed glance at Annie. "We had a good talk. You have wonderful daughters, Zack."

"Thanks." He fidgeted. "So, uh . . ."

Sarah moved away from Zack. "I will head out and let you three enjoy your Christmas together."

Zack touched her arm. "You don't need to rush off."

"Yeah. I do." She picked up her phone and summoned an Uber. "Five minutes away."

"I owe you," Zack said.

Sarah patted his cheek. "Make no mistake. I will collect on that. After your head clears."

Zack shrugged, embarrassed. "I'll walk you down."

"Let me," Annie said. "I need air."

"We can both do it," Zack said.

Annie looked disappointed.

"Okay," Sarah said. "Jenn? You too?"

Jennifer motioned over her nightgown. "Not dressed for it." She gave

Sarah a hug. "Thanks for spending time with us, and for arranging dinner. It was fun."

"Maybe we can do it again before you leave."

"We'd like that," Jennifer said. She started back into the guest room, then turned to Zack. "Is Grant okay?"

Zack shook his head. "Both boys are taking it hard."

"Should I call Grant?"

His daughter's empathy moved Zack. He hoped she'd be that way as a physician. "He might appreciate that."

"Okay."

She turned back to her room.

—⋀—

As they rode down in the elevator, Annie made her decision about what she and Sarah had discussed. She glanced at Sarah and gave a slight nod. They exchanged meaningful looks. Sarah gave Annie's hand a quick squeeze.

The three waited together in the lobby for the Uber to arrive. Freezing rain had begun to fall.

Annie turned to her dad. "Sarah invited me to go shopping tomorrow. I mean the twenty-sixth. After Christmas."

Her dad raised his eyebrows. "Just the two of you?"

Sarah interjected. "We heard that you and Jenn had hospital plans. Plus, you'll probably want to see how Bridget's husband is doing."

"If he's still alive by then."

Sarah tilted her head. "That bad?"

"Yeah. Chance of survival to normal life, zero to zilch."

Sarah gave him a knowing look. "Either way, you'll want to meet up with Bridget." She looked at Annie. "I expect your sister will want to go with your dad. How about you?"

"I'd rather not," Annie said.

"Looks like we have a date, then." Sarah turned to Zack. "We'll be fine. I'll take good care of her."

Sarah and Annie exchanged phone numbers. The Uber arrived.

"Walk me out," Sarah said to Zack.

"Sure."

He opened the door to a blast of frigid air and scattered pellets of freezing rain. He and Sarah hustled to the car. He opened the door for her. She turned and embraced him, kissed him full on the lips.

"Thanks for letting me be part of your life with your daughters."

"Seems to be working out."

"It is. After they leave, you and I can catch up on, uh, other stuff." She kissed him again and opened the car door, then waved to Annie who stood just inside the door. "See you soon, Annie."

Zack watched the car drive off, then returned to the lobby. Annie had already summoned the elevator. They returned to the apartment in silence. Zack couldn't shake the feeling that he was missing something.

When they entered the apartment, Annie walked to the couch and looked over her shoulder at Zack. "I need to get to bed."

Getting the message, Zack retired to his bedroom.

CHAPTER FIFTY-SIX

Emily wiggled out from under Adam Good, leaving him sprawled naked and sonorous on the bed. She'd waited for what seemed like an hour—probably only fifteen minutes—after he passed out to be sure the rohypnol had taken full effect.

As she slipped off the bed, she congratulated herself for finding a new use for the "date-rape" drug.

She dressed quickly in jeans and a sweatshirt, then gathered Adam's clothes from the floor where he'd thrown them. She took them across the hall to the OB room and extracted his wallet and keys. The wallet contained at least a thousand dollars in cash and a half-dozen credit cards.

Emily stuffed the wallet and keys into her jeans pocket, then dumped the clothes into the hamper where they put soiled linens after a birth. Even if he awoke from his stupor, it would take some time before Good could find his clothes and get dressed.

Emily started down the stairs, had a sudden thought, then doubled back to the bedroom. After first peeking through the door to assure Good was still out of it, she tiptoed in, took his phone off the bedside stand, and slid it into the back pocket of her jeans. Then she slipped out and padded down the stairs.

In the front room foyer, she retrieved her heavy coat, stocking cap, and gloves and slipped out the door. Freezing rain shimmered like tiny falling icicles in the light from the porch. She paused for a second on the driveway, letting the rain pelt her for a few seconds, and looked back at the place that had been her home and prison for the last five years. Emotionless, she turned and got into the driver's side of Dr. Good's vintage Mercedes parked on the circular drive in front of the house. Then she did her three-things exercise.

First, drive the heck out of here.

Second, find Interstate Highway 270.

Third, get to Frederick, Maryland.

Emily had not driven a car since Dr. Good had first brought her to The House. One of the ploys he'd used to control her. She'd been with him in his prized Mercedes on several well-orchestrated, closely controlled occasions, such as grocery shopping, so the dashboard and controls looked somewhat familiar. She knew that the ignition required a brand-specific fob, not an ordinary key.

After a few seconds to get comfortable behind the wheel, Emily inserted the fob and turned it. The car started at once. She adjusted the heater to full defrost against the freezing rain, switched on the windshield wipers, put the transmission into drive, and stomped on the accelerator.

The car lurched forward. She slammed on the brakes just in time to avoid hitting the corner of the porch.

"Easy with it."

Emily pressed the gas pedal with a gentle foot. A minute later, she was turning off the long driveway onto the same rural road she'd traveled with Roach. Less than two days ago?

The early light of dawn made it easier for her to navigate. She revised her next three actions.

First, find I-270.

Second, drive to Frederick, Maryland.

Third, find the Greyhound bus station.

At the end of the long driveway, she stopped the car and looked left and right. Which way to I-270? She remembered Roach turning left when they transported Missy and her baby to the rural hospital. Emily turned right.

Free at last!

CHAPTER FIFTY-SEVEN

Dawn had broken when Grant and Dustin returned to the ICU waiting room. Dustin handed Bridget a plastic bag containing three pill containers.

After a group hug, Grant said, "Sorry it took so long. The roads are a mess." He glanced toward the ICU. "Any change?"

"Haven't seen a single person since you left."

Bridget walked out of the waiting room and down the short hall to the ICU's double doors. The boys followed. She pushed the call button next to the doors, a required process to gain entry to the unit for anyone who did not know the combination to the cipher lock.

After a minute, a door swung open and a nurse appeared. "Yes?"

Bridget held out the bag of medications. "Dr. Anderson asked me to get these. They're my husband's."

"Which patient is your husband?"

"Marshall Hilliard." Irritation tinged Bridget's voice.

Deadpan, the nurse replied. "Oh, yes." She took the bag from Bridget. "Thank you." She turned back into the unit. The automatic door started to close.

Bridget blocked the door with her foot.

The nurse turned, frowning. "Yes?"

Seething, Bridget said, "First, how is he? Next, can we see him?"

"He's not my patient," the nurse said. "I'll ask his nurse to come talk to you." She scowled at Bridget's foot still blocking the door. Bridget released it. The nurse retreated into the unit, leaving Bridget and the two boys staring at the closed doors.

Bridget let out a deep sigh. They went back to their seats in the waiting room.

Ten minutes later, a different nurse entered the waiting room and approached Bridget. "Mrs. Hilliard?"

"Yes?"

This nurse sat on the couch next to Bridget. "I'm Jasmine, your husband's nurse." She took Bridget's hand. "I'm sorry for what's happened to him." She glanced back toward the ICU. "I apologize if my colleague was rude."

Bridget shrugged. "Fine. Please, tell me how Marshall is doing, and when can we see him?"

"His condition is unchanged. You can come with me now to see him, but only one at a time, please."

Jasmine led Bridget through the ICU doors. "I must warn you about all the tubes and machines and such. They can seem daunting. He's in deep coma, but you can talk to him. We never know what an unconscious patient hears or understands."

They walked past a workstation bustling with men and women. "It's change of shift," Jasmine said. "Lots of activity. Busy place."

They passed five rows of beds on each side, all occupied by patients either asleep or attended by nurses. Jasmine led Bridget to a private room in one corner of the unit. She stopped and faced Bridget. "Ready?"

Bridget nodded.

The nurse led her into the room.

Bridget stopped and gasped.

Marshall lay like a discarded mannequin in the middle of a hospital bed with the head raised. A plastic breathing tube protruded from his nose, connected to a whooshing ventilator that drove air into his lungs. His chest rose and fell in a rhythm synchronized with the machine. IV tubes protruded from both arms, another one from under his left collar bone. His eyelids were taped closed.

The right side of his head had been shaved, partially covered by a pile of taped-down gauze. A thin plastic tube extended from the center of the gauze to a collection apparatus that hung on an IV pole at the level of Marshall's temple. A cylinder atop the apparatus resembled an oversized thermometer. At the foot of the bed, a bag filled with pale-yellow urine completed the dismal picture.

Not how the next Attorney General of the Commonwealth had pictured himself the day after announcing his candidacy.

Alternating waves of guilt, remorse, and fury washed over Bridget, as if all the conflicting feelings about her marriage teamed up to assault her all at once. She steeled herself, fought back tears, approached the bed, and took Marshall's hand.

"Well, this was unexpected, Mr. US Attorney." She tried to smile. Failed.

Bridget looked at her husband, expecting a typical sharp rejoinder. Nothing except the rhythmic rise and fall of his chest with each ventilator cycle. She saw no movement, no hint that he'd heard or understood what she said. Her gaze wandered over every inch of his body, stopping at the small tubing coming out of his head.

She pointed at it and looked at Jasmine. "What's that?"

"It's called an external ventricular drain. It withdraws cerebrospinal fluid from a compartment inside the brain in an effort to control intracranial pressure."

"Because of his brain swelling?"

"Yes."

"Is it helping?"

"I'll leave that to the doctors to tell you. I'm not the expert."

So, not helping.

"We're doing everything we can to control the pressure," Jasmine hastened to add. "Like hyperventilating him with the machine, keeping his blood pressure under control, administering mannitol as a diuretic to draw fluid out of his bloodstream."

"Are those measures working?"

"Again—"

Bridget raised a hand. "Yeah. The doctors. Got it." She smiled at the nurse. "I appreciate you taking care of him. Thank you."

Jasmine seemed surprised. "Why, thank you, ma'am. We are all doing our best."

"I know."

Bridget turned back to Marshall. She took his hand, leaned down, and spoke into his ear. "You are a self-centered jerk, Marshall Hilliard, but I love you. Always have. Always—" She pursed her lips. "Well, that's up to you."

She'd seen, done, and said all she needed, so she turned to leave. "I can find the waiting room myself," she said to Jasmine. "You have more important things to do." She paused at the door to the room. "The boys won't be in, not for a while. I don't want them to see him until they've had more time to come to grips with what's happened."

CHAPTER FIFTY-EIGHT

December 25.

Dear Noelle,
My heart is breaking.
I assume you are in some place where you know what's going on here in mortal-land. I doubt I can bear to write all the details, helpful though it may be.
I wish I could share Bridget's pain. Of course, that would be inappropriate. Marshall Hilliard may be an asshole, and he's dishonored his wife, but no man deserves where he is now. I hope he recovers.
He won't. Not without a miracle. I don't believe in those.
I think of what Bridget's going through and I remember when you died in front of me and I couldn't save you. To have all my clinical skills and not save the love of my life. Talk about despair.
Bridget doesn't deserve this. Her son and stepson don't deserve it.
I know we don't get to decide these things. You didn't deserve to die the way you did. I didn't deserve to lose you like that. Bridget and those boys don't deserve their pain. And Marshall. Well, I did my best

to save Dennis King after he tried to kill me. I would do my best to save Marshall too.

If I could.

I can't. No one can.

Bridget, those boys, all of us who care about each other—we're spiraling down a dark, awful tunnel.

I remember this from my childhood. Haven't thought of it in years, except when I was in rehab. "Your will be done."

So be it.

Good night, my dear. I will always, always love and miss you.

Zack

CHAPTER FIFTY-NINE

Emily fought the rain, darkness, and her own fear as she wandered roads in rural Maryland. She'd lost an hour before she finally found I-270. She pressed the gas pedal with a hesitant foot as she merged into light northbound traffic, only to back it off when the car accelerated to 60 mph. She let it coast down to 50 mph before she gently returned her foot to the pedal.

Driving a car should be like riding a bicycle. Even though I haven't done it for years, my brain and muscle memory should make it seem like yesterday.

Should.

She squinted against the beams of oncoming vehicles, their flickering reflections in the freezing droplets a dangerous distraction.

Should, unless you're driving an unfamiliar luxury automobile with too many bells and whistles; on an unknown road to a never-been-before destination; in darkness with frozen pellets hitting the windshield like a sandstorm.

Afraid for my life.

She rehearsed her next three tasks.

First, get to Frederick, Maryland.

Second, find the Greyhound bus station.

Third, Ditch the Mercedes.

Headlights appeared in the rear-view mirror, racing up so close behind that she feared the oncoming vehicle might ram her car. She accelerated to 55 mph to gain space. The other vehicle settled in behind her. She couldn't tell if it was a car or truck.

Following the Mercedes? Had they found her already?

After a minute, the trailing car's turn signal flashed, a second before it jerked into the passing lane and shot past the Mercedes. It was an unfamiliar SUV.

Emily breathed a sigh of relief.

Dr. Good should still be unconscious or groggy from the rohypnol. He posed no problem for her yet, unless Spider or Roach had come to The Good House. Even so, how would they know where she had gone with Good's car, especially given her meandering course to the highway?

Emily forced herself to calm down. She had escaped. Now she needed to extend her distance margin and carry out her self-assigned tasks.

Dawn had broken when she arrived in the Frederick area thirty minutes later. The confluence of highways and hodge-podge of road signs confused her. Somehow, she had left I-270 and now found herself on US Route 40. No idea where to find the Greyhound station. Emily had expected road signs telling her how to get there. No such thing.

She would have to get off the highway and ask someone for directions. Fear and anxiety rising, she took the off-ramp to Jefferson Street.

First, find the Greyhound bus station.

Second, ditch the Mercedes.

Third, buy a ticket west. Anywhere west.

Emily saw a lighted McDonald's sign on her left. She barely made the turn and pulled up to the takeout window.

Closed.

The restaurant was dark inside. The Mercedes dashboard clock indicated 7:30 AM. Maybe folks in Frederick were late risers.

Emily maneuvered back onto Jefferson Street and headed in a direction she thought was east, away from the highway. Ahead, a familiar bright yellow sign with black letters appeared.

Waffle House. Open.

She pulled into the parking lot and looked in vain for a takeout window. None existed. She would have to park and go into the restaurant. How much risk in that?

Who could possibly recognize her? Unless her face was on the news. . . .

Get a grip, Em.

She'd left The Good House barely two hours ago. News would not travel that fast. She pulled into a parking spot as far as possible off the street, shut off the car, and got out. At least she knew how to operate the door lock function on the key fob.

Inside the restaurant, a single customer sat at a table sipping coffee and reading a newspaper. A plate of half-eaten pancakes on the table in front of him caught Emily's eye. At once, she felt famished. Did she have time to eat?

Of course not.

A weary-looking older woman with baggy eyes turned from the grill and motioned to Emily. "Just sit anywhere."

Emily approached the counter. "I'm sorry," she said. "I just need directions to the Greyhound bus station."

The man at the table looked up at her, a curious expression on his face. The woman behind the counter gave her the same look, then pointed outside. "Not far from here."

Emily listened closely as the woman gave detailed instructions. "Thanks," she said, then hurried toward the exit. She wanted to get going before she forgot the directions. As she opened the door, the woman called after her.

"It might be—"

Emily didn't stop to hear the rest. She got into the car, started it, and headed further east on Jefferson. She made the first turn onto South Street, then got lost when she couldn't remember the names of the other streets she was supposed to use.

After driving about a mile, she came upon East Street.

"That's it," she said. The woman had told her, "South Street to East Street and turn left."

Emily made the turn and drove about a block to where she came upon a squat red-brick building with a gray slate roof, the Greyhound logo on the side of the building. She pulled into a semi-circular driveway that led to the front of the station. She saw no place to park by the building, but a parking lot across the street seemed a good place to lose the Mercedes.

Emily pointed the car in that direction, then slammed on the brakes when she noticed a sign stuck to the door of the station. A more ominous sign arose in her mind.

Where are the people?

She parked at the curb, got out of the car, and went up to the door. She read the sign three times. Her heart dropped a foot with each reading.

CLOSED CHRISTMAS DAY

CHAPTER SIXTY

A hand on Bridget's shoulder roused her from a fitful doze. She opened her eyes to a blurred figure in front of her, hospital-scrubs-green and lab-coat-white.

"Mrs. Hilliard?"

Bridget blinked several times to clear her vision. She had fallen asleep on the couch in the ICU waiting room. Across from her, Grant and Dustin slept in chairs. She tilted her head and recognized Dr. Anderson, the physician who had asked about Marshall's medications. A male physician Bridget didn't recognize stood next to her.

"Sorry to wake you," Dr. Anderson said. She indicated the other physician. This is Dr. Chang, the hospital pathologist. "We need to discuss Mr. Hilliard's medications."

"Is he—?"

Dr. Anderson glanced down, her expression serious. "No change."

No surprise to Bridget. Marshall's status had not changed since he'd almost herniated his brain in the ER hours ago.

Dr. Anderson looked at Grant and Dustin then back at Bridget. "We need to speak in private. We'll take you to our conference room."

Bridget's head buzzed. "What's going on?"

"Come with us, please."

Grant and Dustin had not awakened. Bridget followed the doctors into the ICU, where they made an immediate right into a small conference room. Dr. Anderson motioned Bridget to sit at the end of the table, then took a diagonal seat, with Dr. Chang next to her. Dr. Anderson placed the bag of Marshall's medications on the table.

In her fog, Bridget had not noticed it in the woman's hand.

Dr. Anderson emptied the contents onto the table. "We can dispense with the Tylenol, multivitamins, Ambien, and Viagra as irrelevant to Mr. Hilliard's current condition."

Viagra? Since when?

"That leaves us with these three," the doctor said. She set a bottle of Bayer aspirin and two prescription bottles on the table so Bridget could read the labels along with her, then set the Bayer bottle aside. "Although aspirin has some anticoagulant function, not enough missing from this bottle to be a factor. We're down to these two."

Bridget sighed. "Can you please get to the point?"

Dr. Anderson scrunched her forehead; glanced warily at the pathologist. "Sure."

She picked up one of the brown medication bottles. "This is Mr. Hilliard's Xarelto. Notice the recent date, and that the bottle is about two/thirds full—what we would expect if he took it as prescribed."

Bridget scrunched her eyebrows. "In other words . . ."

"He didn't overdose on Xarelto." The doctor scratched her head. "We had already come to that conclusion. According to our review of the literature, an overdose of Xarelto, even a deliberate suicide attempt, would not cause abnormal coagulation levels to the degree we found in your husband."

"If he didn't OD, then why . . . ?"

The doctor raised her hand. "I said he didn't OD on Xarelto." She picked up the other prescription bottle and pushed it over the table to Bridget. "Does this look familiar?"

Bridget picked up the bottle. It was empty. Instead of a standard pharmacy label, simple hand-written block text on a plain white label identified it as "warfarin." Bridget studied it, then set it down. "Never seen it, but I've never seen that Xarelto bottle either. I don't make a habit of inspecting my husband's medicine cabinet."

The pathologist, Dr. Chang, spoke for the first time. "Ma'am, do you know what warfarin is?"

"No idea." Bridget scowled. "Again, can we just get to the point? I'd like to see my husband. Soon."

The two physicians glanced at each other. Dr. Anderson took the lead. "Warfarin is the generic name for Coumadin, another type of anticoagulant."

"Also, the main ingredient in rat poison," Dr. Chang said.

Icy fingers squeezed Bridget's chest. "You think . . . ?"

"It would explain the abnormal lab results," Dr. Chang said.

Bewildered, Bridget shook her head. "But how . . . ?"

"We were hoping you could shed some light on that question," Dr. Anderson said.

Bridget threw up her hands. "I have no idea. I've never seen that bottle. Like I said, I don't look into my husband's medicine cabinet."

I would have discovered the Viagra, speaking of rats.

"I'll have to ask my sons where they found it."

Dr. Anderson gave her a sympathetic look. "May not matter."

Bridget shot her a sharp look. "What's that mean?"

"Unlike Xarelto, we have an antidote for warfarin. Vitamin K. We administered that to your husband and got expected improvement in his coags." She paused and glanced away. "His neurological status hasn't changed."

As if all the stress, terror, and anger of the last few days hit a boiling point, Bridget erupted. She slammed a hand on the table. "You could have started this conversation with that, *Doctor*. Instead, you lead me through all this coagulation warfarin Coumadin shit, *then* tell me it doesn't matter?"

Suddenly aghast at her behavior, Bridget buried her face in her hands. She took a few seconds to compose herself, then looked at the two doctors.

"I am so sorry. Please, forgive my outburst. I appreciate your efforts for my husband."

Dr. Anderson touched her arm. "It's okay. We understand."

"May I please see Marshall now?"

Dr. Anderson stood. "Of course. I'll take you."

Bridget smiled at her. "It's okay. I know the way." She stood. "Again, I'm sorry I . . ." She turned, walked out, and went to Marshall's room.

Jasmine, the nurse, stood aside to give Bridget time with her husband. He looked the same as he had hours earlier, brain-drain tubing and all. Bridget grasped his hand. "Me again."

As expected, no response. Raging grief and fury battled for dominance in Bridget's heart and mind. She tightened her grip on Marshall's hand and squeezed as hard as she could, looking for some expression, some indication that the man she'd loved felt the least bit of pain.

Nothing.

"What the hell have you done, Marsh?"

Bridget let go of his hand, turned, and left the room. She didn't look back.

CHAPTER SIXTY-ONE

Zack took the vegan-bacon slices from the microwave and placed them onto a small plate next to the bowl of steel-cut oatmeal and strawberries he'd prepared for Annie. He pulled the sheet pan with the real bacon from the oven and set it on the counter to rest while he whisked the eggs for the omelets he planned for Jennifer and himself.

His phone rang. Bridget.

"How is he, Bridge."

Muffled sobs.

Zack frowned. "Did he—"

Bridget's hoarse voice croaked. "He's alive."

"Good. Any change."

"Not with Marshall."

Zack furrowed his brow. "What's going on?"

He held onto the phone while she coughed and sputtered on the other end. When she could talk, her whispered voice sounded flat.

"They think he overdosed. On warfarin, Coumadin."

Zack's mind churned for a few seconds before he responded. "That makes no sense."

"Does it matter?" She'd stopped crying. Her voice became distant, detached.

"It might." A beat. "Did they give him Vitamin K?"

"Yeah. Made his labs better, but he's still . . . not there. Not there, Zack. Just his body. No signs of a mind."

"Too early for that thought, Bridge."

Her voice hardened. "You don't know squat about it." A pause. "Sorry. I'm . . . a mess. I yelled at his doctors too."

Zack understood, too well. "Do you need me there?"

Long pause. "I can't ask. Your daughters—"

"They will understand." An idea hit him. "Maybe Dustin and Grant could use some time with Annie and Jenn. Better than sitting there for hours with nothing to do."

"I can ask."

"Let me know. I'm about to feed them breakfast. Call or text me after you talk to the guys. Either way, I'm coming. The girls will understand."

Bridget's description of Marshall's status told Zack the crisis would not last through the day.

An hour later, after Bridget's return text and a hurried breakfast, Zack, Annie, and Jennifer drove to the Alexandria hospital.

They left the dirty dishes and cookware where they lay.

CHAPTER SIXTY-TWO

Emily drove the Mercedes northwest on US-40 toward Hagerstown, MD. She had figured out the cruise control and set it to five MPH below the speed limit. She glanced at the rear-view mirror as often as she looked in front of the car. The road seemed deserted. Most people in this rural area would be at home celebrating Christmas with their families.

Fa la la la la la la.

After the disappointment at the Frederick Greyhound station, she had sat in the Mercedes and allowed herself to cry for five minutes by the clock on the dashboard. Then she revised her next steps.

One, bug out of this town.

Two, drive west.

Three, get somewhere safe and figure out a new plan.

Before leaving the station, she pulled out the owner's manual and learned how to work and program the onboard GPS system. She knew better than to travel the interstate system, so she figured out a safer route from the bus station to US-40, thence northwest and west. The road cut across the northern US from coast to coast.

The McDonald's had opened, so she used cash from Dr. Good's wallet at the drive-through to get a bacon, egg, and cheese sandwich, orange juice, and a large coffee. She stopped in the parking area, as far from the road as she could get, ate the sandwich, and sipped the orange juice while waiting for the coffee to cool enough to handle while driving. Last thing she needed was an accident with hot coffee spilled on her lap.

Famished from her long night, the tense escape and drive, and the disappointment at the bus station, Emily devoured the sandwich. She backed out and returned to the drive-through to get another sandwich. She set it on the front seat and drove out of the lot.

Traffic picked up as she approached Hagerstown. She hadn't seen a police car the entire morning. Did they take the holiday off?

Not likely.

Emily also kept a lookout for automobiles resembling either Spider's Cadillac SUV or Roach's black F-150. She did several double-takes when either an SUV or black pickup approached from the rear and slowed down, only to pass in a heated rush when they got the chance.

As if driving below the speed limit in a Mercedes was a crime.

Although traffic was light, Emily took her time getting through Hagerstown. At every traffic-signal stop, she swiveled her head right and left to spot any possible threat. After the third signal, she chided herself.

"Getting too paranoid here, Em."

The sudden sound of a baby squalling and a vibration against her right butt cheek almost forced her off the road before she realized it was Dr. Good's phone.

She pulled into a strip mall, parked, and slipped the phone out of her back pocket. Of course, an obstetrician would have a baby-crying ring tone on his phone. Caller ID indicated Bethesda Metro Hospital. Emily didn't answer it, but the experience had unnerved her enough that she took a few minutes to settle down before returning to the road.

When she reached the west side of Hagerstown, she crossed under I-81 where US-40 became National Pike. Soon she was driving through rural terrain where the speed limit picked up. No other vehicles in sight. Emily breathed a sigh of relief, accelerated the car to the speed limit, and set the cruise control.

What would the hospital do if they couldn't reach Dr. Good? Maybe the call was about a delivery or an OB emergency. What would they do when Good didn't respond? Alert the authorities?

As the near-deserted road wound out in front of her, Emily sipped coffee and got lost in introspection. The Good House, Adam, Spider, Roach, and her sad life seemed to melt away. She tried to think about her future. No idea. She had gotten away, escaped, freed herself from Good and his insane work, from her personal hell. After what she'd suffered, allowed herself to suffer, any new life would be better.

Emily found herself on an on-ramp merging onto a major highway. She glanced at the road signs and the dashboard GPS display.

"Damn."

US-40 had merged onto I-70, a major east-west highway. Lots of traffic, Christmas or not. How did she miss it on the GPS? How far would she have to go on this road before she could get off? To where?

On task three, she had skipped over *get somewhere safe* and gone straight to *figure out a new plan*.

Deep fatigue and a sense of impending failure washed over her. The aromatic sandwich on the passenger seat begged for consumption. She revised her objectives.

First, get somewhere safe.

Second, rest and eat.

Third, make a new plan.

She expanded the view on the GPS screen. US-40 and I-70 went on together for miles and miles. Then she spotted a town, Hancock, and an exit, US-522.

Get off there.

When she looked back out the front window, Emily gasped and nearly slammed on the brakes. A Maryland State Police vehicle occupied the right shoulder just ahead of her, lights flashing. She slowed down, eased into the center lane, and passed it. A sports car came into view; stopped in front of the police vehicle. An officer stood beside it, talking to the driver.

"Caught speeding." Emily blew out a relieved breath.

A few minutes later, she took the exit ramp to US-522 and headed south. She planned to pull the Mercedes into a parking lot or along the roadside to eat the sandwich and catch a few hours of rest before figuring out her next move. Then she thought about that police vehicle.

"Too risky," she said. "What if he comes this direction for coffee or something? What if the Mercedes has been reported as stolen? What if he sees it?"

She needed to get to somewhere less visible, less risky. She drove past a cluster of roadside chain hotels before she came upon a sign.

America's Best Value Inn

Below that, a small white sign said:

$45 & UP

The motel was set back, partially hidden by a large house that fronted the road.

Emily made a hard right, pulled into the parking area, and stopped the Mercedes behind the house, where it would be out of sight from the road.

The house turned out to be the motel office. Probably the residence of the owners. At the front desk, Emily signed up for a $58 room.

"I'll pay cash."

The older hard-faced woman behind the desk reeked of stale tobacco. She gave Emily a knowing look and a sly smile.

"Of course, dearie."

Emily handed her three twenty-dollar bills from Dr. Good's wallet.

The woman eyed the wallet in Emily's hand. She held up a room key.

"I'll need a credit card for incidentals and damage deposit."

No way would Emily consider using any of Adam Good's cards. There could already be an alert out on them.

"I, I don't have any."

The woman scoffed and glanced at the cards inserted into neat pockets in Good's wallet.

"Don't have? Or can't use?"

Emily glared at her. "Doesn't matter. I'm not giving you one." She turned to leave. "I'll go somewhere else."

The woman spoke in a gentle voice. "You could give me a cash deposit in lieu of a credit card. A hundred dollars should cover it."

Emily huffed. "Fine." She kept her back to the woman while taking a hundred-dollar bill from the wallet. She turned around and placed the bill on the counter. "Here."

The woman snatched up the bill and put it into her pocket. She pushed the room key across the counter to Emily. "Here you go, dearie."

Emily took the key but stood her ground. "You owe me two dollars change. The room is fifty-eight and I gave you sixty."

The woman chuckled. "Why, so you did." She took a pair of dollar bills from the register and handed them to Emily. "You get yourself a good rest now, dearie. You look exhausted."

Emily stuffed the bills into her jeans and walked to the front door. She paused and glanced over her shoulder. "Thanks."

The woman held a phone to her ear. She gave Emily a sly smile.

CHAPTER SIXTY-THREE

The opening swish of the waiting-room door rousted Bridget from a semi-fugue state after her last visit to Marshall's bedside.

She looked up, expecting to see Zack and his daughters. Instead, two men entered, dressed in nearly identical business suits. She recognized them as security officers from the previous day at Marshall's announcement. One took up a position by the door, while the other approached Bridget.

Why are they here?

She was about to question them when the door swished open again. Fiona Delaney strutted into the waiting room. She wore a charcoal gray understated outfit, no doubt chosen for its suitability to the dire occasion.

Fury vanished the ennui that had enveloped Bridget through the night. She went after Fiona like a lioness protecting her cubs from an invading wolf.

"What are you doing here?"

Fiona raised her hands in a back-off motion. "I'm sorry, Bridget. This is uncomfortable for both of us." She showed a patronizing smile. "Please, let me explain."

Bridget stood tall and folded her arms across her chest. Her eyes narrowed. "Make it quick, before I call hospital security."

Fiona's fake smile vanished. "Actually, hospital security called us."

Taken aback, Bridget dropped her arms to her sides. "What? Why?"

Fiona stepped forward.

Bridget raised a hand in a "stop" gesture.

Fiona stood still. "When the security dayshift came on duty this morning, they learned that Marshall was admitted during the night. Knowing he's a candidate for state office and realizing the sudden nature of his illness, they became concerned about his personal safety, as well as yours and your family's. So, they called us."

Bridget pointed at Fiona. "They called you?"

Fiona flushed. "We use an answering service when the office is closed. Protocol is to notify me, as the Deputy US Attorney. I returned the call to the hospital security officer-in-charge. To summarize, here we are." She did an awkward curtsy.

Bridget indicated the two men in suits. "So those men are . . . ?"

"From the Virginia State Police security detail assigned to Marshall when he became an official candidate for state office."

Fiona gestured to the men. Both left the waiting room. One turned down the hallway toward the ICU entrance. The other closed the waiting room door and stood outside in front of it.

Bridget pursed her lips and gazed at Fiona with hard eyes, her face cold as marble. "Why are *you* here, Fiona?"

"I was concerned, for Marshall, and for you and your family."

"We're fine. Thank you." Bridget gave her a dismissive wave toward the waiting room door.

"How is he?"

"Not your concern."

Fiona raised her eyebrows but didn't speak.

Bridget moved closer and looked down at Fiona, taking full advantage of her taller stature. "Marshall Hilliard may be the US Attorney, and he may be a candidate for state office, but in this place, he is my husband." She gestured toward Grant and Dustin. "Father to these young men. This is a private family matter upon which you are intruding. You need to leave." She added a gracious smile. "Please."

Fiona stood her ground. "We have a public responsibility here too."

Bridget scoffed. "No. *You* don't, Fiona." She folded her arms and stuck out her chin. "If you need to leave these officers here, fine. They stay outside of this room, and they don't go into Marshall's ICU room."

Fiona relaxed her posture, took a step back, and tried to smile at Bridget.

"I was hoping I could see him."

"Not possible. Sorry."

The hardness in Bridget's voice drove the woman back on her heels. Bridget pointed to the door.

"As you wish," Fiona said. Just as she turned to go, heated voices in the hallway diverted their attention.

When Zack and his daughters walked down the hallway to the ICU, he noticed two men in nearly identical suits. One blocked the ICU entrance. The other stood by the door to the waiting room.

He judged they were not hospital security, based on their physiques, stern faces, and the obvious bulges under their jackets.

With Jenn and Annie behind him, Zack approached the waiting room door. The suit blocked the door. "Immediate family only."

Zack smiled. "I am Dr. Zack Winston, a physician friend, and advisor to Mrs. Hilliard. My daughters here are friends of Mr. Hilliard's sons. Bridget invited us here."

The guard bristled. "What did you not understand about 'immediate family,' Doctor?" He pronounced the last word with same inflection one would use for "vermin."

Zack paused to take a deep breath. "Just check with Mrs. Hilliard. She'll confirm what I'm telling you."

The man stared at Zack with steely eyes. "She's not to be disturbed."

Zack sensed his daughters backing away behind him. He fought to control his temper. Didn't want to make a scene in front of them. He spoke in the calmest voice he could muster.

"As I said, she's expecting us."

The guard shook his head. "I have my orders. No one admitted except immediate family. The lady must not be disturbed."

Zack's eyes narrowed. "Orders? From where?" He looked the man up and down, ending on the jacket bulge. "You're not hospital security."

His adversary opened his jacket to reveal the holstered gun on his belt; spoke in a commanding voice. "You need to leave. Now." He glanced toward Zack's daughters. "Don't make a scene in front of the young ladies."

The waiting room door swooshed open. Zack turned to see Bridget and Fiona staring at him with mouths aghast.

Bridget's hoarse but firm voice. "What the hell is going on out here?"

CHAPTER SIXTY-FOUR

Shaped like an upside-down and backward letter J, the motel consisted of a single level of adjoined rooms with mostly empty parking spots in front of each. Instead of taking the designated space for her room, Emily left the Mercedes where she had parked it behind the house. She double-checked to be sure she'd locked the car, then hurried across the parking area, turned the key to the room door, and stepped inside.

Her sole luggage was the now-cold McDonald's sandwich and Dr. Good's cell phone in her back pocket.

The room featured a threadbare carpet, dingy white walls, a double bed with a sag in the middle, a bedside stand, and a tiny desk/dresser. The latter two were made from wood laminate that was separating at the edges. In lieu of a closet, an alcove with a metal rod and two hangers separated the sleeping area from a single faux-marble sink. A warped sliding wood door revealed a bathroom with a commode and porcelain tub opposite the alcove. The room smelled of mold, stale tobacco, and cleaning fluid.

Without turning on any lights, Emily sat in the rickety wooden desk chair and devoured the sandwich. She washed her hands and face in the sink, then lay on the bed to study Dr. Good's phone. The screen was dark. She pushed buttons on the side at random until the display lit up. It showed the date, the time as almost noon, and some symbols she didn't recognize. At the top of the screen, an icon like a closed padlock indicated she would need a password to get into it. As she stared at the screen, a message appeared above the padlock image.

Face doesn't match

Frustrated, Emily tossed the phone to the foot of the bed. She startled when it immediately rang with a tone different from the previous call. She picked it up in time to see a cryptic message stream across the screen, then disappear.

Code purple. All respond.

From the hospital? Or?

She remembered how the woman at the front desk had sneered at her as she held a phone to her ear.

The state police vehicle had not been far away.

Emily bolted from the bed, stuffed Good's phone into her pocket, ran out the door, and pressed the "unlock" icon on the Mercedes' key fob. She jumped in and started the car, backed out, and drove through the small parking area to the road. She turned right, south, on highway 522—away from the Interstate and US 40. She glanced in the rearview mirror and saw a vehicle turn into the motel driveway. She couldn't make out if it was a police vehicle. She had to assume it was.

Emily couldn't risk driving the speed limit now. She accelerated, but not too fast to risk losing control of the vehicle. Within a minute, she drove across a bridge over a river. As soon as she left the bridge, she heaved a sigh of relief at the large sign on the side of the road.

WELCOME TO WEST VIRGINIA

She drove the Mercedes past the sign, then slowed to below the speed limit. If the car she'd seen enter the hotel driveway was Maryland State Police, she doubted it would cross the state line to look for her.

For the moment, she felt safe. She continued driving as she tried to craft her next three objectives.

First, get somewhere safe.

Second. . . .

She didn't have a clue about the second or third tasks. Time to dump the three-objectives routine and concentrate on the immediate threat. How long before the Maryland trooper contacted a counterpart in West Virginia? Long enough for Emily to get somewhere safe?

She continued along US-522, staying under the speed limit. Ten minutes later, while driving on an open road with dense woods on both sides, the *Low Fuel* light illuminated the dashboard.

"Now what do I do?"

CHAPTER SIXTY-FIVE

Bridget seethed as she sat across from Fiona and the State Police agent at the table in a conference room down the hall from the ICU waiting area. Zack sat next to her. Bridget had sent Grant, Dustin, Jennifer, and Annie to the hospital cafeteria with enough cash to get themselves breakfast, lunch, or both.

Fiona, a phony look of concern badly painted on her face, addressed Bridget. "Please, ma'am. You must understand the need for security here. With the divisive political climate in the state, a high-profile candidate could be a target for an extremist group or a crazed individual."

"Unlikely," Bridget said.

"We don't know the full circumstances of your husband's, uh, medical event," Fiona said.

Zack squinted at her. "What's that supposed to mean?"

Fiona didn't look at Zack but directed her comments to Bridget. "You need to trust us, ma'am."

"I need you to answer Dr. Winston's question." Bridget's hoarse voice trembled.

Fiona turned to Zack. "It doesn't mean anything other than no one really knows what precipitated Marshall's sudden collapse."

Bridget exchanged glances with Zack. Did Fiona and the two men know about the Coumadin? If so, how?

Zack put his hands together on the table. "Marshall Hilliard suffered a sudden, spontaneous intracerebral hemorrhage, a bleed into the deep substance of his brain. It's not a mystery."

Fiona raised her eyebrows. "Spontaneous?"

"As the physicians attending my husband, have stated." Bridget pushed back from the table. "That's all or more than you need to know, Ms. Delaney." She paused and half-smiled. "You are familiar with the HIPAA law and regulations, correct?"

Fiona blinked but did not respond.

Bridget stood up and beckoned Zack to do the same. "Recall that before your men's unwarranted altercation with Dr. Winston, I had dismissed you from further interference with my family. I will ask you, politely, one last time, to leave me, my physician advocate, and my family alone." She pulled out her phone. "Otherwise, I will call my friend, the current Virginia Attorney General, and seek to have you all removed." She leaned across the table toward Fiona. "Clear?"

Fiona shrugged. "Clear." She stood. "I need to leave security here for Marshall. It's required by protocol."

Bridget strained to make her voice strong. "Take your protocol and stuff it up your homewrecking twat." She turned and stormed out of the room.

Zack followed her. "Bridge . . ."

She turned on him. "Don't, Zack."

He didn't speak but made soft eye contact.

Bridget took a deep breath. "I just . . ."

Zack raised a finger to his lips. "It's okay. We all get it." He reached out and took her into a warm hug. They split apart when the conference room door opened for the exit of Fiona and her entourage.

Bridget faced Fiona. "Sorry for my behavior in there. I do understand." She took a breath. "The agents can stay, but not in the waiting room and not inside the ICU."

"Thank you," Fiona said. She beckoned the agents to follow her down the hallway.

"Merry Christmas," Bridget said to their retreating backs.

Zack had never seen Bridget lose control like she did with Fiona.

Not that I blame her.

"I need to check on Marsh," she said.

Zack put a hand on her arm. "Take a few minutes to settle first; for his sake if not yours." He escorted her back into the now-empty conference room. They sat next to each other.

Bridget leaned her elbows on the table and buried her face in her hands.

Zack kept silent, allowing her time to process.

After a minute, she looked up, red-faced, eyes brimming with moisture. "What's going on, Zack? How is any of this right?"

"It isn't." He gestured toward the door. "But those agents need to be here. I've seen the same response in other cases involving political figures."

"Those other cases didn't include the Fiona factor."

"Not by that name, but yes. Yours is not the first triangle to play out in a hospital crisis." He had experienced several episodes in his career where spouse and lover clashed at the bedside of a critically ill man or woman. "It happens."

Bridget stared into space. "Marshall didn't overdose. He's too self-centered to do that."

"Meaning?" Zack answered his own question. "For want of a better term, foul play?"

She shook her head. "Impossible. He was with me the whole time after the news conference."

They traded wary looks.

"Not good," Zack said.

A knock on the door stifled Bridget's reply.

A nurse stuck her head into the room. "Mrs. Hilliard? Dr. Pittman, the neurosurgeon, wants to speak with you. He says it's important."

"Can we meet in here?" Bridget asked. "I'd like Dr. Winston to remain as well."

"I'll ask Dr. Pittman," the nurse said. "If you all could just wait here . . ."

Bridget glanced at Zack. "Should Grant and Dustin—?"

"Your call."

Bridget spoke to the nurse. "My son and stepson are in the cafeteria with Dr. Winston's daughters. I'd like them to sit in on the meeting. I'll call them to come up here. Then we can meet."

"Of course." The nurse left and closed the door.

Zack stared at the wall while Bridget called Dustin.

Only one reason for the Chief of Neurosurgery to talk to the grieving wife of a prominent politician on Christmas day.

CHAPTER SIXTY-SIX

Emily drove a little over five miles before she entered Berkley Springs, West Virginia, and pulled into a Sheetz gas station. She went inside, relieved to see only a few other customers there. She used cash to pre-pay ten dollars of gas, looking down and away from the security camera when she handed the bill to the attendant.

Back at the Mercedes, she searched in vain for a lever or button to access the gas tank. Finding none, she got back into the car, pulled out the owner's manual, and searched for the answer.

A knock on the driver's side window startled Emily. She almost banged her head on the car's ceiling. The young man who had taken her money inside the station stood by the driver's door. Emily rolled down the window.

He smiled. "Need help?"

Emily forced a shy smile. "This is, uh, my boss's car. He was kind enough to let me borrow it."

A wave of fear welled up within her. She shrugged, embarrassed. "I don't know how to open the little door to the gas tank."

The young man cocked his head and smiled. "You must have a nice boss." He looked to be early twenties in age.

Emily shot him what she hoped was a winning smile. "He's a doctor. Has a Mercedes convertible too."

The guy snorted. "Sure, he does." He beckoned her, then walked around the rear of the vehicle.

Emily got out of the car and followed him, careful to take the keys with her. The man pushed against the gas tank door on the right rear fender. It popped open. He stepped aside.

"Benzes don't have a lever or button in the cab. You just flip this little door open."

"Oh," Emily said. "Thanks."

He twisted off the gas cap and showed Emily how it dangled from a cord to prevent losing it. He took the nozzle from the gas pump, inserted it into the opening, and squeezed the lever to start the flow of gas.

Emily started to protest, but he shook her off. "I got it."

"Thank you." She hoped her voice didn't sound as nervous to him as it did to her.

He let the meter run up to eleven dollars before shutting off the pump. "Last buck's on me."

Emily reached into Good's wallet to extract a dollar bill. She held it toward him, but he didn't take it.

"Like I said, it's on me." He gave her a penetrating look. "Nice wallet. Leather?"

Emily quickly returned the wallet to her pocket. "Uh, yeah."

His eyes narrowed. "Did your rich doctor boss lend you his wallet and credit cards too?"

Unable to answer, Emily mumbled, "Thanks for your help." She scurried back to the driver's side of the car. As she drove away from the station, the young man stood by the gas pump, dialing a cell phone.

Terrified that the man had called the police, Emily dared not return to US 522. Leaving the gas station, she turned onto State Route 13 and drove until she had some miles distance from the Sheetz station. While driving, she kept a constant lookout with frequent glances in the rear-view mirror. She felt safer driving the meandering country road while she figured out what to do next. It was now mid-afternoon. Emily was mentally and physically exhausted and needed to find a safe place to stop and rest. She started another three-task list.

One, drive to someplace safe.

Two, stop and rest.

Three, head west.

The sudden baby screech announced a call on Dr. Good's phone.

Spider.

Emily shuddered. What would Spider think or do if Dr. Good didn't answer? What could she do about it?

Nothing.

She ignored the phone and kept driving until she came upon the Virginia border. West Virginia State Route 13 morphed into Virginia State Route 600. Nervous about being back in Virginia, Emily pulled the car as far as she could to the side of the road to study the GPS and weigh her options. The dashboard clock indicated 4:09 PM. The sun had begun to set. Emily needed to get her act together before dark. At least the rain had stopped.

She moved *head west* to the top of her task list.

Dr. Good's phone rang. Spider again.

Emily turned it over so she couldn't see the screen.

Expanding the view on the GPS, she noted that she was not far from US 522 as it headed toward Winchester, VA. That area looked too populated, more prone to police presence. Worse, she was headed in the wrong direction, back toward the National Capitol Area, The Good House, and all the dangers there.

As she studied the map, a solution emerged, albeit risky. She could continue on this Virginia Route 600 to where it joined US 522 for just a few miles, then get off and take a short series of rural roads to join up with US 50, on which she could drive west into the West Virginia hills and go for miles and miles, to Ohio or farther.

She would find a place to pull off the road and sleep for a few hours. She wasn't about to risk another hotel and possible exposure.

Would police search for her on all roads? Probably not, if they were searching for her at all. She nodded as she made her decision. After she rested for a few hours, she could continue west in darkness. For the first time since moving on from the Frederick Greyhound bus station, Emily felt like she'd figured it all out.

Dr. Good's phone rang.

Spider.

With the car still stopped, for reasons she didn't understand, Emily pressed *Answer*, but did not speak.

Spider's voice sounded meaner than she remembered. "Hello, Emily."

She took in a quick breath but remained silent.

"Where are you, Emily?"

Emily clicked the hang-up icon. The phone went to dial tone. She tossed it on the passenger seat, put the car in gear, and started driving toward US 522.

The phone rang again. She ignored it.

It rang again. She ignored it again.

Several cycles of ring/ignore passed before the pattern jangled Emily's nerves enough to distract her driving. She pulled to the side of the road, intending to turn the phone off. It rang again just as she stopped the car.

Caller Unknown

Emily searched the phone to figure out how to turn it off. It kept ringing. Some phantom force moved her finger to press *Answer*.

She knew it was him before Adam Good's voice came over the speaker. "Emily, come home."

A crushing sensation in Emily's chest caused her to hyperventilate.

"Emily, I need you. Please come home."

She spoke in a tremulous voice. "Never."

A long pause. "You don't mean that, Em. Not after all we've had, all we've been through, all I've done for you."

"Go to hell, Adam."

"You don't mean that."

Emily didn't respond, yet she stayed on the line. She could not force her finger to click the *Off* button—as if Adam Good were pulling her into the phone.

"I understand why you did it, Em." A beat. "I deserved it. I am so sorry."

Emily's breathing quickened as if the man's hand reached through the phone and clutched her heart. She reminded herself that she was free from his control.

Turn off the damned phone, Em.

Good's voice turned earnest. "I need you, Em. I promise, I will do better by you. You're my everything. Please, just come home."

"I . . . I can't."

"You can. You must. Emily, you know what will happen if the authorities catch up with you. They will learn about your past, the criminal negligence. They will put it all together and throw you in jail. You'll be tried, convicted, and sent to prison for the rest of your life."

A vision of the dead baby from years past invaded Emily's mind. She remembered Dr. Good's voice. "Run, Emily."

As if he knew her thoughts, his present voice continued. "You're a fugitive, Emily. They will find and prosecute you. Only I can help you."

A brief pause, after which his voice became more sincere. "I'm sorry I mistreated you. I will take care of you. Always. I love you so much. Come home. Please."

Emily hyperventilated. She feared she would pass out. Tears flowed down her cheeks. It took several seconds to find her voice. "I. Can't. Never again."

"We need each other, Emily."

At once Emily's heart hardened. She steeled herself. "No. We don't. You created my fear. You used me. Like you do everyone."

"Those words break my heart, Em. I understand. I do. Please forgive me. We can start over. Come home."

"Goodbye, Adam."

Emily's finger moved as if through unset concrete. She lowered the window and threw the phone into the bushes. The screen still glowed as Good continued to cajole.

"Go to hell," she shouted.

She would buy another phone if or when she needed it.

Darkness would soon follow the dusk. Emily needed to get somewhere soon. An unusual sense of freedom elated her. At last, she was free of Adam Good. For good.

She put the Mercedes in gear and started to turn onto the road just as a pair of headlights sped toward her. She waited until it passed, then her eyes followed it in the rear-view mirror. Cadillac SUV?

As if on cue, the car made an abrupt, screeching U-turn and raced back toward the Mercedes.

Emily stomped on the accelerator. The Mercedes' wheels spun on the icy roadside gravel.

The other car passed on the left, then made a sudden right pivot to stop in front of the Mercedes, blocking it from moving onto the road. For sure it was the Cadillac SUV that Spider always drove.

Emily threw open the Mercedes' door and jumped out.

At the same time, Spider and Roach sprang from the SUV.

Emily ran, but they caught her a few yards past the rear of the Mercedes. Spider grabbed her by both arms, spun her around, forced her to the Mercedes, and slammed her body chest-first over the trunk.

Roach zip-tied her hands behind her back. Spider yanked her head up by the hair and stood her straight, twisting her body to the left.

Adam Good walked up to her casually, as if they were meeting for a date.

"My dear spunky but naive Emily. I have a GPS tracker on my phone, and another built into the car. It took us some time to catch up to you. You helped us by heading east instead of west." He smiled and took her by the arm. With a gentle pull, he led her to the side of the Mercedes and forced her into the back seat.

Roach secured her ankles with zip ties while Good went around and got into the back seat from the other side. Once Roach was sure they had Emily under control and she was no threat to Dr. Good, he got into the driver's seat.

Spider had returned to his vehicle, backed up, and turned down the road to where Emily had planned her escape. Roach pulled the Mercedes into trail behind the Cadillac.

Emily sobbed tears of despair.

Adam Good patted her knee. "There, there, my dear. We will be fine. Trust me."

CHAPTER SIXTY-SEVEN

Ten minutes after the nurse left the conference room, Bridget and Zack remained in their seats. Neither had spoken. When Bridget put her hand on the conference table, Zack covered it with his and gave a gentle squeeze.

Bridget squeezed back. She kept her hand in his.

After another five minutes, Zack stood. "I'm going to go—"

Bridget stopped him. "No. Stop trying to be in control. I need you here as a friend. Please."

He nodded and resumed his seat.

The conference room door opened, and a nurse stepped back to admit Grant and Dustin. "Jenn and Annie are in the waiting room," Grant said. They took seats opposite Bridget and Zack.

Dr. Pittman entered the room. Everyone stood.

"Mrs. Hilliard," he said by way of greeting Bridget. He turned to greet Zack. "Doctor Winston."

Bridget directed him to the boys. "Our son, Dustin, and Marshall's son, Grant."

Pittman offered stiff handshakes, then seated himself at the head of the table. He shot Zack a somber look, then turned to Bridget.

"First, I am so sorry to bear bad news on Christmas day."

Bridget shook her head. "You didn't make it happen, Doctor. No apologies needed, for that, or anything else you tell us."

Pittman cleared his throat. "Very well." Another glance at Zack then back to Bridget. "I understand you are familiar with medical terminology and concepts."

"Two years of med school before I decided to become a lawyer. Decades of malpractice defense work. So, yes."

"Then I won't talk down to you."

Another serious glance at Zack as Pittman cleared his throat. "You understand that your husband has suffered severe brain damage, yes?"

Bridget pursed her lips; gave a polite nod. Her guts boiled while icy hand gripped her heart and terror flooded her brain. How long could she remain in control? "Yes." She gestured toward Dustin and Grant. "We all understand that."

Under the table, Zack grasped her hand. "Please go on, Doctor," Bridget said.

"Right." Another clearing of the throat by the neurosurgeon. "Your husband has shown no signs of spontaneous respiratory or cardiac function for almost twenty-four hours."

"Hence the ventilator and cardiotropic drugs," Zack said.

Pittman shot Zack an annoyed look, then turned back to Bridget. "In addition, since the time of his catastrophic herniation in the ER, he's shown no signs of cerebral function." He paused, blinked, grimaced. "No signs of brainstem function either."

Although expected, the words struck Bridget like a sledgehammer to her chest and an ax to her skull. She couldn't speak. She couldn't look at Dustin or the others. She stared over Dr. Pittman's head at the wall behind him.

No one spoke as Dr. Pittman waited for a response from Bridget.

She let go of Zack's hand. This was her trauma, not his. She closed her eyes. The pressure in her chest and head crescendoed. The events of the past few days, of the past months, the past years—good, bad, or neutral—flitted in and out of consciousness like a swarm of bees, or a flight of butterflies. Bridget took three deep breaths, opened her eyes, and looked at the neurosurgeon.

"You're telling me he's brain dead." Her voice sounded disembodied.

"That's my professional opinion, yes."

Bridget's eyes filmed over as she gazed in earnest at Pittman.

"Are you asking to take him off life support?"

He returned her gaze. "In my professional opinion, continued supportive maintenance would be futile."

Bridget rested her gaze on Grant and Dustin, both of whom wept in silence. She turned to Zack with a pleading look.

He looked back with soft eyes, then spoke in a comforting but firm voice. "Your decision, Bridge."

She swung back to Dr. Pittman, her strained voice as firm as she could make it, and said, "Not before I see him." She gestured toward Grant and Dustin. "Not until his family sees him."

"Of course."

Pittman held out a hand. "I am sorry, Ms. Larsen. Sorry that we couldn't help him. He deserved better." It was the first time he'd addressed Bridget by her professional name.

She gave him a curious look. "Thank you, Doctor. I know your options were limited. I appreciate your honesty."

"And I yours."

He chewed on his lip for a second. "If I may say, I've admired your professional work for many years. A cherished colleague of mine remains in practice today because of your defense."

Bridget's brow furrowed, deep in thought. A look of recognition crossed her face. "Dr. Joshua Green?"

"Yes. An outstanding surgeon and mentor whose career might have ended too soon except for your defense. Thank you again."

Everyone stood. Bridget hugged Dr. Pittman. "Thank you again."

The doctor overcame his initial stiffness and reciprocated. Then he broke off, offered Zack a cursory glance, and hurried from the room.

CHAPTER SIXTY-EIGHT

The Cadillac and Mercedes pulled into the driveway at The Good House. No one had spoken during the drive. Emily had stared out the window on her side of the car, refusing to look at Adam Good until Roach turned off the vehicle's ignition.

Good was asleep.

Emily wanted to choke the life out of him, but she could not move with her wrists and ankles bound.

Roach turned from the driver's seat and spoke to Dr. Good.

"We're here, sir."

Good snorted and opened his eyes. "Very good."

He smiled at Emily. "Welcome home, love."

Adam got out of his side of the car and walked up the porch to where Spider had opened the front door. He never looked back.

Roach got out and opened the rear door. "Come along."

Emily spat out the words. "I'm tied up, jerk."

"No problem." Roach bent through the doorway, lifted Emily out of the vehicle, and stood her up next to it. If she didn't know better, she'd have thought he tried to be gentle.

Dr. Good looked down from the porch. "Be careful, Roach. Don't hurt her. Untie her legs and bring her into the house." He smiled at Emily. "You're not going to run now, are you, Em?"

Emily glared at him.

Roach used a pocketknife to cut the zip-ties off her ankles. As soon as her legs were free, she ran toward the woods. Roach caught her in two steps, clutched her around the waist, and lifted her feet off the ground. She'd had no idea he was that strong. She tried to squirm away, but he overpowered her with ease.

Good came back down the steps from the porch.

"Please don't fight," Roach said in a whisper. "You'll make him angry."

Emily stopped struggling.

Good put his arm around her and steered her toward the house. "Now come along like a good girl."

Emily relented and walked beside him. She would find a way to escape. Soon.

Roach called after them. "If you're all set, I'm on my way."

Good turned to him. "Get some rest. You'll need it."

"I'll be ready by eight, just in case Flossie moves it up."

"Okay," Good said.

Roach got into the Mercedes, started it, and drove away.

With his car gone, did Adam Good intend to spend the night here? At least Emily wouldn't be alone with Spider.

When they entered the vacant living room, Emily searched for an opportunity to release herself from Good and race out the front door. Sensing her intent, he pulled her closer to him. His arm constrained her like a chain around her waist. He guided Emily up the stairs and into the room she'd escaped from that morning. The bed was made, and the room looked untouched.

"Scene of your crime," Good said. "Nice touch hiding my clothes." He gave her a condescending smile. "You should have taken them with you and pitched them into a dumpster. But . . . I'm a genius and you are not. I could have worn surgical scrubs from the pile in the closet. Who needs street clothes?"

Spider entered the room. Dr. Good sat Emily on the bed and stood in front of her while Spider cut the zip ties on her wrists.

She tried to take a swing at Spider, but his hand grabbed her wrist. He pushed her onto the bed. Emily twisted out of his grasp, ready to make a run for it.

Good moved in front of her. "Quit the futile resistance, Em. You're smarter than that."

He grasped one wrist while Spider, from the opposite side of the bed, grasped the other. They zip-tied each arm to a bedpost, leaving her flat on her back with her arms spread above her.

Emily crossed her legs. Her voice trembled.

"Wh . . . What are you doing to me?"

"Don't flatter yourself," Spider said.

"We're not doing anything to you," Good said. "We can't trust you not to try to escape again, so . . ." He patted her cheek. "Here's a little something to help you sleep." He held a small glass of milk under her chin.

"I'm not taking anything you give me."

Good looked at Spider. "Assistance, please."

Spider grabbed Emily's hair and pulled her head back as Good brought the glass to her lips. She clenched her jaw. Spider let go of her head and pressed hard against the angles of her jaw on each side while Good pulled her chin down. Her mouth opened and Good poured a swallow of the milk into it.

Emily spit it out. The milk splashed onto Good's face and trickled down his neck.

Good raised a hand to slap her but stopped in mid-swing. "That's enough." He looked at Spider and nodded toward Emily.

Spider's hand on her forehead forced Emily's head to the pillow. His other hand yanked her chin toward her chest. Good's free hand pinched her nostrils closed as he poured the rest of the milk into her throat. Spider shoved her chin up and held her mouth closed.

She couldn't breathe.

"Swallow," Good said.

Emily swallowed the milk. Spider let go of her chin. She opened her mouth, gasped, and went into a coughing fit from the irritation to the back of her throat. After a few seconds, she let her head fall back onto the pillow.

Defeated. For now.

Good patted her cheek again. "Don't be such a naughty girl." He stood, as did Spider, leaving her flat on her back in the bed.

"Now get some rest," Good said in a sweet voice. "We have a big day tomorrow. Special customer arriving. We'll need you at your best." He leaned over and kissed her cheek.

Emily tried to spit at him, but she had no saliva left.

Good moved away. "I'll ignore that unfortunate gesture."

He flipped the lights off as he and Spider left the room. The door locked behind them.

Alone and restrained in the darkness, Emily broke down and loosed all her pent-up emotion. No one would hear her shrieks except her captors, but she screamed for help anyway.

CHAPTER SIXTY-NINE

Bridget, Zack, Grant, and Jennifer followed Dr. Pittman into the ICU. Dustin had declined Bridget's exhortation to be involved in the decision about Marshall's outcome. Annie had seemed eager to stay with him. Jennifer had volunteered to stay out as well, but Grant asked her to be there with him. She had agreed without hesitation.

Zack had turned away at the ICU door, but Bridget scowled at him. "Really, Doc? You don't get to detach now." She led the group into Marshall's room.

He looked thinner and paler than she remembered from her previous visit just a few hours ago. She looked at Zack. "Don't they feed him?"

Zack pointed to a plastic bag hanging from an IV pole, filled with a creamy white fluid. A tube, filled with the same fluid, extended from the bag into Marshall's nose.

"It's called parenteral nutrition. High protein, high calorie, fed directly into his stomach."

"Well, they're not giving him enough."

"It's done by a complex formula. Calculated nutritional needs, accounting for his anabolic state of burning up calories, plus his protein needs." He looked away. "Eventually they would replace the nasogastric tube with a permanent gastrostomy tube, a larger tube surgically implanted into his stomach. More efficient."

Bridget gave him a withering look.

A "harrumph" from Dr. Pittman drew their attention back to the bedside they'd both avoided with their sidebar conversation.

Bridget and Zack approached the left side of Marshall's bed near his head. Dr. Pittman faced them from the other side. Grant and Jennifer stood at the foot of the bed, holding hands.

"Let me show you the physical indicators," Dr. Pittman said.

Bridget shook her head. "No."

She stood back and motioned for Zack to move in front of her to the head of the bed. "Please."

Zack looked at Dr. Pittman. "With your permission."

The older physician stepped back. "Of course."

Bridget watched as Zack conducted a thorough neurological exam on Marshall. He spoke his findings aloud for all to hear. "Unresponsive to deep pain. Pupils mid-position, fixed. Extremities flaccid. Glasgow Coma Scale equals three."

"Same as last time," Bridget said in a hoarse whisper.

Zack nodded. "He's not cycling the ventilator on his own. No spontaneous respirations. Cardiac rhythm is sinus, no doubt artificially supported by IV pressor agents."

He looked at Dr. Pittman. "Did you consider an EEG?"

Bridget understood he meant electroencephalogram, a measure of brain wave activity sometimes employed in death determination.

"Won't add any useful information beyond the physical exam, and not legally required," Pittman said.

Zack turned to Bridget. "You know about electroencephalograms, right?"

She tossed her head. "Yeah."

"You could demand one."

"No."

"Another option," Zack said. "Wait until tomorrow. See if there's any progress."

Bridget looked at Grant, the stepson who had never accepted her into his life. "Thoughts?"

Tears rolled down Grant's cheeks. He gestured at Marshall. "That . . . That is not my dad."

Bridget gazed at the ceiling and stroked her chin. She thought about Dustin outside. She looked at Zack, then at Jennifer. "Would you two please go out and send Dustin in? We three need to be alone with Marsh. We won't be long."

"Of course," Zack said. He squeezed her hand. "I'll be right outside if you need me."

She squeezed back. "Thanks."

As Zack and Jennifer headed out, Bridget looked at Dr. Pittman. "You too, Doctor. You've done all you can. Thanks."

Pittman nodded. "Of course. You can let the nurse know your decision. I'll be on my way, but feel free to call anytime."

"Thank you," Bridget said.

A nurse led Dustin into the room. Bridget hugged Dustin and Grant. "I am so sorry I couldn't do better for your dad. I tried. He loved you both very much." She broke into sobs.

Dustin buried his head in her chest and bawled, speechless.

Grant put his arm around her. "He loved you too." He stifled a sob. "So do I."

Bridget let out a deep sigh. "Thank you, Grant. I never knew."

He nodded, tears running down his cheeks.

She stepped back, guiding the two young men to their father's bedside. "Time to say goodbye. Whatever feels right to you."

Bridget watched in silent grief as Marshall Hilliard's two sons accepted the reality of their father's death and whispered last words to him. She was thankful she couldn't hear what they said. After a few minutes, they stood next to the bed in silence, their goodbyes done, unsure what to do next.

Bridget tapped them on their shoulders and led them toward the door. "My turn. I need to be alone with him."

Returning to the bedside after the boys left, Bridget noticed the dayshift nurse, not Jasmine, hovering nearby. She smiled at the young woman. "May I be alone with him?"

The nurse spread her hands, apologetic. "I can't do that, ma'am. Hospital policy."

A flash of anger accompanied Bridget's hoarse retort. "Leave."

The woman flushed; a nervous look on her face. "I . . . I can't, ma'am. Please. I'll stay out of your way."

Bridget scolded herself and forced a smile. "I understand. Sorry for my outburst."

"Thank you, ma'am."

The nurse retreated to the far corner of the room and appeared to busy herself by typing on the computer that hosted Marshall's ICU record.

Bridget stood next to the bed, grasped Marshall's hand, and squeezed with all her might.

No response.

"That was just a test to be sure you're really unresponsive because I've quit trusting you." Her attempted chuckle died in the back of her throat. She gazed at her husband for several minutes, watching the ventilator-driven rise and fall of his chest, the lack of tone in his muscles.

"So, this is how it ends. I expected our marriage to go up in flames and explosions, not peter out with a whimper." She shrugged. "You were always better at staging."

Bridget glanced at the door. "I'll do my best with Dustin, and whatever I can for Grant, but I can reluctantly fill the hole you leave in their lives. They will survive. They have your genes, after all."

Looking over her husband's face, Bridget had nothing left to say. The years of her relationship with Marshall Hilliard streamed through her mind in one fast-forward reel like a movie trailer. Their early attraction, their affair that made Grant the child of a broken marriage and her a stepmother. Their early years as struggling lawyers, taking different career paths, hers to defense and his to prosecution and eventually politics.

The gaps in their relationship, unseen and unheeded for too long, coalesced into a black hole that led to his serial affairs and her attraction to Zack Winston. Her rage at losing Marshall to the likes of Fiona Delaney, and Bridget's own shame over a near-dalliance with Zack. The sudden, dramatic, unexpected hemorrhage into Marshall's brain had reduced him to a hunk of non-cognitive protoplasm before they could hope to resolve their issues and maybe save their marriage; or end it amicably. Her own heart and soul wrenched back and forth between grief and anger like some perpetual cataclysmic chemical reaction.

"You would have made one hell of an Attorney General, Marshall Hilliard."

Bridget could think of nothing more to say. No final words of forgiveness, regret, love, or hate. Just an empty heart and a huge void in her soul.

She glanced at the nurse, whose back remained turned as she bent over the computer. Bridget's eyes traced a path from the breathing tube in Marshall's mouth, to the connecting hose, to the ventilator, to the electrical cord stretching from the machine to a waist-high wall plug behind the bed. She bent over Marshall and spoke into his ear. "I loved you so much. We had everything. How could you do this to us? To your sons? To me?"

Bridget gritted her teeth and pursed her lips. Tears flowed freely. She shook her head and leaned back to his ear. "You didn't spoil it. We both did that." She stood straight and stared at Marshall's inert body. "Now we're done."

Bridget stepped to the wall and pulled the ventilator plug out of its socket.

CHAPTER SEVENTY

Zack sat in the waiting room across from Dustin and Grant. His daughters sat on the couch, Annie scrolling on her phone, Jennifer staring into space.

Minutes had passed since Bridget had dismissed them from Marshall's ICU room. Sympathetic as he was to her decision, whichever way she chose, he worried about her mental state. She'd been in such an emotional maelstrom, not only in the last twenty-four hours but the last two years. Strong as she was, even Bridget Larsen had a breaking point. She seemed on the edge of it.

Who wouldn't be?

Zack's clinically tuned ears caught the sound of alarms going off inside the ICU. Seconds later, the loudspeaker blared overhead.

"Dr. Pittman to ICU STAT. Dr. Pittman, ICU STAT."

A loud voice in the hallway from the direction of the ICU. "Officers. Now."

Zack sprang from his seat and rushed out of the waiting room.

A nurse held the ICU door open to allow the two State Police officers to enter. She let the doors close just as Zack got there.

Undaunted, Zack mashed on the intercom button. "It's Dr. Winston. Let me in."

A voice came back. "ICU is closed to non-essential personnel."

Zack started to protest, but he sensed hospital security guards arrive on the scene and move toward him.

A steady hand clasped his shoulder. He turned to see Dr. Pittman, not a security guard. Pittman entered the code for the cipher lock, then allowed Zack to follow him into the ICU.

Outside Marshall's room, Bridget sat on a stool flanked by the two State Police officers. When Zack moved toward her, the officers blocked his path. A hospital security guard entered the ICU and stood near Zack.

He looked past the officers. "What's going on, Bridge?"

She spoke in a monotone. "It's done, Zack."

A nurse came up to Pittman and pointed at Bridget. "She unplugged the ventilator."

Pittman's eyebrows raised. "On Hilliard?"

"Yes."

"Did you plug it back in?"

"Of course."

Pittman looked at Zack and Bridget, the police agents, and the security guard. All seemed in a state of suspended animation, all stared at the neurosurgeon.

"The man was dead already," Pittman said.

"She can't just turn off—"

Dr. Pittman raised a hand. "She can't, but I can, with her concurrence." He looked at Bridget, a question in his eyes.

Bridget returned a slight nod.

Pittman entered Marshall's room, stayed for less than a minute, then returned. He spoke to the nurse. "I discontinued the ventilator and documented Marshall Hilliard's death on the medical record."

Zack looked at Bridget and nodded toward Marshall's room. "Do you . . . ?"

She shook her head and turned toward the exit. The State Police agents turned with her. Zack tried to join her, but the hospital security guard blocked his path.

The agents guided Bridget to the ICU exit doors. "We need you to answer some questions, ma'am."

Bridget held up a hand. "Just a minute. I have to make a phone call." She stood in place, pulled out her phone, and touched the speed dial.

"Fiona," she said. "Marshall is dead."

CHAPTER SEVENTY-ONE

Fiona's unemotional response to her phone call made Bridget wonder whether Marshall's lover already knew he had died.

She accompanied the two State Police agents into the ICU conference room. Zack tried to follow, but they stopped him at the door. The hospital security guards escorted him away from the room as one of the agents closed the door. The other agent indicated a chair. Bridget sat. The two men sat across from her at the long table.

The lead agent spoke without emotion. "Mrs. Hilliard, first let me offer sincere condolences for the passing of your husband."

Bridget folded her arms. "I prefer Ms. Larsen. Please, can you just tell me what you want?"

"We know this is a difficult time for you, ma'am," the man said, "but we need to clarify a few things now."

Bridget stared at him.

The agent stared back. "Why did you unplug Mr. Hilliard's ventilator?"

Bridget huffed. "That should be obvious."

Neither officer said anything.

"My husband was brain dead. The doctors made it clear that it was my decision whether or not to keep him on life support."

"Did Dr. Pittman document that?"

"He told me as much in front of Dr. Winston and my son and stepson. He said further life support would be futile." She leaned forward. "You can ask the doctors if you don't believe me. In fact, will you please call Dr. Pittman right now so I can get on with supporting Marshall's sons in their grief?"

The agent folded his arms and leaned back in his chair. "Wouldn't it be standard procedure for you to communicate your choice to the medical personnel, to allow them to discontinue the life support? Why did you take it upon yourself to do that?"

Bridget stared past the two men into the empty space behind them. "I just did it."

The agents remained silent, scrutinizing Bridget with dispassionate eyes. Finally, the agent in charge spoke. "Did you want your husband dead?"

"He was already dead." She stood. "Unless you have something more pertinent to discuss, I need to take care of my family now."

The man stood. "Very well. We're not done, Mrs. Hilliard. We'll be in touch."

Bridget shrugged. "I'll be around." She walked past him and left the room.

CHAPTER SEVENTY-TWO

Night had long since fallen by the time their dad opened the door to his apartment and stepped aside to let Annie and Jennifer enter. All three moved in slow motion, exhausted from the intense day and excruciating emotions. The young women stopped just inside the door, disgusted by the odor of the leftover breakfast and dirty dishes they'd abandoned that morning when they rushed to the hospital after Bridget called their dad.

"Ugh," Annie said. Her nose recoiled to the stink of old bacon grease.

Jennifer sighed and rubbed her eyes. "I've got it." She walked to the table and started to clear it.

"I'll help," Annie said. "As soon as you get rid of that bacon sludge."

Their dad stood in the middle of the living room, his face frozen, posture limp.

Looks like a zombie, Annie thought. Maybe they all looked like that.

He shook himself out of it. "I have to make some phone calls." He looked at Jennifer as she dumped the bacon grease into a jar. "I'll use the office."

"Sure, Dad."

Jennifer beckoned to Annie. "Ugly bacon grease all gone, sis. Assistance welcome."

Dad closed the office/guest room door behind him.

Jennifer's gaze followed. "I'm worried about him."

Annie squinted. "Why?"

"Think about it," Jenn said. "We just spent most of Christmas day in the hospital with Dad and his friend and her son and stepson while her husband died."

Annie cocked her head. "What are you getting at?"

"Not sure. If we knew him better, we might . . ." She shook her head. "Or not."

"He cares for Bridget. What's wrong with that?"

Jennifer frowned. "I didn't say anything was wrong. I'm just worried by his, uh, willingness to put everything else aside to be with her."

"C'mon, Jenn, we weren't going to do anything today anyway. Christmas Day and Dad had no plans." She waved an arm around the room. "Look. No tree. No decorations. No presents."

"Well, you did get the Kindle . . ."

Annie smirked. "Dad doesn't know the first thing to do with us."

Jennifer regarded Annie with a kind smile. "He didn't make Bridget's husband have a stroke."

Annie furrowed her eyebrows. "You think Dad and Bridget had something going before . . . ?"

Jennifer tossed her head. "Don't know. I sensed weird dynamics the other night when we got back to Bridget's from the pizza place and her husband was there."

"So?"

"So, I don't know. Dad's affect is strange."

Annie shook her head. "I thought you wanted to be a surgeon. You talk like a shrink."

Jennifer smiled. "Channeling my inner Mom, I guess."

"Can you imagine if Mom were here? Now?"

"Oh my God, no. That would be so awful."

They had finished the dishes and returned to the living room when their dad came out of his office. Annie wondered if he'd overheard any of their conversation.

He looked at Jennifer. "We're still on with Dr. Wolfe tomorrow morning."

Jennifer blinked. "Wow, I'd almost forgotten. Seems like ages ago we arranged that."

"You still up for it? I want to visit Nate Young too. Maybe catch up with Dr. Hartman."

"What about Bridget?"

"I just talked to her. We can meet her and the boys for lunch."

"How's she doing?" Annie asked.

Her dad shook his head. "Devastated. But she's strong." His eyes focused on something far away. "She'll be okay. In time."

Annie and Jennifer traded looks.

"That all sounds good," Jennifer said. "Especially if we get some rest tonight. I call first dibs on the shower."

"Go ahead," Annie said. "I'll do mine in the morning. Too tired now."

Jennifer went into the office/guest room, came out a couple minutes later with her nightgown and a towel, and went into the bathroom.

Dad spoke to Annie. "You still meeting Sarah in the morning for your big shopping spree?"

Annie nodded.

"You will be done in time to join us for lunch with Bridget and the boys, right? We could ask Sarah to drop you off wherever we decide to eat."

Annie looked away. "Sarah's expecting to spend the whole day shopping."

He frowned. "Sounds like Sarah." The frown changed to a half-smile. "Up to you. After today, I can't tell you how to spend your time."

Annie chewed her lip. "Well, I did make a commitment." She heaved a big sigh. "I could use some recovery time. You know, retail therapy."

"I never associated you with retail therapy."

She folded her arms. "You don't know everything about me, Dad."

"Yeah. Got it. Maybe we'll plan something for dinner."

Sarah had told her the procedure would not take all day. Annie had to trust that.

"Yeah. Sure."

A flickering look that Annie didn't recognize crossed her dad's face.

"Okay," he said. "I'm going to do an Annie and put off my shower till morning." He helped her open up the sofa bed.

Jennifer came out of the bathroom. "All yours," she said to Annie. "At least brush your teeth and wash your face if you're not going to shower."

"Yes, Mom," Annie said.

Her dad chuckled. "Good night, you two. Thanks for giving up Christmas to spend time with Bridget and the boys."

"It was okay," Jennifer said.

"Yeah," Annie said. "Weird, but good."

Jennifer went into the guest room. Annie's dad headed toward his room. He stopped at the door, turned, and shot Annie a quizzical look.

"You would tell me if something bothered you, right? A problem?"

She blushed. "Of course, Daddy."

Annie waited until she was sure her dad had gone to bed, then pulled out her phone. While at the hospital, she'd traded idle texts with Conner. Merry Christmas and happy crap. She felt guilty leading him on but had to wait till she got back to San Diego before she ended their thing.

He would never know about the—

She couldn't form the word, even in silence to herself. No matter. Juvenile Conner was toast. A nice fling, but she never wanted to, like, be with him. Least of all with a—

Still couldn't say it.

Tyler had texted several times during the day, asking about meeting up tomorrow. She had ignored the texts. With all the emotion around her, she couldn't deal with putting him off.

Now she had other plans.

As if on cue, her phone buzzed. A text from Tyler.

What up we gonna meet tomorrow or not
Can't

Why not

Annie chewed on her lip. What to say? At once she knew.

Call me
Now?
Yeah
It's late
Everyone's in bed and I need to hear your voice
K

Her phone buzzed within seconds. She answered right away.

"Hi."
"So, uh, what's up?"
"Horrible day."
"Talk to me."

She told him about Bridget's husband and how she'd spent the whole day with her dad and sister and Bridget's family, and how the man had died at the end of the day. How she hardly knew Bridget but felt so awfully bad for her.

"Death sucks," Tyler said.
"First time up close for me. Awful."
"I know."
"You do?"
"Yeah. My mom. Couple years ago. Cancer."
"Oh, Tyler, I am so sorry."
"It gets better. The hole never goes away, but, hey, you gotta live your life. It's what Mom would have told me to do."
"I can't imagine . . ."
"So, about tomorrow . . ."
Annie rubbed her eyes. "Can't."

"Can't? Why not?"

She paused, grasping for words. "Can't say."

"Can't? Or won't?"

"Can't."

A pause. "Okay. How about the next day?"

A feeling of gloom swept over Annie. Less than a week here and she would be back in California. Why start something she couldn't finish?

"I don't know." She paused. "Probably not."

Silence for a few seconds, then his voice; less endearing, bordering on angry. "I thought we had something going."

A heavy weight pressed on Annie's chest. "We did." She took a breath. "We do."

"Then what?"

The weight lifted, and Annie felt instant relief. She blurted out the words fast before she could make herself stop. "I can't see you again, Tyler. Ever. I just can't."

He started to say something, but Annie ended the call and turned off the phone.

She laid on her abdomen and buried her face in the pillow to stifle the sobs that welled up with no signs of stopping.

CHAPTER SEVENTY-THREE

December 25

Merry Christmas, Noelle.

I've thought of you often today. So much happening. So many raw emotions. How I needed your voice in my ear. Not to mention your physical presence. My God, how I miss you.

Bridget's husband died today.

I know. I can almost hear you chastising me for my deepest thoughts. You know me. You know I would see opportunity arising from tragedy. That would be the old Zack Winston. The narcissistic Zack. Not me today. Well, not entirely.

You know I love Bridget. You knew it before I did. That love means I focus on her, her son, and stepson. Whatever the conflict between her and Marshall, she's lost her husband. The boys have lost their father. Their lives are forever changed.

Mine isn't, and there's the rub. I must either support her and her family like a devoted friend, or—stay away. You know my impulse. Please, don't let it rise up. Don't let it drive me to do stupid, self-destructive things. Not this time. Please chastise me if I start to go off the right path.

I put down the pen for a few minutes because I heard Annie settling down for the night outside my door. No, that's a lie. I heard her talking on the phone. Wondered who. Maybe her mom, since it's earlier in California, but—

Something's going on with her. She's hiding something, and it's not silly teenager stuff. We were getting closer, but now she's suddenly distant. Avoids eye contact. Gives evasive answers to questions. She even called me "Daddy."

How do I get her to confide in me? Why should she want to? She's in my life for a week, then gone for—how long?

I worry that she's too much like me. Free-spirited. (You would say "impulsive." You'd be right.) Not good with limits. A rebel? Yeah. How do I maintain a relationship with her? Hell, Noelle, how do I establish one, a real one not based on material stuff, a love-bond we can grow into over time. I feel like I'm beginning to have that with Jenn. Why not Annie? Maybe because Jenn is older and remembers some early bonding. Annie was too young. I'm not sure we bonded at all before Natalie—

I hear you say it doesn't matter about the past. Only the now matters.

Tomorrow I'll let Annie have her day with Sarah. I'll figure out how to connect with her for the rest of the time she's here.

I wish I knew if something serious is bothering her—

Time for sleep. Thanks for being there for me, even in this form.

Always,
Zack

CHAPTER SEVENTY-FOUR

Within five minutes, exhaustion and drowsiness overcame the terror in Emily's soul. She stopped screaming. She could not afford to waste energy on histrionics.

Focus on escape.

They had drugged her. Probably rohypnol in the milk. She had a few minutes of deliberate thought left before she succumbed. What "special customer" did Good mean? What did he expect from Emily? Another near-term pregnant runaway would not be a challenge.

Something else was at hand. What?

Why did Roach leave as soon as they returned Emily to The Good House? A mission for Dr. Good, it seemed. Why was Flossie involved? Where had Flossie been since she and Roach left in his truck the day the sixteen-year-old died?

That had been only three days ago. Emily's life had changed so much in that brief time.

She had never understood what Flossie did for Dr. Good. A nurse who seldom participated in the births. What did she and Dr. Good do in the secret wing where Emily was not allowed?

What about the other woman, Nan? Why did Dr. Good call them the "Bobbsey Twins?" Emily had seen Nan only that one time when she sneaked downstairs to retrieve an orange from the kitchen. Dr. Good and the woman were whispering in the foyer by the front door. Alarmed, Nan had turned on Emily. "What's she doing here?"

Good had stepped between her and Emily—his face livid. "Go back to your room, Emily. Now."

Nan had hustled toward the front door.

As Emily turned toward the stairs, Good had called out, "Nan, wait."

Later, he came to Emily's room and scolded her. "Never, ever come downstairs without permission. Never."

Emily apologized, then asked about the woman.

"There was no woman. Forget whatever you think you saw."

To drive home his point, Dr. Good made Emily stay in her room and go to bed without dinner.

Now, laying on her back with arms tied to the bed, Emily fought the drug effect. "I must escape."

Seconds later, she fell into a deep sleep.

CHAPTER SEVENTY-FIVE

Annie awakened in the morning to her phone buzzing. She was alone in the living room. Had her dad and Jennifer already left? The smell of coffee brewing in the kitchen suggested they hadn't.

She answered her phone.

"Annie, it's Sarah. We need to move our, uh, shopping expedition up to nine o'clock. Can you do that?"

An unexpected bolt of fear shot through her. "What time is it now?"

"Eight. Can you be ready in an hour? Meet me at the Starbucks near your dad's apartment? Nine o'clock sharp."

Why couldn't Sarah pick up Annie at her dad's apartment? She squeezed the remaining sleep out of her eyes. "Could, uh—"

Her dad came out of his room, fully dressed. Annie put down the phone, still on the call, and pretended to sleep.

He stopped at Jennifer's room and knocked. "Jenn, we need to get going." Then he came to the sofa bed and tapped Annie's shoulder. "Rise and shine, shopper. I'm sure Sarah will want to be there when the stores open, and you still need to shower and get ready." He didn't wait for a reply but went to the kitchen to fill travel mugs for Jennifer and him.

Jenn came out of her room. "Ready, Dad. Sorry. I hit the snooze button too many times."

Their dad handed Jenn her coffee. "Wouldn't be a problem except Eric is a punctuality nut, and we don't want him in a bad mood." He started to put on his coat, then turned to Annie. "We'll text you when we make dinner plans. I'm letting you skip out on lunch, but that's it. We're having dinner with Bridget and the boys. Sarah will need to make other plans for the evening."

Annie frowned. "Am I supposed to deliver that message?"

"No, I'll call her." He opened the door and hustled Jennifer out of the apartment. He turned to Annie. "Have fun."

As soon as the door closed, Annie picked up the phone. "You still there?"

Sarah laughed. "Oh, yeah. Heard most of that."

"Will we be done by dinner?"

"Way before. We might get to do some actual shopping."

When Annie entered the Starbucks, she found Sarah at a table in the corner. Two grandé cardboard mugs sat on the table in front of her.

"I took the liberty of ordering you a soy latte," Sarah said. "It's vegan, right?"

Annie smiled. "Yes, and I can sure use it."

"Short night?"

Annie sipped the latte.

"Yeah, plus everything that's happened in that last few days. I feel like I've been on a carnival ride ever since we got off the plane."

Sarah touched Annie's hand. "Not to mention the stress of your, uh, condition."

Annie wiped away a tear. "Yeah."

Sarah gave her hand a squeeze. "We're going to take care of that for you." She looked Annie in the eyes. "You still want to do it?"

Annie nodded. It was one aspect of her life about which she had no doubts. She took more sips from the latte.

"Okay," Sarah said. "Here's what will happen."

She moved closer and spoke in a conspiratorial tone. "My car is parked out front. We'll take a short drive to the clinic in Rockville. They'll give you something to relax you, and then you'll have a nice sleep. When you wake up, it will all be over. If you feel okay afterward, we can go shopping. Might be good if you come home with a bag or two, you know." She winked.

Annie sighed. Now that she was so close to it, an uneasy sensation rose within her. Her arms and legs felt a little numb.

Sarah noticed Annie's dismay. "It's normal to be apprehensive. Think how your life will be back to normal by this evening. I promise; it will be fine."

"Thanks."

"Your choice, Annie. You don't have to go through with it."

Annie shook her head. She had no choice. "I want to do it." Just saying the words brought a warm sense of relief over her body. She started to relax and took another sip of coffee.

Sarah patted her arm. "We can go as soon as you finish your coffee, but no rush."

"I'm ready."

Annie chugged the rest of her latte and stood up. At once she felt faint and grasped the edge of the table. "Whoa."

Sarah took her arm. "Are you okay?"

Annie shrugged. "Yeah. Must be more sleep deprived than I thought."

Sarah steered her toward the exit. "Well, you're going to get a nice nap soon enough."

A wave of euphoria wafted over Annie as Sarah guided her out to the car and opened the rear door.

"You might feel better if you lay down in the back," Sarah said.

"Okay." All at once, Annie's legs gave out and she felt herself collapsing to the sidewalk. Sarah held her up under one arm.

A stronger hand grasped her other arm. "Got ya," a familiar voice said.

Annie turned to the source. "Tyler? What are you doing here?"

As if in a fog, she felt Tyler and Sarah lift her up and lay her in the back of Sarah's car. She looked at Tyler's face, all fuzzy. "Wha's goin on?"

"Nothing," Tyler said.

Muffled voices on the periphery, then Sarah's, as if talking to someone through fluffy cotton, "It's okay. Pregnant girl here got a little woozy. We've got it. Thank you."

Next, oblivion.

CHAPTER SEVENTY-SIX

As many nights during her marriage that Bridget had slept alone on the king-sized mattress, it had never seemed so empty as it did Christmas night.

Two days ago, she had banned Marshall from her bed. Now? Be careful what you wish for? Bridget had never imagined that a person could feel both the pain of loss and the euphoria of freedom all at once. Exhausted to the last neuron in her brain, she had still failed to sleep more than thirty minutes at a time.

After the discomfiting interview at the hospital with the State Police, she had contacted Dr. Pittman, who confirmed that Marshall was clinically dead when Bridget pulled the plug on his ventilator.

"Can't kill someone who's already dead," Pittman had told the agents. "I left him on life support only to allow his family time to accept the situation and say their goodbyes."

Bridget had apologized for pulling the plug. "It was an impulse. How I said goodbye."

Although the agents had seemed frustrated, they deferred to Dr. Pittman's and Bridget's explanations.

"Only because they realize they have no case," Zack had said.

Bridget had sent Zack and his daughters home after she begged off on his invitation for a quick dinner respite away from the hospital. She had turned instead to the post-mortem details and minutiae. Funeral home decision, collecting Marshall's clothing and personal effects to take home, signing an obscene number of official papers, and—most important—consoling Dustin and Grant.

She had stood by while Grant called his mother, then spoke to the woman herself. Marshall's ex-wife showed no signs of the animosity Bridget had suffered since she had been the proximate cause of the first Hilliard marriage's break-up.

"Of course, you can come. Grant needs you here." In an odd sense, Bridget did too. "We can collaborate on funeral plans and such. Come as soon as you'd like."

Once they got home from the hospital, Bridget called Marshall's immediate family, an older sister and younger brother. The latter volunteered to break the news to Marshall's ninety-year-old mother who lived in a nursing home in Boston.

Bridget, Dustin, and Grant had stayed up past midnight, reminiscing about Marshall, planning his memorial, or else staring into space or scrolling on phones; whichever provided the easiest distraction from grief. After two double doses of Fiona's gifted Aberlour single-malt scotch, Bridget started to nod off. She bade the boys good night and went to bed where the combined emotions and the alcohol spun her mind like a top.

Just before dawn, sporadic episodes of fitful sleep gave way to deep, dreamless slumber.

The ringing of the front doorbell roused Bridget. The bedside clock read 8 AM. She started to struggle out of bed when she heard Grant come out of the guest room and clomp down the stairs. She rolled over and faced away from the bedroom door, trusting Grant to send whoever it was away.

Could it be Zack? She remembered that Zack and Jenn had morning meetings at Bethesda Metro Hospital, so not him.

Grant appeared at her door. "That State Police guy is here with some detective. They want to talk to you. I asked them to come back later, but they insisted on speaking to you now."

What? I thought we were done with them.

Ten minutes later, after brushing her teeth, combing her hair, and donning sweats, Bridget went downstairs. The State Police officer sat on the sofa typing on a phone. A forty-something woman wearing a dark blue business suit wandered around the room. She studied family photos on the wall and memorabilia on the credenza.

The officer stood and the woman turned when Bridget descended the stairs. The man greeted Bridget, then gestured to the woman, who showed Bridget her badge.

"Sorry to get you up, Ms. Larsen. I'm Detective Kate Melrose from the Alexandria Police Department."

Bridget scowled. "What's this about?" Although the polite gesture would be to ask the visitors to sit, Bridge remained standing. She looked back and forth between them, wondering who would take the lead.

Detective Melrose broke the ice. "Sorry for the loss of your husband."

"Thank you."

Not exactly overflowing with empathy there, detective.

Bridget folded her arms. "You two didn't come here at this hour of the morning on the day after Christmas to express your sympathy, so why don't you cut to the chase." She offered a smile that she hoped looked genuine. "I suppose you know I'm a lawyer."

"Yes, ma'am," the detective said. "May we sit?"

"Sure."

Bridget motioned them to the couch and took a seat in the opposite chair. She sensed Grant hovering at the top of the stairs but didn't acknowledge his presence. A witness to the conversation, however biased, might become useful.

Detective Melrose rolled right into the point. "We understand your husband died from a brain hemorrhage."

"That's what the doctors told us." Bridget gestured to the officer. "This gentleman was there. I'm sure he heard the same as I did."

The man nodded but said nothing.

The detective continued. "Mr. Hilliard's blood clotting mechanism was impaired by, uh,"—She looked at her notepad—"excessive anticoagulant medication, often referred to as 'blood thinner'?"

Wary of where the conversation was headed, Bridget chose her words with care. "The doctors would know more about that than I."

"Right," the detective said. "We've spoken to, uh, Dr. Anderson at the hospital. She said his usual blood thinner, anticoagulant, Xarelto, had been taken as prescribed."

"Seems right, from what I remember. It was a pretty tense time."

"Yes, I'm sure it was. Again, sorry for what you went through."

Bridget waved off the sentiment. "Where are you going with this, detective?" She glanced at the State Police officer. He avoided eye contact.

The detective regarded Bridget with a pinched expression. "I'm getting there, ma'am. The doctor said that an excessive amount of a different blood thinner, called Coumadin or warfarin, caused the abnormal coagulation levels. As a result, your husband couldn't form a clot to keep from bleeding into his brain."

Bridget nodded. "Something like that. Again, I'm not a doctor."

Detective Melrose put down her notebook. "Ms. Larsen, do you know where or how your husband ingested an overdose of Coumadin?"

"I don't know that he did or didn't."

"Could he have attempted suicide with a deliberate overdose of Coumadin?"

Bridget scoffed. "Never."

The detective squinted. "How else would it happen?"

"I don't know. I didn't know he had Coumadin. I don't keep track of his medications."

"Your stepson, uh, Grant Hilliard, found it in Mr. Hilliard's medicine cabinet, right?"

"That's what I understand."

"Other than your husband, you, your son, or stepson, no one else had access to your husband's medicine cabinet?"

"I wouldn't think so."

The detective tilted her head. "Could he have taken an overdose by accident?"

"I have no idea."

The detective closed her notebook. "Thank you, Ms. Larsen. We may have more questions later." She stood. "May we talk to your stepson? Your son?"

Bridget huffed. "Yes, but you'll need to come back later. They're both asleep, and I don't want to wake them." She paused for effect. "They just lost their father."

The detective looked toward the stairs and raised an eyebrow. "Fine. Maybe later today?" She checked her watch. "Would noon be okay?"

No sense in putting them off or they will become more aggressive. We have nothing to hide.

"Okay."

"Thank you, ma'am. We'll want to talk to them separately."

"Of course," Bridget said. She stood and directed the man and woman toward the door.

Each handed her a business card. "Okay," Detective Melrose said. "We'll see you all at noon."

"We'll be here," Bridget said. She found it odd that the State Police officer had not spoken during the conversation.

At the front door, Melrose turned to Bridget. "One other thing, if I may, ma'am?"

Bridget shrugged.

"After he announced his candidacy for Attorney General on the afternoon of Christmas Eve, was Mr. Hilliard with anyone other than you, your son, or stepson?"

Bridget blinked. "No. I was at his announcement, then attended a little reception in his office right after. Then we came home."

"You went straight home and stayed home?"

"The boys went out. Marshall and I had dinner, a few drinks, then . . . he collapsed."

The detective stroked her chin. "Were you and your husband on good terms?"

Bridget's eyes narrowed. "What are you asking?"

"Did you and your husband have a fight?"

Bridget opened the door and nodded toward the outside. "Good day, detective."

The man and woman stepped out. Before Bridget could close the door, Detective Melrose turned to her. "I'm sorry," she said. "I almost forgot. One more question."

Bridget huffed. "What?"

"Is it true you pulled the plug on your husband's life support?"

Bridget closed the door.

Grant came down the stairs.

"You heard?" Bridget asked.

"Most of it." Grant glanced away. "We'll have to talk to them, Dustin and I?"

"Yes, but no reason to worry. Just tell them the truth. They're doing their job. Your father was a prominent politician, so they need to show 'due diligence.'"

Grant stared at the floor, lips pursed.

"Is there something you need to say, Grant?"

He let out a breath and looked at Bridget with fear in his eyes. "That, uh, empty Coumadin container?"

"Yes?"

"I didn't find it in dad's medicine cabinet."

"Where was it?"

"The wastebasket in your bathroom."

CHAPTER SEVENTY-SEVEN

The interval since Zack, Bridget, and Jennifer had met Eric Wolfe for Dr. Gibson's autopsy seemed more like two months than two days. Longer time had passed since Zack had looked in on Nate Young the day he ran into Sebastian Barth.

"When we're done with Eric we can go up to ICU and check on Nate Young," he said to Jennifer.

"Of course, Dad." She eyed him. "I'm guessing you didn't invite Bridget to join us."

Zack recalled his intention to include Bridget in the discussion with Eric Wolfe. Before her world crumbled. "No. Didn't call her. She'll have enough on her plate today."

"We'll see her and the boys at dinner anyway."

"Yes."

They walked into Eric Wolfe's office next to the morgue. Zack offered profuse apologies for their tardiness.

Eric huffed. "Not much going on here the day after Christmas. Other than the four bodies of people who didn't make it through the holidays."

Jennifer did a double-take. "Four?"

"That's a slow day, Doctor Jenn. We've had as many as ten, but only when Christmas came with a three-day weekend."

"That's sad," she said.

"Sad but not surprising," Eric said. "People over-indulge, drive like maniacs, take risks over the holidays they wouldn't consider in normal times. Family disputes tend to surface then too." He smirked. "'Tis the season."

The reference to over-indulgence drew Zack's thoughts to Marshall Hilliard. Had over-indulgence precipitated his sudden cerebral hemorrhage?

Eric beckoned them to sit at a small conference table. Short stacks of documents related to the late Dr. Gibson were set at each place. One seat remained empty.

"I'm sorry about your lawyer friend," Eric said to Zack. "I liked her a lot."

Zack scrunched his eyebrows. "She's still around, Eric. Her husband died, not she."

Eric stared into space. "Yeah, well, it will change her. Always does."

Zack would not allow himself to entertain that thought. He fingered the papers in front of him. "So, about Dr. Gibson."

Eric gestured toward the papers. "The preliminary tox results tell a story, albeit not complete."

"You mentioned the undetermined opioid. And needle tracks between the toes."

"Yeah, fortunately, we still had the body in the fridge when we got the first tox report. Definite needle tracks. Can't believe I didn't look when we did the autopsy."

"Who would?" Zack said.

Eric shrugged. "No one. You can bet I will from now on."

Jennifer raised a hand.

"You don't need to ask permission to speak, Dr. Jenn," Eric said. "Just jump in. Don't let two old guys intimidate you."

Jennifer smiled. "During the autopsy we found no signs of trauma, nothing to suggest the doctor was incapacitated, right?"

"Correct," Eric said.

"Does that mean he self-administered the opioid?"

"Therein lies the mystery, Dr. Jenn. Why does a young emergency physician, with no apparent history of drug abuse, overdose himself via a route commonly used by drug addicts? With no other evidence of IV drug use?"

He eyed Zack. "We know ER docs are a shifty bunch, given to self-indulgence and all, but self-inflicted narcotic overdose is a tough hypothesis to accept without additional data."

Zack turned to Jennifer. "As a pathologist who never sees live patients in distress, Dr. Wolfe has the luxury of seeking additional data." He looked at Eric. "We do have other commitments today, so if you could cut to the bottom line . . ."

"Always in a rush, Zack." He winked at Jennifer. "Typical hair-on-fire ER doc." He turned back to Zack. "What if I tell you I sent a hair sample to the tox lab?"

"You're looking for a drug not tested on a routine tox screen; a substance possibly used to incapacitate Dr. Gibson before the fatal dose of opioid."

"Bingo. My instinct tells me we're looking at a criminal case here."

Jennifer said, "Is there a criminal investigation going on?"

Eric nodded. "The ER nurse found him dead in the sleep room in the middle of a shift. Those circumstances alone trigger an investigation."

"In which the nurse is a suspect, right?" Zack asked.

"That's possible," Eric said. "Maybe he ingested something to knock him out first, then the killer finished him off with an IV injection between the toes."

"How long till you get the results?" Jennifer asked.

"A week. Maybe longer if they have a backlog from the holiday."

"Any guess about the substance?" Zack asked.

Eric shrugged. "Sedative, hypnotic for the takedown, ingested or inhaled. Hence the absence of trauma. Designer opiate for the kill."

"Can you be more specific?"

"What's it worth if I make a wild guess that turns out right?"

Zack huffed. "Box seats, behind home plate, for the first three-game weekend series with the Dodgers."

"I'll take that bet. True confession, and you'll still owe me if I'm right, but I've seen some recent journal articles implicating roofies in similar cases of unexplained incapacitation."

Jennifer's eyes widened. "Roofies? Date-rape drugs?"

Eric puffed up. "I predict the tox test will come back positive for rohypnol and carfentanyl."

CHAPTER SEVENTY-EIGHT

After their meeting with Eric Wolfe, Zack and Jennifer looked in on Nate Young in the ICU. He remained in medical coma. No way to assess his neurological status.

Jerry Hartman joined them at Nate's bedside.

"How long do you plan to keep him down?" Zack spoke in a professional, detached voice.

Jerry smiled. "How diplomatic of you, Zack." He looked at Jennifer. "Your presence seems to bring out the best in your dad. He's usually a 'straight in, no waiting' guy."

"Let's talk," Jerry said. He retrieved the tablet that contained Nate's records and led Zack and Jenn to a small conference room. When they were all seated, he looked at Jennifer.

"So, Dr. Winston Junior, what do you think we should do?"

Jennifer sat back. "I'm not qualified to—"

"Sure, you are," Jerry said. "What if he were your boyfriend, girlfriend, or spouse." He glanced at Zack. "Or your father?"

Jennifer spoke without hesitating. "I'd want to know if he's ever going to wake up."

Zack beamed. "Me too."

"I didn't ask you, Zack, but thanks for your input."

Zack scowled at him, with a hint of a smile at the corners of his mouth.

"Okay, I'll make it unanimous," Jerry said. "We'll start a slow withdrawal of the sedative-hypnotic and see how he does. If he doesn't do well physiologically, we'll have to put him down again."

"You can't keep him in coma forever," Zack said.

Jerry shrugged. "I know, but it's still early in the game. If waking him up doesn't go well, we can let him rest a few more days then try again."

"Sounds fair," Zack said.

Jerry started to get up. "Okay. I'll keep you posted."

Zack motioned him to sit back down.

"One other thing. The tox screen. Did you add anything to the routine one we sent from the ER, or the specific test for carfentanyl?"

Jerry looked puzzled. "No. Why?"

Zack glanced at Jennifer. "We're working another case. Similar, except the doctor is dead."

"Doctor?"

Zack briefed Jerry about Dr. Jeff Gibson. "Eric believes he was incapacitated first, before the opioid. He suspects something like rohypnol, then dosed with something like carfentanyl."

Jerry folded his arms and let out a long breath. "That's . . . fantastic enough to have some merit. What do we need?"

"Send hair and urine to the outside lab," Zack said. "It will take a week or so to get results."

Jerry picked up the tablet and tapped on it with a stylus. "Done."

As they headed out of the hospital, Zack turned to Jennifer.

"Any word from your sister?"

"No, but I wouldn't expect it. She's not used to reporting her whereabouts."

Zack scowled. "Do a dad a favor and call or text her, just to get an update."

Jennifer smiled. "She won't like us checking up on her."

"Not hers to like or dislike."

They continued walking while Jennifer texted Annie.

Zack's phone buzzed. Bridget.

"How are you, Bridge? You and the boys survive the night okay?"

Silence.

Immediate concern gripped Zack. "What's going on?"

Her voice sounded stressed. "Maybe nothing. That State Police guy and an Alexandria detective showed up at our door this morning. The detective asked pointed questions about Marshall's Coumadin and what he and I did since his announcement on Christmas Eve."

Zack and Jenn had reached the parking lot. Zack paused a second to unlock his car. "What do you make of that, Bridge?"

"Don't know. I thought you might have an idea."

"No clue."

He and Jennifer got into the car and he started the ignition. "Jenn and I are just leaving the hospital. Could you use a visit? We can pick up lunch on the way."

"The detectives are coming back at noon to talk to Grant and Dustin."

Zack's head buzzed. "Why?"

"Don't know. Probably just due diligence."

"Yeah. Probably." He paused. "The offer to bring food still stands. We can be gone when your detectives return."

"Okay, Zack. We would like that. Your choice on the food, and no need to rush to leave because of a couple of detectives. If you're still here when they come, they can deal with it."

"You got it. We're still on for dinner this evening, right?"

"You're too kind, Zack."

Zack clicked off the call and drove out of the parking lot. He turned to Jennifer. "How's Annie?"

Jennifer smiled. "She actually texted back. She and Sarah are at Bethesda Row, just getting started on shopping. They stopped at a Starbucks first."

CHAPTER SEVENTY-NINE

A firm grip on her shoulder awakened Emily from nightmare-haunted sleep.

"Wake up, Em. Almost showtime." Dr. Good's voice was soft but stern.

She opened her eyes. Somehow, she had moved from laying on her back to her right side. Dr. Good leaned over her and smiled. She tried to roll away from him, but both hands were tied to a single bed post. She blinked to clear the fog in her brain. For sure she had fallen asleep on her back, each hand tied to opposite bed posts.

Good stroked her hair. "I couldn't leave you on your back all night. What if you vomited and aspirated? You could have died. I would never get over losing you."

Emily remembered nothing after being tied supine to the bed.

Good smiled. "You don't remember, of course. We gave you a little hair of the dog that bit me yesterday."

Emily shook her head. What was he talking about? What had happened overnight?

He chuckled. "Rohypnol. Sub-therapeutic dose after you spit some of it in my face."

Emily remembered that part. She gave him a sarcastic smile. "You're welcome."

The door opened and footsteps entered the room.

Spider?

A woman's voice. "Ready."

Dr. Good untied Emily's hands. She turned over in the bed and recognized the woman called Nan, whom she'd seen only the one time before. Spider entered behind her.

"Get her cleaned up and bring her to the suite," Dr. Good said. "Give her something to be sure she stays awake." He left the room.

Spider and Nan hauled Emily out of the bed and forced her across the hall to the bathroom. Nan oversaw Emily's every move during the forced shower. Afterward, she directed Emily to put on royal blue surgical scrubs over clean underwear. The growing terror in Emily's heart brought her fully out of the effects of the rohypnol. She felt like a trapped animal, desperate to spring loose and run.

Better to violate her captors, then run.

They proceeded single-file—Nan in front, Spider behind Emily—down the stairs and into the narrow hallway that led to the locked door of Dr. Good's private place in the secured add-on wing of The Good House. The place where Emily had never been allowed before now.

Her worst fear was that it was the place where the young women who had given birth went for their final journey; the place from where their bodies were taken after they died at the hands of their captors.

Emily had never seen any of the postpartum women walk out of The Good House.

Nan punched in numbers on the cipher lock, then pushed the door open. Emily stepped back. Spider grabbed both her arms from behind and squeezed, hard.

"Straight ahead, Em." He pushed Emily forward, causing her to stumble over the threshold. She caught herself with a hand against a white-painted wall. They continued into a small alcove facing another cipher-locked door. Metal. Nan unlocked that one, pushed it open, and stepped inside.

Spider pushed Emily through the doorway. She stopped just inside the door, not from fear or desire to escape, but from shock at what she saw. A brightly lit surgical suite.

They stood in a four-by-eight-foot pre-op area. Two scrub-sinks faced a picture window, through which Emily saw a fully equipped operating room. It contained an OR table, large overhead lights, anesthesia machine and related accouterments at the head, a half-dozen IV poles with hanging bags of clear fluid, and a full array of monitoring equipment. She looked across the OR table and equipment to a row of stainless-steel shelves and cabinets that appeared to contain a wide supply of sterilized packs of surgical instruments.

An ultrasound machine and an incubator for newborns stood in the corner.

Emily seethed with anger when she thought of the Spartan converted bedroom upstairs where Dr. Good had used her to assist in delivering the wayward girls with full-term pregnancies. Why had she never been allowed to assist in this space? Now she suspected the real role of the other nurse, Flossie, in Dr. Good's evil enterprise.

She felt sick to her stomach.

Emily brought her attention back to the pre-op area in which she stood. To the left of the scrub sinks, closets and shelves were stocked with surgical gowns, sterile latex gloves, masks, hair coverings, booties, and blue scrub suits. Emily had not seen such a well-stocked operating suite since her surgical rotation in nursing school, years ago.

A door to the right caught her attention. She had not noticed it while her attention was drawn to the OR. It was also made of steel and contained another cipher lock.

That door opened, and Dr. Good stepped through into the pre-op area. He was dressed in a scrub suit of the same royal-blue material as the one Emily wore. A net-like cover like a shower cap encased his semi-bald head. Paper booties enclosed his shoes. He held a surgical mask in his hand.

Emily glared at him. "What's going on, Adam? What is this place?"

"You will know soon enough, Em. For now, please familiarize yourself with the area and supplies. Learn where to retrieve the surgical packs if asked."

Emily stood her ground.

"Get on with it Em. Time is short."

"No." She swept her hand around the area. "Not until you explain all this."

Good snorted, faced her, and stared her down. He grabbed her right arm and squeezed. Hard.

"You will do as you are told. You won't like the consequences if you don't."

Emily pulled away. "No."

Good nodded to Spider.

Before she could resist, Spider and Nan each grabbed an arm and moved her toward the supply shelves. Nan's fingernails dug like claws into the bare flesh beneath the sleeves of Emily's scrub suit. Spider's iron grip squeezed her other arm so hard she thought she would lose circulation to her hand.

Resistance is not conducive to escape.

"Stop." Emily glowered at Dr. Good. "I'll do what you say."

"That's my sweet girl," he said.

CHAPTER EIGHTY

Bridget was just coming out of the shower when the detectives showed up at 11 AM instead of the agreed-upon noon.

Grant tapped on her bathroom door to inform her of their presence.

"Have them wait in the living room," Bridget said. "Don't discuss anything until I get down there."

Ten minutes later, Bridget descended the stairs. She wore a silver-gray Nike jogging suit and had tied her wet hair into a ponytail. She found Grant and Dustin sitting in side chairs facing the couch occupied by the two visitors who had interviewed her earlier. A third person, a man, stood by the fireplace scrutinizing the family photos.

Bridget made a token effort to hide her annoyance. "I'm sorry," she said. "I thought we said noon."

Detective Melrose stood. "Sorry. Unexpected change in plans. We'll do our best to expedite so you can get on with your day." She introduced the new person as Detective Sawyer from the drug diversion unit of the Alexandria Police Department.

Bridget cast Melrose a skeptical eye. "Drug diversion? What's that about?"

"We will share what information we can after we complete these interviews."

"Okay. Please proceed. We are expecting company for lunch." Bridget would appreciate Zack's presence as this uncomfortable process unfolded.

Detective Melrose gestured toward Grant. "We need to conduct these interviews separately. Since Mr. Hilliard here is legally an adult, and you all have no biological or legal relationship, I would like a private place to talk to him. Meanwhile, you can accompany Dustin while my colleagues talk to him."

Bridget looked at Grant. "You don't have to talk to her. You have the right to refuse."

Melrose looked at Grant while gesturing toward Bridget. "She neglected to tell you that we could compel you to talk to us at the police station."

Bridget moved toward detective Melrose. "Please don't threaten my stepson."

Grant stepped between them. "It's okay, Bridget. I don't mind talking to her."

Bridget directed Melrose and Grant to her home office, then sat in the living room with Dustin for his interview with Detective Sawyer and the State Police officer. In response to the questions, Dustin related that he had not gone into his parents' bathrooms with Grant but had waited downstairs. He didn't feel comfortable invading his parents' private domain. He said that when Grant came downstairs, he had some pill containers in his hand. They went to the kitchen, placed the containers in a plastic bag, then returned to the hospital.

The detective turned to Bridget. "You and your husband have separate bathrooms?"

She shrugged. "Yes."

The detective looked back at Dustin. "Did Grant tell you where he found the pill containers?"

"No."

After the short interview with Dustin, Bridget and their visitors sat in quiet discomfort until Detective Melrose and Grant returned to the living room. The detective asked to confer in private with her colleagues, for which Bridget directed them to the kitchen.

Less than ten minutes later, they returned with grim looks on their faces. The State Police officer moved behind Bridget as Detective Melrose approached her. Detective Sawyer stood next to Bridget.

Detective Melrose looked Bridget in the eye. "Bridget Larsen Hilliard I am arresting you on suspicion of the murder of Marshall Hilliard."

Bridget gasped. "You can't be serious."

Melrose nodded to the State Police officer who moved closer to Bridget. "Place your hands behind your back, please, ma'am."

Her mouth agape, Bridget did as directed. She glanced at Grant and Dustin.

Grant stared at the floor. Dustin appeared shocked.

"Don't worry," Bridget said. "This is a mistake."

While the State Police officer cuffed Bridget's hands behind her back, Detective Melrose read her the Miranda rights.

Bridget swallowed hard. "Yes, whatever."

Melrose led the way toward the front door while the officer and detective flanked Bridget.

The doorbell rang. Detective Melrose opened it. Zack and Jennifer Winston stood on the other side.

A shocked look propagated over Zack's face. Disbelieving eyes met Bridget's.

"Bridget, what the hell?"

CHAPTER EIGHTY-ONE

Zack glared at the woman who had opened the door. She stood between him and Bridget, who was flanked by the familiar state police officer on one side and a woman on the other side.

Behind Bridget, Grant and Dustin stared in disbelief.

Only then did Zack recognize that Bridget's hands were cuffed behind her back.

"Hello?" he said to the woman who had opened the door. "Who are you?"

The woman showed a badge. "Detective Kate Melrose, Alexandria Police Department. This is Detective Sawyer from Alexandria PD. The other gentleman is Officer Lansky from the Virginia State Police."

Zack made a clumsy nod to Officer Lansky. "We meet again."

Detective Melrose looked at Zack. "And you are . . . ?"

"Doctor Zack Wilson. This is my daughter, Jennifer." He stepped toward Detective Melrose. "What is going on here?"

"Chill, Zack," Bridget said. She shrugged. "These folks seem to believe I had something to do with Marshall's death."

"That's insane," Zack said.

Detective Melrose took a step forward. "If you will excuse us, please, Doctor, we need to escort Mrs. Hilliard to the police headquarters."

Zack stood his ground.

Bridget offered him a wan smile. "It's okay, Zack. We need to let these folks do their job and allow due process to take its course." She shrugged. "I'm sorry, but we'll have to postpone lunch. Get together for dinner as planned." She glared at Detective Melrose. "I expect to be available by then. For now, please just do what they ask."

Jennifer had already stepped to the side of the porch, out of the way. Zack joined her. He watched as the trio of officials led Bridget to a waiting vehicle, turned her around, and helped her into the rear seat of the vehicle.

Bridget glanced back at Zack and winked.

Zack shouted. "We are all coming with you."

Five minutes later, Zack drove Jennifer, Grant, and Dustin the short distance to the Alexandria City Police Department. When they arrived and parked, Zack shut off the ignition and turned to Jennifer. "Call your sister. Tell her she needs to change her plans and catch up with us. See if Sarah can drop her off here."

Jennifer hesitated. "What's she going to do here, Dad?"

Zack looked at her, pondering. She had a point. He'd already forced her to endure a day in the hospital yesterday. What difference would a few hours make?

He nodded. "Yeah, you're right. Just text and remind her she has to join us for dinner. Even if Bridget's, uh, detained, we'll still have dinner as a family." He paused. "Without Sarah."

Jennifer's thumbs flew over her phone screen. "Done."

A strange sense of foreboding crept up Zack's spine. He shook it off, opened his door, got out, and beckoned to the others.

"Let's go."

CHAPTER EIGHTY-TWO

Annie's head rested on Tyler's lap. Her mind felt encased in clear gelatin, or like she was watching herself through a fogged video lens.

Tyler stroked the hair alongside her temple. His gentle touch reassured her. Waves of sleepiness washed over her. She closed her eyes and dreamed.

Her dad and Jennifer looked at her with blissful expressions.

"I'm so proud of you, Annie," Dad said.

"Way to go, sis," Jennifer said.

Annie fell into a deeper sleep, dreaming she was on a boat rocking in gentle waters like a cradle. A baby was in the cradle with her; a sweet, ruddy, flawless baby. Her baby. She smiled and giggled at the newborn miracle.

Conner appeared in front of her. "Our baby."

Annie trembled and pulled back. The boat lurched from side to side. "Not yours. Never."

Conner raised an arm in protest. Tyler appeared. His strong arm swept Conner away. Tyler put that same arm around Annie and cooed in her ear. "Our baby. Our precious baby."

Annie's father pulled Tyler off her with such force that the boat capsized.

Alone, sinking in the water, Annie reached out. For Tyler. For her dad. Her mother.

No one was there. Annie drifted alone in a raging current. She tried to move her arms to swim, but they lay paralyzed at her side. She cried out for her mother, her father, Jenn, and Tyler. No one came. She would drown in the next few minutes.

The sea calmed. Annie could spread her arms and legs and lay on her back in slow, undulating water. She closed her eyes and floated in absolute peace. Her breathing deepened as she relaxed and allowed her body to move with the gentle waves. She could stay this way forever.

Never imagined such peace.

"Annie."

The voice caused her to open her eyes. Sarah hovered above her, dressed in a flowing white gown like a beautiful angel. Next to Sarah, Tyler wore a brilliant white suit over a white shirt and tie. His hair was golden.

Sarah's voice. "We're here, Annie. Tyler and I will help you get out."

Tyler grasped under her arms and gently pulled her backward, out of the receding water. Sarah wrapped an arm around Annie's torso.

The two angels pulled her from the water. They flanked her and led her to a beautiful white castle with marble steps leading to a porch with splendid white columns. Once on the porch, they laid her onto a magnificent open carriage and whisked her into the castle.

The carriage turned down a golden corridor and stopped at a gilded door. Sarah opened the door and Tyler wheeled the carriage through an emerald alcove into a brilliant white room. He and Sarah lifted her from the carriage onto a grand bed with a soft down mattress and shimmering sheets.

A sudden harsh light forced her to open her eyes. She stared into the powerful lens of a floodlight. Annie looked around and gasped. She was not in a gorgeous room, not on a soft eiderdown bed, not in any sort of castle. This place looked sterile, steel, cold, and ominous. Terrified, she started to get up, but could not move her legs, arms, or torso. She was strapped to a hard, narrow bed.

Annie tried to scream, but she could not find her voice. She moved her head from side to side, searching for Sarah or Tyler. She thought she saw Sarah, but it was an older woman. Not Sarah.

The woman stepped aside and a man appeared. Bushy brown eyebrows looked grotesque between a gauze shower cap and a white face covering. His eyes twinkled, but not in a merry way. His gaze penetrated Annie's soul.

"Hello, Annie Winston. I'm Dr. Good. I've been waiting for you."

Annie screamed and struggled against the restraints.

The man who called himself Dr. Good looked across Annie's bed.

"Ketamine and Fentanyl cocktail, please, Emily."

Annie turned to see a woman dressed the same as Dr. Good, but she had kind eyes. In her hand, was a syringe. She patted Annie's hand, and for the first time, Annie noticed plastic tubing connected to a needle in her wrist. She drew her hand away.

Gentle and reassuring, the woman touched Annie's hand. "I'm Emily, your special nurse." She looked across Annie in the direction of Dr. Good. Her facial expression turned to stone. "I won't let anything or anyone harm you." The kind nurse injected the syringe into the tubing connected to Annie's hand.

In seconds, all went blank.

CHAPTER EIGHTY-THREE

Zack, Jennifer, Grant, and Dustin sat in the waiting area of the Alexandria Police Department. The officer at the reception desk had refused to tell them anything except that Bridget had been detained pending the arrival of her lawyer. The officer had politely suggested that Zack and the others depart and "be about your business."

Zack had given a curt reply. "Right now, this is our business, for all of us."

After about a half-hour, a fifty-something portly man with dark hair and graying temples, wearing a gray business suit, entered the area and went straight to the reception. His manner was authoritarian but not overbearing.

"Norman Jones, attorney for Bridget Larsen."

The officer scanned his book, puzzled. "I have only a Bridget Hilliard."

Norman Jones huffed. "That's her."

Zack intercepted the attorney. "I'm Dr. Zack Winston, Bridget's friend." He pointed at Dustin and Grant. "Her son and stepson."

Jones shook Zack's hand. "I'll let her know you all are here."

"What's going on?" Zack asked.

The attorney offered a confident smile. "Wait here. We won't be long, I assure you."

True to his word, Norman Jones returned a half-hour later with Bridget, two police officers, and Detective Melrose.

Bridget rushed to Dustin and Grant and hugged them. Then she hugged Zack and Jennifer.

Zack looked her in the eye. "What's up?"

She shook her head. "Not here. Can you drive me home, please?"

"Of course."

As they started to leave, Detective Melrose approached Zack.

"Dr. Winston, right?"

"Yes."

"We'd like to talk to you."

"Now?"

"If you don't mind. Voluntary, of course."

"Then I voluntarily decline. I'm taking Ms. Larsen and her boys home."

Melrose folded her arms. "Very well." She gave Zack a piercing look. "We'll be in touch. Soon."

"You do that." Zack turned and led Bridget and the others out the door.

Jennifer asked, "What was that about, Dad?"

Zack spread his arms. "Haven't a clue."

"I do," Bridget said. "But not here." She turned to her lawyer. "Thanks again, Norm."

"I'll see you tomorrow," the attorney said. His brow furrowed. "You're not out of the woods on this."

"Yeah, I am."

The lawyer smiled, shook his head, and walked away.

Twenty minutes later, Zack and Bridget sipped coffee in her living room. They had sent the younger crowd for fast food, since the items he and Jennifer had brought earlier no longer appealed.

Zack put down his coffee and leaned forward. "Fill me in, please."

Bridget took a breath. "In short, the detectives suspect I poisoned Marshall with Coumadin. They questioned me in the presence of my lawyer, who told them after fifteen minutes that they don't have enough evidence to hold me. They had to release me."

Zack fumed. "Of course, they don't have the evidence because you didn't do it. Any clown can see that."

Bridget huffed. "The circumstances don't help."

Zack frowned. "How so?"

"To begin with, the boys and I were the only ones with Marsh between his big announcement and his collapse. That's called opportunity. Second, Marsh and I had an ugly fight over his infidelity with Fiona. That's motive. Third, Grant found the empty Coumadin bottle in my wastebasket. That's means."

Zack shook his head. "As you said, circumstantial."

"Right. They can't connect me with the Coumadin or the time that Marshall consumed it."

"Could have been a suicide attempt."

Bridget rubbed her forehead. "Except Marshall Hilliard has—had—too much self-regard to do that, least of all right after he got onto the path to his dream of becoming Governor of the Commonwealth."

"Reasonable doubt."

"Why I'm here and not in jail. Doesn't mean they won't keep trying. They're under a lot of pressure from higher-ups, and they don't have any other hypothesis."

Zack furrowed his brow. "Why do they want to talk to me?"

"Most obvious reason, they want to connect you to the Coumadin to me."

Zack huffed. "More motive? Secret lover physician acquires the means to eliminate his rival."

"That's my guess," Bridget said. "Would make you an accessory to murder."

"We know the truth."

"Do we? We know we didn't do it. Any clues to who did? Recall there was no prescription label on the Coumadin bottle."

Zack thought a minute. "If we could get a look at his medical record . . ."

"I won't violate HIPAA, Zack, and neither will you. We don't want to avoid being charged with Marshall's murder only to be put away for a HIPAA violation."

Zack shrugged. "Yeah."

They sat in silence for a few moments before Bridget spoke. "As much as I don't want to believe it, Marshall committing suicide starts to make the most sense."

"Maybe you mean it makes the best defense?"

Bridget scrunched her lips. "Yeah."

Zack's phone buzzed in his pocket. He yanked it out. Caller ID indicated Jerry Hartman.

"Jerry, what's up?"

"Nate Young is awake and talking."

"He's intubated."

"Was. He pulled out the tube as soon as he was lucid enough to do so." A pause. "I don't know how well he'll do off the vent, so if you have any unfinished business with him now's the time."

Zack's heart leaped into his throat. "On my way."

He filled Bridget in, then headed to the door. A thought struck him, and he turned back to her. "I'll have to look it up, but I'm pretty sure that the peak action for Coumadin is thirty-six to seventy-two hours after ingestion."

Bridget smiled. "If that's true . . ."

"Marshall would have taken it before his candidacy announcement."

Bridget hugged him. "I love you, Zack. Thanks." She stepped back, chagrined. "Sorry, I meant . . ."

"Got it."

She ushered him to the door.

CHAPTER EIGHTY-FOUR

Near the head of the operating table, Emily scanned Annie Winston's vital signs on the monitor screen. All looked good. Emily's surgical mask obscured the disgust on her face when she cast furtive looks at Dr. Good and Flossie conducting a procedure Emily had never dreamed possible.

Dressed similar to Emily in blue surgical scrubs, cap, mask, and booties, Flossie operated the ultrasound machine that showed on its screen Annie's uterus in the early stages of pregnancy. Dr. Good, gowned, masked, and gloved, sat between Annie's legs spread apart with her feet in obstetrical stirrups. He inserted a slim probe through Annie's vagina. Emily watched in awe as the tip of the probe appeared on the ultrasound, directed toward the bubble-like image that was Annie's embryo. Emily recognized the technique for implanting a donated embryo from in-vitro fertilization into a recipient's uterus. She had never seen nor heard of the opposite procedure, least of all in an uninformed, non-consenting, underage donor.

Adam Good was stealing Annie Winston's embryo.

Emily worried about her own competence to monitor her patient through the semi-anesthetized state known as procedural sedation, also called twilight sleep. Her previous patients at The Good House had been full-term pregnancies who delivered in the usual way, always awake. Emily had no experience with deep sedation, and she had heard tales of sometimes dangerous reactions and bizarre drugged behavior from the recipients.

Annie was not unconscious, but the cocktail of drugs Emily had pushed on Dr. Good's command into her bloodstream via the IV line kept her in a deep sleep. She could not feel or react to the manipulations that Dr. Good performed. When she awoke, Annie would have no memory of what was done to her.

Emily intended to remember for as long as it took to avenge Annie.

In addition to her ultrasound duties, Flossie kept intermittent watch on Emily, scrutinizing her every move. "Watch her blood pressure, Em," Flossie said. "It's dropped a bit."

Dr. Good looked over the girl's abdomen at Emily. "Almost done here. You can lighten her up a bit."

Emily reached for the tubing that ran from one of the IV bags into a Y-connector to a single tubing that ran sedative and narcotic medications into Annie's blood stream.

"Reduce the Fentanyl flow," Flossie said. "That should improve her blood pressure."

Dr. Good's eyes glared over his surgical mask at Emily. "Don't screw up or you'll have this nice girl's death on your soul."

Emily glared back at Dr. Good, but he didn't see her hateful gaze. He had focused back on his task.

"Transfer container," he said to Flossie.

Flossie shut down the ultrasound machine and retrieved a vial filled with clear viscous liquid. Dr. Good's right hand emerged from between the patient's legs, holding a slim suction probe. Tissue that looked like a small clot hung off the tip. Good plunged the instrument into the vial of fluid in Flossie's hand, then released the suction. The tissue dropped into the fluid.

"Get that into the freezer stat," Good said to Flossie. "Confirm temperature is minus thirty Celsius."

"Yes, sir," Flossie said. She hurried out with the vial that now contained Annie's living embryo.

Dr. Good rolled back the stool and stood.

Emily reached to shut off the flow of IV drugs to allow Annie to wake up.

"Don't wake her up."

"I thought you were done, Adam. We need to wake her up, get her vitals and level of consciousness back to normal."

Good looked at Emily, with dispassionate eyes. "Or not. Doesn't matter now. She's a pawn in a larger game. Her part is done."

A chill ran up Emily's spine. Could Good say the same for her now that he didn't need two nurses anymore? Or was this the first of many such procedures?

Good looked past Emily and spoke to someone in a corner of the room. "You're on."

Emily's eyes followed Good's gaze. Roach stood there, looking small next to the steel cabinets. Emily almost choked.

"Yes, sir," Roach said. He looked at Emily. "You're done. I'll take it from there."

Roach went up to Dr. Good. The two spoke in whispered voices.

While they were both distracted, Emily shut off the flow of sedative drugs to Annie's IV. She heard Roach say to Good, "Yes, sir."

Dr. Good left the room in the same direction as Flossie. Roach moved toward Emily and Annie.

Emily stood in front of him. "What are you going to do?"

Roach huffed. "Not your concern."

"You will not harm her."

"Not yours to say."

He tossed his head in the direction where Dr. Good had gone. "I have my orders. You need to stay out of the way, for your own good."

Emily did not move.

Roach reached behind his back and brought out the familiar pistol. He pointed it at Emily's abdomen. "Please don't make me use this on you, Em."

At once terrified, Emily stood aside to allow Roach to approach the table. He put the gun back into his waistband just as Flossie returned to the room.

Roach spoke to Flossie. "Help me get her onto the gurney." He looked at Emily. "You help too."

The three of them moved Annie from the operating table to the gurney. Roach pushed the gurney toward the OR exit.

Emily followed. Flossie grabbed her arm from behind.

Roach turned around to Emily. "You're staying here with Flossie while I, uh, take care of this piece. We'll deal with you next."

Emily pulled her arm away from Flossie and stepped forward. "I'm staying with her anywhere she goes."

Roach pulled the gun and pointed it at Emily.

Sudden movement on the gurney seized the attention of all three of them.

Annie sat up, dazed. Her eyes squinted as she tried to focus. "What's happening?" She looked at Flossie. "Sarah?" She blinked at Emily as if they had never met. Then her eyes shifted to Roach, and she recoiled. "Tyler, what's with that gun?"

CHAPTER EIGHTY-FIVE

Zack rode the elevator up to the ICU at Bethesda Metro Hospital. His knees still shook a bit from his haste to get there when he almost spun out over a patch of ice on George Washington Parkway.

He found Jerry Hartman at the ICU workstation. Jerry shot Zack a concerned look. "Nate's O2 sats have dropped into the low nineties. I need to reintubate him. Soon. I was about to give up on you."

"Traffic," Zack said.

Jerry nodded toward the cubicle where Nate had been since his transfer from Zack's ER four days ago.

Zack entered the cubicle. Yvonne Young looked up from where she'd bent over Nate's face. "Zack. Thank God you're here." She looked at her husband. "He's been asking for you." She squeezed Zack's arm as she left the room. "I'll be right outside."

Nate lay supine on the bed, his eyes closed, breathing labored. Zack looked at the monitor that tracked Nate's physiological parameters. They included a measure of how well he was getting oxygen into his blood stream. Not good enough, despite the face mask delivering 100% oxygen.

If I saw him like this in the ER, I'd intubate him at once.

He approached the bed and nudged Nate's arm. "Nate, it's Zack Winston."

Nate's eyes opened and he turned slightly to bring Zack into view.

Even that slight movement seemed to aggravate his erratic breathing. His eyes blinked several times.

"Winston? Who are you . . . ?" His voice trailed off.

Confused, Zack thought.

Nate focused his eyes on Zack and spoke in a hoarse whisper. "Tried to . . . kill me."

Zack had suspected all along that Nate did not attempt suicide. "Who tried to kill you?"

Nate tried to rub his forehead but stopped halfway when his IV line pulled taut. "Uh, Good."

"Huh? What's good?"

Nate shook his head. His breathing became more labored. "Who." He paused to take a deep breath, closed then opened his eyes. "Doctor. Good."

Zack didn't understand what Nate was trying to say. He touched Nate's hand. "Yes, I'm Dr. Zack Winston. You know me. I hope that's good."

Nate shook his head. "Baby stealer."

"What?"

"Baby seller."

Nate's eyes closed. Zack thought he had passed out. The monitor indicated an accelerating pulse and diminishing oxygen saturation. The man needed immediate intubation.

Zack called out. "We need the crash cart."

Nate's eyelids flipped open, his gaze fixed on Zack. "Wait." He swallowed. "Find. Good House. Girls. Babies." He squeezed Zack's hand.

From behind, Zack heard the arrival of Jerry Hartman and the team with the crash cart.

Zack leaned over Nate to speak into his ear. "Nate, you'll be okay. We need to get you back on the vent now." He gestured to the resuscitation team to take their positions and bring the intubation equipment.

"Go ahead, Zack," Jerry Hartman said. "You're better at it than I am."

"Right," Zack spoke to the ICU team that had brought the crash cart.

"Prepare for rapid sequence intubation." He bent over to speak into Nate's ear. "Nate, we're going to reintubate you now."

Nate whispered to Zack. "I, Dr. Kid." His head slumped to the side. "Sorry."

Hypoxic delirium, Zack thought. He nodded to a nurse, who pushed a sedative into Nate's IV line. Within minutes, they had Nate sedated, paralyzed, intubated, and back on the ventilator. His oxygen saturation and vital signs rapidly improved.

Zack and Jerry watched him for several minutes to assure themselves he was safe.

When they returned to the workstation, Zack said, "Hopefully he didn't kill any more brain cells during that episode."

Jerry gave him a curious look. "What do you mean?"

"He was speaking nonsense. Something about a 'Good House,' selling babies, a Dr. Kid."

Jerry squinted. "Odd, but consistent with hypoxic effect on the brain."

"He also said someone tried to kill him."

Jerry pursed his lips and pondered. "Not so farfetched, given . . ."

"The needle tracks and evidence of sedation and potent opiate."

"Well," Jerry said. "Hopefully, we can get him ready to extubate the proper way. Meanwhile, he's off ECMO, so score one for the good guys."

Zack agreed. "Two steps forward, one step back. Progress nonetheless." He reached out a hand. "Thanks, Jerry."

Jerry shook his hand. "On a happier note, how's it going with your daughters?"

"Nothing like planned." A beat. "Did you know Bridget Larsen's husband died?"

Jerry's mouth dropped open. "I did not. How?"

Zack summarized the events of the last two days regarding Marshall Hilliard's death and the aftermath.

"Sorry to hear all that," Jerry said. "I can't remember the last time I saw a warfarin overdose."

"Ditto," Zack said.

The two men studied each other. Zack said, "Lots of strange stuff happening of late. Nate, Dr. Gibson, the girl who died from DIC, and now Marshall—all from obscure or rare causes."

"Doesn't mean they're related."

Zack's breath quickened. "What do you think of when you hear hoofbeats?"

"Horses, of course."

Zack scoffed. "Sometimes it's zebras. Or wildebeests."

Zack stopped into the ICU waiting room to give Yvonne Young an update on her husband's condition. He was not totally surprised to see her sitting with Montgomery County Police Detective Martinez, whom Zack had met the day Nate came into the ED.

Yvonne sensed Zack's discomfort. "It's okay," she said. "The detective and I have reached a common ground. We both want to know what really happened to Nate."

Zack sighed. "Well, I'm sorry I don't have much substance." He summarized his interaction with Nate, including his bizarre words.

Detective Martinez reacted with unexpected concern. She seemed to weigh her response before she leaned closer to Zack. "I need to speak to you in private."

Zack excused himself, promised to keep in touch with Yvonne, and led the detective to a small conference room down the hall from the ICU.

"You must hold what I'm about to tell you in strictest confidence," the detective said.

"Sure, but what . . . ?"

She raised a hand. "We don't believe Dr. Young tried to commit suicide. Our interest, which includes the FBI and Homeland Security, relates to a suspected conspiracy to capture homeless or runaway women, girls really, in third-trimester pregnancy, keep them prisoner until they deliver, then sell their babies to a foreign interest. To whom and in exchange for what, we don't know."

Zack's eyes narrowed. "That's connected to Dr. Young how?"

"We have only a few facts about this case. One, the lead player goes by the name of Dr. Good. There's also a pediatrician, known as Dr. Kid."

"Nate."

Martinez pursed her lips. "Seems that his words were a confession, not delusions."

Zack stared into empty space. "He said 'Good House.' I didn't know what he meant."

"It's the location of this criminal enterprise. We don't know where."

"Why are you telling me this, Detective?"

She tossed her head. "To enlist your help, in case you become aware of other cases that may be related."

"I already have." Zack told her about the cases that he and Bridget had discussed earlier.

"Thank you, Doctor," the detective said. "They may well be related. Let's stay in touch."

He shook her hand. "Yes, let's."

His phone rang. Jennifer. He excused himself and took the call in the hallway.

"Just got a text from Annie," Jennifer said. "Sarah will drop her off at Bridget's by 4 PM."

"Perfect," Zack said.

Despite his promise to Detective Martinez, Zack shared the information in private with Jerry Hartman. "I figure four sets of eyes and ears are better than two," Zack said.

Jerry shrugged. "Right. Guess we'll keep 'Dr. Kid' intubated for a while too."

"Yes." Zack looked at his watch. "I need to get back to Bridget's before Sarah brings Annie back from shopping."

Jerry's eyebrows peaked. "Sarah?"

"Yeah. Sarah O'Brien. We've been, well, seeing each other for a couple of months. She hit it off with Annie, so they went out for a day of 'retail therapy' this morning."

Jerry's eyes went wide. "Sarah O'Brien lost her nursing license for opioid abuse. That's why she works in utilization review and not a clinical area. She's under investigation by the nursing board and other authorities for allegations of drug diversion." He huffed. "Not someone I'd trust to hang with my daughter all day."

CHAPTER EIGHTY-SIX

Annie rested her head on the pillow, her eyes closed. Was she still dreaming? What happened to her? She had felt woozy when Sarah and Tyler helped her into Sarah's car, then . . . ?

A sharp cramp in her lower abdomen forced her eyes open.

Sarah and another woman wearing blue surgical scrubs watched her. The other woman looked somewhat familiar. From where? Annie looked around. She was laying on a narrow bed in a large living room of a grand house she'd never seen.

"Hello, Annie," the woman in scrubs said. "You're all done."

Annie looked at her, puzzled. "Who are you?"

The woman smiled. "I'm Emily. We met earlier but you may not remember."

Annie recalled meeting Sarah at the Starbucks and the reason for it. But then Tyler? Why had he been there?" She tried to sit up. Pain in her pelvis forced her down. "Where's Tyler?

The two women exchanged looks. "Tyler's not here," Sarah said. "You must have been dreaming."

Annie looked at Sarah with a questioning eye. "I dreamed Tyler had a gun." She looked at the woman named Emily. "You were in the dream too. You were a nurse."

Emily smiled. "I am a nurse. I'm your nurse."

Sarah stroked Annie's hair. "The procedure is all done. Everything went fine." She smiled. "You're not pregnant anymore, Annie."

Annie grimaced and grabbed her lower abdomen. "Ow. Cramps."

Emily grasped her hand. "That's expected after the, uh, procedure. They won't last long. When we get you upstairs to a regular bed, we'll give you something that will help."

Sarah moved to the other side of the narrow bed. She slid her left arm under Annie's shoulders, bent over, and slid her right arm under her knees. With Emily's help, she shifted Annie into a sitting position.

"Do you think you can stand?" Sarah said. "We will help you."

The two women stood on each side of Annie and helped her stand up. They walked her up a flight of stairs in a tandem formation with Emily leading and Sarah behind Annie.

At the top of the stairs, Tyler waited with a wheelchair. "Have a seat, sweetheart." His voice sounded strange.

Emily moved between Annie and Tyler and grabbed the wheelchair. "I won't let you take her, Roach."

Why did she call him Roach?

Tyler grimaced at Emily just as Sarah came up behind her. "You can't stop this, Em."

Emily swung her elbow back hitting Sarah square in the solar plexus. Sarah doubled over in pain. Emily charged at Tyler, but he shoved her aside, sending her sprawling onto the floor. The wheelchair went tumbling down the stairs with a loud crash.

"Run, Annie," Emily shouted. "Run away from here as fast as you can."

Annie took one step toward the stairs before Tyler grabbed her arm and swung her around so that he was holding her from behind with his left arm wrapped around her chest. He had a pistol in his right hand. The same pistol Annie had seen him holding when she first woke up.

It had not been a dream.

Tyler held the muzzle against Annie's head. "I will have to shoot you if you cause more trouble. Please, please don't make me." His voice quivered.

Sarah lurched to where Emily lay sprawled on the floor, grabbed Emily's hair, and pulled her up to a standing position. She wrapped an arm around Emily's neck and looked at Tyler. "How about we take care of them both right now?"

"Stop." A commanding voice came from behind them.

Annie looked around. Her memory cleared; she recognized the man called Dr. Good in the hallway behind them.

He advanced on Tyler and held out his hand. "Give me the gun, Roach." Tyler handed over the pistol without a word. Dr. Good turned to Sarah. "Put her in a room. Stay with her at all times. We wait until dark before the next phase."

Sarah nodded at Emily. "What about her?"

"I'll take care of her, but she has to do some things for me first."

Dr. Good looked at Tyler. "You're on watch here. Expect Spider and Nan to show up soon. Anyone else shows up, call for me."

"Yes, sir."

Dr. Good looked back at Sarah and tossed his head toward the hallway. "Go on. Now."

Sarah hooked her arm under Annie and guided her down the hallway. Annie looked back. Dr. Good tucked the gun in his waistband, took Emily by the arm, and pulled her down the stairs.

CHAPTER EIGHTY-SEVEN

Zack drove from Bethesda back to Alexandria with care to avoid any more spinouts. As he drove, Jerry Hartman's revelation about Sarah's jaded past churned in his mind. What was Sarah's game, and what did it have to do with Annie? And what of Nate Young's ramblings about The Good House, validated by Detective Martinez? He thought about the odd vibes he'd picked up from Annie yesterday and this morning.

By the time he pulled off the Interstate into Bridget's neighborhood, Zack feared his daughter was in trouble. He didn't know what, or where, or from whom?

When he parked in front of Bridget's house, the dashboard clock on his Lexus indicated 4:20 PM. He rushed up the walkway. Bridget and Jenn met him at the front door.

"Annie here?"

Jenn's face became alarmed when she looked at him. "She's late. Traffic maybe?"

"Call her."

Jennifer dialed Annie's number, listened, then scrunched her eyebrows. "Voicemail."

"I'll call Sarah." Zack punched the speed dial for Sarah's number. The call went straight to voicemail. "Didn't even ring," Zack said. "What time did you get the text that they would be here by four?"

"About an hour and a half ago. They were going to shop at Pentagon City Mall before coming here."

"That's twenty minutes away," Bridget said. "Half-hour to forty minutes tops if the traffic's bad."

"Call her again," Zack said to Jennifer.

"Dad, you're scaring me."

Bridget touched his arm. "What's up, Zack?"

"Sarah isn't the person I thought." He summarized what he'd learned at the hospital from Nate Young, Detective Martinez, and Jerry Hartman. "I'm convinced it's all related, and somehow Annie's gotten mixed up in it."

"What do we do, Dad?"

"I don't know." Zack looked at Bridget. "Suggestions?"

She shook her head.

"We should call mom," Jenn said.

"Why?"

"She has an app to track our phones. She installed it a few years ago. I disabled it on my phone." She frowned. "Probably Annie did too."

Zack huffed. "Maybe we should wait a while before we do that."

"Wait for what, Dad?"

"Sarah is never on time. For all we know, she pulled a passive-aggressive and took Annie out to dinner to get back at me for not inviting her tonight."

"Except you just told us she's a fraud," Bridget said.

Jennifer picked up her phone. "I'm calling Mom."

"Go ahead," Zack said.

"I'll make some coffee," Bridget said.

Zack followed her into the kitchen.

She started to make coffee, got a good look at his face, and stopped. "What is it, Zack?"

"I think this may all be related to Marshall's death."

"How?"

"Whoever is behind those deaths, and Nate Young's near-death, has not only knowledge of but access to the drugs involved. Including the rarer ones, carfentanyl and maybe also warfarin."

"And you think Annie has fallen into their clutches."

Zack ran a hand through his hair. "Makes sense. Kill Marshall to get to you, harm or kill Annie to get to me."

Bridget touched his shoulder. "Dennis King is dead, Zack."

"Marshall's task force suspected others, or one other, but they didn't know who."

Motion in the doorway caused Zack and Bridget both to turn in that direction. Jennifer stood there, arms folded.

"Mom didn't answer. I left a voicemail."

Zack let out a deep breath. "Let's hope that by the time she calls back, Annie will have arrived, and we'll all be at dinner."

"I hope you're right, Dad." Jennifer's expression said she didn't believe it.

Bridget finished making the coffee. All three sat in silence at the kitchen table, pondering.

Jennifer's phone buzzed. "Mom." She looked at the screen, did a double-take, and frowned. "Caller ID says unknown."

She answered. "Hello? Who?" A pause as she listened. "Hang on, uh, Conner? I'm putting you on speaker so my dad can hear this too." She looked at Zack as she covered the mouthpiece of the phone. "Some guy says he's Annie's boyfriend in California."

Jennifer placed the phone on the table after putting it on speaker. "Go ahead, Conner."

A voice that conjured up images of a surfer dude or skateboarder filled the air. "Uh, yeah, my name is Conner, Annie's boyfriend. I've been trying to call her all day, but she doesn't answer. Hasn't answered since yesterday. So, I'm, uh, worried. She gave me this phone number for her sister once. So I called it."

Jennifer started to respond but Zack waved her off. "Conner, this is

Annie's dad. Are you saying she didn't answer the phone or respond to texts?"

"Not since yesterday."

Zack looked at Jennifer. "You got texts from her."

Jennifer nodded. "Supposedly. She never answered when I called."

Conner's voice came through the phone speaker. "Can I just talk to Annie's sister?"

Zack huffed. "No, you cannot. If you know something that will help us figure out what's going on with Annie, you need to tell us both right the hell now."

Another long pause before the boy blurted out his response.

"I think she lied to me and is still pregnant."

CHAPTER EIGHTY-EIGHT

Zack sat on Bridget's couch, his head buried in his hands. "I should have seen it. I'm a damned physician. I should have seen it."

Bridget sat next to him, her arm around his shoulder. "It's not your fault, Zack."

He shook his head. "I knew something was going on. I should have seen the signs."

"It's not your fault."

Jennifer sat on the other side of Zack, tears streaming down her face. She took Zack's hand and squeezed it. "You can't blame yourself, Dad. This is the essential Annie. No one controls her. No one knows everything about her, especially what's in her head or what she does."

Zack squeezed back. "Thanks. I do know that. Doesn't help. I'm her father."

"We can't just sit here and mourn," Jennifer said. "Dr. Hartman told you they traffic newborns at that place. According to Conner, Annie is early in her first trimester."

"Maybe they do abortions as a side business," Zack said.

"Or worse," Bridget said.

Zack tilted his head. "What do you mean?"

"Your Detective Martinez described a conspiracy that also involves FBI and Homeland Security. Sound familiar?"

"Marshall's task force," Zack said. He turned to Jennifer. "Marshall's office was conducting an investigation into a deep conspiracy, one with a reach that went well beyond the attempt on my life last year." He pursed his lips. "On the last VTC, Fiona Delaney suggested it's still active. The principal is one Douglas Snyder, whom they believe murdered his wife, Melody, a year ago." He paused. "With a little help from me failing to maintain an airway."

"For which you need to quit beating yourself up," Bridget said.

Zack pondered. "Are you suggesting this is all related, Bridge?"

"It could be. The way these large scale super-secret investigations work, you could be supporting a single component of a multi-pronged, multi-agency affair."

Zack huffed. "Either way, I need to find that Good House. That's where Annie is. Sarah too. I'm sure of it." He worked his fists as he imagined what he would do to Sarah when he found her.

Bridget pointed at him. "First, the investigators have no clue, so how do you propose to find it? Second, if you know where it is, you tell the authorities. You don't go charging in there like Don Quixote."

Zack glared at her. "My daughter, Bridge."

"Both your lives, Zack."

"Doesn't involve you," Zack said.

Jennifer threw up her arms. "You are so clueless, Dad."

Zack stared between the two women. "Fine. Then maybe one of you can figure out how to do something that none of those so-called professional sleuths can do. Find that Good House."

Jennifer smiled. "As I said, Mom has the app that can track our phones. Maybe she can find out where Annie is. If it's that Good House . . ."

Zack interrupted. "Can you enable it on your phone or mine to find Annie's?"

Jennifer shook her head. "Won't help. Only mom has access to the actual tracker."

"Call your mother again."

"Don't be stupid, Zack," Bridget said. She stood between him and her front door.

Zack's ears still stung from the tongue-lashing he'd received from Natalie, but at least he had GPS coordinates to Annie's phone somewhere in the Maryland countryside, nowhere near Pentagon City Mall.

"Stand aside, Bridge."

"No."

"Don't make me push you."

Jennifer grabbed his arm. "You'll have to overcome both of us, Dad."

"My daughter is out there. Your sister."

"You need to call Detective Martinez," Bridget said.

Zack stepped away from the door. "Fine. But then I'm heading out there."

"Not alone, you're not," Bridget said.

Zack stared at her. "Yes, I am."

Bridget and Jenn folded their arms.

"No," Bridget said. "Because if you leave this house alone, I'm calling the police and telling them there's a crazy man on the road who's a danger to himself and others. You won't get out of Alexandria."

Zack huffed. "You are under investigation for murdering your husband, Bridge. You can't leave the state of Virginia."

"Watch me."

Zack's shoulders slumped. "Fine, I'll call Martinez." He pulled out his phone and placed the call.

"Thanks, Doctor," the detective said after Zack told her what he knew. "We've got it." Her voice turned stern. "Don't go there, Dr. Winston. Those people are dangerous."

"Understood," Zack said. "Please keep me informed."

"Of course."

He hung up the phone and handed Bridget his empty coffee cup. "Can I have some more? We could be in for a long night."

She shot him a *Make your own* look, then took his cup to the kitchen.

Zack glanced at Jennifer, who was staring at her phone.

"Be right back," he said. "I left something in my car."

"Dad?"

He gave her a "hush" sign, then bolted out the door.

"Dad!"

Zack activated the remote starter on his Lexus and jumped in before Jennifer and Bridget rushed from the house. He jammed on the accelerator and took off, adeptly correcting a skid as he sped away.

CHAPTER EIGHTY-NINE

Adam Good pushed Emily through the door into the pre-op area of his secret lair.

"Keep moving. Door to your right."

Emily followed his directions to the cipher-locked room off the pre-op area. Adam entered the code, opened the door, and pushed Emily into the room. She thought about slamming the door in his face but saw that she had entered a secured area with no other entrance and no windows.

No possible escape route.

They stood in a room about the size of a small kitchen, Good closed the door behind him. He took Emily by the arm and sat her in a simple straight-back chair. With one hand on her shoulder, he pulled open a drawer and brought out zip-ties. "Hands behind the chair back."

Emily shot him a vicious look. "No."

Without a word, he grabbed both her arms and pulled them behind the chair. Then he zip-tied her wrists together. His breath on her face reeked. He bent down and zip-tied her ankles together, then straightened and stood in front of her.

"You can choose your fate, Em. It's not too late to save yourself."

Emily spat at him.

Good dodged the snot rocket. He moved closer, face-to-face, same reeking breath.

"Listen to me, Em." He pointed to a stainless-steel waist-high medical freezer unit in the corner. "With what's inside there, we can have a future together. We can live in luxury for the rest of our lives. Anywhere in the world you choose. We will want for nothing. We'll be together, free. We belong together, my love."

She glared at him. "I will follow you nowhere. And I'm not your love. You're too sick to really love someone."

He broke eye contact, swallowed hard, stood, and looked at his watch. His voice came out flat. "I must leave in five minutes. You have two choices. You can come with me now, or I can leave you to rot in this room." He shook his head. "We're all leaving this house, with or without you, and never coming back. By the time anyone finds you down here, you'll be a starved-to-death skeleton."

He pulled back his jacket to reveal the revolver in his waistband. "Or you can make it quick. Either way . . ."

She glowered at him, thought about it, then relaxed her face. "Fine. What do you want me to do?"

He squinted. "Sit tight. I'll release you once I'm ready to go, not one second sooner. I don't want you trying something stupid."

She snorted. "You have me trapped, Adam. What could I possibly do now? You leave me no choice but to go with you to, whatever." Her eyes narrowed. "Don't expect me to like it."

He lifted her chin in his hand. "You will learn to like it."

She shrugged.

He turned away.

Emily remained silent and did not move. She looked around the space for any kind of weapon or a way to escape. She saw none.

Just go along. The opportunity will come.

Good opened a cabinet and pulled out a container the size of a milk carton, except this one seemed made of lead. He placed it inside a thickly padded case, like a salesman's sample case, then set it on the counter next to the stainless-steel freezer. He donned a pair of thick insulated gloves, opened the freezer, and extracted a leaded cylinder about six inches long and three inches in diameter.

He showed it to Emily. "That girl's embryo. Proof of concept. Worth more than gold. Sold to the highest bidder." He paused. "Not from this country."

Emily was puzzled. "Embryo? You're transferring an embryo? Different from IVF?"

"Doctors in this country are so arrogant to think we have the most knowledge about science and technology, despite being saddled by human use regulations and crap like HIPAA. Other countries are not so restricted. They can freely research new technology, like human embryo transplantation from uterus to uterus. No need for IVF." He puffed out his chest. "I will teach them how to do it. With or without you as my associate."

Emily's head drooped. "Why are you doing this?"

He smirked. "Part of a much larger plan for which you do not have the need to know."

Emily's heart sank, as if she were conversing with a grotesque imitation of Dr. Frankenstein.

Good sealed the frozen cylinder into the lead carton and padded case, took off the gloves, pulled scissors from a drawer, and cut through the zip-tie binding Emily's ankles. "Stand up."

She did.

"I'm leaving your hands bound until we get airborne."

"Airborne?"

"You and I are going on a trip. For now, you stay right where you are." He lifted the case by a strap over his shoulder and pointed the gun at Emily.

"You go first. Out through pre-op, down the hall to the living room, out the front door, and into my car. You get into the driver's seat. Not one word, not even a peep from you, or I will shoot you. Try to run, and I will shoot you dead."

He seemed to reconsider. "Better, I'll leave you for Spider to finish off."

Spider's here?

As directed, Emily led the way into the front room of the house. Spider and Tyler held a gagged and bound Annie Winston between them. Flossie and Nan stood next to them. They had dressed Annie in the white blouse and jeans she had worn when Sarah brought her to the House. She looked at Emily with terrified eyes.

"Stop, Emily," Good said.

She did as told. He stepped behind her, held the muzzle of the gun to her back, and spoke to the others. "Emily has decided to be a good girl and rejoin the team. Plan A remains in effect. You all know what to do. Do not miss the rendezvous. Anyone late gets left behind."

He poked the gun into Emily's back. "Move along, Em." A brief pause. "Could use some help, Roach."

"Yes, sir." Roach grabbed Emily's arm and forced her outside, down the steps, and into the driver's seat of Good's car. "I believe you are familiar with the operation of this vehicle," Roach said with a sly smile. "You should know we've disabled the tracking functions."

Dr. Good put the case in the back seat, then got into the passenger seat and pointed the gun at Emily's torso.

Roach stepped back. "*Buen viaje,* boss."

Good ignored him. "Drive, Em."

Did Roach just tell me we're going to a Spanish-speaking country?

Emily put the Mercedes in gear and pointed it down the driveway. "Where are we going?"

Dr. Good sighed. "Always trying, eh, Em. You wearing a wire, transmitting on a cell phone?"

"Seriously," she said. "I'm wearing damned scrubs in freezing temperature."

With his free hand, Good turned on the heat to full blast. Then he turned to Emily and gave her a lascivious grin.

"I'll give you directions as we go."

CHAPTER NINETY

When Tyler came back into the house, Annie pleaded with him through the gag.

"Tyler, please."

It sounded like gibberish, but Tyler understood. He shrugged. "Sorry."

The man they called Spider tightened his grip on Annie's arm and pulled her forward. "Come on, gang. We need to get this done and on our way. I, for one, don't intend to miss that flight."

Annie turned to Sarah, eyes pleading.

Sarah tilted her head and shrugged.

Tyler took Annie's other arm. He and Spider guided Annie as they followed Sarah out the door, onto the porch, and down the steps to a waiting metallic-blue SUV. The woman called Nan sat behind the wheel.

They put Annie in the middle of the back seat, with Tyler and Sarah on either side of her. Spider climbed into a white Cadillac SUV parked behind them.

They drove about five minutes, making several turns on country roads, before pulling into a parking area surrounded by foliage. As soon as the vehicle stopped, Tyler opened his door and pulled Annie out of the vehicle.

She shivered, more from terror than the frosty air. "What are you doing to me?"

Spider's Cadillac pulled up behind the blue SUV. Spider got out, stood beside the car, and stared at them. "What's the hold up?" he yelled.

"C'mon," Tyler said. He grabbed Annie's arm and pulled her away from the vehicle. Sarah got out and regarded Annie with dispassionate eyes. Tyler and Sarah led Annie out of the parking area and turned down a short road, past a boat ramp, then a dirt path beneath a narrow bridge. Annie heard the sound of water lapping against a shore. They stopped at the edge of the river.

Tyler spoke without looking at Annie. "Here's the story, Annie Winston. You came to The Good House with Sarah to get an abortion. Afterward, you were overcome with grief and regret. Before Sarah knew you were gone, you ran away and found your way down here. You jumped into the water to drown yourself."

He reached into his pocket, took out Annie's phone, and slipped it into the back pocket of her jeans. "You've been texting your sister all day." He leaned closer. "You didn't throw this away because deep inside you hope someone finds you, before—"

Annie sobbed. "Please, Tyler, don't."

He shook his head. "Sorry, Annie. These people own me." He swallowed hard. "I'm going to untie you now. If you're smart, you'll walk into the water. Otherwise, I'll have to throw you in."

Annie cried. "I'll do it. Just, just give me a moment." She looked at the river. Too wide to swim across, but if she could get downstream. . . .

Sarah shouted from behind. "Get on with it, Roach."

Tyler turned his head toward Sarah.

Before he could turn back, Annie slammed her knee into his groin. He doubled over in pain. She turned and sprinted into the river.

CHAPTER NINETY-ONE

Bridget leaned forward to search through the windshield of her Range Rover as she came off the ramp from Duke Street to I-395 heading toward DC. She had managed to keep Zack's Lexus in sight until the interchange but lost him when she had to slow down to merge.

As soon as it was safe, she flipped on the left-turn signal, jammed her foot on the gas pedal, and maneuvered as best she could across three lanes of traffic. As she crossed over Seminary Road, she reconsidered her decision not to call the police despite her earlier threat to Zack. She hesitated.

I would do the same as Zack if Dustin were missing and in trouble.

She activated the hands-free feature in her car. "Call Zack Winston."

Her call went to his voicemail.

"Zack, I will help you. Don't run from me."

Silence.

"Okay, Zack. With you all the way, BAFERD."

As if by reward, she spotted his car some fifty yards ahead of hers. She settled into trail and matched his speed, following at a safe distance but not so far back that she would lose him again.

She lost him on the transition from I-395 to George Washington Parkway.

From what Bridget recalled of the GPS route that Zack's ex-wife had sent to his phone, he would take GW Parkway to the Capital Beltway, cross the American Legion Bridge, then turn onto River Road. He would then drive northwest into the countryside around Poolsville, Maryland alongside the Potomac River.

She increased her speed to 80 mph. Too fast for this stretch of road, but maybe she would catch up to him again. This time she would follow closer. What difference did it make if he knew she was following him? Not like he would stop and invite her into his car.

Bridget continued on her chosen route, but no sign of Zack. Had he gone a different way? She called Jennifer, who was still at Bridget's house waiting for Grant and Dustin. She would pick up her mother at National Airport early the next morning in the unwelcome event that Bridget and Zack did not get back in time. Natalie had booked a red-eye flight from San Diego after Jennifer called her.

"I've lost him," Bridget said. "I'm on GW Parkway. Can you see any other way he might have gone?"

After a pause, Jennifer said, "He might have crossed the river to Clara Barton Parkway. You two could be on parallel courses on either side of the river." Another pause. "But he still has to get onto River Road. If you are on different routes, you'll converge there."

"Got it," Bridget said. She accelerated as fast she could go, but not so fast as to attract law enforcement attention.

A few minutes later, Bridget made the transition from GW Parkway to I-495. Still no sign of Zack.

As she crossed the Potomac on the American Legion Memorial Bridge, a sign appeared.

WELCOME TO MARYLAND

"I am officially a fugitive," Bridget said. "The things I do for love."
Love? Really, Bridge? Of course, love. Why else would I be here?

She took the exit ramp from I-495 onto River Road. Night and freezing temperatures had settled over the region.

About a hundred yards ahead, Bridget spotted a pair of taillights. She glanced in her rear-view mirror, then accelerated. As she closed within thirty yards, she knew it was Zack. Just as she settled into trail behind his car, three sets of flashing red and blue lights appeared from nowhere in her rear-view mirror, accompanied by sirens.

Captured already for leaving Virginia?

She pulled to the side of the road. The vehicles sped past. Montgomery County Police and unmarked black SUVs. Within seconds they whooshed past Zack's car. He hadn't bothered to slow down.

"Enough charade," she said. Clearly, the law enforcement vehicles were headed to The Good House, based on information learned from Jennifer Winston who had promised to call and give Detective Martinez the GPS coordinates from Annie's phone. Thank God, they would get there before Zack did.

Bridget sped up to within two car lengths of Zack. Her eyes shifted to the flashing lights receding ahead of Zack's vehicle. Why wasn't he speeding up to follow them?

Approaching headlights briefly blinded Bridget and she lost sight of Zack's car. Two SUVs, one white, the other metallic blue, passed her heading south on River Road.

Just as she regained her forward vision, Zack's vehicle made an abrupt left turn off River Road. Bridget hit the brakes. She would not stop in time to keep from slamming into his car, so she veered sharply right, just missing his left rear bumper, then skidded and spun 360 degrees to stop ten feet past the intersection.

She hadn't noticed the ice on the road.

Panting from the moment of terror, Bridget executed a careful Y-turn and drove back to where Zack had turned left. She noted two street signs. To the left, Seneca Road. Bridget turned right to follow Zack on Rileys Rock Road.

Fear ran through Bridget like an electric jolt. Zack had mentioned before that Dr. Nate Young had been found in the Potomac River near

Seneca Landing. Why did Zack head there and not follow the police vehicles to The Good House?

Bridget drove slowly down the road for about a half-mile until she came upon Zack's vehicle, parked at the end of the road, engine running, door open. She stopped behind it, killed the Range Rover's engine, and shut off the lights. She stepped up to Zack's Lexus and did the same in his car.

Her eyes searched the area, which was bathed in full moonlight. No one else around.

Zack's voice from the direction of the river pierced the silence.

"Annie! Annie!"

A small unintelligible voice from further away.

Then the sound of something, or someone, plunging into the river.

CHAPTER NINETY-TWO

Zack had seen Bridget's car in his rear-view mirror as she pulled onto Duke Street from her neighborhood. Of course, she would follow him.

His phone rang. Bridget. He didn't answer.

I won't let her risk her life for me. Not again.

He drove on.

By the time he turned onto River Road and headed along the east side of the Potomac River, he figured he'd lost her. Hopefully, she would turn back and go home. He shook his head. Bridget would continue and try to find him.

His phone rang. Figuring it was Bridget for the fifth time, he started to punch it off. Then he noticed the caller ID. Jennifer.

"What's up Jenn?"

"Mom called. She got an update on the location of Annie's phone. I hope you're familiar with the area. It's at a place called Seneca Landing."

An icy grip squeezed Zack's heart. The site where Nate Young was found nearly drowned.

"Got it," he said. "I'll go there."

The next minutes unfolded like a video on fast forward. Zack saw Bridget's car approach his from behind. Next, a convoy of law enforcement vehicles with lights and sirens screamed past her car, then his. As soon as their lights receded down the road, two SUVs raced past him in the opposite direction. Then, the intersection of River Road and Seneca Road appeared abruptly in his windshield.

Zack made a hard left onto the road, flinching as Bridget's car skidded past his, just missing a collision.

He didn't slow down or look back for Bridget. Annie was at the river. Zack longed for the ten minutes he'd lost trying to evade Bridget. He slammed the accelerator to the floor, then screeched to a stop when the road ended. He jumped out of the car and looked all around.

No one there.

He found a path that ran under a bridge where the C & O trail traversed a creek that ran into the Potomac River. At the end of the path, he came to the water's edge.

"Annie! Annie!"

"Dad!"

Zack plunged into the river.

CHAPTER NINETY-THREE

Annie waded chest-high into the icy water, then turned downstream hoping to get away from her captors without falling all the way into the river. Tyler shouted from somewhere on the riverbank. Fearing he would shoot her, Annie crouched in the water up to her neck. She had to fight to stay upright in the current. Her arms and legs went numb.

Spider's voice echoed over the water's surface. "She's already dead. Come on."

In less than a minute, she heard the cars start up and leave. At last alone, she veered toward the river bank. She could no longer feel her legs. Her foot slipped on a rock, and she plunged back into the river. She got her head above the surface and sputtered. The current carried her downstream. She had no control over the direction the river took her. She flailed in desperation, expending precious energy to tread and keep her head above water.

Annie Winston felt about to die. She would never see her dad, her mom, or her sister again.

She vowed to fight death to the end. She quit fighting the current and went with the flow, looking desperately over the moonlit surface for something to latch onto, a way to stop her momentum so she could regroup and work her way out of the river.

A familiar voice cut through the icy silence.

"Annie! Annie!"

He found me!

"Dad! Help!"

Annie struggled to swim toward the bank from where she'd heard her father's voice. The harder she tried, the more difficult and futile the effort became. A dense inner fog vanished the excitement from her mind. The fog got heavier, darker, colder. Annie couldn't keep her eyes open. Her entire body froze. She quit struggling.

"Dad, I . . . I'm sorry."

Her head submerged. She struggled back to the surface.

Once.

Twice.

The third time, her body sank.

CHAPTER NINETY-FOUR

Zack rushed into the river until the water reached his waist, then he plunged forward and swam toward where he'd heard Annie's voice. Within seconds, the frigid water sapped his energy but not his resolve.

I will not lose my daughter.

He reached deep inside himself, summoned all his strength, and swam out into the river. He switched to breast strokes so he could look forward for Annie. He scanned the moonlit surface of the water. Smooth except for the moving current.

She couldn't have gone much farther than here. I heard her voice.

Treading water, he spun around a full circle. The current carried him further downstream. His arms and legs became leaden. He could not move. A dense mental fog descended over him. His eyes closed. He sank. Water entered his lungs.

We die together.

As he submerged, Zack thought of Bridget. Her voice in his ear.

Suck it up, BAFERD!

Zack made a last powerful effort and forced his body to breach the surface. The current had carried him forward. He spotted what looked like a pile of debris, like a dam, a few yards ahead. As he floated closer, a glint of white reflected by the moonlight caught his eye.

Annie's white blouse from their shopping trip!

He summoned the energy to swim toward the sight. As he got closer to the old dam, he spotted Annie's body washed up onto the flotsam. He closed the last few yards and found he could stand up, although his feet sunk into mud. He sludged his way to Annie and turned her over.

She looked already dead.

Not unless she's warm and dead!

Shivering, Zack assessed the situation. The debris, mud, and eddying water around them would not support adequate CPR. He needed to get her to dry land. He lifted her head, pinched her nostrils, and gave her two quick breaths. No response.

Still shivering, teeth chattering, he labored to pick her up and put her over his shoulder in a fireman's carry. He took one step and lost his balance. He and Annie fell backward into the river.

The riverbank seemed no more than twenty yards away. He could swim her there faster and more safely than carry her. He backed into the river, one arm wrapped around Annie's inert body. Once in deeper water, he kicked his legs and started a one-handed back stroke toward the shoreline. The icy water sapped his energy, but he just needed to swim ten to fifteen yards to shallow water where he could stand and pull her out of the river.

Zack kicked as hard as he could and flailed his arm behind him. Instead of getting closer to the bank, the current carried them further away. Zack kicked and stroked harder.

A hand grasped his wrist and pulled. he twisted his head to lool behind him.

Bridget held a tight grip on his arm, treading water with her other arm.

She pulled herself closer, getting a firm hold under Zack's armpit.

"Kick, Zack. Kick with all your might. For God's sakes hold onto your daughter."

Bridget set a course to the riverbank. Her triathlon-trained swimmer's strokes pulled Zack and Annie behind her. Zack helped as much as he could with the leg kick. It took just minutes for them to reach shallow water. Bridget stood thigh-deep to lift and pull Zack and Annie to the bank.

As soon as they were on solid ground, Zack checked Annie. No breathing. No pulse. He started CPR.

"I'm running back to my car to call 911," Bridget said. She didn't wait for an answer.

Even though he was freezing cold, and his extremities numb, Zack performed CPR on his daughter. He stopped at intervals to check for vital signs. At one point, he thought he felt a pulse, but he couldn't tell if it was real or his imagination.

Bridget returned. "EMS on the way. I'll relieve you here." She pushed him aside and continued the CPR on Annie.

He gasped. "We can do two-person."

Before she could answer, Zack collapsed and passed out.

CHAPTER NINETY-FIVE

During the thirty-minute drive, Emily fretted over how to break free from Adam Good. The unanswered questions gave way to solid resolve.

Wherever he's going with that embryo, I'm not.

"Slow down," Good said. "Take the next left."

Emily did as directed, turning onto a street named Airpark Road.

"Welcome to Montgomery County Airpark." Good smiled. "Our debarkation point. Keep driving. I'll tell you where to park."

Emily followed the narrow road to where it split into an elliptical driveway that circled like a hairpin in front of a small terminal.

"Pass the terminal on the circular drive then park close to it."

Emily did so and picked a space three spots past the terminal.

"Shut off the ignition and the lights. We stay in the car and wait."

"For what?"

"I'll tell you when you need to know."

Headlights approached the drive. A Montgomery County Police vehicle pulled into a reserved parking spot opposite the Mercedes, across the wide part of the hairpin from where Emily had parked. She figured it a twenty-yard sprint across the grass to the police car.

Adam tracked Emily's gaze. "Don't get any ideas." He pulled the gun from his waistband.

"You going to shoot me in front of the police, Adam?"

"Make the slightest move and I will shoot you. With all the aircraft noise, that cop won't hear a thing. Or maybe I'll have to bash your pretty head. That would hurt me more than you."

Emily sat stone-like as the police officer got out of her car and strolled into the terminal.

Adam rested the gun on his lap. "Cops know that small airports have the best restaurants. She'll be in there a while."

Ten minutes passed. Emily shivered as cold air filled the Mercedes. "It's freezing, Adam. I'm cold."

He huffed. "Fine. Turn on the ignition and the heater but leave the lights off."

Emily did so. After a few minutes, she stopped shivering. A plan formed in her mind.

She waited a few minutes then turned to him. "I have to go to the bathroom."

"No, you don't. Stay calm. In just a few minutes we'll be together forever and you'll never have to worry about anything, ever again."

"I really have to go, Adam."

He scoffed. "Don't think for one second that I'm going to let you out of my sight, much less allow you to go into that terminal building where there's a cop and other people who might wonder what a woman in a scrub suit is doing there at this time of night. You hold it."

"I can't."

"Shut up and sit there. It won't be long."

"It's number two." She doubled over as if her lower abdomen cramped. "Feels like diarrhea."

Good glared at her. "You're not getting out of this car until I tell you to."

Emily stuck out her lip. "I hate you."

"Grow up, Em. Some day you will thank me for my devotion to you."

Emily scowled.

Devotion? More like obsession.

Good's phone buzzed. He answered. "Yes. Yes. Yes. Will do." He punched off the call and pointed out his side window. In the distance, airplane headlights approached the far end of the runway.

"That's our ride." Good smirked. "Bathroom and all."

A few minutes later, a sleek Learjet taxied around the terminal to a spot on the tarmac about fifty yards from where Emily had parked. The jet noise diminished as one engine shut down. The other continued spinning.

The passenger door opened. Someone from inside the plane deployed a ladder, then looked in the direction of the parking lot.

"Blink the lights twice," Adam said. He pointed the gun at Emily's head. "Do it."

She blinked the lights.

Good's phone rang.

"Got it."

He pointed to a wide gate in the chain-link fence about twenty-five yards from where they sat. Behind the gate, a straight path to the jet's open door.

The person who had deployed the ladder from the plane walked toward the gate.

Good stared at Emily, eyes like steel. "We're getting out of the car and walking directly through that gate and onto that plane. No funny stuff or you die. If I don't shoot you, I guarantee that other guy will."

Emily stared straight ahead and spoke in staccato cadence, "I have to go to the bathroom."

Good pointed the gun at her. "Stay in the car until I tell you." He got out, retrieved the case with the frozen embryo from the rear seat, and walked around the front of the car to Emily's side.

He showed her the pistol in his right hand. "Get out and stand still."

Emily did as told.

Good held the gun on her with his right hand and the case in his left. He gestured toward the gate. "Walk to the gate."

Emily walked beside and slightly in front of him until they were halfway to the gate. All at once she backed up, grabbed her abdomen, and dropped to her knees.

Now a few paces ahead of her, Good beckoned with the gun. "Keep moving, Em."

"It's coming. I can't hold it." She squatted as if to defecate.

The man at the gate yelled in a heavy accent. "You must hurry."

Good hesitated; stared at her for a few seconds.

Emily backed away in a reverse duck walk.

Good shook his head. "I need you to come with me. Please, Em."

She continued to back away.

Adam Good pointed the pistol at her. "Last chance, Em."

"Must come now," the man said.

"Go to hell, Adam."

"Come now, Emily. Please."

Emily continued to back away.

Good pointed the gun at Emily. "Your choice then." He fired the pistol, but Emily was already diving away. The round struck her upper chest in the front, just below her right collarbone. Good turned and ran toward the gate, clutching the package containing Annie's embryo like a lead football.

From the terminal building, the police officer ran out, pistol drawn. Either she had heard the shot or a passerby had alerted her to what was happening outside the terminal.

The man at the gate ran back to the aircraft, leaving Dr. Good sprinting across the parking area still a few yards from the gate.

The officer chased him. "Stop. Lower your weapon."

The other man had returned to the jet, pulled up the ladder, and started to close the door. The idling jet engine spooled up.

Good stopped, shoulders slumped.

"Drop the gun," the officer shouted, her weapon trained on Good.

He turned and looked at Emily. "We could have had such happiness." He raised the pistol.

In Emily's view, as she backed away, he pointed it at himself under his chin.

The deputy had a different perspective. She fired two shots into Adam Good's chest.

CHAPTER NINETY-SIX

Zack awakened to a sensation of his body hurtling through space. A warbling sound accosted his ears.

Sirens. Ambulance.

He tried to call out, but a rubbery mask covered his face. He opened his eyes. Bridget, wrapped in blankets, looked back at him.

Zack tried to sit up. Tender but firm hands forced him down. Beside Bridget, a paramedic spoke in a commanding voice.

"Stay down, Doc. You're in an ambo. We'll be there soon." The medic reached over Zack to check the IV line running into his left arm.

Zack jerked the mask off his face. Terrified, he looked a Bridget.

"Annie?"

"Another ambulance. About ten minutes ahead of us."

"Is she . . . ?"

"Breathing, some. Unconscious. Cold."

The medic replaced the mask. "Be still, Doc. She's getting good care."

What am I going to tell Natalie?

The sirens silenced and the ambulance motion stopped. Zack roused and looked around.

Bridget said, "We're here, Zack. Bethesda Metro."

"Ma'am could you step out please," a male voice said.

Bridget squeezed his hand. "I'll see what I can find out about Annie."

An ED nurse took Bridget's arm. "Come with me, ma'am."

The medics lifted Zack out of the ambulance on a gurney and wheeled him into the familiar ER where he had spent countless hours caring for the sick and injured. Passing the resuscitation room, he saw a gaggle of nurses and doctors in frenzied motion over a lifeless form on the bed.

Annie!

Among the group striving to save his daughter's life, he recognized Jerry Hartman and Sevati Prakash.

Gotta help them. Warm her up. Call for ECMO.

He tried to get off the gurney, but two pairs of hands pushed him down. The gurney rolled past the resus room and into the main treatment area. They off-loaded Zack onto bed one, the space reserved for the most serious patients not requiring immediate resuscitation.

Bridget sat on the gurney next to his, trying to reassure the nurse. "I'm fine."

"We still need to check you out," the nurse said. She drew the curtain around that cubicle.

A young emergency physician, new to their group, approached Zack. He had met her only a few times, never worked with her, and never changed shifts with her. She looked barely older than Annie.

Zack pulled the oxygen mask off his face again. "I need to get to my daughter."

"Drs. Hartman and Prakash are with her. Nothing for you to do. We need to take care of you."

Zack labored to breathe.

"O2 sats are dropping," the young physician said. She brought her face close to Zack's and spoke in a stern voice. "Dr. Winston, you will be no help to your daughter if you die on this bed. Now settle down so I can take care of you."

Duly chastised, Zack did as he was told.

The young doctor put a stethoscope to Zack's chest. She frowned. "Bilateral rales. Early pulmonary edema."

Zack's breathing worsened even as he realized what was happening. His lungs, damaged from his near-drowning, were filling up with fluid, a condition called secondary drowning.

"Stay quiet," the doctor said, "I'll be right back."

In the cubicle next to him, a nurse was talking to Bridget. "You need to get out of those wet clothes. Here's a scrub suit you can wear."

The emergency physician returned with Jerry Hartman, who repeated the stethoscope exam.

"I've ordered a portable chest x-ray," the young doctor said.

"Fine but irrelevant," Jerry said. He leaned over Zack. "First, we're taking your daughter upstairs to put her on ECMO. She's unconscious, but she has a chance. Her young protoplasm is a plus, more likely to respond than an old guy like Nate Young, or you."

His smile did not resonate with Zack.

"Gotta see her," Zack said, breathless.

"Can't," Jerry said. "Your O2 sat is 89%. You know what that means."

Zack's heart fell. "Intubate and ventilate."

"You got it, BAFERD."

"Shit," Zack said.

Monica Harris, ER head nurse entered the cubicle. She nodded at Zack, then spoke to Jerry Hartman.

"We need to clear resus and this bed stat. Two gun-shot victims coming from Montgomery Air Park. Ten minutes out."

"Okay," Jerry said. "Move Miss Winston up to ICU now. Give me five minutes and then we can move Dr. Winston."

Jerry turned to Zack. "You picked a fine time to be incapacitated, Zack. We need you working, not lying on a damned bed."

Zack tried to laugh, but he couldn't catch his breath.

"We're going to do rapid sequence intubation. Starting . . . now." Jerry nodded to the emergency physician who had taken up position at the head of the bed.

"Wait," Zack said, "Bridget . . ."

The drugs injected into his blood stream rendered Zack unconscious before he could finish his thought.

CHAPTER NINETY-SEVEN

Emily sat upright on the gurney in the back of the ambulance racing down the road. She held pressure on the bandaged wound in her right upper chest. She ignored the pain as she watched in detached silence as two medics worked feverishly to resuscitate Adam Good. They had started two large-bore IVs, one in each arm, and intubated him. One medic squeezed air into his lungs from a Neoprene bag. The other held pressure on the second of two chest wounds, roughly in the region over his heart.

Adam did not move, nor did he breathe. He looked already dead.

Emily didn't care, her nerves were calm despite her own narrow escape from death. Dead or alive, she was free from Adam Good, now and forever.

As the ride continued, she became rapidly short of breath. Inner peace gave way to panic. She reached out to the medic bent over Adam's chest. He turned, and his face paled.

She gave him a desperate look. "I . . . can't . . . breathe."

The medic tried to listen with a stethoscope over her chest—a near-impossible task in a moving ambulance with sirens blaring.

"She may have a tension pneumo," he said to the other medic. "Can't tell for sure." He adjusted the oxygen mask over her face.

"Five minutes out," the other medic said. "Gotta decompress her now."

Even as she panicked, Emily understood their predicament. They feared she had a collapsed lung from the wound to her chest. Air escaping from the punctured lung was filling the left thoracic cavity, like blowing up a balloon. That process was pushing her heart to the right and compressing her right lung so it could not fully expand to draw in air. If they didn't fix it right away, she could die.

Eyes wide, she looked at the young medic. "Do it."

Without hesitating, he opened a drawer over her head, pulled out a large syringe with a needle five inches long. A plastic catheter covered the needle. He pulled back the edge of her scrub suit, measured with his left fingers to find a rib space just below her collarbone. He glanced at her.

She nodded.

The medic thrust the needle through the space between her ribs and into her chest cavity. If they were wrong about what lay underneath, he risked puncturing a working lung and making it collapse.

They were not wrong.

Emily winced as the needle point impaled her chest. When it cleared the inner thoracic wall, a whoosh of air pushed back the syringe's plunger.

She felt immediate relief as her right lung filled with air and her heart returned to normal pumping capacity.

"Thank you," she said.

The medic withdrew the needle but left the catheter in place. He attached it to a one-way flap valve, then secured it all to her skin with tape.

Minutes later, they pulled into the Bethesda Metro ambulance bay. The back doors of the vehicle flew open. Nurses and techs helped the paramedics move Adam Good onto a gurney. They did the same with Emily, except they raised the head to allow her to sit up to keep her lung expanded. The two gurneys moved in tandem through double doors into the ER.

The paramedics in front shouted. "Fiftyish male, two GSWs to the chest, full code."

"Resus," a nurse said.

The medic pushing Emily's gurney shouted. "Thirtyish female, GSW upper right chest. Tension pneumo decompressed en route."

"Bed One," a nurse said.

As they wheeled Emily past the resuscitation room, a nurse appeared at the door and shouted toward the workstation. "This victim is Dr. Barth."

Barth? I knew his name wasn't Good.

CHAPTER NINETY-EIGHT

A few hours after being examined in the ED and witnessing Zack Winston's clinical crash, Bridget dozed fitfully on the couch in the ICU waiting room at Bethesda Metro. She wore a Harvard Law School sweatsuit. Jennifer Winston had brought it when Grant dropped her off at the hospital, then returned home to await the arrival of his mother from Boston and to be with Dustin.

Bridget had asked for the sweatsuit to wear, instead of the hospital-provided scrubs, for her interview with Alexandria PD detectives Melrose and Sawyer. They had come to confront her about leaving Virginia against her detention order. In a contentious exchange, her attorney, Norman Jones, had argued against their intent to take her into custody as their primary suspect in the alleged murder of Marshall Hilliard.

"This upstanding woman deserves a medal, not jail," Norman had said. "She just saved two people's lives, at significant risk to her own." He had pointed to the ceiling. "Up in the ICU, a sixteen-year-old girl and her physician father both live, thanks to Ms. Larsen's unselfish heroism."

He had then challenged the detectives to produce any new substantial evidence to prove that Marshall Hilliard had even been murdered, let alone by his wife. They had none.

"Nevertheless," Detective Melrose had said, "Mrs. Hilliard violated a direct order from the court to remain in Virginia. She now constitutes a flight risk."

Norman had broken into a sarcastic laugh. "Flight risk? From what? Unsubstantiated suspicion? A son and stepson who mourn the loss of their father? Two people whose lives she just saved?" He scoffed. "How do you all think that story will play in *The Washington Post*?"

The threat of adverse publicity had turned the tide, but not entirely in Bridget's favor. She agreed to house arrest, including an ankle monitor, in lieu of incarceration.

"Nowhere else to go at the moment anyway."

In the last seventy-two hours, I've spent two nights on couches in different hospital ICUs. Beats jail.

Bridget had thought of going home once the ED cleared her and the Alexandria detectives backed off.

I belong right here.

Zack Winston had once saved her life. She wanted to stand watch over his daughter's struggle to live while Zack himself lay in an induced coma in the bed next to hers. Drs. Hartman and Prakash had assured her that Zack's hiatus from conscious life would be temporary and brief.

Annie Winston's future was less certain, although the doctors insisted her chances were better than fifty percent.

How much better? Fifty-one percent? A forty-nine percent chance she won't survive?

Bridget wiped the sleep from her eyes and sat up on the couch. Jennifer had left the waiting room.

Maybe she's in with Zack and Annie.

She looked at the clock on the waiting room wall. 1:15 AM. Jennifer would have gone to pick up her mother at National Airport.

Bridget went to the ICU door, from where she was buzzed in to visit Annie and Zack. She nodded at the Montgomery County Police officer guarding the door. At least this officer's presence was unrelated to her.

Most of the staff hovered around a patient in the bed across from

Annie's. One of the two gunshot victims that arrived in the ED before she was discharged.

Judging from the number of personnel, the machines, and the IV bags hanging over the bed, Bridget figured the outcome for this patient remained in jeopardy. A nurse holding tubes of blood broke from the pack. Bridget got a quick glimpse of both Dr. Jerry Hartman and Dr. Sevati Prakash leaning over the patient who appeared to be a man in his mid-fifties.

VIP patient.

The other victim, a woman probably in her thirties, occupied the bed next to the VIP. Compared to the others in the unit, she looked relatively healthy. She sat up, sipping ice water. The only clue to her medical status was a large tube extending from beneath the hospital gown from her chest to a collection apparatus hanging over the bed. Bridget recognized the setup as chest drainage.

She turned away and looked at Annie Winston.

Zack's daughter looked like a beautiful doll, despite the breathing tube in her nose, the IV lines in both arms, and the ECMO tubes running beneath the sheet from her groin circulating blood to and from the heart/lung machine. The nurses had cleaned her up and combed her hair. The Goth jewelry had been removed; hopefully, put in a safe place.

Annie looked peaceful. Had she realized the depth of her dad's love? That he risked his life to save hers?

Bridget approached the bed, leaned over, and spoke into Annie's ear. "Your dad is a good man, Annie. He loves you so much. He'll do anything for you."

Movement behind her startled Bridget. She turned. Zack was awake. Still intubated and encumbered with IVs, he looked at her from his bed next to Annie's. His eyes shone brightly.

She smiled. "You heard me, didn't you?"

A slight nod answered her.

Bridget moved next to Zack, grasped his hand, and squeezed.

He squeezed back.

A nurse appeared at the bedside. "Time for his next sedative dose."

Bridget did not try to hide her annoyance.

Zack glanced at the activity across from Annie's bed, a quizzical look on his face.

The nurse also looked in that direction. "Dr. Barth. Two GSWs to the chest. Not good."

Zack started to raise up, but the nurse pushed him down and injected the sedative into his IV line. She watched as his consciousness drifted away, then she left.

Bridget squeezed Zack's hand.

Maybe a slight return squeeze. She wasn't sure. She spoke into his ear. "Your daughters love you, Zack. Get well for them. Please." She started to turn away, then leaned back in. "I love you too."

Seeing no response, not even a blink, Bridget felt foolish.

She turned and left the ICU.

CHAPTER NINETY-NINE

Natalie Lewis, Zack's former wife and mother of his daughters, impressed Bridget as neither warm nor cold. She carried an air of superiority but not haughtiness, privilege but not dominance. When Jennifer brought her mother into the ICU waiting room, Bridget rose and introduced herself.

The two women exchanged cordial greetings. Natalie gave Bridget a look that implied, "So you're the current squeeze."

Bridget hated that she felt the need to correct the woman; gratified that she did not do it.

Jennifer led Natalie into the ICU to see Annie.

Bridget stayed behind. They had endured a moment of embarrassed confusion when a nurse addressed Bridget as Zack's spouse and the girl's mother. Given the chaos in that unit over the last several hours, and the fact that Jennifer and Bridget had visited both Annie and Zack together, it was an honest if embarrassing mistake.

"I am the mother of Annie Winston," Natalie said.

The nurse blushed. "Sorry. This way, Mrs. Winston."

To her credit, Natalie did not correct the nurse any further.

Bridget sat alone in the waiting room, contemplating the events that had brought them all together to root, pray, or wish for the full recovery of Annie Winston.

The waiting room door opened, and a nurse wearing the purple scrubs of the ED staff entered. She looked at Bridget.

"Are you by any chance Bridget Hilliard?"

Bridget hesitated. "Yes, but I prefer Bridget Larsen."

The nurse nodded. "We have a patient in the ED asking for Dr. Winston. When we told him we couldn't divulge that information, he asked if you might be here. We didn't confirm or deny but thought you should know."

"Who is the patient?"

"A young man. Tyler Rhodes."

The nurse led Bridget to the ER, where she found Tyler on a treatment bed. He wore a hospital gown that did not cover bruises and abrasions on his face, arms, and legs. A plastic bag containing wet clothing sat on the bed next to him.

When he saw Bridget, he cried.

The nurse took Bridget aside. "We're ready to discharge him. No serious injuries." She opened her mouth to speak, paused, then continued. "He's eighteen, legally an adult." Another pause. "He says his parents are out of the country. We're reluctant to let him out on his own. He seems too distraught. Can you help him?"

"Of course," Bridget said. "I know him and his parents."

"Thank you," the nurse said. She turned and left.

Bridget scowled at Tyler. "What the heck, Tyler?"

His expression looked harried, eyes wild. "Is . . . is Annie here? Please tell me she's here."

"She's up in the ICU." She cocked her head. "Why?"

Tyler buried his face in his hands. "Thank you, thank you." When he looked up at Bridget, tears ran down his face. "Is she . . . ? Is she okay?"

"She's in critical condition, but she has a chance. She almost drowned."

A glance at Tyler's wet clothes triggered her.

"Tyler, what do you know about Annie?"

His face scrunched up and his breathing quickened. "I need to talk to the police."

CHAPTER ONE HUNDRED

Bridget agreed to stand in as Tyler's legal counsel until she could help him find a criminal defense attorney. While it seemed the right thing to do, it took her away from her primary desire to stand watch over Zack and Annie. She reminded herself that Natalie and Jennifer had that watch now.

Tyler Rhodes was alone and terrified. He kept glancing around the ED as if he feared someone would attack him. As soon as she could, she got the ED staff to agree to move them into the quiet room, an environment more conducive to privacy and a sense of safety. What light would Tyler throw on the converging events that had led them all to this place and time?

After an hour's delay to get the right people into the room, the first of several interviews took place in the ER quiet room. Detective Martinez from Montgomery County Police Department led the questioning, accompanied by agents from the FBI and Homeland Security.

Tyler described his alternate life as Roach, a factotum for a clandestine enterprise that ran The Good House and trafficked in selling babies to customers unknown to him. Everyone there used fake names. He didn't know anyone's real identity.

His primary role had been to recruit unattached and unsupported young women and girls, runaways, homeless, whatever, in the late stages of pregnancy. They would be set up, "imprisoned," he said, at The Good House until they delivered their babies. A nurse called Emily was in charge of delivering them.

He paused. "I think Emily is her real name. Dr. Good had something on her. She seemed to be a prisoner herself in The Good House. Another nurse they called Flossie sometimes showed up there. She seemed to be over Emily, but she wasn't there very much."

After they delivered their babies, Tyler would assist his immediate boss, a man called Spider, to dispose of the women. Usually, they would abandon the girls in a remote area, where they either resumed their prior states in life or. . . .

He hesitated to continue. "Or, they died." More tears came. "Some of them died at The Good House. I didn't know how they died. I assumed it was from complications, until . . . until tonight." He broke down, sobbing and rocking in his seat. "They kill them. I swear I didn't know."

Bridget called for a break, asking the others to leave her and Tyler alone so she could confer with her client.

"You need to tell me the whole story, Tyler. I need to know what to advise you to say or not say to the police."

Tyler stared at the ground, bit his lip, then raised sad eyes to Bridget. "About a week before Christmas, Dr. Good told me to change my focus. Instead of recruiting girls in late pregnancy, I was to find one in the early stages. He said he had a new procedure that would make us all rich."

He shook his head. "I didn't know how to go about doing what he wanted. Then, like a gift, I met Annie Winston and learned she was pregnant." He let out a long breath. "Dr. Good got all excited when he figured out she was Dr. Winston's daughter. He immediately called Spider to tell him, then gave me the order."

Bridget leaned forward. "You kidnapped Annie?"

His shoulders slumped, body bent. "Yeah, me and Flossie."

"What then?"

Tyler described how he and Flossie had taken Annie Winston to The

Good House, where Dr. Good had performed some special procedure that involved retrieving and freezing her embryo. Tyler didn't know why.

"Dr. Good was really uptight after he did the operation on Annie."

"Who else was there at the time?"

Tyler huffed. "Spider." He shivered. "That guy gives me the creeps."

He paused, thinking. "Another woman. Haven't seen her much before. They call her Nan." He pondered. "She bosses Flossie. Dr. Good calls them The Bobbsey Twins. I don't know what that means."

"What happened after the procedure?"

Tyler buried his face again, struggling to compose himself. "Dr. Good had the embryo in some insulated case thing. He left with Emily. Flossie and I forced Annie into the back seat of Nan's SUV and sat on each side of her. Nan drove. Spider followed in his Cadillac."

He took a deep breath. "We went five minutes to Seneca Landing. There's a boat ramp there, for the Potomac River. Spider knew it from something he'd done earlier. I wasn't involved in that."

"What happened at Seneca Landing?"

"Sarah and I took Annie out of the car. I had her phone. We'd been using it to text her sister so she and her dad wouldn't get suspicious. I put it in Annie's pocket because they wanted everyone to think she still had it when she . . . when she drowned. We were supposed to untie her and throw her into the river. Make it look like she committed suicide."

"Did you?"

He shook his head. "She kicked me in the groin and ran." He choked. "She ran into the damned river."

Bridget thought for a minute. "So you didn't push or throw her into the river?"

He shook his head. "She did it herself. Like she wanted to die."

Or escape.

"Did you go after her?"

"Couldn't. Spider and Nan insisted we needed to leave. We had to meet Dr. Good and Emily at the airport." A sigh. "Spider told Flossie and me to get into his Cadillac. Nan drove away alone in her SUV."

"What happened at the airport?"

"I don't know." He looked at her, eyes sincere.

"When Spider stopped at the next intersection, it's a road to another boat ramp and a dam, I opened the door and tried to jump out of the car. Spider hit the gas and I was thrown from the vehicle. I saw the brake lights go on and the Cadillac backed up. I knew then that Spider would kill me. I got up and ran to the river. Jumped in."

He swallowed hard and scrunched his face in agony. "You see, I really liked Annie. If I had to die, I wanted to be with her.

"As soon as that icy water hit me, I knew I'd made a mistake. I swam a few feet back to the bank and hid in the bushes until I heard the Cadillac drive away."

He sobbed. "I realized I would never find Annie in that river." He stared at the floor. "I am such a loser."

Bridget touched his hand. "Her dad rescued her. They are both up in the ICU. Dr. Winston will almost surely recover. We hope and pray that Annie will."

Tyler collapsed into Bridget's arms. She held him as if she were his own mother.

A knock on the door interrupted them. Detective Martinez opened it and stepped into the room. The FBI and Homeland Security agents stepped in behind her. "We need to continue the interview. Now."

Bridget looked between the officer and the agents and shook her head. "No. My client is too distraught to continue. We'll have to continue at another time."

CHAPTER ONE HUNDRED ONE

The sound of Natalie sobbing next to him awakened Zack. When she confessed to an affair and told him she wanted a divorce, Zack had been the sobber. What was going on now? Why was she back?

He opened his eyes. The harsh lights of the ICU and uncomfortable pressure of the tube in his trachea brought him to the present. Zack managed to turn his head enough to see his ex-wife bending over the bed of his younger daughter, comatose after a near-drowning.

Jennifer stood next to Natalie, an arm around her mother's shoulders.

No sign of Bridget. Changing of the guard.

Zack tried to sit up but caught an IV tubing on the siderail of the bed. Like a rubber band, it yanked him back to the bed.

The sound got the attention of Natalie and Jennifer. Both turned to him.

How has Natalie not aged in twenty years?

When Zack looked into her eyes, he saw the same pity and contempt that he remembered from their final parting.

"You miserable excuse for a father," she said. "I hope you die in that bed." She turned and walked out of the ICU.

Jennifer held back and touched Zack's arm. "She's stressed out. You know she didn't mean that."

Zack tried to force a smile, but of course, he could not do so around the endotracheal tube taped to his face.

"Jennifer. Come." It was Natalie's voice.

"I love you, Dad." Jennifer turned and went after her mother.

As soon as the women left, Zack pushed the call button slung over the siderail of his bed. Seeing no response, he pushed it again. Then he pushed it in rapid sequential bursts.

A nurse hurried to his bed. "Are you okay, Dr. Winston?"

Zack made a gesture as if he were writing on something.

The nurse brought him a tablet.

He wrote, *Call Hartman. I have to get out of here.* He started to hand it back to the nurse but pulled it from her hand to write in large letters, *NOW!*

Fifteen minutes later, Jerry Hartman completed examining Zack and reviewing his vital signs record. "Okay, Zack," he said. "Here goes."

With a nurse standing by to assist, Jerry removed the tape from around Zack's mouth, used a syringe to deflate the small balloon that held the endotracheal tube in Zack's windpipe, and pulled out the tube.

Zack coughed and sputtered a few times, sat up, then dropped his head back onto the pillow. "Thanks," he said in a hoarse voice. "Now get me out of here."

"Not yet," Jerry said. "You still have some rales in your lungs, residual pulmonary edema. You're not yet out of the woods."

"The hell I'm not."

Zack would be damned if he'd let Natalie see him at anything but his best.

And he had to find Bridget.

And, of course, look after Annie.

Jerry gave him a kind smile but spoke in a firm voice. "We need to monitor your vitals and O2 sats another day before I feel safe letting you go."

"That's why I'm the BAFERD and you're not. No time to be conservative. I'm getting out of here, with or without your help." To illustrate his point, he started removing the tape on the dressing around the IV site in his arm.

Jerry stared at him and shook his head.

Zack motioned toward Annie's bed. "I'm not leaving the hospital any time soon. If I crash, you can put me back in here."

Jerry's scowl turned to a smile. He shrugged. "If I have time. Otherwise, you'll be on your own."

Zack smiled back and continued to pull on the tape around the IV site. "Deal."

Jerry put a hand over Zack's to stop him. "At least let the nurses do their jobs. Meanwhile, I'm writing your discharge orders."

"Thanks," Zack said. "I owe you one."

"Make that *another* one, Zack. I'm running a tab on you." Jerry smiled and started to walk away, then turned back to Zack.

"You're not the first patient I've extubated today. We just moved Nate Young to the step-down unit. He's going to survive. Neurologically intact."

CHAPTER ONE HUNDRED TWO

When Zack was out of the bed and dressed in a fresh set of scrubs, he leaned over Annie's bed and scrutinized his daughter from head to toe. His mind filtered out all the medical accouterments, and saw only his Annie, his beautiful, spirited, intelligent, passionate daughter, sleeping peacefully in her bed.

The vision lasted only a few seconds. Zack came back to the reality that Annie was fighting for her life. He thought about their last conversation, the morning she supposedly went shopping with Sarah. He had sensed something was bothering Annie, the way her voice pitched up, how she avoided eye contact. He'd been unable to break through her facade.

Should have tried harder to reach her.

If she had confided in him, they might be in a far better place right now. Would she have confided in him, whatever he did or said?

Doesn't matter. Now is all we have.

He grasped her hand, leaned over, and spoke into her ear. "Annie, I love you so much. I am so sorry for what happened, but I believe with all my heart you will recover. We have wonderful times ahead of us. I will wait for as long as it takes for you to wake up and come back to me. To us. All of us. We all love you."

Zack looked at her face. No signs that she had heard or understood anything he said. "I love you more than my own life, Annie." He squeezed her hand.

She squeezed back. A deliberate, firm squeeze, not a reflex.

A tear filled Zack's eye. He squeezed back, leaned over, and kissed Annie's cheek.

"Welcome back, my beautiful daughter."

Zack turned to leave the ICU to tell Natalie and Jennifer and Bridget what Annie just did. He ran straight into Jerry Hartman. How long had he been standing at the foot of Annie's bed?

Jerry's face looked uncharacteristically stressed. "Now that you're for sure alert and oriented times three, Zack, I need to tell you something else."

"What?"

Jerry pointed to the cubicle across from Annie's. "Sebastian Barth was brought in here last night. GSW to the chest times two."

Zack's mouth gaped. "Barth? Shot? Who? A patient?"

Jerry shook his head. "Police."

"What?"

"We don't know the whole story. Cops aren't talking. Apparently, he was trying to depart on a private jet from Montgomery County Airpark. He had a frozen-tissue container with him."

Zack's mind started to churn. "Go on."

Jerry tilted his head toward the bed opposite Annie's. A young woman lay asleep there, a chest tube emptying into an underwater seal.

"Barth shot that woman first. Upper right chest. Tension pneumo."

Zack's jaw dropped. "Barth shot her?"

Jerry nodded. "So say the cops."

Zack looked closer at the woman. "Who is she?"

Jerry shrugged. "Emily Morgan. May not be her real name."

Zack's mind started to clear. "Barth had a tissue container? At Montgomery County Airpark?" In his head, Zack envisioned the location of the airpark, its proximity to Seneca Landing where he had rescued Annie, and the first location of the GPS track from Annie's phone.

He looked back at Annie, then at Jerry. "On her exam, did—?"

Jerry nodded. "Physical evidence of recent transvaginal procedure. Hormone levels consistent with recent pregnancy no longer active."

A torrent of rage shot through Zack. He moved toward the cubicle that Jerry had indicated. "I will kill him."

Jerry blocked his path. "No, Zack, you won't. He's dead already."

CHAPTER ONE HUNDRED THREE

Emily had feigned sleep and kept her eyes closed except for furtive glances at the men standing by Annie Winston's cubicle. She had heard most of what transpired there, especially the outburst from the man who was obviously Annie's father, apparently a physician.

Dr. Hartman was escorting the man out of the ICU, away from Dr. Good's cubicle. Emily could not bring herself to refer to Adam Good as "Barth." Not yet.

When they passed by her bed, she took the chance and called out.

"Annie's father?"

Both men stopped and turned to her. She stared at Dr. Hartman, who took the hint and retreated.

Red-faced, with cold, hard eyes, Annie's dad approached Emily. "What?"

"My name is Emily Morgan. I worked at The Good House." She put a hand to her mouth. "I mean that Dr. Good, you call him Dr. Barth, forced me to stay there."

The man's face tightened, and his eyes narrowed. "Talk."

"I, uh, took care of Annie. I know what they did to her."

The floodgates in Emily's heart and soul burst. "What they did to many women. And their babies. I am so, so sorry. I didn't mean to—"

Annie's father put up a hand. "Stop."

Emily didn't know what to think or say. What would this man do to her? What would the others do? She didn't care. It was time to face consequences.

The man moved closer to her. His face changed. Intense but no longer angry. "I want to know everything, but not here." He looked around. "Too many ears."

She gave him a puzzled look.

"I believe you," he said. "From what I've figured out and what I see in your face, you're telling the truth." He beckoned to a nurse, who walked up to the bed with a curious look on her face.

"Move this girl to an isolation room. She shouldn't be here in the midst of all this, this, melodrama."

The nurse scoffed. "I'm sorry, Dr. Winston, but you're not in charge here. Dr. Hartman needs to order that, and he's busy." She motioned toward Dr. Good's cubicle.

Annie's dad is a physician.

Dr. Winston started in that direction, but the nurse blocked his way. "You can't go near there. Dr. Hartman's orders."

He started to protest, but then Dr. Hartman came out of the room and walked up to Dr. Winston at the foot of Emily's bed.

"I just pronounced Barth. He's officially dead, Zack."

Emily broke into sobs that diverted both their attentions. She lay with hands clasped over her chest.

"Thank you, God. Thank you, thank you, thank you."

CHAPTER ONE HUNDRED FOUR

After they moved Emily Morgan to the isolation room, Zack pulled up a chair next to her bed. He sent the nurse out and hoped Emily would be comfortable talking to him alone. He moved closer to the edge of her bed and offered a kind smile. "Talk to me."

She hesitated. "I don't know you."

"You know my daughter. You know she's an innocent victim in whatever this, thing, is that almost took her life. And yours."

Emily blinked away tears. "I . . . I don't know how much I can tell you."

She's terrified. About what? Who?

Zack lightly touched her hand. "Your 'Dr. Good' is dead. He can't hurt you anymore."

She turned away, took a deep breath, then turned back to him, her face agitated.

"There are others."

"Other women?"

She shook her head. "Other people who can hurt me. Hurt Annie."

A chill pierced Zack's chest. "Who?"

"I don't know their real names."

Zack furrowed his eyebrows. "How could they hurt Annie? Here in the hospital?"

"They have a wide net in many places. For sure in this hospital, and others."

Zack wondered how much to believe. This woman had been an integral player in whatever happened to Annie. Was she blowing smoke?

He needed help.

"Emily, I'm going to invite someone else to join us. A woman you can trust. Is that okay?"

Emily shrugged. Zack took that as consent.

"I'll be right back." He went to the workstation and spoke to a nurse. "Could you please ask Ms. Larsen to join us? She should be in the waiting room."

Zack wondered how Bridget and Natalie were getting along. Even though discharged, he had not yet left the ICU.

He returned to the isolation room. He wanted to engage Emily in small talk, to break the ice, but he'd never been good at that. Instead, he sat next to her in silence. She seemed to appreciate that.

The nurse entered the room. "Sorry, Dr. Winston. Ms. Larsen isn't in the waiting room. She was called down to the ER."

Zack furrowed his brow. Strange. "Okay. Just send her in when she returns."

If she returns?

He would have to fly solo for now. He turned back to Emily. "Tell me about your relationship with Dr. Barth."

She frowned. "I only knew him as Dr. Good." She took a deep breath. "I'm a nurse. I met Adam, Dr. Good, when I was a student midwife . . ."

Zack listened in horror as Emily related the incident when she practiced home midwifery without a license under the patronage of Dr. Good, aka Sebastian Barth. How a difficult delivery ended with a dead baby. How Barth had used the incident and the threat of imprisonment for criminal negligence to manipulate and gaslight Emily into helping him operate The Good House. How he had subjected her to emotional, mental, and sexual abuse.

"He made me his prisoner. I'd have been better off facing the consequences of what I did."

She told Zack how Dr. Good had gotten into a new scheme, one that required a woman, or women, in the early stages of pregnancy. Emily didn't know why. Dr. Good had become more and more abusive and Emily realized she was in imminent danger. She described her futile attempt to escape on Christmas day, and how Dr. Good had found her and brought her back to assist in his new venture.

"These other people involved, that you don't know their real names. Can you describe them?"

Emily told him about a young man who came and went, who seemed to be both a recruiter of young women and an overall errand boy for the Good enterprise.

"They called him Roach. He was a pothead, but he seemed to have a soul somewhere."

"Others?" Zack asked.

"Two women, Flossie and Nan. Dr. Good called them 'The Bobbsey Twins.' They weren't twins, but they may have been related. The older one, Nan, wasn't around much."

"What made you think they were related?"

"Both had red hair and freckles."

A chill ran down Zack's spine.

"Who brought Annie to The Good House?" He already knew the answer.

"It was Flossie, the younger of the Bobbsey Twins."

Sarah!

"Do you know where this Flossie is now?"

Emily shook her head. "She was with the others when Dr. Good and I left for the airport." She wiped away a tear. "They were to, uh, dispose of Annie then meet us at the private jet."

Zack rubbed his eyes. "But they hadn't shown up by the time you and Sebastian, Dr. Good . . ."

Emily stared at the ceiling. "I don't know where they went."

Zack swallowed hard. "Okay, you mentioned this Roach guy, and the Bobbsey Twins. Anyone else?"

The young woman shuddered. "The scariest man I've ever met, other than Dr. Good. They called him 'Spider.' He terrified me." She looked away.

A nurse entered the room. "Dr. Winston, a call for you at the desk. Ms. Larsen."

Zack stood. Emily turned on her side, sobbing. He touched her shoulder.

"Thank you for your courage, Emily. We're going to take good care of you. No one can hurt you now."

She didn't turn around, but he heard her whisper, "Thank you."

Leaving the room, Zack said to the nurse, "Get a psychiatrist to see her. Sooner is better."

The nurse nodded.

Zack went to the work desk and picked up the phone. "Bridge?"

"I hear you're discharged." Her voice sounded strained.

"True, but I'm still in the ICU. Lots of drama here." He paused. "The so-called Dr. Good is dead. He was an obstetrician on our staff, Sebastian Barth."

Brief silence. "They said you wanted to talk to me."

"They told me you were called to the ER."

"You remember Tyler Rhodes from Christmas Eve?"

"Of course."

"Well, he was treated in the ER and asked for me. Turns out he had another life connected to this Good House thing."

Zack sighed. "Did he go by another name at The Good House?"

"Roach."

"Shit."

"What's going on, Zack? How's Annie?"

"She's the same." A beat. "We've found out what happened with

Annie, and more. I just had a chat with the woman who came in with Sebastian Barth."

"Emily?"

"Yep. She seems to be the only one who used her real name."

"Wow. We need to confer. I'm in the ER quiet room with Tyler. I'm doing my best to hold off Montgomery County PD, FBI, and Homeland Security."

Zack pondered, bit his lip, and let out a deep breath. "Bridge, we need to turn this criminal mess over to those authorities and take care of our personal issues. I'll check on Annie, make sure Emily's okay, deal as best I can with Natalie, then come to you."

"Okay," Bridget said. "I think Tyler's okay to talk to the law now. I'll work to get both him and Emily good criminal defense lawyers."

"They may need protection too."

"On it."

"See you as quick as I can, love."

The last word came out of Zack's mouth without premeditation.

CHAPTER ONE HUNDRED FIVE

A week later, a nurse pushed Annie Winston in a wheelchair out of the ICU, took her up an elevator, and down a hallway to a regular hospital room. Her mom and dad followed. Earlier in the day, Annie had hugged Jennifer and said goodbye before their dad drove her sister to the airport. Now that the doctors had pronounced Annie on the road to full recovery, her sister returned to medical school where she was already a week behind in her classes.

At least Annie's mom and dad weren't so awkward around each other as they had been the day Annie woke up. That had been so weird that she wanted to go back to sleep. A few times she faked being asleep when they both came into the ICU to see her, just so she wouldn't have to deal with them competing with each other.

They must have figured something out because after that first day they came in separately. Until today, when they both showed up for the big transfer. The awkwardness between them had disappeared. Did this mean they were always going to visit her together? She needed to get her dad alone to tell him her request. No, her decision.

"This is a nice, bright room," her mother said. "Much better than that ICU. That place was like a dungeon. No wonder there's such a thing as ICU psychosis."

The dad smiled at the mom. "Spoken like a true shrink."

Her mom feigned a dirty look; the same one Annie had seen her use before when she wasn't really angry.

"I happen to agree with you, Natalie. One day in there and I was ready to bolt."

"I hear you tried to pull out your own ET tube," the mom said, joking.

Annie's dad shook his head. "Not true." He paused and chuckled. "It was the IV line."

"Hello," Annie said. "Daughter who almost drowned over here."

They both turned to her.

Her dad spoke. "It will take more than a cold-water drowning to put out your lights, Annie Winston."

Her mom came up and hugged her. "I'm glad you're alive enough to make jokes."

Annie squinted. "What joke, mom?"

Her mom looked embarrassed. "I, uh, mean that soon you'll be making your usual lame jokes."

Annie smiled. "Yeah, mom. That's what you meant." She winked at her dad.

An awkward silence filled the room.

"Tell you what," her mom said. "Your dad has things to do today, so I'm going to give you two some time alone." Annie's mom looked at her dad. "I'll be in the coffee shop. Just let me know when I can come back up."

Her dad shrugged. "You can come up any time. You don't need my permission."

Annie's mom scoffed. "Oh, I wasn't talking about permission, just notification."

He smiled. "Okay. I'll notify you when I leave."

After her mom left the room, her dad came up and hugged Annie. "I am so happy you made it."

A tear formed in Annie's eye. "You saved my life."

He shrugged, embarrassed, then broke into a smile. "Hey, I would do it for any daughter of mine." He got serious. "I'm just glad I got to you in time. And Bridget. She saved both of us."

"I love her, Dad."

"So do I."

"I know."

"Really?"

"Duh, it is so obvious."

"How would you know? You're still a kid."

She shook her head. "You can be so lame."

"I'm glad you are well enough to say that. I don't know what I'd have done if . . ." He couldn't finish.

Now or never.

"So, Dad, how much longer do I have to stay in this hospital?"

He shrugged. "I don't know. It's up to Dr. Hartman. Maybe a week, maybe less."

"A week? I'll die if I have to stay here that long."

He gave her a solid look. "Listen. You may be out of the woods, but you're not a hundred percent. You could still get complications, like pneumonia. You need to stay under competent medical care."

She gave him a sly grin. "Aren't you a competent medical guy?"

"Yeah, but—" His eyebrows shot up. "What are you saying, Annie?"

Annie gulped. "I could stay with you."

He eyed her, curious. "The plan is to keep you here in the hospital until it's safe for you to fly home with your mom."

"What if I don't want to?"

"Don't want to what?"

She gave him her best teenager eye-roll. "Seriously, dad? You really don't get it?"

He tilted his head. "Annie?"

She blurted it all out. "I don't want to go home. Not this week, not ever. I want to live with you. Here. I want to live with my dad."

His mouth fell open. He couldn't speak.

"I'm serious," she said.

"I get that."

He looked away then turned back. A tear hung off the corner of his right eye. "I would love to have you with me, but are you sure it's what you want?"

She nodded her head with vigor. "Yes. Yes."

"How can we be sure it's not the lingering effects of hypoxic brain injury?"

"So what if it is?"

"Your life would be a lot different than what you have in California. You know that, right?"

"I have no life in California. Mom works so much, and her social life . . ." She put a hand to her mouth. "Don't get me wrong. She's a great mom and I love her."

She folded her arms, face serious in a half-pout. "I want to know my dad better. What the heck is wrong with that? Jennifer has some early memories, but I . . . I don't. I was too young when you left."

Her dad raised a hand. "When your mom kicked me out."

Annie's voice turned sharp. "Really, Dad? It doesn't matter who did what to whom way back then. It felt like abandonment." She looked him in the eye. "We can make it right." She folded her arms again. "Unless you don't want me."

He came up and put his arms around her. "Of course, I want you. Not having you in my life never stopped hurting. I would love for you stay with me."

"Is that a yes?"

"It will be a big change for both of us."

"So, not a yes."

He broke into tears. "Of course, it's a yes. I am thrilled. Yes, Annie. We'll make it work."

They hugged, then her dad said, "Your mother has to agree, or we can't do it. Should I ask her, or . . . ?"

"We don't ask. We both tell her."

Her dad huffed. "Annie, she has to agree. We need to play it straight."

"Fine."

He pulled out his phone. "I'll call her to come back up now."

Annie nodded. "Oh, one more thing, Dad."

"What?"

"You can tell Bridget."

CHAPTER ONE HUNDRED SIX

Later that day, Zack called Bridget from his car as he drove to a location in Alexandria different from where she lived. Since Zack and Annie had been discharged from Bethesda Metro Hospital, Bridget remained confined at home 24/7. She remained the only suspect in the alleged murder of her husband.

Dr. Pittman's attestation that Marshall was already brain dead when Bridget pulled the plug on his ventilator cleared her of any charge that she had killed him by cutting off his life support. However, law enforcement and prosecution still suspected that Bridget had poisoned her husband with the Coumadin anticoagulant, perhaps with the assistance of Dr. Zack Winston. Their inability to provide substantial proof of that issue was keeping Bridget out of custody, but not out of reach.

Because Zack was considered a possible accomplice, he and Bridget had been ordered not to see or talk to each other. They were to have no contact, direct or indirect.

Zack broke that rule when he called her.

"Zack, what the hell are you doing?"

"A message from my daughter. Has nothing to do with any pending case, no matter how frivolous, of no interest to anyone else listening to this call."

"Make it quick."

"Annie wants to live with me. She said to tell you."

"That's wonderful, Zack."

"I just wanted . . ."

"Hanging up now, Zack."

She clicked off the call.

"Screw the prosecutor," Zack said before he ended his side of the call.

Twenty minutes later, Zack walked into the reception area of the US Attorney for the Eastern District of Virginia, the former office of Marshall Hilliard. The woman manning the desk recognized him. "Dr. Winston. How may I help you?"

"I have an appointment with Fiona Delaney."

The receptionist picked up the phone. "I'll let her know you're here."

"No need. I'll just go up."

Before the receptionist could respond, he bounded up the stairs. He heard the woman at the desk speaking into the phone. "Dr. Winston is coming up."

Zack hit the top of the stairs and looked into Fiona's office. Empty.

Her voice behind him verified his thought. "Hello, Zack."

He turned to see her in the doorway to Marshall's office. His seat was not yet cold, but it appeared she had moved into there; even though she was only the acting US Attorney.

"Here for our meeting." He gestured between the two offices. "Yours, or his."

She looked at him with narrowed eyes. "We can use my office. I only use Marshall's for certain, uh, security issues."

I'll bet you do.

Zack followed Fiona into her office. He shut the door behind him. She sat in the chair behind her desk. Zack took a chair directly across from her. Fiona gave him a questioning look, but Zack just stared at her. Silent.

She broke the ice. "Well?"

Zack leaned forward. "Before the tragic events that led to Marshall's death, you asked me to research the possibility of using bee venom extract as a murder weapon."

She leaned back. "Oh, yes. I remember." Her eyes narrowed. "I'm sorry I didn't call you off on that. With Marshall gone, and the political uncertainty about the next AG, we're suspending the task force."

Zack shook his head. "Really? Maybe you will reconsider once I tell you my findings."

She squinted and sat back. "Go ahead."

"I would be willing to testify that Douglas Snyder, whom you all believe is the kingpin of the cabal that also included Dr. Sebastian Barth, did murder his wife, Melody. Aware of her severe allergy to bee stings, he substituted her fresh EpiPens with outdated, inert replacements. Then he dosed her with bee venom extract in her sports drink, just before she went on her daily run on the C & O trail. He knew she would go into anaphylaxis, that her self-treatment with ineffective EpiPens would fail, and she would succumb."

Zack squirmed in his seat. "She was brought to the ER in time for us to save her." He took a deep breath. "So he tried it again a few months later."

"That time she died in your ER, because you failed to establish a patent airway."

"True enough. But the substantial cause of her death was poisoning with bee venom extract."

Fiona leaned back, folded her arms, and looked out the window. Silent.

Zack stared at her.

After a bit, she wheeled back to Zack. "I'm sorry you came all this way to tell me that, Zack. A phone call or email would have been sufficient. I don't see your analysis stimulating a re-opening of the investigation. Especially since Douglas Snyder's whereabouts remain unknown."

"I figured as much." He paused. "I, uh, had another reason for coming to see you in person."

"Yes?"

"I'm concerned that I haven't seen nor heard from my girlfriend in over a week."

Fiona's eyes narrowed. "How is that an issue for the US Attorney?"

"It's not. Well, it is. Just not yet."

She shook her head. "You'll have to explain."

"Her name is Sarah O'Brien."

Fiona kept a stone face, but Zack caught the brief sideways glance.

He continued. "She's implicated in that Good House conspiracy. I didn't know it at the time, but she was working for Sebastian Barth aka Dr. Good."

Fiona's body took on the posture of a cat poised to run. She spread her arms. "That case is closed. What exactly are you asking of me?"

"I was hoping you could help me find Sarah."

Fiona rose from her chair. "I'm not in the missing persons business, Dr. Winston. You should contact the police." She moved toward the door to see him out of her office.

Zack stood and blocked her path. "At The Good House, they called her Flossie. She was one of the so-called Bobbsey Twins."

He stared at her. "I figured you would know Sarah's current whereabouts. She is your sister, is she not? Nan?"

CHAPTER ONE HUNDRED SEVEN

Less than a week had passed since Marshall's memorial service, yet it already seemed remote to Bridget. With Grant back at Harvard, Dustin at school, and herself confined to the house, she settled down to read a new novel. She couldn't remember when she'd had so much leisure time. After the cryptic phone call with Zack the previous day, she had spent some time on conference calls with her office and reviewing a new case with Ange Moretti. The young lawyer was acting on Bridget's behalf as the primary malpractice defense attorney for the firm. She had grown into the role with predictable alacrity and competence.

"You'll be the lead all the way on this case," Bridget had told her. "I'll be away for a while."

Hopefully not a long while.

Bridget had confidence that the Alexandria District Attorney would never find jury-convincing proof that she and Zack Winston had conspired to murder her husband. They had not committed the alleged crime, so no proof existed. On the other hand, she knew more than a few cases where innocent persons had been convicted and incarcerated on less evidence.

At least Virginia abolished the death penalty.

She failed to laugh at her attempted gallows humor.

A knock on the front door surprised her. Who would come calling at mid-day without phoning first? She went to the door and looked through the peep-hole.

Zack Winston stood on her porch, holding a large white bag. Bridget cracked the door but did not release the chain.

"I brought lunch," Zack said.

"You can't be here. Go away."

"Open the door, Bridge. I bring tidings of great joy. And sushi."

She glared at him. "Have you lost your mind?"

"Please, just let me in, Bridge." He shot her an exasperated look. "Oh, hell. I'll just tell you from out here. You, and I, have been cleared from any and all potential charges related to the death of Marshall Hilliard."

"What?" She opened the door to let him in. "This better not be a joke."

He stepped inside. "I'm surprised your lawyer hasn't called."

"I turned off my phone." She pulled out her phone and turned it on. Three missed calls and two voice mails from Norman Jones. She looked at Zack. "Do you want to tell me what's going on, or do I need to return these calls?"

"I'd be delighted to tell you."

Zack went through to her kitchen and placed the take-out bag on the table. He extracted a bottle of sake and put it in the refrigerator. "*Junmai Daijingo.* For later."

She faced him with hands on hips. "What's going on, Zack?"

He led her into the living room. They sat on the couch. He faced her and took her hands. "Fiona Delaney confessed to the murder of your husband."

"What? They were having an affair."

"It was all a setup. As was the romancing of me by her sister, Sarah."

"Sister?" Bridget's face scrunched. "Explain."

"Fiona and Sarah, aka Nan and Flossie the so-called Bobbsey Twins, are sisters. They were co-conspirators with Sebastian Barth and company to eliminate Marshall and deter you and me from further pursuit of the cabal that we first encountered when we chased down the bogus malpractice case."

Bridget shook her head. "That seems preposterous."

"That criminal organization has tentacles in many high places, and they play hardball. After you and I uncovered Dennis King's assassin role last year, whoever runs the show decided that Marshall was getting too close. They put out a hit order on him and plotted to put you and me away by framing us for his murder."

Bridget shuddered at how close the conspirators had come to succeeding. If such a conspiracy had existed. She remained unconvinced.

"How do you know all this, Zack? More importantly, how did the authorities figure it out?"

"Between the two of them, Tyler Rhodes and Emily Morgan painted an almost complete picture. Emily identified Sarah as Flossie, one-half of the Bobbsey Twins. Although she had only seen the other half, Nan, a few times, Tyler could describe her in more detail from his encounters as 'Roach.'"

"I had a pretty good idea of Sarah's features." He paused, embarrassed.

Bridget smirked. "I'm sure you did."

"I had also spent time with Fiona on the task force. I hadn't noticed the resemblance to Sarah until Emily and Tyler mentioned it."

"I imagine you didn't spend much time looking at either Fiona's or Sarah's eyes, face, or hair color."

Zack's head hung a bit. "I showed Emily and Tyler the US Attorney's website with Fiona's official photo. They both identified Fiona as Nan."

"Those women have different last names."

"Fiona was married in law school; kept the Delaney name after the divorce because it was on her degrees and official documents."

Bridget stroked her chin. "Doesn't prove that Fiona had anything to do with Marshall's death."

Zack assumed a 'gotcha' pose. "Not until Annie woke up."

"Huh?"

"She verified that both Sarah and Fiona were at the river with Tyler and the guy called Spider when they tried to drown her. Nan told Tyler to make it look good. Spider retorted that Nan had 'botched' Marshall's murder. He was supposed to die sooner."

Bridget shook her head. "That won't fly in court. Hearsay."

"Right." Zack smiled. "Then I got to thinking about that mysterious unlabeled bottle of Coumadin they suspect I had supplied for you to overdose Marshall. Neither one of us had seen it before Grant found it in your bathroom wastebasket."

He gave her a sly look. "Are you following me here?"

"Please go on, Zack. Admit you violated HIPAA, again, and dug into someone's health record."

"Smart lady. Still. Yep. Fiona's and Sarah's father, the distinguished honorable former judge O'Brien, was prescribed Coumadin for a past history of pulmonary embolism. That's a blood clot to the lungs."

"I know what a PE is. Move this along."

"Okay. Judge O'Brien's loving daughter, Fiona, picked up his most recent refill on the day she and Marshall went to Richmond."

"Fiona slipped Marshall the Coumadin while they were together in Richmond?"

"Yep. Peak onset of action of Coumadin is thirty-six to seventy-two hours after administration. Marshall's sudden cerebral hemorrhage matches the time interval from his, uh, dalliance with his deputy. Fiona poisoned him, pre- or post-coital. Maybe both."

Bridget scowled. "Don't be gross, Zack."

"Sorry. All that remained was for Fiona to pay you and Marshall a visit on Christmas Eve, wherein she planted the empty Coumadin container in your wastebasket, wiped free of her fingerprints, of course."

Bridget pondered, then shook her head. "I still don't see this flying. Okay, you can establish motive, means, even opportunity, but you still can't connect a chain of custody from Fiona's father's prescription to Marshall's collapse. Even if we can prove she picked up the Coumadin at the pharmacy, we have no evidence that she gave it to Marshall instead of putting it in her father's medicine cabinet." She frowned. "Beyond that, you broke the law when you violated HIPAA to find out about Judge O'Brien's medication. That makes it inadmissible, Zack."

He sat in silence, smiling at her.

"Wait. You said Fiona confessed."

"Yup."

"How?"

"Promise you won't hate me when I tell you."

She shook her head. "I can't promise anything, but I can't imagine ever hating you, Zack. Out with it."

"I made a deal with her."

"What?"

"I paid a visit yesterday to the acting US Attorney for the Eastern District of Virginia, one Fiona Delaney."

Bridget's shoulders slumped. "Oh, Zack."

He raised a hand. "I confronted her with her secret identity as Nan, her involvement with Sebastian Barth and the Good House, and the conspiracy to murder Marshall Hilliard. I told her I could trace the medication that killed Marshall back to her. I opined that a concerted investigation would surely prove her connection to the deeper cabal."

He paused. "Then I mentioned how much I love my daughter, Annie. How I'm not only a physician but a father, an aggrieved father who can and will exact revenge on anyone responsible for her near-death."

He tossed his head and smiled. "I might have said something like, 'If you thought Dennis King was a skillful medical assassin, meet Zack Winston. I know so many ways to kill you without leaving a trace."

"Come on, Zack. If Fiona has any smarts at all she knows you may be capable of many things, but murder isn't one of them."

"Almost her exact words. So I took the syringe of carfentanyl from my pocket and . . ."

"You didn't."

"I did. Well, it was a placebo but she didn't know that. I told her I knew they used rohypnol to induce unconsciousness in Nate Young and

Jeff Gibson, then killed them with carfentanyl. I put the syringe back in my pocket and assured her I was not so stupid as to kill her in her own office, but she should never underestimate a father's rage. Being a patient man, I would wait for the right opportunity to strike when she least expected it. That got her attention."

"Still not seeing a confession."

Zack sat back. "Before I went to Fiona's office, I had a conversation with our prosecutor friend off the record. I told him he was way off base charging you and me with Marshall's death. You couldn't have given Marshall the Coumadin, because he was in Richmond when the overdose happened.

"I told him I had a solid idea of the actual killer's identity, but she is not the leader of this conspiracy. Putting her away will do nothing but further endanger you, me, and our loved ones. Only a matter of time before someone else comes after us. We would live in constant fear for our lives."

Bridget nodded. "That's true."

"I suggested we could trade places with Fiona. Make her the one living in constant fear, then turn that fear into a deal. Turn her into a confidential informant, get her to give up Spider, the real leader of the cabal."

"Clever."

"I thought so. The prosecutor agreed to let me deliver the message to Fiona and offer the deal. She accepted. The authorities were waiting in the reception area to take her to a secure location."

Bridget picked up her phone. She winked at Zack. "Trust but verify."

Ten minutes later she hung up. "My lawyer confirms what you said, Zack. We are both free of any charges or suspicion."

She pointed to her ankle. "They're sending an officer over to remove this tracker thing."

"Meanwhile, sushi is best when consumed fresh."

It took some time for the officer to arrive. In the interim, Zack and Bridget sat together on her couch and ate the sushi.

Halfway through, Bridget asked the follow-up question that had bugged her since Zack's narrative. "I imagine it will be some time before the authorities get all the information they need from Fiona, or they catch up to Douglas Snyder and whoever."

Zack held a piece of *hamachi* sushi halfway from the plate to his mouth. "Not only that, whatever happens will be confidential, except for those with a need to know."

"Not including us."

"Yeah, I'm looking forward to being a simple ER doc again."

Bridget scoffed. "There's never been anything 'simple' about you, Zack Winston." She thought a moment. "I gather the information about Sarah is also confidential since you didn't close that loop."

Zack hesitated. "Fiona swore she doesn't know her sister's whereabouts."

"Doug Snyder, aka Spider, and Sarah are still out there?"

Zack shrugged. "Suppose so."

Bridget looked away. "In other words, you, we, are still at risk."

"Yeah. I suppose we are, but so are they."

"How so?"

He glared. "I was dead serious about that avenging father role."

Bridget tilted her head. "Zack . . ."

"Tyler Rhodes was just a pawn. In the end, he risked his life for Annie." Zack's eyes hardened. "Sarah, on the other hand, would have let her die. Spider, too."

"Don't go there, Zack."

Raw, fiery emotion raged inside him. "I'm going after them, Bridge."

Bridget moved closer to him on the couch, put an arm around him, and pulled him close. "You know that's not you, Zack Winston."

When Zack looked up, tears flooded his eyes.

"Bridget, I . . ." He buried his head in her lap and sobbed.

Evening was on the horizon when the officer arrived to remove the tracker from Bridget's ankle. By the time he was done, Dustin came home from school and basketball practice.

Zack had recovered from his break-down and cleaned up. He looked Bridget in the eye. "Raincheck on the sake?"

"Of course. Anytime."

She walked Zack to his car.

He opened the door and was about to get in, then turned and faced her. "Good night. Be safe."

"You too."

They shared a warm embrace that turned into a brief but passionate kiss.

"I'll take you up soon on that rain check," he said.

"I'll be here, Zack." She smiled. "Always."

CHAPTER ONE HUNDRED EIGHT

A week later, Zack and Annie drove Natalie to the airport for her flight to San Diego.

Annie had been out of the hospital for two days and had taken up residence in Zack's office/guest room. At the end of the month, Zack and she would move into a new three-bedroom apartment in the same building, where Annie would have her own bedroom. Natalie would ship her belongings from San Diego. They had enrolled her in high school, where she would start only a week behind her classmates.

"She'll make up the deficit in no time," Natalie said.

"Her mother's daughter," Zack said.

During Annie's continued recovery in the hospital and the few days since discharge, Zack and Natalie had made peace. After Annie told her mother she wanted to live with Zack, the process mirrored the stages of grief. It had taken several days of intense emotional discourse before Natalie reached the acceptance phase. Now she supported the move.

"Nothing like a crisis with a child to bring estranged parents together," Zack said.

"She deserves better from both of us," Natalie said. "Jennifer too."

"They will have it. I will make it my first priority."

He was almost shocked when she believed him. Maybe because she saw he believed himself. For once.

Zack and Annie waited until Natalie went through airport security, then stopped for dinner on the way back to the apartment building. At Annie's request, it was the same restaurant where he'd taken her and Jennifer when they first arrived three days before Christmas.

"A lifetime ago," Annie said.

"You're not even close to a lifetime on earth yet," Zack said.

She sniffed. "I almost died, Dad."

He reached out and touched her hand. "Thank God you didn't."

"God, and Bridget." She looked him in the eye. "Now that mom's gone..."

"We'll have Bridget over. Maybe after we get into our new place."

Annie gave him a knowing smile and a wink. "Yeah. More privacy for you and her there."

For one of the few times in his life, Zack Winston was speechless.

After dinner, they returned to the apartment and watched a movie together. Then Annie went to bed. Zack went into his bedroom and pulled out his journal. He hadn't written to Noelle since Christmas night, a lifetime ago.

Dearest Noelle,

I write with a full heart. My daughter is asleep in <u>her</u> bedroom in <u>our</u> apartment. <u>Our</u> home. Never did I imagine such a gift would come into my life. All the more wonderful because it was her idea. She wants to live with me, to know me, to build something together that we never had.

I am ecstatic.

Someday soon I will tell her all about you. How you were and still are the love of my life, my soulmate, even now in separate worlds. I hope to teach her what it means to love and be loved without guile, with complete vulnerability, and absolute trust. She and I both will become better persons for it. I will do my best to model you for her.

I realize it's possible to have more than one love of my life. You. Annie. And ... But you know that.

There's still that dark side of me that wants to tear Sarah apart for what she did. If I ever find her again. Something tells me that by the time that happens, Annie and Bridget will have helped me close that compartment in my life. I know you would.

Thank you for loving me, Noelle, for showing me true love, and for helping me become capable of giving that gift to another.

I am nearly at peace tonight.
I love you.
Always.
Zack

CHAPTER ONE HUNDRED NINE

Emily held her head high as she followed the uniformed officer down a short corridor. She tried to adjust her body in a futile effort to get the one-size-too-big, borrowed clothing to hang straight over her thin frame. She failed.

Whatever.

The officer opened a door and stood aside for Emily to pass through. Norman Jones, the defense attorney that Bridget Larsen had procured for her, *pro bono*, greeted her at the doorway. She entered a brightly lit courtroom, empty save for the judge and the people in the front row. Mr. Jones led her past an empty jury box to a table that faced the judge from the left side of the courtroom.

A solitary Assistant District Attorney sat at the table to the right.

Six months after her release from the hospital and transfer to the Maryland Pretrial Detention Facility in Baltimore, Emily would soon learn her fate for the rest of her life. She had pleaded guilty to the crimes of kidnapping, performing/assisting in unlawful medical procedures, and criminal negligence from her prior misadventure as an unlicensed nurse midwife—the event that had leashed her to Adam Good until the police officer shot him in the chest at the airpark.

Emily expected to go to prison for decades, perhaps for life. The ill fit of the borrowed clothing became irrelevant. As she took her place at the defense table, she nodded in turn to the people sitting just behind the railing.

Detective Tina Martinez had responded to Emily's call from the hospital offering to turn herself in for her role in the Good House atrocities. The detective had become Emily's advocate and, to the extent possible given their roles, her friend.

Dr. Stephanie Argyle, psychiatrist, had first seen Emily in the Bethesda Metro Hospital ICU and had continued to be her refuge, sounding board, and mentor. Also *pro bono*, because her former patient, Dr. Zack Winston, had so insisted.

Ms. Bridget Larsen, whom Emily had met in the hospital after Tyler Rhodes had come forward to reveal The Good House and all its shame. Bridget had also become a friend and mentor. Emily considered her the strongest and kindest woman she'd ever met.

Dr. Zack Winston had become Emily's most ardent supporter and advocate.

A person whom Emily had not noticed sitting next to Dr. Winston leaned forward to get her attention. Emily almost burst into tears when she recognized Annie Winston, now a poised and confident young woman. An inspiring contrast to the troubled youth whom Emily had coached through a heinous assault.

"You got this," Annie whispered.

The judge rapped his gavel and called the court to order. He confirmed that Emily had pleaded guilty to all charges, thereby waving her right to trial by jury. He then announced his intention to hear testimony from the witnesses and defendant before pronouncing his verdict.

The Assistant District Attorney produced no witnesses.

Emily's witnesses took the stand in turn, each one attesting that Emily was a good person trapped in terrible circumstances by a psychopathic predator posing as a kind physician and loving patron. Detective Martinez and the psychiatrist both testified to Emily's full cooperation with both the investigation and her mental health recovery.

Annie Winston took the stand. "Emily risked her life to save mine. I will owe her for the rest of my days. Moreover, she brought an evil man to deserved justice. Vulnerable women everywhere owe her for that."

Emily took the stand. She looked at each of her supporters, her eyes lingering on Annie Winston. "I'm so sorry. My foolishness in trusting Adam Good, I mean Sebastian Barth, over my own instincts will forever haunt me." She stifled a sob. "I thought he loved me. I . . . I needed that so much." She paused and shook her head. "I make no excuses. I knew better. I should have done better." Another sob. "I'm glad it's finally over." She looked at the judge. "I'm ready to take my punishment, Your Honor."

Tears ran down her face as she stepped off the witness stand.

The Assistant District Attorney offered a bland argument that Emily had confessed to the terrible acts, for which she deserved just punishment under the law, no matter how compelling her character witnesses. He added that Emily herself had confirmed as much in her own statement.

Norman Jones rose to speak for Emily. After a long pause, he gestured to the empty jury box. "Imagine those seats occupied by young, desperate women, alone and pregnant. Imagine others there, after giving birth, alone, forsaken, even murdered. Imagine dead infants."

He turned toward Emily. "Look upon this young woman, herself a victim of diabolical cruelty and abuse. Suckered and manipulated by a psychopath. Snatched from a life filled with hope to a life consumed by the desperate need to survive, to escape, to get free from this tormentor and his evil deeds."

Norman turned to the judge, then pointed back to the jury box. "I ask you, your honor, who harmed those young women, who killed them, who stole their babies?" He pointed to Emily. "Was it this woman, herself kidnapped, alone, forgotten, and almost murdered?"

He stood beside Emily. "This woman harmed no one. She suffered the same torture as those other women, at the hands of the devil himself, Sebastian Barth, and his band of demons. Barth has already paid the ultimate price. In due time the others will be brought to justice. But no one in this courtroom, not even the ADA here, wants to put Emily Morgan in prison to pay for the sins of Barth and the others. She deserves only one sentence from you, your honor. To be free at last. Free at last. Free at last." He walked over and stood next to Emily.

"Thank you." He resumed his seat and patted Emily's hand.

The judge sat in silence for several minutes, his eyes gazing at the documents in front of him. Finally, he looked up. "I am ready to pronounce sentence."

The bailiff's voice boomed. "The accused will please stand."

Emily stood and locked her eyes on the judge.

A tiny hint of a smile crossed his face. "Emily Morgan, of all the victims of Dr. Sebastian Barth—I refuse to use the word 'good' in reference to him—of all the victims of his evil empire, you are arguably the most defiled, the most victimized, the most damaged. I cannot make you pay for his despicable sins." He paused. "I sentence you to time served and three years' probation."

He pounded his gavel. "Emily Morgan, you are free to go. May God bless you."

Thank you so much for reading *Warm and Dead*. If you've enjoyed the book, we would be grateful if you would post a review on the bookseller's website. Just a few words is all it takes!

OTHER BOOKS BY MIKE KRENTZ

Dr. Zack Winston Series (Medical Conspiracy Thrillers)
Dead Already (Book one)
Warm and Dead (Book two)
Near Dead (Book three, coming Summer 2023)

The Mahoney and Squire Courageous Military Women Series
Her Show of Force (Book one, coming February 2023)
Her Spratly Showdown (Book two, coming Fall 2023)

Standalone Psychological Thriller
Angels Falling

ACKNOWLEDGMENTS

This second Zack Winston novel represents the support, input, and encouragement of a cherished team of family, friends, and colleagues. Mere words of praise or acknowledgment cannot do justice to what these people mean to me.

My wife, Kathryn, who supports, patiently goads, kindly edits, and selflessly praises my meager efforts. You are the perfect life companion.

My adult children and stepchildren, Debi, Michael, Jewls, Lisa, Kate, James, and Matthew. You've endured more than a fair share of your imperfect dad's life meanderings, family disruptions, and challenges. You remained loving and loyal through it all. You will always have my constant and unconditional love and gratitude.

Jayne Ann Krentz, cherished cousin-in-law, for your encouragement, support, gentle nudges, and solid counsel. Your confidence helped me to believe in myself as a writer. A special salute to Frank, who is more like a brother than cousin to me. Thanks especially for marrying Jayne and bringing her into the family!

Sheri Williams, Ashley Carlson, and the TouchPoint Press team for opening the door to traditional publishing, then guiding and supporting me through it.

Jenn Haskin, not only my editor but a fellow-writer and friend. Your editing skills improved and polished the manuscript yet preserved my original voice. I so enjoy working with you. Best wishes on your own writing.

My colleagues at The Muse Writers Center studio. Your cogent commentaries and enthusiastic support elevated the quality of my writing: Kelly Sokol, John Cameron, Kim Engebrigtsen, Susan Paxton, Kelley McGee, John Aguiar, Hope Dahmen, Lea Ann Douglas, and Tamako Takamatsu. You all are fabulous writers whose works deserve publication. A huge thanks to Michael Khandelwal, founder and guiding light of The Muse for establishing a world-class writers' community in our hometown, and to Shawn Gervin and Susan Deutsch who keep the wheels turning.

Lauran Strait and staff at Hampton Roads Writers. Their annual writers' conference rivals those hosted on a national level.

Cissy Hartley, Susan Simpson, and Degan Outridge at Writerspace/Killer Books for guiding me through the book promotion process and managing my website, email list, and newsletter. True professionals whose efforts give me more time to write.

Dr. Pat Connell, fellow BAFERD, college roommate, colleague, and friend since grade school, who reviewed my original manuscript and pointed out clinical anachronisms by virtue of his current emergency medicine practice. Best wishes on your continued practice in both US academia and Honduras.

Most of all, thanks to my readers. I appreciate your investment in my novels, in time as well as money. I hope you enjoyed reading this story as much as I did writing it. If you are so inclined, I would appreciate a review on Amazon, Barnes and Noble, Goodreads, BookBub, and/or other retail platforms.

ABOUT THE AUTHOR

Mike Krentz writes medical suspense, psychological thrillers, and military fiction based on his experiences as an emergency physician and US Navy medical officer.

Born and raised in Arizona, Mike earned a classical degree in English from the University of San Francisco, a Doctor of Medicine degree from the Medical College of Wisconsin, and a Master of Public Health Degree from Johns Hopkins University.

Following a civilian career as an emergency physician, (including a term as president of the American College of Emergency Physicians, Mike rededicated his professional life to serve America's Navy and Marine Corps heroes and their families. His last active-duty assignment was as 7th Fleet Surgeon on board the USS BLUE RIDGE.

After retiring from the US Navy, Mike continued his service as a consultant to the Navy and Marine Corps Public Health Center, Health Analysis Department. Upon completion of that mission, he returned to his earliest life passion as a full-time writer.

Mike sits on the Board of Directors of The Muse Writers Center, where he also teaches fiction writing and participates in advanced fiction studios.

Mike, his wife Kathryn, and miniature schnauzer Yoshi live in Norfolk, VA.

Free Book

If you enjoyed *Warm and Dead*, you can read more about Dr. Zack Winston, emergency department drama, and real-life ED scenarios in Mike's free 70-page novella, *ER TALES: Stories from "The Pit."*

Just sign up to receive Mike's periodic newsletter that contains insights into emergency medicine, news about Mike's books, dogs, and other non-spammy content.

Claim your copy and sign up for the newsletter here:

https://mikejkrentz.com/newsletter/

CPSIA information can be obtained
at www.ICGtesting.com
Printed in the USA
LVHW092113160922
728592LV00010B/680